FORGED BY FURY

Demons of New Chicago

KEL CARPENTER

Forged by Fury

Kel Carpenter

Published by Kel Carpenter

Copyright © 2022, Kel Carpenter LLC

Edited by Analisa Denny

Proofread by Dominique Laura

Cover Art by Okay Creations

E-book ISBN: 978-1-960167-15-6

 Created with Vellum

For Jude

You are the love I didn't know was possible.

"We all have our edge, Auren. One day, you're going to find where yours is." The darkness of his essence brushes against my skin like a whisper's caress. "You're going to find out just how far you can be pushed until you're tipped over. And when that happens, when you find your edge, just promise me one thing."

My voice comes out like a croak, a single tear dashing down. "What?"

"Don't fall." Time stands still as he leans in and places a kiss on my temple, lips turning to whisper into my ear. "*Fly.*"

Raven Kennedy, *Gleam*

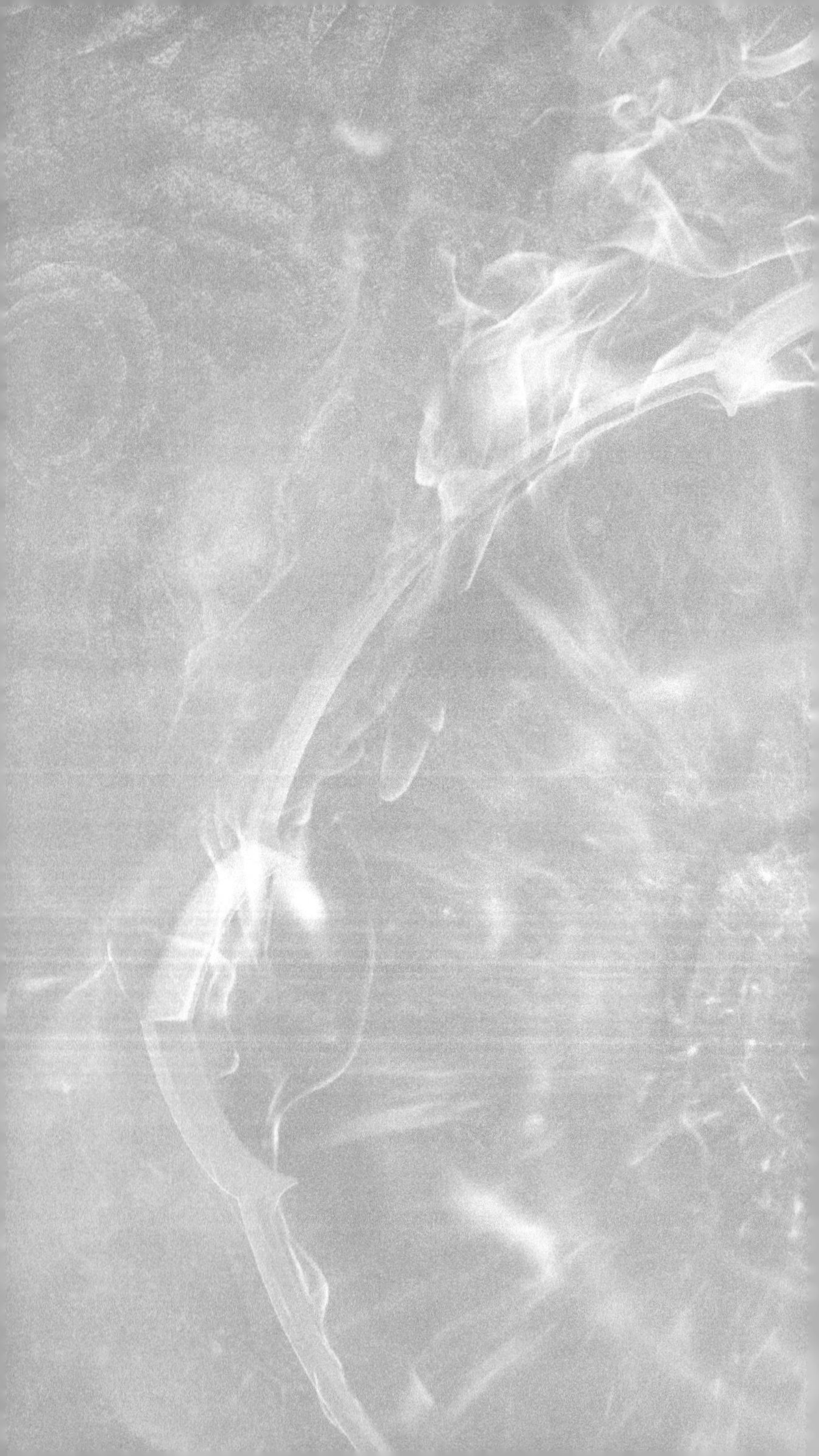

NATHALIE

Welcome back to New Chicago, readers. It's been a while since we've all seen each other. Unless you've done a reread knowing this day was coming, I'll do a quick recap for you on what happened last time we were all together.

We started off after Ronan and I helped Piper bring her sister back. Bree is none too pleased to see Piper. I'll tell you what. The hate-filled look she had on her face was intense. Definitely not the sister she remembered.

Bree made it known too. She wanted to go back home immediately. She'd built herself a life in the Otherworld. Hell was her home and had been for ten years. She had an atman of her own. Of course, Piper refused. I was only present for the last leg of her journey, but my best friend didn't fight for a decade to bring her sister back to Earth just let her walk away. Didn't stop Bree. She turned on a heel and walked right out the door. I can't say I was all that sad to see her go.

But Piper was.

So to deal with that rejection and the rollercoaster of emotions she was experiencing, what did Piper do? Surprisingly, she didn't make good on her threat to shoot me. But she did drown her sorrows in a bottle of liquor. Several bottles, actually. So many. She went off, getting into bar fights and all sorts of other crazy things. Ronan and I eventually pulled her head out of her ass. Her purpose in life had been Bree. That was shot to Hell. Pun intended. She needed something to do other than drink herself stupid.

I made her start earning her keep. If she was going to live with me, she needed to learn how to work. In the meantime, she and Ronan just fought a lot because—surprise—she was still buried in her self-loathing and he's not great at communicating. They eventually figured out how to get a little better at it.

I've always had my hands in a great deal of what goes on in our city, and I try to do the best I can for people. While Piper had been trying to poison herself with alcohol, I got into magical arms dealing. Why? New Chicago was sort of getting worse. Hard to believe, I know. How could this place actually get worse? Because Lucifer died. Humans thought they had a chance at gaining back some control. I couldn't blame them. They'd been through so much since the start of the Magic Wars. But this was more than protesting. It was hurting innocent people. Riots and bombing. Working with a group calling themselves the Illuminati. A group that wanted to end magic, and anyone who had it.

Remember Sasha and Sienna? They're the twin succubus-shifters. They worked for Lucifer. Sienna got hurt in a bombing. She was going to die. Sasha brought her to my apartment and begged Piper to save her. Piper refused, because doing so would mean Sienna entered a blood oath without consent. Sasha agreed to take the oath willingly so her sister wouldn't be alone in it. She just wanted her sister to live. I'll never know what went through Piper's head that day, but she gave her blood to save Sienna, forever tying the twins to her.

So we have them in our little group now—and living in my apartment. Everyone that lives with me needs to go to work instead of being bumps on a log. Thems the rules. So I take them on as well. Having the extra hands doesn't hurt, and the twins are good at what they do. Piper, less so, but she learned.

Now the Illuminati wanted to end supernaturals, right? But to fight magic, they *needed* magic. Rumor had it there was a gun that could steal magic, allowing the wielder to turn it on the supernatural and kill them. Not good. I set it up that Piper was going to 'exchange' Sasha (her pretend captive) for this magical weapon. Who shows up? Flint. Piper's incredibly stupid ex-boyfriend. He shoots her, thinking he can steal her power. Instead, the power ends up killing him. Not really a big loss there. But the weapon wasn't recovered, and that was a problem.

Piper is still reeling from what happened with Bree, so she makes a deal with her. If Bree spends a month with her, Piper will open a portal for her at the end of their time together so she can go back to the Otherworld. Bree reluctantly agrees. Piper doesn't even know what to do with her —none of us did. It's not like they could bond much since she had no desire to see her sister. So Piper brings her to work with us. I'm trying to do good around the city, and then we have Bree tagging along, who—let's face it—is kind of a bitch, especially to Piper. But what's good in all of this was that the people of New Chicago were seeing Piper. They were seeing her out there, conversing with humans and supernaturals that continue to suffer. Learning of their plights. Empathizing with their stories.

She didn't know it, but she was learning to be a queen.

Bree had some really surprising magic. It's impressive what she can do with metals and how much control she has over it. So naturally, she goads Piper about being unable to use her powers well, which leads to Piper taking lessons from Bree. Not the worst thing that could happen. It was quality time together, even if they didn't realize it. Their relationship improved some, and that was what Piper needed. Bree too, if I'm being honest.

Now we're coming up to Bree's departure. It would be a bittersweet send-off if it weren't for another plot twist. The Illuminati sent a teenage suicide bomber . . . and she had Bree's magic in the bomb. Bree swears she didn't know what they were doing when she was collaborating with them. She was just trying to rile Piper into helping her get home. She left when she learned they were crazy assholes. Piper agrees it's best to send her back to the Otherworld that night.

Ronan surprises the hell out of her by telling her she couldn't open the portal. Why? She was pregnant. I mean, I knew about it. I could sense it. I just thought she was processing it and would tell me when she was ready. Turned out, she had no clue. But Ronan won't allow her to open the portal. It was too dangerous.

So Ronan and I open the portal. Bree and Piper have a meaningful goodbye, where Bree uncharacteristically softens for a brief moment. She tells her sister she loves her, letting her know she forgave her. That even worlds apart, they would always be sisters. Whispering to her that she did this for her, knowing that she would never understand what that meant.

Then Lorcan, her atman, walked through the portal, and everything in our world stilled as Bree looked at him in horror.

That's where we left off, and that is where you will begin.

As for me? I'm pretty sure I'm losing my mind. When not tethered, witches eventually do. My moment is coming. I'm being followed by phantom shadows. Hearing voices.

I only have a matter of time.

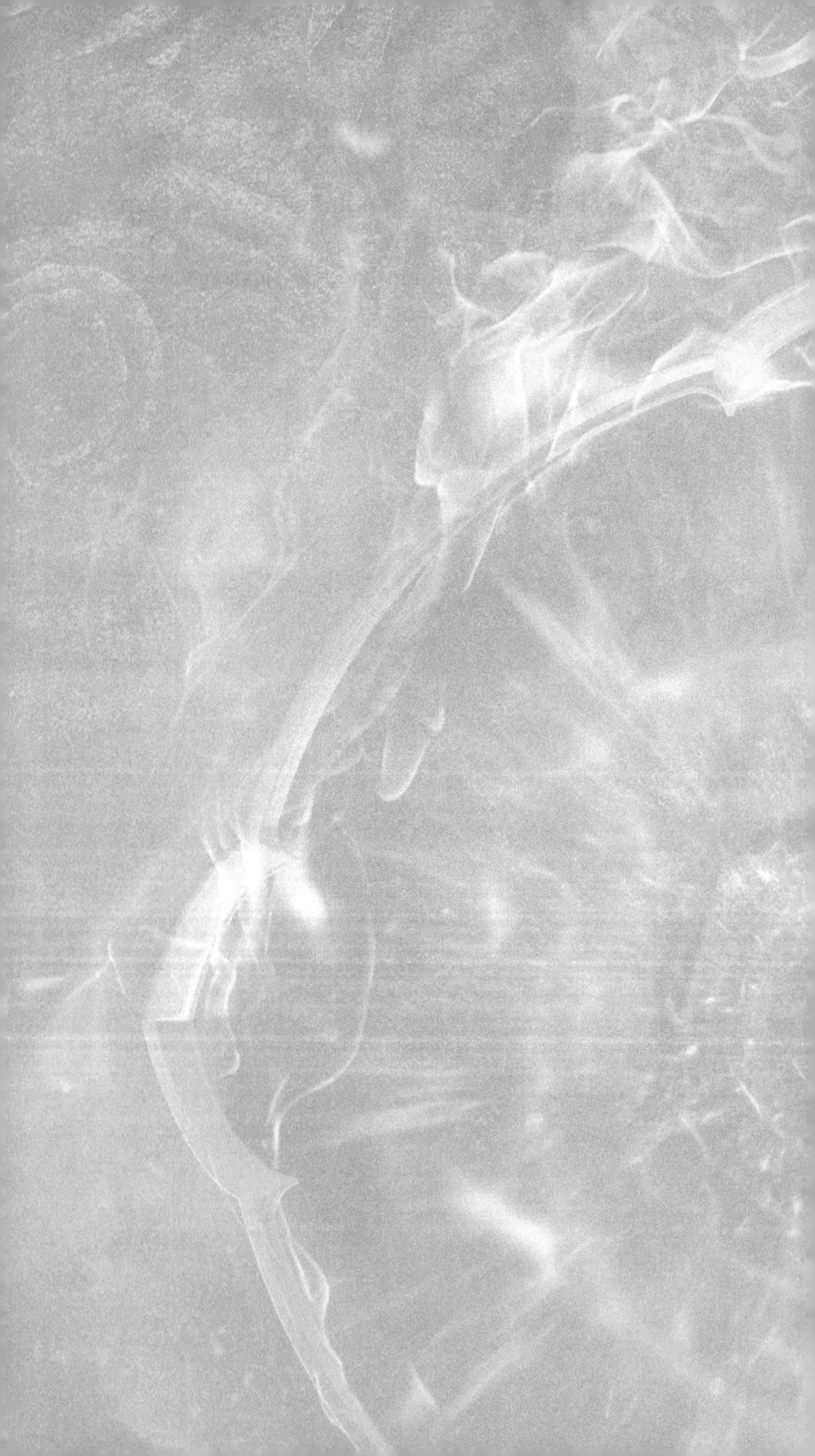

I

PIPER

Thunder clapped.

Its echo was loud enough to make the walls shake. Dust fell from the fan. Not a single person moved. Not a twitch. Not a blink.

An unbearable tension thickened in the air, making it hard to breathe.

"Lorcan." I repeated the name Bree had said in surprise. My words were coming out in a breathless tone. "Your atman," I added, needing to say it. Needing to clarify it for myself. The way she stared at him was nothing like what I would've expected from the woman who professed only love these last weeks. They were destined for each other. Their bond so much like my own . . .

Or so I thought.

"I can see that this is confusing for you," Lorcan said, stepping further into the small living room. He walked with ease like he owned the place. "I'll simplify it, seeing as my atma is at a loss for words in my presence." His blood-red eyes flashed toward Bree for a second, making a chill shiver down my spine. He didn't look at her with awe. Nor with love or adoration.

He regarded her like a petulant child. One who'd clearly disappointed him.

My sister stared at her supposed mate with nothing short of fear. Her mask was in tatters, shredded by the realization that he was here—and had been for some time.

"Bree is my soul-bound mate. We met some time ago, but upon realizing what she was, I had"—he tilted his head to the side, eyes slowly perusing her form, a flicker of sexual interest showing—"reservations." Lorcan took another step forward, this time in our direction. I grabbed Bree's hand, holding it tight, but her fingers remained loose. Impassive and cold. "Bree was not of my world. She was made, not born. Her customs were human. Her way of life was so vastly different, and I had to be sure she was committed to me and the Otherworld. That she'd truly embraced it if she was to be my atma in all ways."

"What did you do?" The words fell from my mouth in a horrified whisper.

"I gave her a task. A challenge," he replied, completely unbothered by my tone. "After living in the Otherworld, she understood the importance of culture. Tradition. Our world existed on a precarious power dynamic for so long that when the Harvester left, it was chaos. Chaos unchecked leads to ruin."

His gaze shifted from me to Ronan. My heart thrummed in my chest like a thoroughbred galloping harder at the end of a race. I was only just beginning to realize what came after the finish line.

"I was tasked to find the Harvester," Bree said suddenly and quietly, her voice strong despite its softness. "Find him so that the new one could challenge him, and the world could continue on as it had been."

My heart clenched. I turned to stare at her, but the fear I saw was gone. Her horror evaporated. Apathy and careful calculation were all I saw beyond the shutters she'd closed around herself, her true feelings buried deep.

"You were searching for Ronan when I called you home."

The truth settled in, but it didn't fit. I couldn't stomach that I'd brought her back after so long only to find out her mission was to find my atman.

"If it's any consolation, I was there with her that day in the courtyard in the Otherworld. When you opened the portal, I don't believe she realized he was here. I sensed it. As for Bree . . ." He tsked, taking another step in our direction. "Her weak human sensibilities weren't as diluted as she'd tried to convince me they were. You called out, and she walked right into the portal. Didn't even glance back to see if I was following."

He reached out and ran a single clawed fingertip down her cheek. The gesture wasn't sweet. It was possessive. Aggressive. Controlling.

"But I wasn't simply going to let her walk into another world without me. Certainly not the world that held the Harvester I'd been searching for. So I came behind her and masked my magic as her own. I stayed hidden and watched. I waited to see what she would do upon finding out that the demon she was supposed to locate was bonded to none other than her sister—the infamous Piper Fallon. Witch Hunter. Rage Demon. Queen of New Chicago." He chuckled as he drew out the last title, mocking me and finding false amusement in the names.

Pale fingers closed around my sister's throat. He jerked once, and her hand slipped from mine as she moved forward, stepping into him. Her electric blue eyes stared intensely into his. "You almost failed," he said quietly, his lips brushing over hers. "I saw it in the dark of night when you wept over her. Over your loss. Over what you had to do." His thumb stroked her cheek as his other arm came to wrap around her waist. "But when the time came, you were prepared to return to me. Despite your time here, back on Earth. You were going to return and bring the knowledge of the old Harvester with you."

I inhaled sharply. "No," I said, shaking my head. She wouldn't—

"Yes," Lorcan snapped. "In the end, she made a choice and proved she is worthy. Now we will bond, and then I will take my place as Harvester, returning to Hell as the rightful ruler and most powerful demon to have ever walked the realms."

There was a maniacal glow in his expression. Power hungry. Blood thirsty.

His lips dipped from hers to the pale column of my sister's throat. He hovered for a brief moment before his fangs descended and met flesh. A look of wide-eyed alarm crossed her features.

Then he savagely bit into her.

Red dribbled down her neck as a low moan escaped her lips.

Her head tilted back, giving him better access as the effects of the blood exchange took over. I knew better than anyone how little control she would have once he started to drink from her.

Whether she wanted it or not, she would be in his thrall

until someone either forcibly parted them or the blood lust ran its course.

Beside me, a strong arm snagged me by the waist. I sensed Ronan's familiar heat as he pulled me back into his chest, his low laugh rumbling against me.

Lorcan stilled in his greedy drinking. His hand slipped down my sister's waist to her ass and gave it a firm squeeze before releasing her neck.

Red smudged his mouth and ran down his chin.

A true monster.

"You laugh," he commented, regarding Ronan coolly.

"Because you foolishly believe you'll beat me in a challenge." Ronan's clawed hand remained protectively cupped over my stomach. "You forget yourself. It was a thousand years ago, but I remember you. Chaos demons are so rare I made a point to meet and assess every one of you for potential. You had power, but you were hungry for more. I saw the terror you would be if unleashed upon our world. I sent you back to Nephilania and haven't thought of you once since. That is how unworthy you are of being the Harvester."

Lorcan smiled and my blood chilled in my veins. "Yes. You sent me home after mere hours. I spent over five hundred years training for the day I'd finally get to meet you, and you *dismissed* me without ever letting me near the Source—when the Source is the only true decider of who is worthy." He reached up to the collar of his button-down shirt and pulled at the top. The buttons popped and unraveled, falling, landing with tiny pings against the wood floor as he continued to pull the material down—revealing a collar of a different nature.

A dark red brand coiled around his neck. It was an exact replica of the one Ronan wore.

My atman froze, though I'd gander his face didn't show it.

"You went to the Source," Ronan said solemnly.

"After you left, the Council was desperate. They let every chaos demon approach it, but *I* was the one it chose to be the next Harvester. And now that I've found you, I challenge—"

"No," Bree snapped.

My lips parted at her outburst. The lustful thrall that Lorcan pulled her into had cleared.

She shoved against his chest. Hard enough his grasp on her loosened.

"I'm not doing this, Lorcan—"

"Yes," he hissed. "You are." A dark rage crossed his face. He narrowed his eyes down at her. "You're *mine*, Bree, and you will do as you're told and complete the bond with me so that I can take what is mine."

"No," she repeated firmly. "I won't. *You won't.* If you want me, then we will return to Hell and complete the bond there, but I'm not doing this here. You can't challenge him —" She shook her head, trying to back away. His grip on her tightened and righteous fury rose up within me.

"You're lucky I am a benevolent demon and have grown attached to you over the years," Lorcan said acidly. "You would do well to accept my blood and let me fuck you how I please—"

"I reject you."

I couldn't believe the words I'd heard. It seemed neither could Lorcan because, for the first time, his own expression cracked. Something akin to alarm began to seep in.

"I don't accept your rejection—"

"I, Bree Fallon, daughter of no one, reject your claim— as is my right." The words fell from her lips, soft but lethal.

After all that she'd done to return to him, I was beginning to understand.

His eyes darkened, going black at her refusal of their bond. "You're going to regret that," he said quietly. It reminded me of Ronan when his muted anger was louder than shouting.

He squeezed my sister's neck, and my hand came up, white fire bursting to life in my palm—ready to burn him alive. But when Lorcan spoke again, his words . . . they changed everything.

"I, Lorcan, son of Eris and Anhur, challenge you, Bree Fallon, atma mine, soul of my own, to claim the bond between us—as is *my* right. Either submit to me here and now, or I will take pleasure in forcing you to."

I gaped at him—at her. To deny him meant they would fight. If he won, he'd take what he believed was his, enslaving her to him instead of bonding. If she won, she'd have no choice but to kill him. Love or not, he was her soul-bound mate.

It was a horrible situation; one I couldn't believe he forced them into.

But my sister was steel and iron. To her very core, she was strength itself. Hardened resolve and cold calculation.

Unwavering, she looked him in the eye and said, "I accept."

Her words sealed an unseen contract.

Lorcan released my sister, taking a step back. He straightened the lapels of his suit jacket and turned his hate-filled gaze toward me and Ronan.

"After I bring my bitch to heel, I'll be coming for you and your queen." He focused on me and the hand of fire I wanted nothing more than to hurl at his head. "Congratulations on the baby. It's a shame it won't survive."

"Get out of my house," Nathalie growled, reminding me that she was here this whole time. Her athame sailed through the air, nicking his cheek before planting itself in the drywall behind him. He smiled cruelly, and then disappeared.

2

PIPER

Silence reigned.

Only the vibrating hum of Nat's athame wavering back and forth broke it up. She must have struck a joist when she threw.

"You don't have to fight him," I said quietly. The first to speak. "Ronan can take him—"

"No." She still hadn't turned to look at any of us. Her shoulders were drawn back, strong and stiff. She held her head high despite the emotions that must have been eating at her. "I have to do this."

I sighed, exasperation seeping out of me. "Now who's being the stubborn one?"

"You can't save me from everything, Piper." She tilted her chin to the side, looking back at me over her shoulder. "Lorcan is my atman, and he believes he's destined to be the next Harvester. Maybe he is . . ." Her eyes dropped a fraction. "But either way, there can only be one. Him. Or Ronan. I'm not bonded yet. I don't have a baby on the way. I —I can survive this loss." Her electric eyes lifted to my face once more. "You can't."

"Ronan won't lose—"

"You don't know that," she said, shaking her head. "And if we bonded and Ronan did win, I'd either die or be crippled by his loss. I won't do that to myself. Neither will I bond and take the chance that Ronan could lose. I wouldn't be able to live with myself if I brought him back here and led him right to you, then let him slaughter your atman and risk your child."

Her blue eyes dropped to my belly and her bottom lip tightened.

My shoulders sagged, the fire in my palm winked out. Helpless.

Despite all the power in the world, I couldn't do a damn thing to change this.

"I can't lose you," I admitted. "I was prepared to let you go when I thought you were running toward something, but this—" I waved my hand to the spot where Lorcan disappeared. "I can't lose you like this. If it's too much of a risk for Ronan to fight him, how could you possibly think it's safer for you?" I demanded. "By not letting him, you'll either have to kill your atman—or be forced into bonding with that monster. You're a rage demon. Not chaos. If he's really been chosen by the Source, he could devour your magic—"

"He won't." She sounded surer of that than I would have been. "Lorcan wants me in his own twisted way. The bond wouldn't let him kill me unless he thinks there's no other choice."

"There isn't," I snapped. "Not if you're unwilling to bond."

"He'll either make me yield, in which case I did everything I could to prevent this—or he won't, and I'll win. There's no changing it now, Piper. The challenge was issued, and I accepted. This is why I wanted to return as soon as I realized where I was—and that he was here." She nodded toward Ronan. "I wanted to spare you from this. From Lorcan. But he followed me, and he doesn't care for me enough to not go through with it."

"You were leaving to protect us," I said, before she could turn away. "You wouldn't have told him the truth, though. You were going to return and risk never completing his task—never bonding—weren't you?"

Bree stayed quiet long enough that a trickle of anxiety ran through me. If not for her actions, I would have questioned it. But she wouldn't . . .

"I was confident in my ability to persuade him. That with enough time he might give into his baser urges and claim me anyway, even if he couldn't find Ronan, and therefore never become the Harvester." Her fingers shook, the only outward hint that she wasn't as put together as she wanted me to believe. "I underestimated him. His lust for power. His drive to become more."

"You deserve better."

She laughed once. "Fate picked him for me."

"Fate chose wrong," I said.

She tilted her head in agreement. "Out of everyone in the universe, Lorcan is the other half of my soul. The only person that can stabilize me and my magic. Without that bond, I'll rot away. It won't happen immediately, but as the centuries pass, and eons go by—my power will grow and so will my own insanity." Her eyes closed and her hand clenched into a fist to stop the shaking. "Not all of us get happy endings. I'm happy you found yours, truly, even if I am jealous. I won't take that away from you just to try to find mine."

"Lorcan isn't your happy ending," I disagreed.

"Maybe not, but he's the one I was given—and he chose himself. Now it's time for me to choose *me*."

Without further delay, she faded into nothing—an astral form of herself. I sensed Bree's magic linger a moment longer before it disappeared, the only true way to tell that she wasn't here anymore.

I sighed, wanting to follow after her with everything in me—even if I didn't have the first clue where to look.

"Can you track her?" I asked Nat without turning.

"Yes," she replied, striding forward to rip her athame out of the wall and inspecting the blade. "But I won't."

I narrowed my eyes, and she lifted both brows. "Don't give me that look. Tonight was a shitshow by the best standards. Anyone could see that while she stood up to him, it's a lot to process. I'm not going to help you hunt her down when she's not in any immediate danger."

"We don't know that," I started to argue.

"She's not," Ronan agreed. "When a challenge is issued, she has six hundred and sixty-six hours to get her affairs in order—they both do." One might think the universe had a sick sense of humor, but six-six-six only became associated with demons because of Lucifer. I wondered if he had a personal qualm with that number, or the subsequent challenge associated with it. Not that we'd ever know. "That's roughly twenty-eight days. He won't come for her before that."

"If he does?"

"He can't." Ronan shook his head. "His magic won't allow it. That's why she cut him off. Had he fully issued a challenge to me, I would have had no choice but to accept. There's no way around it. For better or worse, our magic enforces demon law."

I suppose it was a blessing in disguise at the moment,

because I had little doubt Lorcan would leave her be if that wasn't the case.

"That doesn't mean he won't find other ways to get to her," I said, crossing my arms over my chest. Outside, the storm had calmed, but not dissipated. A heavy cloud hung over New Chicago with ominous intent.

"Or us," Nathalie added. "Something I'd be more concerned about, frankly. If Ronan is right, their magic should keep them from interacting with each other till the challenge, yes?" She glanced at him, and Ronan nodded. "That won't stop him from coming at any of us in the meantime. Can he issue a challenge to you still? And will it also be the same length of time before it takes place?"

Ronan stayed quiet for a moment, considering her question.

"He can . . . but the fact he didn't and intends to bond with Bree first leads me to believe that he needs her power before taking me on. He's not strong enough yet, and he knows it."

"And Bree?" I asked. "Would her power make him strong enough?"

My atman's lips thinned.

I had my answer.

"There's a chance I may survive, but your sister is unnaturally strong. Not quite to where you are, but she's steadily approaching it."

"Will she stand a chance against him?" I asked. It was the question that weighed on me most, because if she didn't . . . I couldn't think about that outcome. I refused.

"I don't know," Ronan said honestly. "Normally, I'd say no. She's a rage demon, as you pointed out, and he was chosen by the Source. Lorcan's abilities to mimic others' magic is clever, but not particularly useful here. He does have a few thousand years on her, though, and he may have developed more abilities than what I'm aware of." He ran a blood-crusted hand through his dark hair.

"I can't lose her," I said, knowing I sounded like a broken record but unable to stop repeating myself. "Not to him. Not like this." I shook my head, clenching my hands into fists.

"Have a little faith," Nat said. Her hand wrapped around my shoulder, giving it a gentle squeeze. "Your sister is one tough bitch. I can't imagine her doing this knowing she'd die. She's not that self-sacrificing."

Under different circumstances, I might have laughed, or at least let out a snort, but worry ate away at my unflappable sarcasm. My stomach churned with acid.

Through it, a cold resolve worked its way through my mind.

Fueled by something stronger than hate and less fickle than love.

It felt like a burning in my chest that warmed my face and would have set this whole building aflame if I let it.

"I hope he comes for us," I murmured. "I hope he thinks me weak. Vulnerable."

"Piper," Ronan said, and I wasn't sure if it was an admonishment or warning or begging. Maybe it was all three. All I knew was that I didn't give a damn.

"He thinks that he's owed your position, my sister's life, and the power to control an entire realm . . . but he doesn't have the first clue about what it means to take responsibility for something. He doesn't understand love or family. He doesn't know what it really means to protect what's yours. That the depth of that love means that you'd risk anything because losing them is losing everything."

"You can't hunt him down," Ronan started.

"Or rather you could, but that's not wise," Nat added with a grimace.

"I won't need to," I answered, lifting my chin to stare at them both. Rage burned in me, but this time, I had a purpose for it. A mission. "He'll come for me." I was sure of it. After the little conversation I'd had with him in *Sin*, there was no way he wouldn't. It wasn't in his nature to leave things be. Just like leaving Bree to this monster wasn't in mine. "And I'll be ready. If I can cripple Lucifer without trying, I will destroy this asshole. He'll be a husk of a demon. A sliver of magic. I'll make him wish he never came to Earth, so that when their challenge gets here—he won't stand a chance."

"Not to interrupt your moment—I'm all on board with the maiming of abusive pricks—but you might be getting a little ahead of yourself here. While a badass, you're still new to learning your magic." Nat flashed me a tight-lipped smile in apology. "And we know very little about Lorcan's— including how he got past the wards without anyone knowing."

"His mimicking ability," Ronan sighed. "He can disguise himself and his magic as any of ours because of chaos. The wards will be entirely ineffective at keeping him out."

Nat's eyebrow lifted. "There's nothing that can be done? At all?"

"Short of being attached to Bree's side—no. They can't harm each other right now, but everyone else is fair game."

He didn't look any happier about this outcome than she did.

"Well, in that case, prepare-and-be-ready-to-light-him-up, it is."

3
RONAN

The cold settled like morning fog. It seeped in, eventually freezing enough to jar me from sleep.

I don't need to reach over to know the right side of the bed was empty.

Piper's magic still permeated the air, but thinner. Less dense. My own sought her out on instinct, and I breathed a sigh of relief to feel her down the hall. Rising, I pulled on a pair of sweats and stepped through the void, into my living room.

She sat on the floor, one leg bent, the other straight while she leaned over. Her blonde hair wasn't pulled back as it usually was, instead hanging in thick ropes around her shoulders and down her back. She wore a tank top and plain cotton panties, giving her a vulnerable look—if not for the firearm in front of her. Her hands worked in feverish motions, dissembling the pistol, reassembling, point and aim. The gun clicked when she pulled the trigger.

She did it again. Then again, and again.

Her fingers were rubbed red and would likely be bruised

if not for her healing. She wouldn't stop, though. Not without another outlet.

When the stress or the fear or the worry drove her from sleep, this is what she did.

It was a compulsion of sorts. A coping mechanism that developed from growing up in a war-torn world, where every day was a battle. Some people might count or repeat their actions. Some might do things in patterns. Some might clean until their fingers were raw from the abuse.

My atma assembled and disassembled her guns.

"Have you slept at all?" I asked, half expecting no answer. It wasn't unusual for her to retreat so deep in her mind that she didn't register me talking when she was like this.

"No."

She was cognizant tonight. More alert than her answer would leave me to believe.

I took a seat on the couch behind her, lifting my leg to the other side, so she sat between them. Piper continued what she was doing without missing a beat.

"Is it Lorcan?" I asked, my voice darkening on the syllables of his name. I should have killed him all those centuries ago. I knew he was power hungry. I sensed the cruelty just waiting to blossom. But I had a policy in the Otherworld of not killing demons until their actions called for it.

If I'd known what would happen, that I would be sitting here one day in this position, I wouldn't have hesitated—instead draining his magic where he stood.

"Yes," she answered after a moment. "But not for the reasons you think."

I reached for her, running my fingers through her hair

till they caught a snag. Her head tilted back, hands still moving at a blistering speed.

"Explain."

"I'm not afraid of him. Maybe that's foolish . . ." Her eyes strayed downward, and I tugged again, drawing her attention back to me. "But I'm not. I fear what he means for Bree. This challenge. The outcome . . ."

"I wouldn't write her off so quickly. I might not be a fan of Bree, but she isn't stupid—and her confidence in this challenge makes me wonder why."

"It's not just that," she said. "Even if she wins, she'll have to kill him. I know she thinks of this as her problem to deal with, but I can't help feeling like if she'd told me sooner —said anything at all—we might have found a solution."

The gun clicked as she pulled the trigger once more, and with a heavy sigh, she set it aside, leaning back into the couch. Her head rested against the seat, turned up to alternate between watching me and the ceiling.

"But she kept it to herself, and now there's no avoiding the outcome," she said.

"Ruminating on what could have been doesn't help you now," I pointed out. She made a sour face, pressing her lips together in annoyance.

"I'm angry with her," Piper said after a moment. "She refused the bond for your sake—for us—but I'm angry with her for it. If I thought she did it for herself for one second, I wouldn't be—but she made this choice and wants me to respect it when it could end up meaning her death, or Lorcan abusing her for as long as they're together. How could she do that and just expect me to stand by?"

Her hands clenched into fists as she scowled at the ceiling.

"Have you considered that for so long you've taken responsibility for her, sacrificed yourself again and again for her sake, and this time, she's doing the same in her own way?" Before last night I wouldn't have thought it, but nor had I thought Bree capable of lying so well that not even I realized what was really going on these last months with her.

The hatred toward Piper was feigned. Fake.

Perhaps some of her was still angry, similar to the way Piper was now, but the way she treated her . . . it was to help her in the end. She thought she had to return to keep the knowledge of my whereabouts from Lorcan so that he could never challenge me.

But she failed in that, and instead of letting it play out, she forced his hand.

Her, or his lust to be the Harvester.

In her own way, she had cared for Piper while here, thinking it easier for my atma to let her go when the time came if she were horrible to her. She pushed her away in a vain attempt to help her move on. She underestimated Piper's love for her, though.

In the same way I underestimated Bree's love for her sister.

Despite all they'd been through, they would both protect each other to the bitter end—even at their own expense.

"I know that's what she's doing," Piper said, eyes squeezing shut. "I just wish she wouldn't. All this time I wanted her to choose me over him, and now that she has— I don't know how to deal with it. This guilt—"

"Is misplaced," I insisted, tugging on her long tresses again. The hair at her scalp pulled taut. "This is Bree's decision and hers alone. You have no reason to feel guilty when she chose this, not you."

"I know," she sighed. "But knowing something doesn't make it any easier."

"Would you want her to beat herself up over this if the situation were reversed?" I asked, trying another tactic. "Or feel guilty about all the times *you* chose to try to protect her, like when you entered a summoning circle and almost died from it?"

A steely glint entered her violet gaze.

"No . . ."

"Then don't focus on it. Choices were made. There's no changing it. We all have to move forward. Besides, there are greater things to concern yourself about." I pointedly looked toward her stomach, where that flare of magic pulsed with life. Piper shook her head.

"Nope, still not going there with you."

"You can't ignore it forever."

"I'm not," she said defensively. "I'm taking time to process it since my atman didn't do me the courtesy of telling me weeks ago—like he should have."

I sighed. "We've been over this—"

"Good reasons or not, I still need time and to talk to Señora Rosara. Nat said she might have a clue about how to handle a demon baby."

"I want to be there for that," I said, smoothing my hands over her scalp and down her neck to massage the tense muscles in her shoulders. Piper groaned, then shot me a glare, silently telling me she knew what I was doing. "I've seen a lot of demon babies born and know what to expect. I want to be sure that she doesn't do anything, accidental or otherwise, that could hurt you or the baby."

Her lips twisted as she slowly relaxed into my touch.

"You can be there on one condition," she said after a moment. I lifted an eyebrow, waiting for her to continue. "We continue training. I was serious earlier; I know he'll come for me, and I want to be prepared. I need to be. Bree may not get a happily ever after, but I'm sure as shit not letting that asshole have one either."

I leaned down, inhaling every breath she released. Our lips met and my cock stiffened. Nothing turned me on more than that fire in her. That strength to stand her ground and burn everything in her way to ash.

"I'll make you the most lethal thing to walk this earth, not a demon on this side of the portal will cross you when we're done."

"You say the sweetest shit," she murmured, smiling against my lips.

"For you?" I breathed. "Anything."

4

PIPER

Sunlight warmed my skin. I rolled over, the satin sheet slipping from my shoulders just as the scent of magic tingled my nose. Juniper and cinnamon. Chaos and desire.

Nat was here. So were the twins.

"It's almost two in the afternoon," she griped. "If we're going to do this, we need the element of surprise."

"I told you, I can handle it."

"I don't want you to *handle it*, Ronan. I want Piper to. You know as well as I do, she needs to get ahead of these things if she wants to stand a chance of swaying the humans—"

"I'm aware," he replied, his voice full of gravel.

"Then wake her up," Nat said. "We're burnin' daylight."

I didn't need to be in the same room to know she was giving him a headache. I sensed the building pressure through the bond.

Sitting up, I stretched my arms over my head and let out a grunt. The joints in my shoulders popped, relieving some of the tension. I slipped from the bed and dressed in jeans and a tank top, the kind with the built-in bra.

Running my fingers through my hair, I pulled it back in a sloppy bun, using the ends to hold it in place. Nat and Ronan were still going at it in the living room. I hadn't heard a peep from either of the twins, but it was only a matter of time.

With a sigh, I stepped out of our bedroom, closing the door behind me. Down the hall, Nathalie grunted, "*Finally.*"

"What's this about burnin' daylight?" I strode forward, plucking an apple off of the kitchen counter and taking a bite. Juice dribbled around the corner of my lips as the slightly sweet, but not quite ripe tang, touched my tongue. I didn't care. It was fresh and juicy, soothing the dryness in my throat from sleep.

"Sasha." Nat nodded, tipping her chin in her direction.

"While we were out last night"—she motioned to her sister who sat on an empty barstool at the end of the counter, drinking what looked like a fruit smoothie from a coffee mug—"we watched a woman get taken off the street. Anders glamoured us so we could follow them undetected, and they led us straight to a feeding den that doubled as a brothel. Given this lady's response and the couple of screams I heard coming from inside—I'd say it's not consensual."

Cold washed over me, making my skin pebble. My stomach turned and I had to set the apple aside, only half eaten, because I couldn't take another bite.

"You declared yourself the Queen," Nat said, taking over for the succubus that was eyeing me shrewdly. "You promised things would change and that you'd protect them. So what's your move?"

I glanced at Ronan, not for permission, but to silently communicate my thoughts to him.

"*I can't abandon them.*"

"I'd expect nothing less from you, both as my atma and my queen."

I blinked, expecting more push back. Ronan shook his head.

"Even though you had an issue with me opening the portal?"

"How much magic the portal required was an order of magnitude larger than dealing with a rogue band of vampires," he explained. *"You don't even need your magic to handle this, though it would make good practice."*

My heart skipped as something warm spread through my chest.

This. This is what I wanted from him. Not the chest-banging alphahole that tried to lock me away for my own good, but someone who let me be *me*.

I'd never be a housewife. I'd never be someone's wife period, given the antiquated and religious act meant nothing to me in this age. I'd never be a stay-at-home mom, even though I saw the merits in it. The mere concept of being a mom was so supremely foreign still, I struggled to wrap my head around it.

But I'd always be Piper.

Gun-toting and driven by my own moral code. I'd spent ten years taking care of a sister that I never knew would return and worked at making my city better—at least in some capacity. I was still doing that, but I was doing it for myself now. Because I was sick and tired of watching people kill each other in the streets and use others for their own personal gain.

I'd seen enough for a lifetime, even a demonic, immortal one.

"I hate when they do that," Nat complained. "Would it kill them to speak?"

"Yes," both Ronan and I answered at the same time.

A wry smirk spread across my lips.

Nat huffed, throwing herself down on the couch.

"If you two need to fuck and get it out of your system, make it quick because I'd like to do something about this den today."

I rolled my eyes, breaking contact from Ronan and going to take a seat across from her. "Give me a rundown of where this den is and what we're walking into."

For twenty minutes they laid out every detail they could tell me about it, from the number of windows to how many people they estimated were in there.

Their guess? Dozens. At minimum.

With a two-story building and no idea how much of it was occupied, it could be in the low hundreds. The idea of that many men and women being held captive and tortured . . . I wouldn't be eating anytime soon.

"Do you need my help?" Ronan asked as we were finishing off the details.

I lifted an eyebrow. "Need?"

Ronan cocked his head, appearing unamused even though there was an inkling of it coming from the bond between us. "I will take that as a no. Very well. I have some matters to attend to with Anders, but if for any reason you need me—"

"I'll holler," Nat said, not even looking his way. "She's in good hands. Go deal with Anders and see if he's found anything to help us deal with our *other* predicament."

I looked between the two of them. It's clear I wasn't the only one holding silent conversations with Ronan, given the way she'd phrased it. I knew she was referencing Lorcan, and to a lesser extent, Bree. I trusted them both implicitly to report to me if there was more on that front, though, and left it be when Ronan nodded once and entered the void.

"I don't think we should drive to the den," Sasha said, not a moment later.

"Hm?" I prompted, flipping through Sienna's phone where she'd photographed as much of the building as they could from the outside.

"Nat's car is recognizable," she said. "It's not like there's many of them in New Chicago anymore, certainly not as nice as hers."

I tipped my chin in acknowledgement. This was true.

"We'll need to have a glamor created for it at some point," I mused, zooming in on a window at the ground level. "Not that it'll help us this time, but for the future. I prefer we not take the L, if there's another alternative."

While my hatred of all things magic was no longer the case, I hadn't changed my mind on New Chicago's public transportation. I disliked the idea of being pricked and a machine stealing a drop of my blood for payment—even if it was to power the train. Knowledge might be power, but so was blood, and ever since I'd become a full-fledged demon as Nat called it—mine was a lot more precious.

"I can take us there," Sasha said. "Through the void."

I looked up from the phone, eyebrows scrunching in skepticism.

"You have enough control to take all of us and get there in one piece?"

The succubus-shifter narrowed her golden gaze on me. "Yes. I've been practicing."

"I can vouch for her," Sienna chimed in from her seat next to Nat, where she'd moved when we started planning.

"I don't need a voucher. I can't lie to her," Sasha said, watching me coolly.

"That you can't," I muttered, the wheels turning inside my head as I stared at a window on the building. "We can go through the void, then. What are the odds you can get us into this room on the other side?" I lifted the phone, flashing her the screen.

Sasha walked over and plucked it from my grasp, her long fingers flicked and scrolled as she pursed her lips in thought.

"If there's no wards, I should be able to," she said after a minute. "If there *are* wards, we'll bounce off them and appear just outside the window, which may be worse than walking in the front door, depending on how long it takes you to get through them."

"My solution to wards is blowing the door off its hinges and shattering the windows. If that won't work, I'll take down the front wall of the building."

Nat snorted. "Real subtle."

I shrugged. "Wards are nuanced if you want to untangle the magic in them. I don't have the time or practice for it. Eliminating the barrier is usually enough to weaken or kill them. Unless you have a better idea?"

"Unfortunately, no. And getting someone to go in and tamper with them will take longer than I'd like. I think your break and enter strategy is really our best option."

I nodded. "Let's gear up."

5

PIPER

The chill from the void barely registered past the adrenaline coursing through me. Magic wrapped around my fingers, up my arms, creating bands around my chest as both I and the rage within waited for the inevitable.

"Brace yourselves," Sasha whispered, her voice coming from everywhere around us.

Light pierced the darkness and the void recoiled, turning to smoke on our heels.

I took a step back, the cracked brick wall in front of me sharpening as the disoriented feeling faded.

"Wards," Sasha grunted.

No shit.

I eyed the front of the building as I called wind and fire. Sparks shot from my fingertips as my hair lifted on end. I rallied the magic into a single bolt that would strike the den where it stood.

Power thickened the air, rage oozing from me in spades.

Then Nathalie's hand came down on mine.

She stopped me with a single word. "Wait."

So I did. Pulling all that aggressive magic in, I held onto

it with a vice-like grip as she slowly approached the building.

She lifted her fingertips to it, almost gently. As if she were caressing the bricks.

"It's Katherine's magic," she said in a hush. "She laid their wards."

I lifted my eyebrows. "I didn't know your sister survived Lucifer . . ."

"Me neither," Nat said, her voice not giving anything away. She stared for a moment longer before glancing back at me. "I can undo them."

"Now?" I asked, looking toward the window for signs of movement. There was none, but that didn't mean a whole lot.

"Now," she said with a nod.

Nat stepped back, lifting her hands. A glow started in her palms as she chanted an unbinding spell under her breath. In an instant, gold erupted from her.

It spread up the building and around the windows, forming tight vines. It took me a moment to realize that the vines weren't her, but the wards themselves.

Nathalie reached out, plucking them apart like blades of grass.

She snapped them in pieces, and one by one they fell away until only the strands of magic coming from her remained.

She stopped chanting and the magic died out, the scent of juniper and raspberries fading slower.

"About that window—" I started. A click had my head whipping around to where Sienna stood, leaning against the brick wall, one of her long cat nails crooked under the edge of the seal.

Slowly, she slid it upwards, the pane lifting smoothly

until it caught on something and let out a screech. Sienna winced. Her lips silently formed the word, "Oops."

I sighed. "So much for a 'subtle' break and enter."

"You were going to take down the wall," Nat pointed out.

I shrugged, not arguing her point, then I picked up movement inside.

I drew my gun as I approached the window. Squinting, I tried to make out the figure in the corner, but they were cloaked in shadows.

Vampire or victim?

Only one way to find out.

I swung my leg through the opening and ducked down under the mostly open windowpane. My eyes adjusted quickly, gun already focused on the person waiting before I even pulled my second leg through.

On a rumpled bed, black hair hanging in sweaty clumps around her face, was a human woman that appeared to be in her later twenties. I lowered my gun slowly as I approached, pressing my finger to my lips in the universal sign of *be quiet*.

Her eyes didn't widen. There was no quickening of breath. The shallow rasping continued as she watched me with bleary eyes—not entirely cognizant.

Understanding washed through me.

I lifted the edge of the comforter and pulled it aside. The woman didn't react to what was likely the first fresh air she'd felt in a long time—if the sunken hollow cheeks and bruised naked flesh from several dozen vampire bites were anything to go off of.

A sharp inhale behind me told me the others had entered the room.

"Blood slave," I said quietly. "There's likely to be a lot here. Not all alive."

Beside me, Nat pushed forward. Her brown eyes soft and sad with empathy.

She leaned in close to the woman, who let out a soft moan, stretching the purple and blue column of her throat in invitation.

Bile churned in my stomach as Nat whispered an incantation, and the woman drifted to sleep instantly.

"You shouldn't use too much of your magic on them," Sasha said quietly. "Not when you don't know what we'll face."

Nat's lips pinched together in a thin, harsh line.

I understood her anger, but as much as it sucked to admit—Sasha was right. We could help them when all the threats were neutralized.

Instead of arguing, Nat nodded toward me as if to say, "*I'm ready.*"

Part of me doubted it. Even as a witch, they weren't subjected to the kind of horrors that went on in these places. But she'd have to be, because this was just the tip of the iceberg, and there was no way I planned on leaving a single one of these assholes alive now.

"We move as one. I'm in the front, Sasha in the back. Let's go."

The door handle clicked faintly as I turned it and pushed outward. It swung slowly, a low squeak emitting from its hinges that had me grimacing. I stepped into the hall right as the room across from us opened. A vampire peeked his head out, revealing bedhead and dried blood caked around his mouth. Muffled cries came from the room behind him.

Something dark and wicked settled over me as I shot between his eyes.

Shock emblazoned on the monster's face, he crumpled, but never hit the ground. I summoned white fire to consume him, wiping real evil from the earth.

His ashes hadn't even settled when all hell broke loose, the gunshot announcing our presence to the rest of the den as surely as a doorbell ringing.

"Couldn't have led with the fire, could ya?" Sasha griped as half the doors along the hall opened and vamps swarmed us.

I lined up my shots, firing one after another as they came for us.

Bam.

Bam.

Bam.

The shots echoed back-to-back as I mowed down nine vampires—three females and six males—incinerating every single one. Behind me, the screams of Sasha's victims followed as she decapitated them with her wicked claws.

Unlike the legends, a wood stake did jack shit—but decapitation?

Yeah, there was no coming back from that.

Just as the last shot sounded, so too did their screams reach a satisfying crescendo before dying out.

I started down the hall, letting Nat and Sienna check each room as we went for stragglers. At the end, it opened up into a grand foyer that gleamed with wealth and age. White and tan flowers decorated the wallpapered room. Wood floors, the darkest shade of mahogany, gleamed to perfection beneath plush antique rugs and oversized furniture. Bookshelves lined the walls with texts I didn't bother to read, instead turning for the sleek, dark staircase that ran up the right side.

"Sasha," I grunted, starting for the stairs.

She dropped into place behind me, moving swift and silent in my footsteps.

The top of the landing opened up to a smaller, cozier version of the main foyer, with two hallways. One right. One left.

I turned and thrust my chin toward the left, cutting a look to her where she stood at my back. She nodded once, stepping around me. I turned, leaving her to it as I took the right.

The floorboards creaked under the weight of my boots. I drew back, bringing my heel up into the center of the first door. The lock smashed through the frame, splintering as the wood gave way.

"Put the gun down."

I cocked my head, lowering my pistol a fraction.

Standing behind a disoriented human woman, if the flush in her cheeks and haze in her eyes were to be believed, was a piece of shit holding her hostage. Woman was a bit of a stretch. Her skin was smooth and youthful, with no wrinkles or age spots.

If not for the swell of her breasts, I wouldn't have thought she was much older than a young teen. As I eyed the way he cupped her distended belly, along with her throat, horror washed over me.

She's pregnant.

Shock tore through me, intensifying the threat of his next command.

"Drop it, or I'll rip her open right now."

Her lips moved, mouthing words without sounds. I narrowed my eyes, focusing on what she was trying to say.

Me. Something *me.* Maybe save me? Help me?

Right as his hand tightened on her belly, nails digging into the bruised flesh, understanding washed over me.

Kill me.

That's what she was trying to say.

She didn't want me to save her . . . she wanted to die.

In the split second where the truth and desperation of her demand really hit me, the captor acted.

The hand around her throat tightened in a fist, crushing her trachea.

Pain contorted her face, even if it's what she wanted. He shoved her toward me, jumping back toward the window.

That wicked thing inside me, born from seeing too much shit in this life, lifted its head and marked him for death.

Without moving a finger, light encapsulated him, pulling him from this realm into my own.

He disappeared in a flash as he entered the light dimension.

When I was done here . . . I would come for him to exact the punishment all these vampires had deserved. They'd died too easily because I didn't revel in death or pain.

Seeing this woman, hearing her dying breath . . . no.

Not anymore.

Maybe they needed more than death to fear me.

Maybe they needed pain. Rage. Destruction.

Clearly their own desires won out over the worry I'd come for them . . . but I could do things so heinous that they would never forget. Not in a hundred years. A thousand.

If the monsters of this city wouldn't fall in line, I would *make* them.

The woman—girl—in my arms slumped over. Life was

draining from her as quickly as water poured from a spout, and eventually she'd run dry.

But she didn't have to die.

I could save her.

Even if she didn't want to be saved.

Indecision warred inside me, because if I did this, there was no taking it back. I was taking her choice and binding her to me for as long as she'd live. This would not be like the twins or Nat.

But neither would it be like Lucifer.

I didn't have time to talk to Nat or Ronan or anyone else. I had only seconds to decide.

Falling to my knees, I rearranged her in my lap. I bite into my wrist roughly, without regard for my pain. The adrenaline would keep me from feeling the worst of it, anyway.

Blood dripped from the wound in a messy stream.

I shoved it between her lips, forcing it—my power, my will—down her throat.

She could end up hating me for it, but that was a sacrifice I'd make.

Because she would *live*.

The girl's two words told me everything I'd needed to know. She'd been through unspeakable horrors. Things that many never recovered from.

But I would pull her out of that. I would give her the chance to live, to heal, and see if she could find her way on the other side. She might not see it now. A year from now. Ten years, even.

With the right tools, though . . . one day she would.

A creak at the door made me jump. I grabbed my gun with my free hand and lifted it to the figure there, finger poised on the trigger.

Sasha stood, head cocked to the side.

"I cleared the rest of the hall. She going to make it?" She nodded toward the girl.

"If I have anything to say about it, she will."

I hadn't even finished the sentence when her heart started to speed up. It raced in her chest, hammering away as the magic rushed through her system. It healed the bruises, bite marks, and broken bones. The yellowing in her skin disappeared and her hair became fuller, shiny despite its unwashed state.

"Looks like it," Sasha said after a moment. "I wonder what she'll be."

"No idea," I murmured. When a human changed, what they became was usually influenced by who they were in life.

A succubus or incubus could be born from a love of sex or power.

Shifters often struggled with rage and anger, something I related to. Their new form giving them an outlet for that animalistic nature.

Ghouls never died, and their kind seemed more often than not to come from fear. Fear of death. Fear of what came after. People that clung to life because they were afraid would become something that ultimately lived in-between.

This girl didn't fear death. She didn't have the fire to fight for her own life out of anger. I doubted there was a deep desire and love for sex, although there might be for power.

Only time would tell what she became after this.

"Was anyone hurt?"

"A few of the women were drained almost entirely. A desperate attempt for their captors to be strong enough to get away. They didn't, but the women might not make it."

"Take me to them."

The first one wasn't conscious, but it was clear she'd put up a fight. Blood congealed under her nails from where she'd tried to kill her attacker. I didn't have hesitations saving her, but a thread of unease pulled at me when I realized she was pregnant.

Two that are pregnant?

My lips thinned into a hard line when Sasha took me to another.

She was close enough to giving birth that I was surprised the ordeal hadn't caused it.

There was no way this was a coincidence.

But why would a vampire den be keeping pregnant women?

Was it possible these were hybrid children that their abusers had impregnated them with?

The thought sickened me to my core.

"What are you doing?" she rasped, trying and failing to sit up. While conscious, she was weak and the wound at her neck was still bleeding.

"I'm a demon. I can save you if you take my blood."

I lifted my wrist that had already closed again. She wouldn't need much blood to save her, though. I could get away with a finger prick for this one.

Still, the woman eyed me warily. "Will it hurt my baby?"

My lips parted. I looked up at Sasha who stood at the door, a passive, steady presence. She lifted one shoulder in silent answer, as if to say, *I don't know.*

The thing was, neither did I.

"I—" My lips pressed together. "There's no way to

know if the magic will take—in you or the baby. Some people do, some don't. But if you don't get help, there's a good chance you won't make it. That wound on your neck doesn't look good, and I don't even know the other ones you might have."

She swallowed hard, tears pooling in her eyes. "I can't chance it. Not if—" Her voice cracked, a hiss escaping her lips as a hand dropped to her abdomen. "Oh no."

"What is it—"

Liquid and blood quickly dampened the dirty sheets just below her waist.

The baby was coming.

Fuck.

"Sasha," I said in alarm.

"What do you want me to do? I don't know how to deliver a baby—"

No. She didn't.

But I knew someone who did.

"Take her to Señora Rosara. She can help her."

Her cat ears twitched as she approached the woman with trepidation.

"She can deliver the baby, but she may not be able to save her," Sasha said quietly.

"Ask her if she can keep her stable, or at least stop her from dying. I need to finish up here. Come get me if she says she can't."

Sasha nodded before awkwardly shifting the woman in an attempt to pick her up and not jostle her neck wound or belly while she was at it.

I left her to it, taking a quick glance inside every room on the floor.

Twenty-three women. All pregnant.

That unease inside me grew with every room. Every woman and girl.

Some of them looked barely old enough to even physically be able to *have* children.

Nausea rose, but it was only through sheer force of will that I kept from retching when I reached the end of the line.

I needed to find Nat and figure out what the hell was going on here.

6

NATHALIE

I shouldn't have taken down Kat's wards.

I should have let Piper do it.

Now I was paying the price.

"I know you can hear me, Nathalie," the low growl said from behind me. A ghost of a touch skated over my shoulder. I must have imagined it because he wasn't here.

This wasn't *real*.

I refused to respond. To give the voice an inch. Since it had started months ago, I'd learned to keep it at bay, only losing my grip when I used too much magic.

The portal was an acceptable sacrifice, but the wards? No. I wanted to kick myself for being so stupid and careless on such an important mission.

"I'm going to check on the survivors down here while we wait for them," Sienna said, casting a worried glance up the stairs. Sasha would be fine. Piper would be fine. If I had any doubts before, I certainly didn't after that show in the hallway. The way they mowed them down, slaughtering without mercy . . . whether Piper realized it or not, she'd found her match in Sasha. The shifter-succubus had an inner fire that burned in likeness to my best friend. She was nearly as stubborn too.

I waved Sienna off, appreciating the reprieve from others' eyes. I had to watch myself around Piper, and Sienna was starting to catch on too. Whenever my gaze strayed too close to that figure, or I found myself listening to his voice . . .

I needed to get a grip.

Straightening my shoulders, I pointedly ignored the other presence in the room as I traced the lines of magic through the wall.

Unlike Kat's magic, that was a dark, royal blue and felt like the first snow of the year—the magic in this room was dark. Seedy. Nearly black in color and filled with sour intent. I couldn't shake my own apprehension.

If I used magic to find it and unravel the spell, it would give *him* a greater foothold in my mind—even if temporarily. I'd already all but opened the door and invited him in when I took down Kat's wards.

I was in deep with no immediate end in sight, so I gave in, and gold blossomed.

It started as sparkles, like glitter in my palms, falling to the ground where it would have dissipated if not for that ink-like magic running along the wall of bookshelves.

A single spec touched it.

My magic erupted.

Spreading like a contagion, the magic coated everything that was tainted, turning it into my own.

A disease spread and compromised all it touched, but my magic did the opposite. Instead, giving it life—and handing me control.

As it morphed before my eyes, I recognized the spell in place.

Locking enchantment.

But what it locked . . .

I wasn't sure.

"How far you've come from the witch that didn't know who or what she was," he whispered, taunting me.

My mouth tightened in a grimace.

Focus. Focus. Focus—

"Nathalie Opal Le Fay, the greatest chaos witch to ever exist. It has a ring to it, doesn't it?"

"Stop it," I said through gritted teeth, knowing my mistake as soon as the words left my lips. *Shit.*

I had one rule with myself.

Never, ever respond.

He may have assumed I could hear him, but it was another thing entirely to talk back.

"Finally," he purred. A phantom hand wrapped around my neck as his lips ghosted my temple. It shouldn't have been possible. It *wasn't* possible, but the mind was a crazy thing in what it could make you believe—and right then, I felt him.

Perhaps not as solid as the ground beneath my feet, but I felt *something*.

It unsettled me more than I could admit.

"You've been playing games with me for months now, little witch. Pretending you can't see—can't hear. I knew it." His thumb brushed over my jaw. Real or imagined, the touch made goosebumps break out along my skin.

"You're my guilt. My remorse. My demon—"

"I might be your demon, but not in the way you think," he hissed, inhaling my scent despite the fact he didn't need to breathe *because he wasn't real.*

And now I'd really lost it. Talking to myself.

Great. Just flippin' perfect—

"And I won't tolerate being ignored any longer," he added, the sound a rumble in his chest.

"No," I snapped, stepping out of his imaginary hold. My body went through his hands as if they were smoke—but I could have sworn I felt their loss. "I'm not doing this with you. I am not going to be one of those witches that loses their mind. If I can't handle you on my own, I'll start taking medications to get rid of you. Even if it costs me my magic . . ." Something in me wilted at the thought. Anti-hallucinogens, anti-psychotics, anti-depressants—they all had the same effects on a witch. We couldn't access our magic. For that reason, there was stigma that prevented witches from ever considering it. We were known for going insane, much like my great ancestor, Morgan Le Fay. Magic drove us to extremes, and when we were unwilling to part with it, it stole our minds. Without a psychic bondmate, it was the price we paid.

I'd found mine . . . but I'd never completed the bond. And now it was going to be my end.

Unless I stopped it.

"I won't do this. I won't lose my mind to it. Damn it all, I'll take whatever I have to, to stay *me*."

"Brave little witch," he murmured, equal parts reverent and infuriated. "No medication will ever get rid of me. No drug will cure you of this disease. You ensured that when you tied us together."

I shuddered. "No . . ." I shook my head. "It's not possible. I tried, but you *died*."

"Move this bookcase." He tapped it with his foot. "Slide it to the left and unbind the lock. There's a stairwell that leads to a basement of children."

My lips parted.

I blinked, frozen to the spot.

"You can't know that. *I* don't know that—"

"And I'm not you. I'm not your guilt. I'm not part of your psyche." He strode forward, and for the first time, I let myself really look and take him in.

Golden eyes and stark white hair. High cheekbones and full lips. He came to me in a button-down shirt with the sleeves rolled up, revealing his golden brands.

Lucifer.

Not in the flesh, but just as imposing as he stood before me.

His head canted forward, leaving only inches between our forms.

That unnamable energy that connected us burned hotter than Piper's fire.

"I'm the devil, and I'm not going anywhere."

He disappeared, but that energy . . . those words . . . I was shaking and I didn't even realize it.

"Nat?" Sienna said, her voice making me jerk. "You okay?"

I clenched and unclenched my hands, subtly wiping the sweat from my palms on my jeans. "Fine. Can you help me with this? I think there might be something behind here."

I motioned to the bookcase Lucifer had pointed to.

Sienna walked over and gripped both sides. On the right was another bookcase. On the left was a blank space where a portrait hung. The staircase slid easily under her grip, and my heart hammered.

He was right.

There was a door.

I chanted under my breath and unlocked the binding spell. The door clicked open.

My chest tightened, threatening to cut off the air from my throat.

There, in the dark, was a staircase.

My feet descended on their own. Needing to see the truth of it with my own eyes.

"Wait, we don't know if there are any vampires down there—"

"There's not," I said, feeling eerily assured. I shouldn't have been. But I was.

And he was right.

In a damp basement that smelled of mold and rot, cages lined the walls.

Children of all ages, both genders, some magical and some not . . .

My knees gave out. Bone hit cement as my world—both metaphorically and physically—was pulled from under me.

I wasn't going crazy.

I'd killed the devil.

Now his ghost was haunting me.

7

PIPER

I scrubbed a hand down my face.

Thirty-four children.

The youngest was a two-year-old half-succubus, with curly black hair and sad brown eyes. The oldest was eleven, and just on the cusp of maturity. She was human and mute. No doubt she'd been abused, but I just wasn't sure to what extent.

"This is a fucking nightmare," I muttered, surveying the basement as Nathalie and Sienna took charge, trying to place them in groups for kids that either didn't have parents or weren't sure, and kids that were stolen.

I wasn't sure what we'd do with all of them. How we'd find something resembling a family or homes. The sad truth was they'd likely end up in orphanages for the most part. It wasn't the horror they'd come from, but it was a far cry from parents that could actually help them recover from this ordeal.

Shaking my head, I started up the staircase to check on our other survivors. Maybe one of them could tell me what the hell had been happening here. Children in cages and an entire floor of pregnant women . . . there was no possible misunderstanding in all of this, but I needed to find out what exactly it amounted to.

My footsteps were heavy. Dragging. I reached the top of the staircase and had to pull my shoulders back and lift my head up because it wasn't coming easily right now.

"You look like you've seen better days," Sasha said from the couch in the main foyer as I entered. Usually there was snark that couldn't be hidden. A caustic tone that was unmistakable. Not this time.

"They were keeping kids in cages." I shook my head. "Nat and Sienna are sorting that out downstairs if you want to help."

Her cat ears twitched. "I'm good. I'd rather be up here."

We stared at each other for a long moment. The thing neither of us said was that we couldn't look at them. That to see kids that way . . . there was something so fucking depraved about it that it made us incapable of actually helping them. Not when the anger and the rage and the darkness closed in.

No. In that, we were alike. She didn't need to say it. Unspoken, we both saw the truth in each other, plain as day.

"Was Señora Rosara able to save the woman?" I asked, needing to focus on something else. Something good, even if it was only the flickering flame of a single candle in an endless night.

Sasha shook her head. "The baby was dead. Had been for a while. It didn't develop right in the womb." She looked away, closing her eyes. "Señora let her go because she lost the will to live when she found out. She didn't want to force her through that."

I inhaled sharply through my nose in reaction, slowly letting it go.

Apparently, not even candlelight was allowed today.

"Thank you for taking her," I said. "I need to start talking to victims. Figure out where they're from, how long they've been here, if they know anything about the kids . . ."

"I know of a women's shelter that takes humans and supes. Would you like me to contact them and see how many spaces are available right now? I doubt they can take everyone, or that all these women would want that—but something tells me enough will."

I nodded. "That would be good. Let me know what they say, and we can start getting people where they need to be." She stood to leave, and I paused. "I haven't forgotten what we talked about. I just haven't had a chance to speak to Nat."

She gave me a half smile that could have been mistaken for amusement if not for the darkness I could see raging in her eyes. "We've had a bit more important things to deal with. I don't mind waiting when I know you're not just putting me off."

With that, she stepped through the void.

Despite my previous reservations, today went a long way in showing me how useful Sasha could be as a second. But that was a thought for another time. Like she said, there were more important things right now.

My feet seemed to know where to go, even though I hadn't fully realized it until I stood in front of the same door where I'd watched a girl's throat get crushed—before I consequently turned her, despite her dying wish. There were so many people that needed my help, but something about this girl and knowing how alone you are those first moments when you realize you're no longer human . . . I needed to check on her.

My knuckles rapped against the wood door. No answer came, but the shuffling from inside told me she was still there.

I took a deep breath, preparing myself for whatever I'd find.

Courtesy of the shattered frame where the lock was, the door swung open all on

its own.

"I know you don't know me, but I'm—"

"My maker," a soft, melodical voice said from the far corner of the room. She sat in a tight ball, between the edge of a desk with peeling paint and a wood chest that had seen better days. Something dark blocked most of her body from view.

Everything obscured except large, pewter-colored eyes.

"Piper," I said, correcting her. "I gave you my blood because you were dying."

"I wanted to die," she said softly, unflinching.

"And now?" I asked. "Do you still want to?"

Her lips pressed together.

Yes and no.

Fair enough.

I took a step toward her, and she instantly focused on my feet. I stilled, then dropped to one knee.

"What's your name?"

"My parents called me Mist. For mistake." Her voice didn't waver. "The vampire who they gave me to in return for protection called me *mio preziosa* when he . . ." She didn't finish the sentence. She didn't need to.

Her bottom lip quivered, the first hint of emotion. She

shut it down immediately, taking a deep breath to steady herself.

"What do you want me to call you?"

Her lips twisted almost sardonically. "I don't care. Just not that."

All right, we'd have to come back to that one.

"How old are you?" I asked, changing direction.

"I was fifteen when he brought me here. That was . . . a long time ago." Her eyebrows drew together in concentration. "I counted at first. Months went by. Eventually things blended together. Their bite, it does things to you. Makes it all fuzzy."

"Vampire venom makes humans high," I said, filling her in. While young, she wasn't as educated as I was on what supernaturals could do to you. I wondered if it would have helped her, had she known. Would she have found a way out? Or would that knowledge not matter in a place like this?

"Were you pregnant when he brought you here?" I asked her.

Slowly, that wide gaze dropped to her belly, completely hidden in shadow.

"No," she said. "That happened after."

"Is it his?" I asked. While rare, sometimes vampires could procreate with humans. If she'd been human when it was born, she would have died.

"I-I don't know," she said after a moment. "Mostly it was just him. But there was a stretch of time when they brought in another man. Just one. He would pay to rape me while the vampire watched. He stopped coming once I was pregnant."

Acid ate its way up my throat.

"Was he human?"

"I don't know."

I nodded slowly. They were trying to impregnate her. That much I was sure of. If they brought someone else in and he stopped coming after she was . . . I had to wonder how many other women in this house were subjected to the same treatment.

"I don't want it," she said after a minute. "This baby. I'm just a kid." Her lip began to quiver once more. She sucked in another tight breath, but it didn't stop this time. Shock was setting in. I was surprised it took so long.

"You don't have to keep it," I said quietly. "When you give birth, we can take it away and you'll never have to see it again if that's what you want." She let out a terse breath and nodded. That answer seemed to ease something in her.

If it was fully human, it might be hard to place the kid was what I didn't say.

And if it wasn't . . . we'd face that when we got there.

"What am I?" she asked after another long pause. "What are you?"

Her order of questioning implied she knew enough to understand that most of the time, if a supe turned you, you'd be the same as them. I was the special exception.

"I'm a demon," I answered her honestly. "But I'm not sure what you are yet. The shadows—" I motioned to her body with my hand and gave a half smile.

It was tight, and hard for me to put on my face. It probably looked like a grimace more than anything. Her eyes squinted in confusion.

"I've heard about demons," she said. "My parents said they'd steal your soul." How unoriginal. "But the vampire . . ." She paused, trying to search her memory. "He talked about a demon that hunted demons. A woman that killed vampires and witches. He said she was worse than the devil." She looked me over in a new light. "Is that you?"

Never before had I been proud of being called worse than Lucifer.

But there was a first time for everything, it seemed.

"It is."

She nodded once. A knock against the wood frame startled us both. Her eyes snapped up over my shoulder, turning from pewter to a glowing silver that bordered on white. As soon as the color changed, it winked out. If I didn't know better, I might have thought I'd imagined it.

Whatever she was, she had power. A lot of it.

I turned my cheek to peer over my shoulder. Sasha stood in the doorway, holding a pile of clothes. "The shelter thought we might need these." She lifted the heap in her arms pointedly.

"Would you like some clothes?" I asked her, not knowing for sure but sensing she had nothing on given she was naked when I found her, and it didn't seem like these sick fucks were big on giving them clothing.

The girl nodded almost enthusiastically.

I stood up and turned toward Sasha, plucking some clothes off the top. A simple tank top and sweats. They might be a little big, but they'd do for now.

I set them down on the bed. "We're going to step out while you get dressed, okay?"

She nodded again but didn't move, waiting for us to leave first.

I closed the door shut as firmly as I could, leaving her to it.

"She looks better," Sasha said.

"She's been through a lot, but I think she'll be okay. Eventually."

Sasha nodded, understanding. "The shelter has sixteen spots. I guarantee we'll need more, but maybe Nathalie will have some ideas there. Giving them clothes is a start, then we can see who needs to go to the shelter, and who needs to find their family. Should probably see if any of them have kids in the basement and want them," she added, quieter than before. "You find anything out on that front?"

"They purposely impregnated her. No idea if the fetus is human or not. She doesn't want it, but that's a problem for the future."

"One thing at a time," Sasha said.

I nodded. "See if any of them will talk to you and let me know how the one who was unconscious is doing."

"Will do."

As she was disappearing into the next room, the sound of something shattering from the one I was just in had me cracking the door.

"You all right?" I called, trying not to barge in on the poor girl.

"Y-yes," she answered. "You can come in."

I stepped inside and my breath caught in my chest.

"What?" she asked defensively, a hint of aggression showing.

"Your wings," I murmured. They weren't shadows. They were wings. Pure black wings that held a touch of the void in their depths. They spanned at least twelve feet, tip-to-tip, and a shattered lamp was just below the end of her left one. "I didn't realize you had wings."

"They're clumsy," she replied. "I had to tear the tank top to get around them."

"We'll figure out a better clothing situation in the future," I started, then paused when something else caught my eye. Iridescent scales ran up her bare arms, shifting from clear to opal and grey to black, absorbing light within them. They started at her forearm and ran past her collar bone, along the slope of her neck, before trailing off.

Wings and scales.

Talons replaced her nails, bloody from where they'd sprouted on her hands and bare feet.

Instantly, I knew what she was.

And it told me so much more than the words spoken between us before this moment.

"You're a siren."

"What is that?" she replied.

A creature of fury. Of wrath.

The legend of the harpy came from sirens. Whereas harpies aren't real, sirens very much were. But oh, were they rare.

And hunted.

In trying to save her, I'd both given her impossible power and put a target on her back. But I wouldn't say that now. Not when it was new. That would come later, after she learned to protect herself.

"You'll eventually be able to fly with those wings. The only time they'll go away is when you get in water. Your legs will turn to a fish tail, and you'll be able to breathe under water." I hesitated to tell her the next part. Her beauty and allure would be incomparable now as well, but it wasn't the reason sirens were hunted. In fact, that had everything to do with being the hunter. Beauty was just a pretty face and a supernatural pull to make lesser creatures of vile intent enter her trap. The real weapon was her voice. "You'll be able to make people do anything you want. Even if it's against their will."

Her lips parted.

I waited.

This was the moment she'd tell me I made her a monster. That she hated me. That she—

"Can I stop them from hurting me?"

Weak, but not. Fragile, but strong. There was something in her that defied all logic and reason. In every way, this world had beat her down, and yet she wasn't breaking.

She wasn't running, despite telling me to kill her.

She was on the cusp of becoming something new. Someone she'd never been.

A creature of wings and talons and scales.

"Yes, and I'll help you."

She smiled, and I could have sworn that a whisper ran through my mind and called her *vengeance.*

8

RONAN

"It's about damn time," Anders griped as I walked into the bar called *Sin*. It was the same bar I'd followed Piper to when she killed Greta McArthur, and then later when she trashed our apartment. The gyrating lights assaulted my senses, but the spell woven to keep the peace helped settle the agitation.

Standing on the other side, serving drinks, was the vampire hybrid we'd agreed to meet. Her purple and green hair blended in with the technicolor lights that strobed throughout the club she owned. "No rest for the wicked," Dahlia Le Grange said as I approached. With a sidelong glance at the patrons to Anders' left, they got up and moved —clearing a space for me.

"You've no idea," I muttered, taking a seat.

"Anything I can get you?" Dahlia asked, hands splayed on the bar as she leaned against it. While her face was youthful, childlike even, I knew better than to assume. This hybrid had been around a long time, slowly gaining power along the west coast and only settling in New Chicago when the Magic Wars hit nearly two decades ago. While she appeared sixteen, I had it on good authority she was over two hundred.

"No," I said, answering her question.

"Hm," she responded, amusement flashing in her eyes. "No alcohol, drugs, or sex? Your mate said the same thing, though she was here for a different reason, I suspect."

My knuckles tightened at the mention of Piper. Dahlia's eyes flicked downward, then back up, a wide grin settling in. "Touchy about your uncrowned queen—though she's not so 'uncrowned' as she was before, now is she?"

"We're here to discuss an alliance," Anders said, not-so-subtly turning the conversation. "You've ignored our inquiries for weeks. Time is running out for you to choose a side, Dahlia."

She snorted. "All business, you two are. I can respect that. Lucifer wasn't enough business. All fucking and frolicking about, swinging his magic dick around like New Chicago was a high school locker room." She shook her head, the green and purple pigtails swinging with the movement. "Unfortunately for you both, I've already made my choice. Sorry to waste your time." She turned to walk away, dismissing us.

"Who?" The tone of my voice clued her in. I wasn't simply asking.

She paused, peering at me over her shoulder. "Piper Fallon."

I inwardly released a sigh. Again.

"Piper isn't on the table right now."

"I beg to differ, demon. She declared herself a player in the game—and not just any player—the queen. You're her mate and king, so I mean no offense when I say I'm not interested unless it's her I'm speaking to. I've watched men rise and fall, crumbling beneath their own flaws. I didn't follow them then, and I won't follow one now. My choice is made. It's her or *no one*."

My fingers drummed against the bar top, pointed nails nicking the veneer. "And if she isn't prepared to take the blood oath with you?" I asked.

"I'll wait. I told her to come find me when she's ready. I haven't changed my mind, and I don't plan to." Something flashed in her eyes. A coldheartedness that told me she wasn't afraid of me—even if she should have been. Supernaturals often had a certain arrogance that came with power and age. The vampiress was no different, except in the singular fact that she didn't flaunt whatever power she held. She was confident, but not overly cocky.

"You've been around for a time, Dahlia," I said. "Your clan is one of the biggest in New Chicago, yet you're the only one that never submitted to Lucifer. I wonder how that is, that a hybrid vampire never took blood from a demon, yet managed to stay on top *and* evade him," I mused aloud, watching the twitch of her lips.

"Power comes in many forms, Harvester," she replied, tipping her hand. "Now if you'll excuse me, I've got other business to attend to." Her eyes flicked to the far side of the club where two vampires stood, silently waiting for their mistress.

Anders opened his mouth to push the topic, but I placed a hand on his shoulder and tipped my chin. "Thank you for speaking with us."

I stood and turned for the exit to the club. Anders followed my lead, waiting to speak until we'd exited.

"Well, that was a bloody waste of time," he muttered, scratching the back of his head.

"Not necessarily."

He lifted an eyebrow in question. I responded by grabbing his shoulder and taking us through the void, exiting into his apartment.

Anders wrenched himself away the first chance he got, shaking off my grip. "You could warn a man before doing that, you know?"

"I could," I answered. The unspoken 'or not' coming across plain as day.

"Prick," he muttered, pulling out a cigarette. With a snap of his fingers, the tip of his thumb caught fire. He used it to light the blunt end, then inhaled the sweet tobacco.

"Dahlia is right. Whether or not Piper meant to put herself out there, she's now made it clear who and what she wants to be. If they won't accept a blood oath from me, she'll need to take it—whether she likes it or not."

I could only imagine how this conversation was going to go down with her. But knowing my atma, there was no way to predict how she'd really respond.

"Does it bother you?" Anders said. I lifted an eyebrow. "Their refusal of you? That they picked her."

"No." I shook my head. The thought hadn't even crossed my mind. "Not at all, why?"

"Curious," he hummed, releasing a breath of white smoke from his nostrils. "Does it bother you they will take her blood? I know demons can be . . . territorial with their atmas."

That wasn't as simple to answer. It had occurred to me already that I may not be thrilled with the prospect . . . but them swearing it with Piper instead of myself suited my ends better than any of them knew.

"Piper will have control over them. The bond isn't a mutual exchange. It's a bargain for power. She gives them a drop and they sign away their souls. So while I don't like anyone taking her blood, this will give her a measure of protection and power in this city—and I will sacrifice anything—certainly my pride—to keep her safe."

Anders nodded along, considering my words. "And the baby."

I stilled, tilting my chin to glance sideways at him.

"You know?"

Anders lifted his hands in mock surrender. "Half-fae, remember? We have an affinity for these things."

"How?" I said through clenched teeth.

"Heard the Señora talking to herself about a demon baby and herbs she needed," he deadpanned. I cursed the universe. While Nat was trustworthy, the old witch who owned the building had no one to answer to but herself. That situation would have to be rectified. "Given you had me handle the arrangements for your apartment and I knew about the extra room, it wasn't exactly a stretch. Especially when you opened the portal without Piper last night."

I sighed. "Who else knows?"

"If I had to guess? Bree and Lorcan. The twins might suspect, particularly Sasha. Not to mention Nat."

"The witch knows," I confirmed. "Bree and Lorcan as well."

He nodded. "My mother was pregnant with me for thirteen months. Fae typically spend two years pregnant, though. I don't suppose that's the norm for demons?"

"No."

Far from it.

Six months—give or take—was a rough estimate. The truth was every pregnancy differed, and the length often had more to do with how strong the fetus was above all else. Babies in the human realm follow a set path because they're all the same there, with only slight variations. But demons? We were as varied in power as day and night, with everything in-between.

"My mother gave birth to me at three months," I said quietly. "Lucifer was five months. Our child . . ." I looked away. Anders understood and let out a heavy sigh, putting out his cigarette in the ashtray on his kitchen counter.

"Piper is strong," he said, clapping me on the back, albeit somewhat awkwardly.

"That's what I'm worried about." He frowned in confusion. "The stronger a demon child is, the earlier they're born. They develop at a rate that correlates to their magic."

"Well," Anders breathed. "Magic doesn't always pass linearly. You have no way of knowing how strong your kid will be, or when she'll give birth. But that does bring up the question of what we're going to do about Lorcan. He knows, and while he can't touch Bree right now, Piper is another case entirely."

"I know."

"She lacks the temperament to back down, nor does she have the ability to fight someone who can get to her on a psychic level. Bree has shields; Piper has *nothing*."

"I know," I growled, shoving him off me. "In every way, she's pure rage at its core. Her elemental magic is stronger than any I've seen. She has created another realm that didn't exist before. She possesses the ability to shift, but she can't block out psychic attacks. She's heavily susceptible to magic, particularly spells. She has sheer strength, but she needs more than that." I shook my head, biting the inside of my cheek. "The blood oath will help. They'll have no choice but to assist her if something were to happen."

"Lorcan is a demon—one capable of masking his magic as easily as I can mine, if not more so," Anders sighed, flopping down on the overstuffed armchair. He hooked his ankle up over his knee and rested his elbow against his bent knee—hands steepled. "You need more than a supernatural guarding her."

"She won't tolerate me at her side day and night. Not even for this," I admitted, much as it pained me to.

"I'd be shocked if she did, but that's not what I was thinking."

"You're not enough." My response came out flat. No room for argument.

"I wasn't thinking of me, but thank you again, asshole. That's the second time you've insulted me today—"

"The point, Anders," I ground out. "Get to it."

"Bree," he said, like it was obvious. "Lorcan can't attack Bree, and she knows what he's capable of better than anyone. Have Bree guard her, at least until the challenge is over."

I considered it. Her sister was a force to be reckoned with, and furthermore, she was probably the only guard Piper would actually accept. The greater question there was, would Bree agree?

"I'll talk to her."

Anders lifted his eyebrows. "Word to the wise, insulting her likely won't get you far if that's how you plan to go about it—"

"Oh fuck off," I muttered, standing to take my leave.

His chuckle followed me all the way through the void.

9

PIPER

Blood dripped from my fingers. It leaked all over the sidewalk, seeping between the cracks, painting a grotesque picture.

Never before had I enjoyed torture or reveled in death. But today . . . today I crossed a line.

And I didn't regret it.

Of all the vampires that resided in this place, there was only one left to take the brunt of my anger. My rage. Only one left that could answer my questions.

Answer, he did.

I made him sing like a canary as he begged for death.

In the end, it came too soon, but wasn't that always the case?

He told me how they'd bring in humans and the occasional incubus to impregnate the women they held captive. Afterwards, when the children were weaned, they were placed in the basement. Neglected. Only kept alive to act as feeders. And when they came of age, the process began anew.

They were breeding them, entire lines, simply to feed. To gorge themselves.

And to stay under the radar.

The more they bred, the less they had to pull off the streets or steal from their homes. It helped them avoid suspicion for decades.

To think if the twins hadn't been walking by when they were—we never would have known. Things needed to change. It started here. Now.

On the blood-soaked pavement outside this disgusting place.

I summoned rock from the ground in a spike that impaled his body in a vulgar display for all to see. His flesh was stripped away, then burned, the layer underneath bubbling and oozing. The chest cavity had been opened; his heart ripped out. Preserved in my freezer for the day the little siren girl needed to feed. While she had time, it wouldn't be long before the effects of her transition finally caught up to her. Just as vampires needed blood and ghouls needed flesh, she needed the hearts of men. Her magic demanded it, and I made sure her abuser would be the first.

"You've been busy," Ronan said from behind me. I was surprised that I hadn't heard from him all day. The silence wasn't unwelcome. Just unexpected.

"He deserved it," I murmured. "The others died too quickly."

"I know," he said quietly. His presence wrapped around me, familiar and comforting. "Sasha told Nathalie, and she contacted me after you went to the light dimension."

"You didn't try to stop me," I said, staring at the gory figure in front of me. His body was poised nine feet high, in front of the double doors to the den. It had been evacuated for several hours now. All the women were taken to shelters and other temporary hiding places. The children were split between several orphanages, while Nathalie tried to work out a more permanent solution for them. It turned out very few of them had family, and the ones that did—their family were the women held captive, few of which were still alive or wanting to claim them. It was a horrible situation.

"There was no need. You are rage. You have to have an outlet, that's the price of your magic—and exacting it on people that deserve it is the least of my concerns."

I might be rage, but in the wake of my own destruction, I was numb.

Mentally and physically exhausted.

"I hope they learn," I said into the quiet of the night. "Because every infraction, I'll go further. I'll punish more. I'll make an even bigger statement. If these depraved fucks don't get it together . . . I'm going to become the monster I always feared I was."

Ronan wrapped an arm around my waist, pulling me in.

"And if that's what you have to do, I'll be beside you to pull you back from it. You can be a monster to protect your own, and I'll be one for you."

The thought warmed me, bringing just enough life to my numb senses that I was able to finally step away from the entire mess. To leave what happened here, here—where it would stay.

Without lifting a finger, I lit the building on fire.

White light ravaged the antique wood and drywall. It ate through the bedrooms, through the sinister memories this place held—cleansing it.

And with the fire still burning, and the body still hanging on display, I said, "Take me home."

"Gladly."

The void closed around us, its cold bringing me peace.

I didn't register that we'd stepped out of it until the sound of thundering water hitting the shower tiles pulled at my senses. Steam filled the bathroom as Ronan undressed me. Nothing sexual about it, but intimate all the same. He pulled the blood-soaked fabric from my body, yanking it in places it had dried too stiff to stretch. One by one the pieces fell away, like armor being removed. I stood in front of the shower glass, my reflection smudged red and brown, eyes tired, feet sore.

I recognized the girl staring back.

She was the same beat down, exhausted survivor that worked as a bounty hunter on the city streets—before anyone knew her name or what she truly was.

They may call me queen now, but part of me would always be her.

Particularly on days like this, when the bad shit was just too much.

The glass slid open. Ronan nudged my back, guiding me beneath the spray.

My head tilted back on instinct. The first touch of hot water scalded enough to make me release a small groan. I reached out blindly for the soap and started the process of washing it all away.

Flakes of blood and grime trickled down my body, through the reddish-brown stream. The scent of honey and vanilla chased it away as I lathered my body.

Ronan retreated to the bedroom, letting me have this time for myself. I was thankful for it. A moment of reprieve to decompress.

After my body was clean, I moved to my hair, then scrubbed underneath my nails. I wasn't sure how much time had passed when I flipped the water off, then stood there for a moment, wringing my hair.

The glass shower door slid open. Ronan extended a fluffy grey towel. I took it wordlessly and started patting my skin dry, then twisted it around my hair in a wrap.

I stepped out, coming to stand before Ronan. He didn't ask. He didn't speak. He just let me lean my forehead against his shoulder and wrap my arms around his neck.

Warm calloused hands grabbed my waist, his fingers sliding along my lower back.

"I know we've got a lot to work through, but I don't feel like talking tonight. I don't have it in me after today."

"What do you need?" The low rumble started in his chest, and everywhere we touched, skin-to-skin, I clung to it. To him.

"Oblivion," I said, without thinking. "Release."

One hand slid up my back, nails trailing along my spine while his thumb skimmed over my ribs and along the curve of my breast. He continued up over my shoulder blade, past my neck, to the towel wrapped around my hair —unceremoniously pulling it from my head and dropping it on the floor. Wet locks of hair cascaded down. He ran his fingers through it, tugging on my ends to tilt my head back.

I looked into his face. It was so strange, so different, so *other* from the people of this world. The way his brands curled up his neck, just barely touching his jaw—to the swirling power in his eyes—to the fangs I knew were aching with the need to bite. I reached up and caressed the tip of my finger down one, pressing into the point just enough to break the skin.

Ronan inhaled sharply. Dark hunger pooled in his gaze. Shadows descended over his features that made him equal parts terrifying and unearthly beautiful.

His hand darted up from my waist, gripping my wrist

firmly in place as he leaned forward, sucking the tip of my finger into his mouth—drawing a single drop of blood.

It sent a line of pleasure through me, from finger to chest to cunt. My lips parted, fangs lengthening on their own. He grabbed a fistful of my hair and pulled me into the warmth of his body, placing my head at the crevice where his neck met his shoulder.

"Bite me, atma," he growled in command.

I pressed against his skin, tasting sweat and salt and something musky that was entirely him. My fangs pierced his flesh, chaos ichor welling on my tongue. I moaned into him, sucking without abandon.

Ronan groaned, the hand in my hair tightening almost painfully. I didn't mind it. The pleasure. The pain. It was better than thinking, so I took it all.

He released my wrist, letting my finger slip out of his mouth as he dropped that hand to my ass, giving it a firm squeeze. I lifted my leg to hook it around his waist and he took the invitation to haul me up along his body, my core pressing into his slacks-clad length. My hips rolled, trying to gain friction. With one arm wrapped around his neck, I clamped my free hand on his shoulder, nails pressing into his branded skin.

"Fuck," he ground out as I continued to roll into him.

Please, I sent down the bridge between our minds.

My back slammed into the bathroom wall. The cool tiles pressed against my heated skin, making me hiss. I released his neck with a pop of my teeth, sucking as I pulled away.

His grip in my hair shifted to keep me from cracking my head on the tile.

My tongue snaked out to lick the blood off the corners

of my mouth, Ronan's magic filling me in the way I needed his cock to do the same.

I dropped my hands, wedging them between our bodies just enough I could dip my fingers into the edge of his pants. With a sharp tug, the button popped and zipper split, tearing fabric along with it.

I rolled my hips again, this time feeling his thick shaft, hard against my wetness.

Ronan lifted me several inches, angling my opening at the head of his cock. His hips thrust forward as he brought my body down, forcing me to take his full length in one go.

My jaw nearly unhinged itself as a low moan escaped me.

"Give it to me hard," I said as he shallowly thrust, trying to give me a second to adjust. The moment the words were out, his control flew right out the window.

Hips pressed to mine, he pinned me against the wall and thrust in and out at a rapid speed, never fully withdrawing. I couldn't wiggle or writhe or roll. Instead, I tried to spread my legs as wide as possible to let him closer, accepting every inch as he gave it.

"Is this how you want it?" he said through gritted teeth.

"Harder," I breathed. I wanted to feel like he was splitting me in two.

Ronan's fingers slipped through my hair, and it was the only warning he'd let go before my head bounced back against the tile, eliciting a sharp crack behind me.

He grabbed one thigh, wrenching it higher than the other, pushing my leg up so my knee was nearly to my shoulder.

"Oh my—"

"If anything other than my name comes out of that mouth, I'm going to take it too."

His wicked words set off a chain reaction. My pussy convulsed, tightening around his cock like a fist. As the first blinding wave ripped through me, I said, in hardly more than a whisper, "God."

Then the riptide eased and finally let me breathe. I opened my eyes to see a cruel smirk pulling at his lips. Ronan lifted me off his length, still thick and hard.

I should have known he wasn't going to be gentle. After all, I'd asked for it.

He stepped back, releasing me before my feet even hit the ground. I canted forward, trapped between him and the wall as I caught my balance and then let myself slide backwards, down to my knees.

"Open," he commanded. I licked my lips. In truth, I was going to enjoy this. But I knew he loved the power plays. The push and pull when I denied him.

"Or?" I asked, lifting an eyebrow.

That smirk deepened.

Then he said my name. My true name.

"Open wide," he said, knowing I had no choice but to obey. I glared at him, even as my jaw ached from opening as far as it could. He cupped my face, skimming his thumb over my cheek. "Good girl," he said condescendingly as he pushed the head of his cock into my mouth. "Now suck."

Almost robotically, as if he had a remote that could control my every movement, my lips clamped around him and began to suck.

Ronan rocked forward, thrusting deeper. The thick muscles of my throat objected. "Relax your throat," he ground out. The sticky stuff trickling from the sides of my mouth told me he loved this. "That's *right.*"

His cock shoved halfway down my throat, cutting off air. I panicked for a moment, seizing up but unable to stop.

"Take a deep breath, Piper. Through your nose," he said, pulling out so I could do as I was told. He prepared himself to go in deep once more, but first continued his instruction. "Open your throat again." Under normal circumstances, I might not have recovered so fast, but unable to control my own body, it adjusted to each and every one of his commands.

"Reach between your legs and finger yourself," he said, eyes hooded with lust as he slid in and out of my throat. On command, I slipped two fingers around my clit, rubbing it in slow circles. It didn't take long for that familiar feeling to build.

"Pinch your nipple."

"Now twist it."

"Do the other."

"Snap your fingers before you come."

His instructions continued one after another while he fucked my face, giving me intermittent moments to gasp for air and then take him again. It didn't take long for that climb to reach its peak. I snapped my fingers quickly, rubbing my clit with fervor.

"Stop touching yourself," he groaned, grabbing onto both sides of my face. I growled around his dick, eyes no doubt flashing. "Don't gag. Swallow."

His cock pulsed. Ronan went deep then stilled. His eyes closed as his lips parted as hot come shot down my throat in one salty jet. He stayed there for a moment, till his own release abated.

Slowly, his eyes opened once more, pure molten silver.

"Very good," he purred, his cock slipping out of my mouth. "Now thank me."

"Thank you," I spluttered, eyes narrowed. "For being such a prick."

Ronan let out a roaring laugh. He should have known, though. He said to thank him, but he never said what for. "For someone that doesn't want to talk, you're being very mouthy now."

"Didn't mind using that mouth, did you?" I retorted, still on my knees.

"Stand up and bend over the counter." He punctuated the statement by using my true name again. "I think you need a little more of my cock. You're still too tense."

I wasn't going to argue. Wordlessly, I walked to the edge of the bathroom counter and bent at the waist. Dripping wet and more than ready, I waited, locking eyes with him in the bathroom mirror.

"Do you want me to fuck you?" he asked, knowing I'd have no choice but to answer honestly.

"Yes."

"How?" he demanded, voice hard as his touch was soft. One hand smoothed down my back and around the curve of my ass.

"Like this," I spat. "From behind." A thin sheen of sweat dampened my skin from the way my magic both riled and submitted under him.

"Where? In this pussy?" He ran two blunt fingers through my folds, dragging them all the way back to my ass. "Or here?" He toyed with the outer ring of muscle, a glint of possessive lust running through him at the idea. "Maybe I should take your ass."

While I wasn't opposed, the idea gave me some trepidation. I hadn't actually let any of my past partners go there. Either my face or my thoughts must have given me away because that wicked smirk was back. Sensual, yet cruel. Challenging, yet safe in the absolute power he held.

"Answer me, Piper."

"I . . ." The words scrambled in my brain. I hadn't considered the other option, but now that it was out there, I was intrigued. Not enough to ask for it, though. "I don't know," I said eventually.

"Have you ever had anyone take your ass before?" he asked, confirming his suspicion. I pressed my lips together, not wanting to answer but unable to help myself.

"No."

His gaze further darkened. He liked that. Possessive alphahole that he was.

"You know I can't help wanting every part of you," he whispered softly. "Especially the pieces you haven't shared . . . but I'm a patient demon. I won't take anything you won't give me."

My breath quickened. The precarious edge I was dangling off of finally sliding out from under me.

"Don't break me," I uttered, giving my permission.

"Only when I get to remake you," he said back, giving my hip a comforting squeeze.

Between my legs, his length brushed against me. Using both hands, Ronan spread my cheeks. My chest tightened a little, but I wouldn't take it back. Not with him.

A bottle appeared out of thin air, and he snatched it up, popping the top. A trickle of cool liquid hit my ass, sliding along my skin. I jumped at the feeling as he set the bottle aside.

"You need to relax," he said, before grabbing his cock and thrusting it between my thighs. I was so focused on what he'd been doing with his hands I wasn't prepared. My muscles contracted around him, taking his length with ease, albeit a little sore after our rough fucking. He rocked into me in quick, shallow thrusts, reaching one hand around to toy with my clit. The tension drained from me as I gave myself up to him, to this feeling.

I was just starting to find the edge of my release when I felt his other hand, and the thumb that was circling around the puckered flesh. "Don't fight it," he insisted, pressing down. The muscle tightened, but the lube made it easier as he slipped his thumb in there. Intrusive but not painful, I took in the new sensation while skirting around my next orgasm.

"How's that?"

"Good . . . I think." He chuckled, and another finger started to prod at me. I tensed once more and he quickened his pace on my clit, pulling his thumb in and out to match the rhythm. Unable to help it, I felt my core tighten, ready and waiting to shatter.

The muscle gave. A second finger pushed into my ass, the tight fit coupled with his cock hurled me over the edge. "Come for me," he urged.

I blacked out.

Reality broke apart and time stopped as my channel convulsed. I vaguely heard Ronan let out a string of curses, both English and something foreign as my body locked tight, spasming out of control and unable to find its way back. Longer than any orgasm I'd had before, it dragged me under and wore me out. I wasn't sure how I was still standing when I came back to it. Only that I never wanted the mind-numbing bliss to end.

That's when I felt something a lot bigger than a finger pushing into me, but my muscles were too tired to tense. I couldn't fight it if I'd wanted, which is exactly why he did it.

"You have no idea how difficult it is to hold myself back right now," he panted. His hips thrust forward more, gaining another inch inside me. The more time that passed post-orgasm, the more feeling I got back.

"It burns," I managed.

"Almost there," he groaned. In a quick movement, he shoved the rest of the way in, seated to the hilt. The air hissed between my teeth as the burning turned into a searing.

While I was good with pain, there was a limit before it overshadowed pleasure.

"Shh," he breathed, leaning forward. He kissed my neck before sucking on a patch of skin. "I'll make it better."

His teeth sank into me and the instant my blood touched him, our connection flared to life. Heat pooled low in my core, sliding down my thighs. I moaned, pushing back against him. Feeling empty, and yet not.

Slowly, he pulled out, not all the way, but enough to rub at the nerve endings before pushing back. We started a slow rhythm once more. This wasn't the savage fucking against the bathroom wall, or the brutal way he'd fucked my throat. Neither was it love making, per se. But it was deep and intimate and perhaps the rawest we'd ever been with one another.

There was no power play here.

No games.

No demands.

I gave him this out of trust, and it shook me so much more when he didn't rush through it—though I could tell he wanted to from the way his hands shook where they held my hips. His breaths were labored. Sweat slicked us both, but we didn't speed up—instead I reveled in the way his lips felt against my neck. The way my magic sang as he pulled it from me, just like I'd done to him. The way his hands caressed me softly, yet firm. Unyielding, but compromising.

My release wasn't blinding this time, but the flutter of me tightening around him and the relief that filled me as I let go was so much more.

I called out his name, letting it reverberate off the walls for us to hear as he finished inside me. Hot liquid dripped down my body as I slumped against the counter, utterly boneless.

"I think I need another shower," I grunted.

"We both do."

After another rinse and lather with soap, we climbed into bed. The moon was high in the sky already, painting us in silver and shadows. Tired and content as I was, the weight of the truth was heavy when there was only darkness and nothing left to distract me.

"I don't know if I can do another day like today," I said quietly into the night, but I knew he was awake. That he was listening. "I'll have to. I know that. There will be more, as much as it kills me . . . but I need to bring the supernaturals to heel quickly. That's the only way I can stop it from happening again." I rolled on my side, facing Ronan. He was already looking at me.

"The only thing that can do that is the blood oath."

"I know."

There it was. The truth I didn't want to say.

"There's no going back if you take it. Anyone that you give blood to will be bound to you until death."

"I know," I repeated, quieter. "I never wanted to control anyone. But after seeing those kids and knowing what was happening there . . . the blood oath is the lesser evil. It's the easier thing for me to live with. I can make that sacrifice again and again if I have to. But I can't deal with cases like today over and over again. That will break me."

I knew it in my soul as well as I knew my name.

People used to say that god only gave you what he knew you could handle.

But there was no god, and the universe didn't give a damn what we could handle.

It was up to us to decide that, and enforce it, if need be.

"Then you'll take the oath, and this city will have no choice but to bow, or bleed by your hand."

IO

PIPER

"I really don't think this is necessary." My feet dragged behind Nat and the elevator idled. "Ronan would tell me if something seemed off."

She stopped and turned, eyeing Ronan. He stood behind me, supportive, but just as pushy as she was being. "Do you think this is necessary?"

"I do."

Ass. Even if he did, he didn't have to agree with her.

"I'm not that far along," I started.

"That would be true if you were human," he said. I flashed him an irritated look over my shoulder. One corner of his mouth twisted in amusement. "Don't look so sour. Pregnant demons are checked daily in the Otherworld."

My eyebrows rose. "Why on earth would anyone do that? I don't have anxiety, but I'm getting it just thinking about that."

"Pregnancy is rare. A successful birth, even more so. My mother was revered for having two children over the eons she lived, for a sense of understanding."

My jaw slid a little. Two. In thousands of years.

I couldn't truly grasp the magnitude of that.

"I'm only twenty-six."

"I know."

"That makes the odds of this being a full-term pregnancy . . ." My words trailed off as I considered it all. I hadn't truly wanted this. While family was a priority, kids weren't. Until they were. Knowing that something was growing inside me changed that perspective. It made me somewhat protective of that tiny life, however feeble and short-lived it may be.

"I think it will be different with you," he said, hand settling on my lower back. "That your origins will work in our favor, but there's reason for concern, nonetheless."

My lips pressed together. I let out a sigh and stepped out of the elevator.

"Going to stop fighting me now?" Nat asked, arms crossed, hip leaning against a side table with jars of pickled eyeballs sitting on it.

"I'm not doing it daily," I said. "That's excessive. But if I have to see the good Señora once a week, I'll acquiesce."

"Twice," both Nat and Ronan said.

My eyes flashed between the two of them.

"How about this, we see what she says first, and if she wants me back again so early, then fine. Fair?" I gave it good odds she wouldn't, given she harbored no great love for me and merely tolerated my presence due to her fondness of Nat. I figured there'd have to be true concern for her to want me once a week, even if demon pregnancies were shorter.

Before either could answer, the old witch's voice fell over us.

"I don't have all day, you know." I blanched, turning

toward the direction it came from. "If you don't want to see me, then move on. Your aura agitates my cats."

As if to prove a point, a fluffy tabby poked its head out from under the table and hissed at me. I pinched the bridge of my nose and sighed.

"Let's just get it over with."

"Follow me."

We waded through the cluttered shop, toward her counter in the corner. It was small and squared off to the wall, with a wooden flip top panel on one side and a curtain-covered doorway opposite of it. Señora Rosara stood, holding the gauzy fabric aside. Her nose wrinkled in annoyance as she tapped her foot. I didn't comment on her less than stellar bedside manner given I didn't have great social skills to speak of.

"On the table," she said as I walked through. It opened up to a larger hallway, one side filled with shelves and a long table along the other. I glanced at the black door at the end. Power radiated from it. Cool, but velvety soft. It felt almost like—

"Lay down, shirt up."

Señora Rosara stepped in front of my view, blocking the door at the end. The move roused my suspicion, and I lifted an eyebrow. She didn't even blink. "You want my help, you mind yourself."

I glanced over at Nat, who nodded. Swallowing any comeback I might have had, I kicked my legs up onto the table and flattened my body. My hands pulled at the hem of my tank up, pulling it up to the edge of my sports bra. "Will this work?"

"Sí."

All right then. She turned around and began rummaging through a bag. It took a moment, during which

I glanced up at Nat and Ronan. She sat at the very end of the table, knees crossed, and elbows braced on top. Her encouraging smile was a stark contrast to Ronan's intensity. My atman watched me with some kind of concentration that neither love nor duty could replicate. I wasn't simply a romantic partner or the would-be mother of his child. I was his everything. His entire universe. Salvation and damnation wrapped up in one.

I didn't realize how intently I was watching him in return until the Señora turned toward me, and Ronan didn't simply move—he struck. Out of nowhere, he grabbed her wrist, not painfully, but firm and immovable. "What is that?" he demanded, motioning to the instrument between her fingers. She moved them aside to show him a simple tape measure.

"Calm yourself, demon. I mean no harm to your mate."

Slowly, he released his grip and stepped back, but was no longer hovering at the door.

The Señora turned around and pulled on the end of the measuring stick, lining it up from my pubic bone to just below my ribs.

"I doubt you'll see anything. I'm only—"

"This gives me a base to work from." Her eyebrows furrowed, then her thin lips twisted. Something was off.

"Everything all rig—"

"How long do demons gestate?" she asked, cutting me off again.

"Six months," we all answered, having had this discussion before we came here.

Her eyes narrowed. After a suspended moment, she closed the tape measure and set it aside.

"Have your clothes seemed tighter?"

I blinked, surprised by the direction of questioning.

"Not particularly." I tried to think back, but it wasn't like I was paying attention to my fashion choices.

"I often clothe her with my magic. If her size changed, she wouldn't notice," Ronan interjected.

"Do your breasts hurt?"

"How is the nausea?"

She continued on like this, running through the list of symptoms. The only thing I could definitely pinpoint as different was my sense of smell.

A troubled pucker formed between her brows from scowling.

"Hmmm."

"Is something wrong?" I asked flatly, unable to dance around it any longer.

"Wrong? No," she answered. "Off? Yes. I need to see inside you. Harvester, would you join me while I mix the potion? I'd like you to fill me in on what symptoms female demons usually experience."

She turned for the store and made a shooing motion when Ronan didn't move.

I knew why he was stalling.

"I'm fine," I said into his mind. *"She hasn't done anything but measure my belly. Go with her. Nat will wait with me."*

I was pretty sure they were only moving a good ten feet or so, but saying as much was pointless with him.

My atman stepped aside, letting the old witch lead the way. When the curtain swished closed behind them, I looked at Nat and motioned for her to come closer.

"Was it just me, or did she look concerned?"

Nat chewed her bottom lip, unable to lie. "A bit, but you shouldn't worry too much just yet. She said nothing seemed wrong, just off."

I lifted both eyebrows at her. "Yeah, because that seems

so much better."

Nat rolled her eyes. "Just relax. I'm sure everything is fine, and if it's not—we'll deal with that. One problem at a time, right?"

My lips pinched together, but I sighed, then nodded.

"Speaking of problems . . . I've been meaning to talk to you about something. Sasha approached me the night Bree was supposed to go back. She wants to be my second."

I spoke slowly, gaging her expression. Her lips didn't move, and her eyes didn't squint. Her heart rate remained the same. The only tell she felt anything at all was the way she was studying me in turn.

"What do you think about that?" she asked after a suspended second.

I frowned. "I think she's a solid choice, but that's not why I'm telling you. For as long as we've been friends, you've been my second. Maybe not officially, but you have."

Nat nodded slowly. "That's fair, although I begrudge being called second."

"That's just semantics."

"I'm aware," she said, picking at a cat hair that stuck to my tank top.

I groaned. "You know, you're really not making this easy on me. I don't want to get rid of you. I'm not trying to drop you—I just want to know what you want. If I'm donning the title of Queen around here, I've gotta earn it. I'll need whoever is taking that spot to be the person that both questions and supports me. Especially when I start taking blood oaths with the leaders of each faction."

Nat stilled. "You're going to take the oath?"

"Yes, but that's not the point."

She sighed. "Honestly, I'm relieved you brought this up. I've been avoiding it because we have bigger things, but I'd already been thinking on it." She paused, and when she didn't continue, I made a motion with my hand.

"Are you going to tell me what you're thinking, or do you expect me to guess?"

"Okay, asshole," she said bluntly. "It's called 'thinking about what I'm going to say.' The short answer is I think you should take her up on it. Sasha compliments you well, but she doesn't put up with your bullshit. You need that."

When I broached the topic, I expected her to say she wanted it. While there was a chance she might not, I hadn't put much thought into it. So her telling me to take Sasha up . . . I was surprised by the little bit of hurt I felt. Which was crazy. And yet, it was there.

"The long answer?" I asked.

Nat sighed. "I don't think I'll be able to do the job you need me to do. Not with what's coming. When we raided the vampire den the other night, and I discovered it was Katherine's magic, it did something. For a while now, I've thought I was hallucinating and hearing voices. Well, one voice. Now I know I'm not losing it . . . I'm actually being haunted."

"Haunted?" I repeated. "From the other side?"

She nodded.

"Who?" I asked. She looked down and her voice dropped to a hushed whisper.

"Lucifer."

My lips parted. For Lucifer to be haunting her meant . . . "He's not dead."

Her head dipped in acknowledgement. "Somehow part of him exists despite the fact he's not a death deity, and it's locked onto me. When we get this business with Lorcan settled, I need to deal with that. Find out why he's attached to me."

Toward the end of her speaking, her eyes wavered to the side. Toward the black door.

"He's here, isn't he?" I said quietly.

Nat nodded again. "When I use my magic, he gets stronger. Somehow we're linked. When I took down Kat's wards, he came to me and told me where those kids were. He's real—this isn't in my head."

I sighed. "I believe you, but what do you plan to do about it when you do find answers?"

She looked away again. "I don't know."

"If you need my help—"

"I'll ask, but I'd rather not have to, given your history with him. I'm the one that dealt the final blow. I killed him. This is my problem."

I reached out. The angle was awkward as hell, but I grabbed her hand and squeezed her fingers. "He was once my problem, and you helped me. My sister has been a problem for a month now and you helped me. Now we have Lorcan to contend with and you're still helping me. So don't hesitate. If you need me, I'm here."

She smiled softly. "And you say you're not good at being sappy."

I groaned, dropping her hand. "Oh eff off."

She chuckled. "I think that's what I'm getting at, though. Second or not, I'll be here when you need me. It doesn't change that we're friends, or that you can't get rid of me. Not only are we blood bound, but I'm also fixing to be an aunt, and you're going to need a babysitter for when you're off busting heads and whatnot." She grinned, but it faded. "And there's still the illuminati to contend with. That's not just a you-problem. That's an everyone-problem."

I nodded. "One thing at a time, though, yeah?"

"Precisely," she said. "That's why I think you should take Sasha up on it. If you're the Queen, then I'm the Queenmaker, and she's the guard dog. Few people know this city as well as me, and she's one of them. While rough around the edges, she knows how to turn on the charm and she's a straight shooter. You're in good hands with her backing you up, so I can handle what I need to get done and still keep all the wheels of this city spinning, so to speak."

"Thank you—"

The curtain swished to the side.

Señora Rosara came in first, carrying a wooden bowl. The contents glowed blue.

Behind her, Ronan stepped in. The black fabric fell into place behind him.

Nat stood up from where she squatted beside me, moving back to her spot at the end of the table.

"I'm going to paint this on your belly and then cast the spell. It will let me see through you, to your baby. Safe and painless."

I nodded.

The liquid was cool to the touch. It smelled faintly of mint and citrus. A strange but not unpleasant combination. I tried to focus on that and ignore my beating heart.

It was safe. She said it would be painless.

So why was I feeling this way?

"Because you're worried."

I met his eyes from across the room, over Señora Rosara's shoulder.

"I've killed people and felt less than this." Sad, but true.

Ronan chuckled. *"What will be, will be. This is why I wanted to be here."*

"To micromanage the old lady?"

"For you," he corrected. *"Anyhow, my instincts wouldn't allow me to be elsewhere while the witch was doing this."*

It was my turn to snort. *"Nice way of saying micromanage."*

Señora turned her head and gave me a look. "Hard as this might be, I'll need you to not move." Her lips were pencil thin.

I tipped my chin.

Nat smothered her giggle with a cough, but did the Señora give her a dirty look? Of course not. Nat could do no wrong unless she was bringing in strays like me.

She set the bowl aside and then started chanting.

The language she used wasn't Hebrew, Egyptian, Gaelic, or Latin—as was most common for spells and incantations. It was one I'd never heard before, and I made the mental note to ask her when she was done.

The sounds coming from her mouth were low and gruff. Sharp and jagged.

My stomach warmed everywhere the potion was painted.

I glanced down past the valley of my breasts.

The color changed from blue to orange.

She stopped.

Silence spanned for a beat as she peered down. Her lips parted.

My chest tightened and my nails bit into the palm of my fist, but I waited for her to speak.

"Your babies are perfect, but they're much further along than you thought. You're at the end of your first trimester."

My mouth fell open.

She said—

"Babies?" Ronan repeated, sounding as shocked as I felt.

II

NATHALIE

"You lied."

His words were a whisper that crawled up my spine. A cool breath of air against my flushed skin. I tried not to fidget, to react, to respond—from the corner of the table where I perched.

Easier said than done when he towered over me. His body curved into mine, head bowed like some dark knight. While I didn't believe he was the villain—I knew better than to think him a hero. Flawed or otherwise.

"Or shall we say, omitted the *real truth* to why you want her to accept Sasha," he continued when I didn't respond. "Though, I *am* surprised you shared my existence, considering your insistence on ignoring me." I blinked slowly, focusing on my surroundings—the room, the table I sat on, my best friend in front of me as Señora Rosara wiped the goop from her stomach and gave her instructions to return by end of the week. Piper didn't seem to have registered her instructions yet, given the slack expression she wore. If I had to guess, she was scared shitless that she'd be having not one kid, but two. I didn't need to be a mind reader to see that. But it wasn't me she needed at this exact moment either. While I'm sure there would be a later time for her to process it with me, at this exact moment, it was Ronan's job to step up and show her what kind of father and partner he'd be when she was this vulnerable.

I slipped off the table, my body passing through Lucifer's incorporeal form. He hissed at my continued silence as I quietly left to give them the room and give myself space.

When the curtain fell back into place, the tension in my chest eased.

I walked around the counter, feeling better with every step that I put between myself and them. It wasn't that I didn't love Piper, or that I wasn't happy for her. Far from it.

But Lucifer was onto something when he said he was surprised I'd told her about him. Originally I wasn't going to, not when she had the whole of New Chicago to worry about, let alone her growing family. Telling her I was seeing ghosts seemed small by comparison. Even if that ghost was the devil.

She was hurt when I told her to take Sasha on. While she wiped her expression quickly, I'd known her long enough now to tell when something was bothering her— and me turning her down did just that. I needed to make sure she knew that it wasn't *her*. That I had no plans of abandoning her in her hour of need.

Piper needed a reason to understand why I said no.

Lucifer, if anything, was a great scapegoat for that.

While she would help me with him if I needed it, I knew she didn't *want* to. There was bad blood there. He forced the atma bond on her after kidnapping us, then went and got himself captured by witches. Those choices led to his death and millions of others, as well as Piper losing control.

I don't think she blamed him, per se, but she hated what he stood for. What he created.

And what Piper hated, she avoided.

"Running from me won't change the truth, Nathalie." He growled my name, and I felt the power in it riding my heels as I exited the shop.

"I'm not running," I corrected once the door to the shop closed. "I'm walking, and what I do with my two feet has little to do with truth." With the curtain acting as a sound barrier and the door a second one, I could respond without one of the Señora's many cats listening in. The last thing I needed was for my landlord to find out that I was being haunted. Superstitious as she was, if she knew the devil's ghost had locked onto me, it could create problems with me living in her building.

"Your sharp tongue won't distract me, little witch," he purred. I felt that phantom touch against my hips, as if his hands were trying to grasp me.

I shifted, flitting away from his ghost touch and the strange feelings it elicited.

"Considering that you're always lingering, I'd be surprised if it did." I turned my cheek, lifting my eyes to the figure that shadowed me. Brilliant white hair hung loosely over his forehead in his eyes, the same length it was when he died. His eyes were just as golden and piercing.

Few saw me. Really saw *me*. He always had an uncanny way of making me believe he was one of them.

"And what, pray tell, would you rather I do?" His voice dropped, becoming low and sensual as he took a step toward me.

I tilted my chin, considering his question. "I'm not sure. I imagine being dead is rather boring and lonely. Seeing, hearing, watching the world go on around you, but unable to interact with it . . ." I pitied him, now that I knew I wasn't going insane. "I should put on reruns of *Friends*, just to give you something to do."

His eyebrows drew together. "*Friends*?"

"TV show from the 90s."

"Why would I want to watch a show from the shittiest decade in the last century?" He scoffed, crossing his arms over his chest.

I wrinkled my nose. "Shittiest decade?" I tsked. "I'll have to disagree there. The Magic Wars were a dumpster fire, but if we're going to ignore those, I'd have to give the shittiest decade award to the 80s."

His eyebrows lifted in incredulity. "The 80s? That's the universally renowned decade."

"Just because lemmings think it doesn't make it so." I wagged my finger. "That was the decade of big hair, really bad crime shows, and lycra. But I digress, the music makes up for it." I shrugged. "If you'd rather I put on *Golden Girls* for you, that can be arranged."

Lucifer didn't react. Most people would sigh, grow annoyed, and walk away. He was a ghost, so I didn't expect him to do any of those things. My rebuttals were just words buying me time from the deeper things I could tell he was on the edge of broaching.

"I don't need TV," Lucifer eventually settled on in response.

"I'd offer a book, but turning the pages may prove difficult."

"I've seen the romance novels you read," he said dryly. "My imagination would serve me better if that's what I was looking for."

I huffed. "Given you're several thousand years old, I'd be disappointed if that weren't the case."

One corner of his mouth curled into a sensual smirk. He took another step toward me. "Was that a challenge, little witch?"

My tongue traced the edges of my teeth before I sucked the air between them. "No. Simply an observation. Seems rude to tempt the ghost of the devil when there's not much you can do about it."

His nostrils flared, but before he could respond, the shop door opened. Bells tinkled against each other, breaking up the tension that was building in the space my words left behind.

"We were looking for you," Piper said slowly. Her gaze travelled between me and the spot where the demon that plagued me stood. I knew she couldn't see him, but my conversation must have given us both away.

Sasha followed behind her.

While the twins were truly identical in features, they were easy to tell apart in how they interacted with the world. Sasha walked like a predator stalking her prey. Sienna swayed her hips, preferring the prey come to her. They were two sides of a coin, the same, and yet utterly different.

"I wanted to give you a moment," I said, avoiding the 'why.' Last I knew, she hadn't told anyone she was pregnant, though I wouldn't be surprised if Sasha had figured it out already. "Where's Ronan?"

"Off doing whatever business it is he does with Anders." Piper rolled her violet-colored eyes. "We were just finishing up when Sasha came looking for me. Apparently, one of our victims from the vampire den is causing trouble at the women's shelter."

Lucifer's gaze bore into me as I turned away from him entirely.

"What kind of trouble exactly?"

Piper and Sasha shared a look. They were already more in sync than Piper likely realized.

"The magical variety," she said after a moment. "I may have changed one of the women shortly before she started staying there . . ."

"Changed," I repeated, knowing damn well what she meant. "What did you *change* her into?"

"A siren," Sasha said, cutting in when she saw the reluctance on Piper's face.

Smacking my hand to my forehead, I groaned. "Only you," I lamented. "Only you would make a siren."

She frowned. "It's not like I get to choose what they become."

"You don't like giving the blood oath, and yet the first creature you actually *make* is a siren. One of the rarest, deadliest, and most dangerous. I shouldn't be surprised because this is you we're talking about. There, rephrased it for you."

"Are you coming with or—"

"Of course I'm coming," I scoffed. "But I wasn't going to pass up the opportunity to give you shit, either."

Sasha wrapped one hand around Piper's shoulder and the other around my wrist. Darkness crept in, spewing from the cracks in the concrete and shade on the sidewalk.

For only the briefest of seconds, I glanced back at the spot where Lucifer stood.

My memory was perfect in every way. I could recall the smallest details of a person or place that I'd seen in passing, but there was something about the way he looked at me that was different than before.

"We're not done here, little witch."

I dipped my chin in acknowledgement just before the

void swallowed us whole and darkness so absolute blinded me in its depths. It was only there in the space between one shadow and the next that I thought about our encounter.

He was right that I lied. He was right when he said I was running.

But he was also dead wrong.

I wasn't running from something, but toward it.

The real problem was I'd yet to figure out what *it* was.

12

PIPER

I WRINKLED MY NOSE AT THE SCENT OF PISS AND DESPERATION.

If not for the lines of women, I would have thought we were in the wrong place. Sasha had recommended it, after all. But the large warehouse with port-a-potties and a small broken concrete parking lot wasn't what I'd thought it would be.

I glanced sidelong at her but didn't say anything.

Sienna came bustling out of the open double doors carrying a stack of towels that started at her waist and ended just under her tucked chin. Her dark braid whipped back and forth, caught in the wind, and the baggy T-shirt she wore flapped along with it. Her jeans were ripped and stained. The boots on her feet scuffed and dirty. It was a stark contrast to the clothes they had donned while working for Lucifer, and certainly not as chic as she usually was when working with Nat. I wondered if she intentionally dressed down when helping the shelter.

"Where is she?" I asked, my voice ringing. Several of the women in line for the bathrooms flinched, making me inwardly frown. Scaring them wasn't my intent.

"Inside." Sienna jutted her chin toward the open door behind her.

As we were walking by, one of the women whispered, "Thank god."

I turned my head toward her, lifting a brow in question.

She pressed her lips together, and the other women looked away.

"Why do you say that?" I asked.

She swallowed. A trickle of sweat formed at her temple despite the cool temperatures. Her pale skin turned rouge in the sunlight.

"You're coming to take that girl away, aren't you?" Her voice grew quieter with every word as she questioned herself and whether she should have said anything at all.

"That girl," I repeated slowly, giving nothing away.

"The one with scales on her arm and black wings like death. I–I don't know what she is," the woman admitted, her pale bottom lip trembling. "But whatever it is, it's not right." She lowered her eyes. Fear was eating her up inside. Fear of the girl. Fear of me. Fear of this world.

"How surprising," Sasha mocked, her honey-sweet voice dripping with poison. "A human that hates what they don't understand." I lifted my hand and she stopped. While I sensed anger radiating off her, it wasn't my focus. *Both* of them lacked empathy for what they couldn't understand.

But I did.

"I was like you once," I said after a moment. "Scared of supes. That fear turned to anger, then hate. I killed them with little regard for their lives, their families, their pasts or futures. I didn't think there was a possibility they could've been changed against their will, or question if they turned for reasons other than power. I . . ." My throat closed, making me stop and take a slow breath. "I didn't care.

Enough of them had hurt me and mine that I didn't have it in me to. They were dangerous, so I hunted them out of fear."

Her eyes reflected my truth. My regret. While she wasn't where I was now, she knew I understood. It was a hard world to be human, but it was hard to be anything. That was living.

"They can't change what they are any more than you can. Human or supe, none of us can go back in time. There's good and bad that exist in both. I've seen it from humans without mercy that kill anyone that has magic, just like I've seen the reverse. That girl in there," I thrust my chin toward the door, "she's been through hell. She doesn't know who or what she is or wants to be." I shook my head because I understood that too. More than they knew. "She can't control herself yet, and if anything, it's my fault for sending her here when she was so newly changed. I take responsibility for that. I'm . . . I'm sorry."

There were perks to being powerful and in charge, but there was also an incredible amount of responsibility. If you didn't own up to that, you'd end up like Lucifer. Like Lorcan. Like all the shithead leaders that just shunted their duties onto someone else for authority.

I made the choice to change that girl. She had no idea how to use her powers. She'd undergone immense trauma. Sticking her in a situation like this with other women that had also been through similar traumas . . . it was a mistake. I didn't need to see her to know that.

This was on me, and as uncomfortable as it felt, I wouldn't shy away from it.

Because that's the only way things would change.

Slowly, the woman lifted her eyes. A scar marred her cheek. A bruise on the other. They caught the light as she nodded a couple times and then continued forward in line. I let her go, not needing to make a bigger scene than I already had.

A light touch on my shoulder made me jerk. Nat smiled at me and nodded once. We headed inside, meeting Sienna at the door. She handed off the towels she was carrying to someone else, then started leading us down one of the many rows. On one side, cardboard boxes and crates lined it, likely filled with supplies; on the other, makeshift tents that were really sheets held up by rope hung above us. Every row appeared like that. Supplies on one side, people on the other.

"Interesting setup they have here," I murmured.

"It's to give them some semblance of privacy," Sienna answered quietly. "They only have so many resources. Using the sheets to create four walls around them helps protect from the windchill and lets them have a safer space, even if it isn't safe." I nodded as she continued. "Rugs and extra blankets are given to them for sleeping since there aren't enough actual beds. Same with pillows."

"Wouldn't it be better to pair them up in tents so they can maximize bedding?" Nat asked.

"They do. That's where we ran into problems with Mist."

I paused. "That's the name she gave you?"

Sienna nodded.

"She tell you why she picked it?"

She shook her head. "No. She actually didn't tell them her name until she told them to call you. They couldn't, so they came to me to pass the message along."

"Anything else I should know?" I asked, as Sienna slowed. We must be approaching her tent.

Her cat tail flicked to the side while she hesitated.

"She had a nightmare and severely injured her room-mate. Since then, she's refused to speak to anyone but you. Anyone that tries to get near her is sent away against their will."

"Any idea what the nightmare was about?"

"Not a clue. She sent me away too."

I sighed. "Thanks for the heads-up."

She dipped her chin in acknowledgement. "Good luck."

"Thanks." I turned to the tent we stopped outside of. If I tried, I could feel her inside. Her magic. Her darkness. But also her light.

Taking a deep breath, I pushed the stiff fabric aside.

Much like the day I'd changed her, she sat on the floor, legs pulled up to her chest, wings wrapped around her.

Her large pewter eyes tracked me from the moment I entered the tent.

"I hear you picked a name."

"I had a name," she replied, wings slowly unfurling. "I chose to keep it."

I plopped down on the floor in front of her, crossing my legs. "Why?"

She blinked once, like she was surprised I asked. Surprised I cared.

"Because . . . they thought I was a mistake they could get rid of. It might've been one thing if they'd just kicked me out and I had to make my own way, but they didn't. They sold me to be a blood slave in return for their own protections." She looked away. "I'm going to show them the mistake was leaving me alive."

My lips parted.

"You want revenge."

"No." Her eyes cut toward me, becoming hard and unyielding. "I *need* it."

Behind me, Nat inhaled sharply.

"Is this why you asked for me?" I responded, not delving too deep into the darkness of her mind just yet. Mist shook her head. "Okay . . ." I trailed off, not exactly the most well trained in working with traumatized pregnant teenagers. "Is there something wrong? Did your roommate do something?" It was a shot in the dark, but I had to get answers out of her somehow.

She shook her head again. "I told them I didn't mean to hurt her. I just didn't realize fast enough . . ."

"Realize what?" I prompted, watching as she shifted uncomfortably.

"I was awake."

So it was the dream. I didn't want to be an asshole about being called down here for a nightmare. She was only a kid, and I'd taken a certain amount of responsibility for the girl, especially where her being a siren was concerned.

"What were you dreaming before then?"

Her hesitance spoke volumes. She glanced up at Nat and Sasha again, indecision warring on her face.

"They're friends of mine," I said.

"I know," she whispered. "They were there. We all were."

I froze, tilting my head. "Where?"

"I don't know. The ground was made of glass, but harder. There were people fighting. A man and woman. He had white hair and red eyes . . ." She broke off, shaking her head slightly. "He looked like them. The vampires."

Lorcan. I had no doubt. Which meant whatever she was dreaming, it wasn't just a dream. It was the future. Or some version of it, at least.

"What did he do?" I asked.

"He was fighting with a woman. Her hair was white too. Her arms looked like yours, but green."

Bree. She was seeing their challenge. The duel that would decide their fate.

"Who won?" I asked, unable to help myself.

"I don't know," she said. "I died before it happened. We all did. Me. Them. The other one that looks like her." Mist nodded toward Sasha. "The man with the red eyes bit you and our blood turned to fire. Our bones became ash. White flames consumed us. But before we died, there was another person. Another man." She swallowed hard. "He was dark. Hard to see. The shadows clung to him like they do my wings." Mist reached out to stroke her hand down the tip of one. Soothing herself. "He ended it."

I had to take a second to gather myself. My thoughts. My strength. "Ended what, exactly?"

Her eyes seemed to reflect the very shadows she spoke of. Light danced on her scales. I could practically smell the fear as her voice trembled.

"Everything."

13
RONAN

I STUMBLED THROUGH THE VOID. MY FEET MOVING FASTER THAN my mind was capable of.

While I'd dreamed of finding my atma for millennia, I never saw past that. I wasn't able to imagine what life could hold after—if she accepted me. That a child was possible. Let alone twins.

My body hurled through time and space in the blink of an eye. I landed on the other side on Anders' couch. The scent of tobacco, leather, and wood was heavy in the air.

"You look like shit."

"She's having twins."

He stood leaning against the kitchen countertop, a cigar between two fingers, white smoke escaping from his lips. At the mention of Piper, he was alert.

"Well, she's never done anything in half measure." He sighed. "I don't suppose congratulations are in order and the shock on your face is how you show being happy?" He lowered the cigar from his mouth, stamping the hot embers into his palm to put it out.

"I can count on two hands how many demons have had twins in the last ten thousand years," I said. "I can count on one how many times the children survived."

I lifted two fingers.

Twice.

That was it.

"Yours will be the third," Anders said without pause.

"One child is already hard on the body, but two . . . there will be complications. There always is." I stared at him without really seeing. In every case of twins, I was there for the birth. In half, neither child made it—and that was just the pregnancies that went to term.

"You don't know that," Anders said, taking a seat across from me. His hair was pulled back in a bun, stretching the skin around his eyes, making the red blood vessels even more apparent. "If that few have been born, you don't have a true sample size to say one way or the other, and even if you did, it overlooks the fact that she wasn't born a demon. As you've said yourself, it should be nearly impossible for her to be pregnant already. But Piper is different, and she's strong. If anyone is going to carry your two hellions into this world safe and sound—it's her."

I wanted to believe him. I desired nothing.

The fact remained that I couldn't.

It was one thing to be the Harvester and see it, but another entirely to be the father and experience it.

"There's already a complication. The children . . . they're past the first trimester."

Anders's eyebrows lifted, and while he said nothing, his expression spoke volumes.

"Exactly."

It was what I'd worried would happen. That our

combined strength would create children that were more than my world had ever seen—and were perhaps too much for hers to handle.

"At that rate, they'll be due shortly after Bree's challenge," he said.

I lifted my head, scrubbing my hair back with one hand. "If he wins and then challenges me, I may not survive. Assuming Piper somehow escapes his wrath afterward, that loss will damage her, perhaps beyond repair. If they survive birth, she'd be in no place to actually be a mother. She'd be rage. Nothing less, nothing more."

Anders sighed. "If—and that's a big if—it came to that, you know I would do my best to care for and protect them. As would Nathalie, Sasha, and Sienna. This isn't news. Whether it was one or two, that would be the case."

He wasn't wrong, but fear was a strange thing. Before I'd seen them, I was able to keep my concerns at bay. I didn't express them to anyone—not Piper, not Nat, not him. But now, when reality began to set in, I couldn't escape it.

"If that future comes to pass, Lorcan will come for them. You'll have to leave."

"I already assumed as much."

"I'm not talking about New Chicago."

Anders quieted. "Earth. This dimension."

I nodded. "Nathalie will need to open a portal. Not to the Otherworld, but one of the dimensions in-between. Somewhere he can't track you."

It wasn't a small thing that I was asking him. To not only care for my children, but to leave everything he'd ever known behind and take them to an unfamiliar world.

I knew that was the only way they'd be safe.

Too many people on Earth knew of demons and how to bind us. Lorcan would have the power to kill them so easily, or worse—enslave them all.

I couldn't leave their futures to chance because of my own arrogance and belief that I could protect them and my atma from everything and everyone.

"If it comes to that, I promise I will take them to another world with Nathalie's help and keep them safe."

Promises were no small thing among creatures with magic.

For demons, they were binding. Anders was not a full demon, but he was the strongest fae to walk this planet—and the fae could not lie.

I dipped my head in acknowledgement. "Thank you, my friend."

Anders snorted, looking away. "Just a few days ago you were insulting me, and now we're friends. I see how it is."

"I'm ten thousand years old and you're my first friend. Being Harvester . . . there is no room for friends. The courts of the Otherworld are filled with vipers. I knew better than to trust anyone there."

"And before you were Harvester?" Anders asked, leaning back in the armchair and crossing his ankle over his knee.

"I was raised in isolation," I answered. Recalling my early years was difficult, with so much time to wade through. They were more like a dream or a storybook than memories. "My father was the previous Harvester, which put us in a certain level of danger by association. My mother and I lived far away from demon civilization for a long time. When it became clear to her and my father that I had the potential to be the next Harvester, I was then trained in the matters of our court and history. They taught me what would be expected of me, and when I was reintroduced into society, my parents made sure I understood that I could trust no one. Any friend I tried to make betrayed me. Any lover I took was just an empty fuck. The only person I was raised to trust implicitly was my future atma."

Anders let out a low whistle. "That explains why you weren't put off by Piper's cold demeanor."

One corner of my mouth curled into a smirk. "I quite like her cold side. It's ruthless, befitting of a queen."

Anders shook his head. "That. It's not normal. You're just as emotionally damaged as she is."

There was more truth to that statement than he could understand.

"I am," I agreed. "Likely even more."

"When this is over, and Bree has ended that piece of shit, and Piper gives birth to two healthy children, you should see someone about that."

"See someone?"

"A therapist. A real one. Not me." He motioned to himself. "Great as I am, that's not my area of expertise. But you had a real dinger of a childhood, not to mention your years as the Harvester, and it's impacted you. Processing it could help."

I shook my head. "It was so long ago I don't remember most of it."

"Doesn't mean it won't affect you—or your kids. You may not remember most of it, but what you remember shaped you, and then those memories continued to. This anxiety surrounding Piper and your kids—it's not going to disappear when Lorcan is gone." He looked at me with true concern. It was something I'd never seen before, apart from Piper. "There will always be someone or something gunning for you and your family. It comes with the position you've put yourself in, and the power you hold."

"There's safety in power."

Anders inclined his head. "To some degree. There's also envy, which often leads to violence and, by extension, danger. Humans and demons are alike in that. It was dangerous for you as the Harvester in Hell, and it's dangerous for you here. Different reasons, but the outcome is the same." I considered that.

"What would you do, in my position?"

He tilted his head. "Well for one, I would have used protection so I didn't end up in the position you've found yourself in."

I narrowed my eyes, and he chuckled.

"For another, I have no desire to rule. While I haven't escaped all the territorialism that demons possess, it doesn't move me the same way. I find safety in the shadows, shifting pieces into play where no one else sees me."

"You hide," I said.

Anders shrugged. "To some extent. In all seriousness, I'm not entirely sure what I would do in your situation. I had a wife and child once, and I lost them. It nearly destroyed me—and I'll never have another child again." I sensed the pain in his voice. Heard the anguish he experienced at their loss. "That trauma changed me. I have my own issues because of it, and that influences how I handle situations."

"Like?"

"You cling to Piper as your everything. Partly because it's your nature. Partly because she really is all you have ever had, and you waited a very long time for her. I only meet others halfway. I'm not afraid to make friends, but when I take a lover, I don't get attached. I leave before that ever happens." He shrugged, flashing a sympathetic grimace. "Neither is healthy."

"Hm." I ran my palm over my jaw in consideration. "If things play out the way you think they will, I'll consider 'seeing someone'."

He lifted his brows.

I shrugged. "You've made valid points. I may struggle to change, but change is the only true constant in the universe. If it's going to happen either way, it should be for the better."

"Very few people seem to understand that," Anders commented.

"I don't think that's it," I disagreed. "As you've pointed out, humans and demons are more alike than they'd like to believe. Both driven by emotion. I think many of them do see, but when it comes down to it—it's far easier to be a hedonist like my brother, or a liar like your father, than do the right thing." He inclined his head in agreement. "Improvement is difficult, but my atma and children deserve nothing less."

"Do me a favor," Anders said. "Have this conversation with Piper when you get the chance. You're not the only one that could benefit from it, but I know better than to broach the topic with her. She'd likely shoot me for even trying."

She probably would.

The thought made me smile.

Anders groaned. "You would find that amusing."

I got to my feet, adjusting my suit jacket. "I find a great deal amusing where she's concerned."

Anders rolled his eyes. "I can see that you're feeling better. My job here is done."

"Actually," I said, "the appointment with the Señora

wasn't my only reason for coming. I need you to pay Dahlia a visit for me."

"Oh?"

"Piper agreed to take the oath."

Anders stared for a moment, waiting for me to continue. "You're serious?" He blinked and blew out a breath when I didn't do anything more than lift an eyebrow at him. Like I would joke about this. "We'll have to move quickly. The factions that turned us down may try to pull something when word gets out she's taking the oath with them."

"I'm aware. That's why you're going to make the arrangements for tonight."

He jerked to a stop in between sitting and standing, before slowly straightening. "Tonight? They won't take kindly to the short notice. I don't suppose you'll be coming with to relay that to them?"

The corners of my mouth tightened. "Unfortunately not. I have a more important matter to attend to."

Anders squinted at me. "I'm doubtful of that."

"Bree," I bit out. "I can't put it off any longer."

Not with the news of how fast Piper's pregnancy is progressing. Lorcan would have yet another reason to come after her when she takes the oath and begins assembling her pieces on the board. I needed her protected before that happened.

"I see," Anders said slowly. His voice lost all amusement, something deeper smothering it. "Give her my regards." There was an odd inflection in his tone. A tightness I didn't want to place. I was aware he had a fascination with Piper's sister, but just how far that feeling went . . . I didn't know, and I didn't want to know. It wasn't my business. If she failed to win her challenge against Lorcan, I'd be forced to cripple her when I fought her atman. If she survived, she wouldn't be the woman he knew. If she didn't, well, his feelings would be the least of my worries.

The Otherworld would feel Piper's grief if she lost her sister—and New Chicago would suffer the wrath of its queen.

14

BREE

I PACED.

The sound of my boots echoing off the walls was like a metronome. There was a comforting rhythm to it, but it didn't keep track of the time. For that, I watched the shadows as they moved across the room.

She was never late. She'd be here.

The abandoned building was empty during the day, but by evening, stragglers and the homeless would crowd in downstairs to escape the dangers of the cold, dark streets. I'd watched the coming and goings of this location for a while. As best as I could tell, this particular group of humans called it home. Moldy blankets and piles of dirty mattresses were scattered about what used to be a bustling storage warehouse. Broken bottles and trash littered the floor, but it didn't deter them from returning every night. Most of them left the upstairs rooms alone, with the exception of a few looking to get a quick fuck before heading back to the common areas. The upper floors weren't useful to them. Shattered windows weren't conducive to keeping warm, and the old supervisor's office I stood in was no different.

Back and forth I walked, waiting, as the wind picked up.

A whisper of footsteps registered in my ears, and I paused, listening for more. She had the stealth of a thief, but I knew by the gait it was her coming down the hallway.

"In here," I called out to her.

The door opened, and she stepped into the room quietly, shutting it behind her without making a sound.

Robin should've been a wraith for how she could appear and disappear so quietly.

Or an assassin.

I suppose I should be happy she didn't have the stomach for it. But in this world or any other, the ability to kill was not only useful, it was sometimes necessary.

"I'd ask if you were followed, but I know the answer already."

She shrugged. "I was, actually. That's what took me so long."

A slight surge of alarm went through me.

"Who?" I asked, concerned it would be my atman. That would mean I was too late.

"Brandon," she answered, surveying the room. I hadn't heard that name before and Robin saw the questioning look on my face. She waved it off. "Don't worry. He's a no one. One of the pets meant to keep track of people they don't entirely trust. He's shit at it, though. He has lead feet and can't hide in the shadows."

I narrowed my brows. "Why are they following you?"

She tilted her head and gave me a pointed look. "They suspect I have magic."

I breathed out a heavy sigh.

"I never meant for that gun to bond to you," I said, and

meant it. "When I agreed to work with them, I laid out conditions that I wouldn't turn anyone. I refused to give blood. That you ended up turned from my magic—they won't let you go easily."

"Don't put this on yourself. It was going to be this way whether you changed me or not, Bree." She crossed her arms, shifting her position. Dark green hair draped over her shoulder in a tight braid. Her black trench coat moved with her, snagging something she kept hidden beneath the fabric. My gaze dropped to see the gun peek through before she closed the jacket around it. "The minute I joined the Illuminati, my old life was over. They never let anyone go easily, magic or not. You were the exception, not the rule. If anything, I dragged you in."

Dragged was a stretch. She'd been on Piper's tail when I caught her. When she realized what I was and assumed I would kill her, she told me who she worked for, and where to shove it.

My chin dipped in acknowledgement. "Still. I didn't exactly make things easier for you on that front," I said, looking pointedly at the magic weapon she kept with her.

She lifted a shoulder and huffed out a small laugh. "It is what it is, right? Not much can be done about it now. Besides, better me than one of the zealots."

I couldn't help but smile. She was right.

"Can you imagine what would've happened if that dickhead Flint bonded to your magic instead?" She wrinkled her nose, referring to the singular time the gun was not in her possession since she'd bonded to it. Of course the person who stole it, and then used it, was my sister's ex. The universe had a sense of humor. It was morbid. "No, it's better off with me," she added quietly, shaking her head.

"We're lucky I was able to track it before someone else managed to."

If my magic had to be attached to anyone, I was happy it was Robin. She had fight in her. A kind of spirit a lot of humans didn't have anymore. She had direction and purpose, and she was fighting for the right reasons, but she ended up with the wrong people.

We were alike in many ways.

"I suppose calling it luck is one way to look at it."

"Always look on the bright side of life," she said in a sarcastically chipper tone. "Or some such shit."

I snorted, taking in her form and seeing the dark circles under her eyes. "You doing okay out there?"

"It's New Chicago. No one is doing okay out there," she retorted. "But yes, in comparison, I'm okay. I'm surviving, so that's better than most."

Saying nothing, I watched the shadows creep along the wall a little bit more. The minutes ticked by as I debated how to ask this of her, knowing she wouldn't like it.

"You are good at that. Surviving, I mean. That's why I asked you to meet me."

Scrunching her eyebrows together, she said, "I don't understand."

"I need you to leave the city."

Her mouth slackened, and she blinked a few times as she processed my words. "You want me to run away? What the hell for?"

"The finer details are somewhat complicated for this world, but to break it down, I have a mate—called an atman—and he's . . ." I paused for a moment, twisting my lips.

"An asshole?" Robin supplied, holding her hand out in offering.

"Ha," I barked out a bitter laugh. "That's the gist of it."

"What does that have to do with me?"

"I rejected him, and he challenged me to a fight. It's a custom I'd rather not explain."

Robin raised a dubious eyebrow. "So does this duel take place at dawn, or . . ."

I exhaled loudly. Leave it to Robin to use humor instead of taking me seriously. I suppose from the point of view of a human, someone that had never been to the Otherworld, it seemed extreme. Demons and wilder creatures often were.

"Something like that. He can't come near me until we fight . . . but that doesn't mean he can't go after those I care about." She waved me off again, but I kept going before she could interrupt. "I know you're going to tell me how good you are at losing a stalker. That you can hide. That's not going to help you in this case. If I could capture you once, he could at any minute. Lorcan has chaos magic. No wards can keep him out. No spell can shield you. He's more powerful than you can imagine." But I could, and I knew better than anyone what he'd do to her if he found her. After I defied him, rejected him . . . he'd be out for blood, and until he had mine, nothing would stop his thirst. "I need you to leave the city before he finds you. If Lorcan even catches a whiff of my magic in you—he won't simply kill you, Robin. He'd keep you alive to get to me, breaking you apart piece by piece—stealing the magic in you—until you wish you were dead."

Robin's expression softened, and she uncrossed her arms, sticking her hands in her pockets instead. With her coat moved back, I could see the gun tucked neatly into a holster. Moments passed while she considered my words. "Your boyfriend sounds like he'd be right at home with the Illuminati."

Caught off guard, my cool expression slipped for a split second before I corrected myself. "What does that mean?"

"He's not the only threat you need to worry about. The Illuminati can't have you, so they have Piper in their sights. Again."

I groaned inwardly. Their timing was terrible.

"What do they want?"

"What do you think?" she huffed. "They're pissed off to hell after what you did. They want revenge, and they want magic—same as before." My eyes shot down to her holstered weapon. "I'm still safe. They don't know the gun and I are bonded yet. I told them I had no magic of my own, but they're getting suspicious. Both my hair and eyes turned green during the accident, and some of the higher-ups don't believe that's possible without having retained something from you. Ben is trying to keep them at bay for now, insisting they can't experiment on one of their own unless I wanted it, but time is running out."

My lips pursed, and I hummed. This was a mess, and it was my fault for getting involved. I'd only joined in to make a big scene to Piper about getting that portal and going home. That and the small part of me that wanted to help the race of people I was once a part of. I jumped ship as soon as I realized what they were doing. I never would have given them access to my magic if I'd known they were going to create weapons with it and try to start another magic war. No matter the reason, mistakes were made on my part, and it was too late by the time I understood what was happening.

I was many things, but a terrorist wasn't one of them.

But the Illuminati were, and now they wanted revenge on me for not only taking my own magic away, but also for depleting the supernaturals that worked with them. When

I'd severed ties, they attempted to use magic to bind me. But Lucifer was dead, making almost all black witches weak, and the fae that could control minds stood no chance against my shields. I lashed out and killed them all—then left their bodies to send a message.

To say they were pissed was an understatement.

Robin was right. It sounded like a perfect place for Lorcan.

Turning my head, I looked out the window as the sun moved across the hazy sky. My atman was out there somewhere, waiting to strike. Now, so were the fanatics.

"Thanks for letting me know," I said, looking back at her. "I'll do what I can, but I need you to do the same. Leave and don't look back. Keep moving around so they don't catch up to you."

She leaned her shoulder against the wall. "And where exactly would I go, Bree? Old NOLA? Nuevos Prados? Dos Ciudades? They're no better off than here. In case you haven't noticed, it's the same everywhere. There's no safe haven."

"Fucking find one," I snapped. As soon as the words came out, I regretted my tone. "I'm sorry—"

Robin held her hand up. "Don't. I know why you said it. But it doesn't change the fact I don't have magic the way you do. I didn't get your ability to astral project. I can't just hop on a plane or catch the bus bouncing between cities. Forget crossing the ocean. Unless you're volunteering to take me somewhere yourself, I'm stuck here. Something tells me that's not the case, or you'd have already said so."

I sighed, pressing my fingers to the bridge of my nose. I couldn't tell her that Lorcan had the possibility of winning or what that would mean for me. If I took her somewhere, he could pluck the location straight from my mind. An atma and atman that were fully bonded couldn't shield themselves from each other. My barriers would be useless. He'd chase her down, keep her alive, and taunt me with her torture. I wouldn't take that risk, but she couldn't stay here.

"Lorcan is going to kill you," I said bluntly, dropping my hand. "And if he doesn't, the Illuminati will."

"I know that," she said, pushing herself off the wall and walking toward me. "But what better choice do I truly have? They have people everywhere, not just in New Chicago. If I run, they will know I have magic and track my ass down. At least here I have some measure of protection from them. There is nothing that can protect me from a demon. If he finds me, I'm done for." Her lips formed a grim line, eyes heavy with the weight of it all.

"Everyone is a pawn in this game, but so long as the hand moving me is in my corner, I can survive."

Damned if we do, damned if we don't. I cursed under my breath, considering our options.

"If you can't get out of New Chicago, stay on the outskirts. Get into the old suburbs, the forests, anywhere but here. Move around. You're crafty. Sly. Maybe you were a fox in a past life. Let me take care of this thing with Lorcan, and then we'll get you away from the Illuminati."

Her eyes twinkled, almost like she knew I was challenging her skill. "I can take care of myself, you know. I've been doing this for a long time."

"Thing is, you don't have to," I said. She may have been older than me, but I felt responsible for her. Cared for her in a way I couldn't explain. We weren't sisters, but we were more than friends. Bonded not by blood, but instead by magic. Whatever we were, I knew she felt it too, but neither of us were touchy-feely enough to share it. I levelled her with a stare, trying to convey how important this was to me.

Pressing her lips together, she nodded. "Okay. I'll stay on the move. I have supplies stashed around the city. That will keep me moving for at least a time."

"Good. You've only got to do it for three weeks, then I'll come find you." I walked over to her, wrapping my arms around her shoulders. The embrace was small, but the simple fact that we did it at all meant something genuine on both our parts.

As I released her, she cleared her throat. "I'll lie low until then." I dipped my head in thanks. "In the meantime, keep Piper safe. They won't stop looking for her."

A shift in the air made the hair on my arms raise. The air tasted of power. Pure and potent. It twined with the threads of my sister's rage, casting out hints of smoke and roses.

Ronan.

Of course he'd show up here.

"What is this about Piper?" he asked.

Robin moved to defend herself, but I blocked her arms and stepped between them. "Don't—this is Piper's mate. He's not familiar with the concept of knocking. Ronan, Robin—Robin, Ronan."

She narrowed her eyes at him. "Charmed."

"I won't ask again," he said through clenched teeth, silver eyes turning black as he spoke.

I held my hand up to him. "Robin was just leaving. I'll tell you what you need to know."

"You'll tell me everything," he said, his voice rumbling. "If you don't, I'll have a look into the changeling's mind and see for myself."

I pinned him with a glare that said, 'piss off.' Turning

back to Robin, I said, "I need to have a word with Ronan. Use what daylight you have left to get on your way. I'll find you. Stay safe, keep hidden. Do whatever you need to do to protect yourself. Whatever you have to do to survive." My eyes quickly flicked to the magic gun hidden beneath her coat.

An unspoken agreement passed between us, and she nodded. "Same to you. Whatever it takes."

She turned on her heel and walked toward the door, her green braid swishing. "Robin," I said, and she halted, looking at me over her shoulder as she placed her hand on the doorknob. "Get a scarf or something. A hood, maybe. The hair is sort of a giveaway."

She winked over her shoulder and slipped through the exit, barely making a sound as she found her way through the maze of hallways to the staircase.

I continued to look at where Robin had last stood. Crossing my arms, I didn't make eye contact with him. "What do you want, Harvester?"

"I'd like to know what this was about," he said, stepping forward.

Turning to him, I tsked. "No, before that. You showed up here not knowing I was with someone. So again I ask, what do you want?"

"I need you." His features were stone cold, and his tone gave away nothing.

Need. It was an interesting word coming from him. I cocked an eyebrow.

"I'm listening."

15

PIPER

THE RUINS OF THE UNDERWORLD STRETCHED OUT BEFORE US. Black crumbling stone and ash as far as the eye could see. A glass veneer reflected the sky off its black depths where the sand had liquified and hardened.

This place was once a thriving city. After the night Lucifer died, and my power consumed me in the process, ash and glass were all that was left.

"This is it," Mist said quietly. She stepped forward, looking across the wasteland. "This is the place I saw."

I nodded, catching both Nat and Sasha's stares. A grim understanding passed between us. I sighed heavily.

"What you saw in your dreams was the future." The siren girl turned her pewter eyes on me. So mysterious. So *other* in the way she didn't stare with shock or fear, though she had to feel it.

"It felt fluid . . . like water. But the intensity seemed so real." She looked away again, her face wistful. Lost. "I'd feared it was the future the moment I saw your friends."

"The fluidity is because it's not set in stone. Every choice made can impact it. What you saw was the conglomeration of events if we were all to go forward with the choices we're leaning into now. If even one person changes course, the future changes."

"The outcome felt different. It was solid, like stone."

I didn't let my face show how much that concerned me.

"The Magic Wars weren't foretold. It wasn't until mere hours before that seers began to see what was coming. By then it was too late." Dryanda Abernathy hadn't made her choice till that morning. And it was her sole decision that changed the fate of us all. Permanently. "What you're seeing can't come to pass for three weeks. That's a lot of time for new decisions to be made; for things to change."

She was silent. Unresponsive. I'd wondered if she'd checked out, unable to handle the vision she saw when she now knew there was a chance it could happen.

"The person I saw—the man. He ended the world because of you." She didn't phrase it like a question, but the confusion in her voice begged an answer.

"My atman," I said in another sigh. "We're mates. He's a powerful demon. More powerful than any other as far as I know." The number of times Ronan told me he'd destroy the world for me, for grief, for the inexplicable reason that we could never be parted . . . I'd known that our magic meant he wouldn't survive my death. What I didn't know, or consider, was that those weren't simply words for him. He wasn't filling my head with declarations of importance. He was trying to make me understand the very real truth of what would happen if he lost me. That whether he wanted to or not, he wouldn't be able to stop himself—and he'd end life on this planet as we know it.

"I don't know what that would be like," Mist confessed. "To be so important to someone that they'd end the world if something happened to me."

My lips parted, but I wasn't sure what to say.

Before him? Me neither. But after?

It's hard to remember what it was like before. He'd only been in my life half a year, but so much had changed in that time. I changed.

"None of us do," Sasha said. "And I'm glad for it. That's a heavy burden to bear."

"Not to mention toxic in any other situation," Nathalie added. I narrowed my eyes, and she shrugged. "What? I'm just calling it like it is. Love may not be the sunshine and roses people like to think it is, but to love someone to that extent—to be so attached that you'd do something like that because they were taken from you?" She shook her head. "The horror I feel thinking of it can't be conveyed."

"He wouldn't have a choice," I said, defensively. "Just like I didn't have a choice in this." My arm swept wide, motioning to the destruction I'd caused single-handedly.

Mist's eyes blew wide, taking the destruction in with a new lens of understanding.

Nathalie approached me, hands up in the universal sign of surrender. "I'm not talking about you two. He *can't* choose—just like you couldn't. That option is stripped from you both, and that by itself is a crime. My heart bleeds for you—for what was done here," she said earnestly, holding my gaze in hers. The sincerity in her voice couldn't be denied. "You couldn't control it, and for that you shouldn't feel guilty, as I know you do. But *no one* else holds the power you do, and no others are bound the same way you are. One supernatural partner's death doesn't mean death for both of them in any other situation."

I stared at her quietly.

While I'd never intentionally end the world for Ronan . . . I couldn't say the same of him. The way he felt, the depth and intensity of our bond, the only thing that would now give him pause were the twins. He wouldn't for them, and only them.

I wasn't the only one who remained mute while uncomfortable silence settled between us. Mist also remained pensive. If I didn't know better, I'd say that she felt longing for what I had. Not jealousy, but a deep desire born from loneliness and being abandoned and abused.

"We need to move on," I said, clearing my throat. "We've established that Mist is indeed a far-sighted seer. She's going to need training. I'd like to bring her back and see if Señora Rosara would take her on as an apprentice."

Nathalie ran her hand over her jaw in consideration. "She'll need somewhere to stay that's safe." Not just for her safety, but for those around her was what she'd left off. "She can take Sasha and Sienna's old room now that they've moved into yours." I started to nod in thanks when she added a condition. "But I need you to use the blood oath."

I froze, my hackles rising.

She knew I didn't take the blood oath lightly, and I *never* wanted to use it to enforce my will unless absolutely needed.

"She can't control her powers, Piper," Nat said slowly, calm but unyielding. "I won't endanger the other people in the house. All I'm asking is that you give her the same terms you gave the twins—that she can't use her powers on anyone that shares your blood. Alternatively, you can name just the three of us, if you'd like it to not include anyone else you might take the oath with."

I released a tight breath. That wasn't unreasonable. Not when her last roommate was severely injured and had to receive critical care from white witches.

I nodded. "Mist, if you choose to come with us and stay in Nathalie's home, you can't use your powers on anyone that lives in the building." Which included Señora Rosara if she were to take up this opportunity. "You'll be taken care of. Fed. Clothed. We'll make sure you have everything you need, and we'll work on training your magic so that the only time you're a danger is when you choose to be."

Mist cocked her head. "And if I said no, what would you do?"

"Let you go," I answered simply. "But next time something goes wrong, don't expect me to come fix it. I don't mind being there for you, but I only help people that want to be helped. The choice is yours."

She nodded. "I want to come," she said without thinking. "I need to learn control—which, after you changed me, you promised you'd do." I inclined my head. "And if this other person, Señora Rose?"

"Rosara," Nat corrected.

"Rosara," she repeated. "If she can teach me how to control the visions, or at least my response to them, that would be good too. I'm scared to fall asleep right now. Worried it'll take me back there. I used to fear being awake, and I'd count the moments until exhaustion took me, but I'm tired of being scared of everything. I need to do this so I can live my life."

I knew what that was like, to be so scared that it consumed you. I'd turned to rage to smother my fear. There was no reason to fear the fire if I became it.

It seemed that despite her desire for revenge, she recognized that there was something more important than anger.

Control.

~

THE SHOP DOOR jingled as the four of us stepped inside.

Señora Rosara called out, "Bring her here."

Old coot must have been expecting us. I led the way back to her desk where she stood, arms crossed, lips pursed.

"I take it you saw us?" I asked. She ignored me, waving Mist forward.

"Let me take a look at her—and watch the wings."

At the reminder, Mist tucked them in tighter, still somewhat awkward with them. While she seemed to grasp the mechanics, she'd yet to accommodate for the fact that they moved with her emotions the same as the twins' ears and tails. Her wings were an extension of her, and it was impossible to clench a muscle all day, every day.

After a slow circle around her, Señora lifted her head and said, "She'll do."

Mist cocked her head. "You're strange."

Nat grimaced and Sasha's mouth dropped at little. I waited a beat as the Señora's face went flat as stone, then she bent at the waist letting out a full bellied laugh.

"Sí. I am, and I like it that way." She smiled and it was genuine, shocking the hell out of all of us. Who knew the crotchety witch just needed a blunt teenager to bring out her better side? "When you're different, people either covet you or fear you. The key is to be just a bit of both so that they won't hunt you, and you can tell them to fuck off."

A slow grin spread across Mist's face.

Great. Now I'd done it.

"Come down tomorrow afternoon and we'll begin your training." Then to Nat she held out a small cloth bag. "Brew this for her before bed. It will prevent her from having visions while sleeping."

Nat took the bag and nodded. Mist said, "Thank you."

"De nada," she nodded. "I need to talk to the demon alone."

My curiosity and dread piqued simultaneously. This was either about our appointment or the girl. When the elevator doors closed behind them, I waited for her to speak.

She waved her hand at me. "You don't have to see me for another four days. Don't look so pissed off."

"I'm not. That's just my face."

"Hm." She wrinkled her nose, clearly not believing me. "The girl has death magic. A lot of it."

My eyebrows lifted. I didn't know. I couldn't see magic like Nat. I could only taste it. Pregnancy had allowed me to smell it to some extent, but they were specific to the person, not the type.

"I'm surprised it's not rage magic. She's got enough anger for it."

"Darkness," she said. "It starts here." She tapped on her chest. "She would have longed for death before you changed her, and she will revel in it with her newfound power."

The door chimed once more, and a cold breeze sent the hairs on my arms sticking straight up. Her words sounded an awful lot like a prophecy. "Did you *see* that?"

"No." She shook her head. "I saw her arrival, but nothing more. This is what I felt when I circled her. She will struggle to straddle the line between dark and light. Ultimately it will be decided by her heart."

"Should I be concerned about her staying with them?" I asked, leaning against her counter, and rubbing my temple.

Señora Rosara shook her head as an arm wrapped

around my waist. Warm and solid. I recognized the chaos in him the moment he walked in the shop.

"I will work with her. Train her in death magic, but I am only so strong. She will need a stronger tutor eventually."

"Ahh," I said. "Understood. Keep me updated on her, please."

She made a shooing motion, dismissing me. Ronan tugged me toward the elevator with a nod in her direction, to which she rolled her eyes. I felt him stiffen.

"Are you okay?" I asked, eyeing him more closely.

"Fine," he grunted. "Long day with Anders."

That I understood. The days felt too long and the nights too short. More often than not we both got back and rolled into bed after a quick shower with few words exchanged. It wasn't ideal, but I had to hope it got better.

I hit the button for our floor.

"The siren girl I changed . . . she saw the future."

Ronan grunted that he heard me, the hand around my waist tightening. His lips skimmed my neck, inhaling my scent.

"Bree and Lorcan's challenge," I added. He paused.

"And?"

"Lorcan kills me before she can see a winner," I said quietly, expecting his magic to fluctuate any second. He remained still. Steady. The elevator chimed and the double doors opened. He released me, stepping out in one fluid motion.

"What happens after?"

I frowned, tilting my head.

"You destroyed everything. Everyone."

He didn't respond at first. With his back to me, I couldn't read his expression. He turned toward the kitchen counter and rested both hands flat on its surface.

"I see."

That's all he said. No emotion. No inkling as to what he thought or felt or anything. Ronan had always been a man of few words. He didn't prattle on endlessly about things that didn't matter. He didn't express extreme emotion outside of where I was concerned.

I reached across the bridge between our minds to brush his. Without turning his back, Ronan answered, *"Is everything all right?"*

His response didn't make any sense. After what I'd told him . . .

My feet turned sluggish. My blood turned to lead in my veins.

Slowly but surely, the imposter turned around.

White fire ignited in my right hand as I stepped forward, my expression as flat as his own.

"You should have known better than to come here," I said. My brands glowed red-hot like the ends of a fire poker.

His skin lightened and his hair turned bone white. The silver of his eyes drained away as crimson bloomed. The process only took a second, then Lorcan was standing before me.

"On the contrary, Ms. Fallon, you should know better than to challenge me—given the future already sees your death."

16
RONAN

I paused. Waited.

Her response didn't come.

Over a minute ticked by, uncertainty pricking my skin. Uneasiness scraped along my scalp.

"What?" Bree asked. A single question, though she demanded it with the haughtiness of a queen. The arrogance of a demon.

"Piper."

She blinked. "Where?"

"Our apartment," I said, pinpointing her magic from across the city as easily as I felt my own.

Bree disappeared as I stepped into the void.

But when I came out . . .

The air left my lungs. Rage hissed between my lips. Death sat heavy at my fingertips.

She stood face-to-face with Lorcan; fearless and determined. Her fists were consumed by white flame. It might have been enough to actually kill him. Her power itself was greater than his, but Lorcan wasn't without tricks.

"Atman," Bree's voice rang out, commanding and dangerous.

Despite the white fire only inches from him, the essence of pure rage itself—the bastard smiled. Cruel and cunning.

His dark magic was wrapped around Piper. Burying her beneath its strength—or trying to, at least. Hers was so bright he was struggling to smother it.

"Ah, good. You're both here for me to deliver the message in person," he said. "Ronan, you will not see my atma again. You will not seek her out. You will stay impartial if you desire me to leave this one be." Lorcan reached out to brush Piper's cheek with his fingers. Her hand moved to strike him. To ignite him. She lifted it to his chest, then froze.

Her eyebrows drew together.

With ease, he lowered his hand to cup her cheek, then curved it around the slender column of her throat.

I didn't give a warning. I didn't lift a hand. My own magic rose in the space between one second and the next. The power of the true Harvester.

I hadn't been him since coming here, but I slipped back into that mask so easily the moment Piper was threatened. It was as simple as embracing my atma.

I didn't care that Bree had her own challenge.

I didn't care that she wanted to deal with him or that Piper likely wanted to strike him down.

I didn't care about the outcome or their feelings.

He touched her. He was trying to cage her.

He would die for it.

"I wouldn't do that if I were you." Lorcan spoke calmly, self-assured despite the precarious position he was in. "While Piper here is truly exceptional in some regards . . ." His eyes lowered, drinking in his fill of her. "She is weak of mind. Like a child. Her magic is so potent . . . and yet she has no true protections." Piper turned, her back settling to his chest. While her face showed alarm, her body moved robotically. Entirely out of her control. My fists tightened. The building shook. Picture frames rattled the walls. Kitchen drawers slid open. Glass fell to the ground, shattering around us.

"Leave my sister out of this, Lorcan," Bree said calmly. "Your fight is with me and Ronan. Not her."

"Ahh." He smiled, tilting Piper's head with one hand. His lips skimmed her neck, fangs grazing the skin. "That's where you're wrong. She declared herself the queen of a city I intend to take. By demon law, she's opened herself up to a challenge of her own . . . one she has no hope of winning against me."

The fire in Piper's hand swirled as her magic continued to gather. It grew impossibly bright to the point that it was difficult to look at.

"Challenge or no challenge—if you hurt even a hair on her head, I will end you," I said through clenched teeth. "Without her, nothing will stop me from ripping the magic of your soul apart and feasting on it piece by piece. I will make it a slow, agonizing death. Keeping you alive for centuries. Millennia. You will wish for me to finish the job long before I do—if ever."

Lorcan stared, red gaze unimpressed.

"He won't touch me," Piper spat. While her body couldn't move—it seemed her mind was still her own—for now. "One sip of my blood and he'll be eaten alive."

Lorcan smiled against her neck. "I would consume your power first, then let you give birth—before I drained you of every last drop."

Her face blanked. I could only describe it as a dam being

slammed into place, locking everything she thought and felt behind it.

I called down the bridge between our minds, but she didn't answer me.

"If you do, you know what future awaits you." A chill ran through the room. A cold air that wasn't present before. "We know that you need Bree's power to actually take on my atman. Without her—you are *nothing*. Which means as much as you like to threaten and scare, you're all talk and no action."

Her eyes began to glow, turning violet.

Lorcan's hand around her throat tightened, knuckles turning white.

It seems that she'd hit a nerve. Under ordinary circumstances, I liked that about her, but here? Now?

I didn't want to chance that she was wrong, and yet, I could not act. If I came for him, he'd go for her.

There would be nothing left.

"You think that?" he asked, but it wasn't a question. It was a challenge. "You think that my lack of action is because I don't have the power I need?" He lowered his head and let out a laugh. "It's too bad that you are his atma. I might've liked to keep you when this is over. If my own atma had been half as loyal, things might have ended differently." He kissed her neck once, squeezing her hip. "I may need Bree's power; I'll give you that. But there's one thing in all of this that you haven't accounted for." Silence ticked by, each second worse than the last. "*You.*" She didn't let her own mask slip. Neither did she open the bridge between our minds. "Ronan won't touch me because of you. You are his greatest weakness—and he can't protect you from me. Not when all I need to do is reach into your mind and break you. I can make an hour of torture feel like a year." Lorcan met my eyes across the room. "He may not be able to stop himself if you die . . .but if you lose your mind? Your sanity? Well . . . he won't end the world when his unborn twins are still here."

Despair filled me because he saw the same thing the Morrigan did.

For all the power I held, Piper was young and still had much to learn of her own. She had weak points and each one was a fracture in her armor that someone exploited.

I'd taught her how to use her magic so she'd never be chained again, but she had no shields. No true protections from the magic of others. Hers was aggressive to a fault, but not defensive in the slightest. I couldn't teach her something she did not possess.

And Lorcan knew that.

"I may not have my sister's shields or my atman's chaos —but I killed Aeshma when I was only human. I imagine if push comes to shove, I could find a way to kill a false harvester too."

"Perhaps," Lorcan acquiesced. "I've heard the rumors. The stories. With time, you might live up to the impossible feats you've managed . . . but time is not on your side, and neither is the future. One way or another, I will win and take everything each of you holds dear." He looked from Piper to me to Bree, settling on her last. "I'm giving one warning as a courtesy. You will regret denying me, but don't for a second believe I cannot make your punishment worse if you do so again. Come to me and beg forgiveness before the challenge—or Piper will pay the price."

I stilled. Waiting.

Lorcan released her and stepped back. Then he lifted his hand, and I knew it wasn't over. Not yet.

"I'll leave you with a parting gift. A bit of 'action,' if you will."

He smiled. Piper shuddered, then fell to her knees.

Her body convulsed. Then she lifted her head, staring straight out, but not at me . . .

"Run," she whispered to her sister.

White fire exploded.

17

PIPER

I couldn't stop it.

My body was not my own.

My power had multiplied in the minutes Lorcan was here. I delved deeper and deeper into the pits where my magic rested, spurring it forth—dragging it to the surface with every intent to wipe him off the face of this planet. Or as close to it as I could.

I hadn't planned on him using my power against us. I didn't know it was possible. Not until my hand shot forward without my consent, unleashing fire upon them. It burned in my blood. Raged in my veins. The flames ate at me from the inside out as Lorcan, for all intents and purposes, pulled the trigger.

Like a bullet released, there was no taking it back. I couldn't do it, no matter how much I tried. It was the episode with Flint and the gun all over again. Fire and fury coiled around me with nowhere to go but out.

Ronan barreled through the flames, taking the brunt of the initial wave.

While Bree would not survive it if she came into contact

with it, Ronan was my atman. Not quite invincible against me, but as close to it as one could be. He pushed through whatever pain he had, tackling me to the ground.

Except the ground never appeared.

In an instant, the cool touch of the void nipped at me. It smothered the fire, depriving it of air. The inferno turned to strands, then wisps, until nothing more than smoke remained. Chaos magic wrapped around me like a weighted blanket. It pressed into my magic, my skin— filling my pores like a cork did a wine bottle. It put a stopper on the outpour of fire, if only for a moment, instead shoving it back inside of me with a firm push.

I gasped.

Finally back in control.

My chest heaved with exertion as I crouched in the fetal position, taking deep, laboring breaths. "Fuck," I ground out, my forehead touching my knees. I wanted to pull at my hair and scream, but it wouldn't do any good. I couldn't change what had just happened. Only hope the damage wasn't irreparable.

Ronan's rough fingers grasped either side of my face as I sat up.

"What were you thinking?" he demanded. Mercury pooled in his gaze, his magic going wild.

"I didn't go searching for him," I said, yanking back. He didn't release his hold, fingers knotting in my hair and scraping my scalp. "I thought he was *you*. He looked like you. Smelled like you. His magic . . ." I trailed off. Ronan had warned us he could disguise his magic to mimic anyone.

I didn't grasp how dangerous that made him until now.

"Why didn't you call me as soon as you knew it wasn't me?" He spoke quietly, but not softly. Fierce chaotic energy swirled around us as his self-control tried to unravel.

"I didn't think—"

"*Do not lie to me.*"

I swallowed and tried to look away. He didn't let me.

"You didn't answer me when I asked if you were all right. How long did you know it wasn't me?" he said, grip firm and unyielding.

"About a minute."

The void shuddered.

"A second is all it would take—"

"I know."

"*Then why didn't you call me?*"

I didn't have a good answer. I had an ignorant one. A selfish one. I didn't know it at the time, but it didn't change the facts. I should have called him. As much as it riled me to ask for help, Lorcan could have killed me.

"Can we talk about this later? I need to see if Bree is okay—"

"No. She's fine. We'll talk about this right now."

I lowered my eyes, and he tugged on my roots, demanding I pay attention. That I answer.

"I thought I could handle it. I thought—" I broke off and he stared at me, jaw clenched, eyes tight, waiting for me to continue. "I thought I could kill him. Or at least try."

He closed his eyes, shutting me out. "I told you not to—"

"I'm not a dog," I snapped. Any feeling of remorse drained out of me, replaced by a familiar anger. "You can't tell me to do things and expect it to just happen. I didn't search him out. I wasn't looking for him. But like I told you —he came looking for me. I stood my ground—"

"You overplayed your hand," he snapped. "You thought you could be the hero and save the fucking day instead of listening to me. He could have killed you right then and there."

"I didn't know he could control my body or make me use my magic," I replied icily with painstaking calm.

"You knew he could mimic magic. He impersonated me well enough that you believed him to be me—your atman. We are literally bound together for eternity. Your soul is intertwined with mine. My magic runs in your blood, and you mistook him for me. He's a chaos demon. Did you really think that's all he could do?" The condescending edge of his voice had me biting the inside of my cheek till I tasted blood.

"No," I said honestly. I wrenched my head back, forcing him to either let go or risk hurting me. While I'd heal from it, I knew he wouldn't do the latter, no matter how pissed he was. "I knew he likely had tricks up his sleeve. I just didn't know what they were. Now I do." I scrambled back further into the void. He was right there in an instant. Arms caging me in.

"If you think I'm letting him near you again—"

"In case you didn't realize the first time, *you can't stop him.*" My words must have hit like a slap to the face. I felt his hands warm despite the drop in temperature through the void. "That's the whole reason this happened to begin with. None of us can stop who he goes near or hurts—not even me, apparently."

"That's where you're wrong," he said. His breath fanning my skin. "I could find him, given time. As the Harvester, I can kill without having to justify it to anyone. Even him."

"Then why haven't you?"

"You," he answered. "If he got to you before I found him . . ." Power rippled through the void, making me shudder.

He gripped my forearms harder, keeping me on my feet. "I can't lose you."

I held my breath as claws wrapped around my chest and squeezed at the very idea of losing him. Our children.

"I fucked up," I said eventually. Slowly, I wound my arms around his waist. He released his grip, running his palms up my arms and around my back, pulling me into him. "I thought because I'm powerful that I might be able to kill him. That all this fire in me could be enough. We already have plenty of enemies before adding him to the mix. Maybe if he could be dealt with before Bree's challenge, then we could have two seconds to actually breathe before the twins get here." I sighed, shaking my head.

"You are powerful," Ronan said, his forehead tilted forward, touching mine. "I'm in awe of the strength you have for one so young. Neither me nor Lorcan were anywhere near as strong at two hundred, let alone twenty-five." His thumbs rubbed small circles into my back, easing the tension there. "But you are only a quarter of a century old, and he and I have been alive for millennia. If he were not a chaos demon and chosen by the Source, you would be able to finish this . . . but he is what he is, just as you are."

"You yourself said Bree's not as powerful as me," I pointed out. "It can't be both ways, that she has a chance to defeat him, and I don't."

Ronan sighed, and he nodded slowly. "Bree's particular skill set protects her mind. He wouldn't be able to control her or turn her own power against her. She may not be as strong as you, just as he isn't as strong as me, but she has shields, and that gives her an advantage you don't have. A complicating factor is that I don't know the extent of what powers he possesses. Demons grow in strength as they age until they bond. Because he hasn't bonded with Bree, they don't share power yet, but that also means his is growing slowly with every passing second."

"But so is Bree's, then."

"Yes," he agreed. "But not yours. Your sanity is safe now, but your power will never grow or change. We've yet to learn what all you can do, but whatever your gifts are at this moment, that's all you'll ever have."

It didn't bother me that I couldn't become even more powerful. The only reason I'd bargained for power to begin with was to protect my own. What bothered me was that I became a demon, the literal source of magic in my world—and it wasn't enough anymore.

The more power I had, the bigger my enemies were.

When you're an ant, wolves don't try to kill you, but they squish you anyway.

When you become a wolf, they circle you. Target you. Pick apart your every weakness until they can strike the killing blow.

"Three weeks isn't enough time for her to gain some new ability that could change the outcome," I said, shaking my head. "And as it stands, the siren I created saw their challenge. It didn't matter what either of them could do. Lorcan killed me in the middle of it, and you detonated like a bomb, destroying everything. The world was gone."

Ronan froze. His fingers pressed into my skin. The void wavered. If I hadn't been his mate, the sheer force of it would have crushed me. My muscles tightened under the strain, but I didn't buckle or bend or break.

"She foresaw this?"

I nodded. "She dreamed it. When I talked to her, she described Lorcan and Bree in exact detail. She knew Sasha had a twin. She talked about you . . ." I took a shaky breath. "I told Lorcan how it ended and that's when I realized he wasn't you. His reaction wasn't right. I couldn't pinpoint why, so I reached out to you. Your response helped me put the pieces together."

"He won't do it now," he said quietly. "He knows the outcome. He won't kill you. That's why he wants to break you and keep the twins alive." He released a slow breath. "The future she has seen will have shifted. He's planning something else now."

Mist could possibly see what had changed, but there was no guarantee. She hadn't even started learning to use her powers. I couldn't rely on that. Even the Señora couldn't see that far into the future, and she was remarkably accurate.

"If he's making new plans, so can we," I said.

"There's no way to have a contingency for all the possibilities." His claws had retracted, and he dragged his fingertips over my skin, almost as though he were calming himself. Grounding himself in this moment.

"Of course there's not. That shouldn't stop us from analyzing him and what he could do."

"My focus is keeping you safe. That is all I care about."

I exhaled, tilting my head to the side. "Don't you think I know that? My death ended the world in that vision. That's a heavy weight to carry." I twisted my lips, thinking in the silence of the vast darkness.

"I considered putting you in the void at the first sign of danger," he admitted quietly. "But if something should happen to me—if I didn't survive—you would be stuck here for eternity."

"Sasha can enter the void," I reminded him.

"If she could find you. Its very nature is endless," he countered. "When she brought you into it unknowingly, I only found you because of our bond."

I pressed my face into his chest. I could enter the light realm. I could hide there. Stay safe. Wait until this was all over. For . . . three weeks? I'd been alone long enough that I could handle that. But for what? Survival? The 'what ifs' were too great.

If Lorcan won, the world as we knew it would change. He wanted control and power and the subjugation of its inhabitants. If he won, Bree was dead. Ronan was dead. My throat thickened with emotion, and I tried to swallow it down. What was I supposed to do then? Bring Nat, Sienna, and Sasha into the light realm to live? Give birth to the twins and stay there forever. It wasn't possible. It wasn't a home. There was no food or water. It was the polar opposite of the void. Endless light. A vast expanse of nothingness.

"I wouldn't want that for you," Ronan whispered, his chest rumbling against my face as he spoke. I tilted my head up to gaze at him. "Your mind is open to me, and your thoughts are loud right now."

"I don't want to survive this. I want to live," I said after a long pause between us. Before he could interrupt me, I kept going. "The only outcome in this that works in our favor is if Bree wins. Anything else is death and destruction. I don't want to go into hiding for the next three weeks."

His arms tightened around me. "Piper—"

I stepped back, removing myself from his embrace. "No, listen. I've been here before. I spent the last day with my family, not knowing that it was our last day. Not knowing it was our last hug, or our last words. If we *knew* the world was going to end, I wouldn't spend it hiding from everyone I love until the doomsday clock ran out. I would make time to be with Nat and let her sing terrible eighties music, and I would be by your side every night. I would talk to my sister and make amends before everything was gone." I shook my head, placing my hand on my stomach, feeling the life growing inside me. "It's not enough to simply survive this. I've survived before, but I won't do it again."

"I know." Ronan cleared his throat. "I can't pretend to understand human emotion, but I know enough from you to plan for it."

Confusion filled me, and I blinked rapidly, trying to piece together what he meant. "What plan?"

"While today didn't go accordingly, I expected Lorcan to seek you out at some point. So I spoke with Bree about moving in."

"He can't come to her. . ." Understanding filtered through me, and a gruff chuckle escaped my lips.

"I don't understand why this is funny."

"The role reversal," I said. "After everything I did over the past ten years, in the end, she's quite literally my body-guard. Now she's protecting me while trying to save me. It's just . . . ironic."

"And you're not going to argue this with me?" he asked, hedging carefully.

I shook my head. "No, I think it's a good plan. It's as good as it's gonna get, anyway. We carry on with life while we do what we can to prepare for their challenge."

After everything that had happened today with Lorcan, the message he sent was crystal clear. So much was at stake, and I'd been incredibly stupid trying to face him by myself. I'd spent the last decade trying to do things without any support. If there was one thing I'd learned over the past several months, it was that I did need help, and I had it if I was willing to accept it. The earlier showdown was a much-needed reminder that I couldn't do this on my own.

None of it.

Ronan wrapped his arms around me once more, caging me in. "Bree is still waiting for us in the apartment."

"Good. I have to meet up with some supes that have been demanding my attention, or so you've told me." He rumbled against me in confirmation. "If that's the case, I need to prep my sister, so she knows what to expect."

Sasha said I can't be everything to everyone, and she was right. An entire city was looking to me for protection. The burden was heavy. I had cracked under the weight of it for years. I didn't take care of myself, my sanity—all in the name of surviving.

Now I had people that I trusted to help me. I wasn't alone, and only together would we be able to drag this city into a new age without succumbing to our enemies.

Or so I hoped.

Either way, it was our best shot—our only shot—and I would take it.

18

PIPER

MY WHITE BUTTON-DOWN PULLED IN THE MIDDLE.

I pinched my lips together in a frown as I turned to the side, examining my stomach. Sure enough, just about where my belly button was, I had a small, asymmetrical bump. I placed my hand against it, feeling the hardness there I hadn't noticed before.

"You're progressing quickly."

I turned at the sound of my sister's voice. Bree stood in the doorway, her white hair braided back in a fishtail. It was one of the simpler hairstyles I'd seen her wear since she'd returned. Her blue eyes were lined in black, making her pale skin appear even lighter. A black crop top squeezed her beneath a leather jacket with faded patches. Her green brands ran down either side of her abdomen, the strokes sharp and jarring. Unlike mine, hers had a distinctly harsh edge to them. Jagged and uneven. It made me wonder what her name was, not that I'd be dumb enough to ask.

"Faster than I'd like," I said, turning back to the mirror. I dropped my hand and the black blazer fell into place, hiding the bump—unless you knew to look for it. "I won't be able to keep their existence a secret much longer."

Bree tilted her chin in acknowledgement, slowly stepping around the bed. She appraised the wall of windows the headboard sat against, overlooking part of the city. "It's a good thing you're taking the blood oath with Dahlia Le Grange. She'll be able to hear their heartbeats tonight," my sister remarked. "As will the werewolf representative Ronan chose to endorse."

I nodded, somewhat absently. After everything that happened leading up to this, it was strange to think she was standing here, in my bedroom, commenting on the twins.

"You don't agree with his choice?" I asked, not particularly caring one way or another. It was small talk.

"I have reservations," she said, tapping her fingernails along the metal bed frame. Her vagueness scratched at my composed exterior, like sticking fingers in a festering wound. This is why we were in the situation with Lorcan to begin with. Bree never showed her cards. I blew out a quick, frustrated breath and turned on my heel.

"It's time—"

"I want you to make up your own mind," Bree said as I passed. "Ronan shouldn't be choosing your inner circle any more than I should. He may be your atman, and a good one at that—but you put yourself in charge. It's your reputation on the line if they fuck up. You should decide. No one else."

I paused, lowering my head.

"Thank you."

"For?"

"Telling me," I said. "I'm sorry that I'm prone to not thinking the best of you right now. It's complicated."

Bree snorted and her hand squeezed my shoulder. "When has it not been complicated for us?"

She had a point.

Even when we were younger, our differences put us at odds with one another, and yet made us love each other all the more fiercely. Why else would I bargain with witches and demons for power as a kid? Why would she deny her mate for me? For my children?

"I know that you don't want to talk about what happened with Lorcan—"

"I don't," she said instantly, cutting me off. I pressed my lips together and nodded.

"I'd like to spend these next few weeks we have getting to know you again—the real you. Not the faces you've worn for me." I turned, squeezing her shoulder opposite to me in return. "I want to see the places we talked about visiting as kids, and I want to know about your life in the Otherworld, what of it you're willing to share. You don't have to tell me about Lorcan if you don't want to . . . I just want to know about you."

Bree stared and stared. Some small amount of surprise lingered in her gaze, despite the way her eyes searched me as if looking for signs of deceit or some other underlying reason. It was telling of the life she'd lived, if that's what she went to first.

"Okay," she said eventually. "I'll tell you my stories . . . but I want to know yours. After I was gone, you became something of a legend around here, enough so the supernaturals want you as queen." One side of her mouth quirked up, a sly amusement that treaded a cruel line. There was no questioning my sister had changed irrevocably in her time away. Her very nature may have been fearless, but not so callous as it was now. I wanted to know why.

"Let's get through tonight without any fights breaking out, and I'll tell you whatever you want to know."

"Likewise."

"If you're both done, we can go," Nat said, coming around the corner to stand in the doorway of my bedroom. "We're late—and while being late can be a power move—it's a dick one. No one likes having their time wasted." She stuffed the last bit of a croissant into her mouth, groaning in appreciation. It smelled fresh and buttery. Mouthwatering. My stomach grumbled.

I frowned. "Where did you get that?"

"Sasha." She thrust her head in the direction of the living room. "She popped over to France for snacks while you were getting ready. Found this upscale bakery that has survived over there."

"Is there any more—"

"No, but tell you what, get through this and I'm sure someone can go pick up another dozen of them." Nat motioned for me to start walking toward the living room with a sweep of her arm.

"It's rude to not think of the pregnant lady, you know," I said under my breath.

Nat bent at the waist, letting out a raucous laugh. "Oh, *now* you want to pull the pregnant card?" She shook her head.

"What? I haven't eaten since this morning."

Sasha tossed me a banana from across the room. I caught it easily and quickly devoured the fruit. "Now that the cat's out of the bag, we'll need to talk about that," she said with a pointed glance at my stomach. "But later. Nathalie is correct that being late will only piss off some of the people we're trying to bring to heel. You need to exert power, but in a way that will get you their respect."

I nodded. It occurred to me how at ease I'd become with Sasha and Sienna. It wasn't like Nat, exactly, but in some ways they felt like family all the same. Family you might argue with and butt heads with, but you always had each other's backs.

I didn't know if it was the blood oath I took with them, particularly Sasha, who offered herself willingly. If my magic in their veins had changed something in all of us, but I didn't hate it. I'd always wanted a family, especially after mine had been stolen from me. I never imagined I'd find it in complete strangers, supernaturals at that.

The thought made me laugh a little, under my breath.

"Hm?" Sasha asked.

"Nothing." I shook my head. "I'm ready."

EBONY DOUBLE DOORS SWUNG OPEN.

With Sasha on my right and Bree on my left, I stepped forward into my future.

Everyone stopped and turned.

Conversations died out, till not even a whisper could be heard. I regarded each of them shrewdly. Vampire. Were-wolf. Ghoul. Incubi. Witch. Fae. Banshee.

Seven leaders and their seconds, representatives of the seven largest supernatural factions in New Chicago.

Ronan and Anders stood off to the side, also pausing mid-conversation.

"You all know who I am and what we're here for. This is your last chance to back out of our arrangement if you're having second thoughts." My voice carried on a wind I created to project my power. "Once you take a seat, there is no going back. Each and every one of you will either swear a blood oath or die in flame. As it is, some of you may not survive my power. If you fear death, this is not the place for you."

I waited for a suspended heartbeat.

The purple-and-green-haired bartender I'd met not long ago was the first to take a seat, followed by her second. Both were vampires.

The banshee clan leader went next. I was unsurprised. They were matriarchal. Banshees may run their homes and be dominant in personal relationships, but it was the women that ruled clans. They hadn't submitted to Lucifer during his reign, and it was a good sign they were among the first now.

Rafael, the incubi leader, and his mate, Rajvi—who also served as his second—were the next to take their seats. He nodded in my direction once, as if to say that he was firm in his choice. I certainly hoped so, otherwise he would die tonight. While I reveled in killing that vampire from the den, I didn't enjoy killing for the hell of it. These two were good leaders. They had kept their people in line for several decades now, and actively worked to put an end to the trading of incubi and succubi children as slaves. Their actions had earned them goodwill in my eyes. I hoped they lived up to their names.

Our white witch coven leader and her daughter came next. They were descendants of an old line and had moderate power before Lucifer's fall—and an even stronger hold now that most black witches were dead or depleted. My own bias against witches made me hesitant, but I knew the covens had chosen them intentionally—with my reputation in mind. They were well-known healers and didn't engage in the darker arts. Little did they know it wasn't the arts themselves that turned me off, but the people that were often hurt through them. Still, I regarded them evenly as they took their seats.

Next came the ghouls. Both men with white-gray skin and black eyes. They were the group I knew the least about. While I'd been hired to bring in a ghoul once or twice, I tended to stay away from their kind. They were toward the bottom of the totem pole when it came to power. Their leader, Thaddeus, was a preacher in his past life, and took those in who sought to live a peaceful life. Ghouls that were made often feared death and carried that into the afterlife. Ghouls that were born were raised in the faith, at least those under Thaddeus' care. While I wasn't a believer, I could respect any man that had morals he stuck to till the bitter end.

Eidelyon and Etheria, the current ruling fae, were next. While there was a great deal of divisiveness in the lineage of Seelie versus Unseelie, I didn't care what their bloodline was. I only cared about what they could do and who they would choose to be. These two had a history of staying out of politics unless it directly affected them. They did the bare minimum of Lucifer's requirements, giving just enough to stay under the radar despite the numbers I knew they were building. Toward the end Lucifer found out, and a number of fae warriors were enlisted in Lucifer's ranks. I'd heard through the grapevine how much this angered them, and knew they'd be slow to trust because of it.

The very last to take a seat was Kai Winters, the current reigning shifter alpha, followed by his beta—Leonard Daunte. Kai cast me an appraising glance, not lustful, but calculating, as if weighing my worth. I did the same, meeting his eyes without reserve. Leonard took his seat first, something that irritated Kai if the flick of his eyes and tightened jaw were any indication. He followed after a suspended second.

The showdown of powers was done, but the hard part had yet to begin. Ronan and Anders took their seats, followed by Nat and Sienna. They weren't official heads, but Nat dealt with business in this city that impacted every person in this room. As the single wealthiest and most influential non-leading party—she had a role to play in this as well.

Sasha, Bree, and I were last.

I leaned back in my chair, letting my hands sit loosely on the armrests in a feigned mask of aloofness.

"Each of you were asked here tonight to swear a blood oath to me because my atman deemed you worthy—but it is my blood you'll be taking, and therefore my own agenda you must come to terms with."

I felt Bree's eyes on me, casting a sidelong glance in approval from my left.

"What agenda is that, precisely?" Rafael, the incubi asked. "We've heard rumors. Seen the evidence of what it means to be on the other side of your temper, but what is it exactly that you want from us?"

Lucifer would have silenced him before the third word, but I let him speak. Respect went both ways, and he was right to question.

"To keep your people in line," I answered honestly. "I want an end to the slave trading business in this city. Children. Adults. It doesn't matter their age, the practice is barbaric. We should be focused on protecting our city, and therefore our own. Building a better life for ourselves and a better future for anyone that entrusted their lives and loyalty to each of you—just as you are entrusting your lives to me."

He nodded, pleased with that answer. His mate, Rajvi, smiled at me.

"How do you plan to do this?" Etheria asked. Her hair was a pale lavender color that shifted iridescently beneath the lowlights of the domed conference room. "These are pretty words, but I've been around longer than you can grasp—"

"And I longer than all of you combined," Ronan rumbled. He didn't like the tone of her voice.

Etheria inclined her chin, pale lips pinched together stiffly. "I want to know how she plans to enforce this. How she plans to punish transgressors." Her eyes swept back toward me. "The fae have long opposed the flesh trade. Not in the least because our children are kidnapped twice as much as any other group in this room. How will you put an end to it, when neither Lucifer nor any soul in this room has been able to?"

I nodded in understanding. Her question came from a place of concern, filled with hesitation to believe in a claim that was too good to be true.

"It won't be instant," I acknowledged. "But it will be easier with each of you entering a blood oath. The things I ask for are different from Lucifer. There will be less wiggle room for error, and if someone manages to find it—I'll be doing regular visits with each of your people. I want to get to know them. See their homes. Meet their families. Understand their struggles so that I can better help you help them." She opened her mouth to interrupt, and I held up a hand, not quite done. "I'll also be doing these so I can monitor for abuse and corruption of the system. I can more easily hunt down a trafficker than anyone in this room. It's what I did for years, as you well know. And when I find them, which I always do—I will make an example of them. Like I did with the vampire den this past week."

She settled back in her chair and nodded. Not completely convinced, but not as skeptical either.

"I am only one person," I continued, addressing another part of the equation that had yet to come up but was relevant. "Which means you will often get visits from my second and third—if I choose to take one. They will be my eyes and ears as much as my fist and fury when needed."

"On behalf of the banshee clans, I offer myself as an option for second or third," Siobhan, the leader, said. "I will happily step aside and leave the clan to my sister's ruling if I can further aide you—"

"The witch covens also offer up one of our own, anyone of your choosing—"

"A shifter would better complement your rage magic," Leonard remarked. "We are a loyal species with respect to hierarchy and power."

Rafael leaned forward, likely to offer himself or one of his own as well, but I cut him off. "I've already chosen a second." I tilted my chin to my right. "Sasha Loren. She's already taken the blood oath and proven she can be trusted beyond measure."

"With respect, demoness," Eidelyon said, motioning to her. "Sasha Loren was close to Lucifer's hand and in his ear, but you saw how well that worked out. Surely a stronger candidate would be a better fit." He put a hand to his chest. "My own son has power over the air—"

"Your son is an arrogant jackass with difficulty controlling his temper," Anders interrupted. "And before you suggest it, your daughter's power may be great, but her mental state is not. One panic attack and she could wipe out a city block. This isn't about which faction is best to serve. Piper has a second that meets her needs and requirements." He nodded in my direction. It was still strange for me to see him like this, his own fae heritage on display. "One would think you'd know how to respect her choices. After all, a good second knows when to do what is asked of them and when to shut up."

With a pointed remark and a lifted eyebrow, he brought that argument to a close.

"Thank you, Anders." I tipped my head to him. "If I choose to pursue a third, I will consider all of you and your people—but this is not a job that you can interview for. It isn't a matter of power or name. If I need one, I will choose one and let you know my decision when I do. Either way, Sasha is *my* second and under *my* protection. Disrespect toward her is a disrespect to me."

Several of them nodded and others looked away unhappily, not thrilled about my choice or their inability to get a leg up on each other. I did find it interesting that two of the seven parties hadn't yet spoken.

"Thaddeus," I called out. "What concerns of yours haven't I addressed?"

He blinked. I wasn't sure he'd planned on being asked his thoughts on anything. "We ghouls have been ignored. Our kind aren't as strong as the shifters or as fearsome as the banshee." Siobhan smirked at the compliment. "We don't speak pretty words like the fae or have the speed and reflexes of a vampire. Nor the guile of a succubus. Or the sheer power of a witch. My people are often overlooked and undervalued." He wasn't wrong on any of those counts, but he interested me more than anyone that had spoken yet because he said it. "We can give you loyalty and respect. We can obey your laws. However, we need to not be treated as second-class citizens. Our people struggle to get jobs and most live in poverty. I need assurance that you will help us. *Help me help them.* With food. With shelter. With education and training and childcare. Out of every faction here, that is what we are in most dire need of."

Honesty. Vulnerability. He'd shown his hand but played it perfectly if his aim was to be heard by me.

"At the conclusion of this meeting, Nathalie Le Fay will be meeting with each of you to discuss goods and trade as well as job opportunities. She will meet with you first, so we can get things underway."

Thaddeus murmured his thanks, gratitude and sincerity reflecting in the depths of his black eyes. I turned to Dahlia Le Grange, the vampire leader, and the only one I'd met personally before this meeting.

"Any requests? Concerns? Questions you need answered?"

She smiled, her hand curling into a fist that she propped her chin on. Her incisors peeked out from her top lip.

"Much like you, I have a soft spot for the humans and want to see them treated better. No longer being turned against their will or used as unwilling meals to my kind and others." She glanced at Thaddeus, who sighed. While vampires needed blood, ghouls needed flesh.

"We only eat the newly deceased," he said defensively.

"And my clan only take from willing donors," she said. "But the requirements of our kind and yours need the humans for survival. The fae may oppose the slave trade, but they've had no issues with using humans for indentured servants. The witches have long been using them as test subjects to experiment with spells and potions—"

"Those were black witches," Isadora, our white witch leader interrupted in a nasally voice.

"When you were twelve years old, your mother led a

ritual where we sacrificed an old lady to use her life's energy to heal your sister," Nathalie said. Her voice cutting Isadora's argument to shreds. The white witch's face turned ashen. "It was a new moon, and the first ritual you were allowed to participate in. You needed the help of my family for the transference of life."

Nathalie lifted a brown eyebrow, daring her to dispute it.

She didn't.

"My point is," Dahlia continued with a leisure glance around the room, "that humans are the least protected group of individuals. Their desire to be heard has turned many of them against us and toward a terrorist organization known as the Illuminati. You've run into them before, have you not?" The question was directed at me.

"I have."

She dropped her hand from under her chin and leaned forward, elbows resting on the aged round table, fingers laced together.

"Then you know we need to give them a voice. Protection. If not for the fact that some of us actually need them, then because keeping them on the bottom has created an enemy—one that is learning to bend magic and science into something truly terrifying."

Her eyes were shrewd. Intelligent. Measuring. She and the others were waiting for my reply. I took a moment, considering my words. While not having an immediate response could make me look indecisive, having a poor one would show incompetence.

"As many of you have probably heard, I was once human. Part of the reason I decided to finally step up and claim this city as my own is for them." I had to tread carefully with this part. Too much sympathy would make me look like a bleeding heart. "The protection laws placed on humans will be tightened, and the punishments more severe than before. Any humans working for or with your factions will need to be documented, along with their pay and benefits. Sasha and I will also be taking a deeper look at each of your books and assessing where positions for humans could be created."

"With all due respect, demoness, not all of us have the means to take on charity—" Eidelyon started. I silenced him by narrowing my eyes.

"If you have no positions that could be filled by humans being paid a reasonable wage, then you really should not be at this table. I'm only interested in speaking to those that have the power to control change and steer it in the direction I see fit."

His face slackened, then went blank. He lowered his eyes, Adam's apple bobbing as he did so.

"Going forward, a minimum of ten percent of your expenses needs to be payroll and benefits paid to humans."

As predicted, that didn't go over so well.

"Ten percent?" Siobhan repeated.

Rafael leaned forward in his seat, placing his hands on the table. "I am all for change, but an adjustment in structure and spending this great and so sudden, when there's war brewing on our streets—"

"War is good for business," Nathalie said lightly. I lifted my eyebrows at her as if to say, *seriously?*

She shrugged. "It's sad, but true. Employing men and women to fight opens space for someone else to step into creating goods or delivering services. The key is paying them well enough they spend their money, so you make it back. That's how we'll keep the economy rolling— assuming a war does eventually break out."

"You assume we have the funds to begin with," Thaddeus said, shaking his head. "I can barely take care of my own. How do you expect me to add several thousand humans to the mix?" I tapped my nails on the wood ends of the armrest, the picture of ease and arrogance and power that these people needed to believe I could be.

"We will be supplementing your income to allow for the increase without it affecting your own. Subsidies will be given to those in need, with the understanding that you will go through Nathalie for trade outside these city walls. If something needs to be imported in, whether it be food, clothes, supplies for housing—you'll go to her. Because she and I will be personally funding the initial startup, she will also take a cut of the profits when you start seeing them." I didn't mention my own money came from Ronan, who stole it from the members of the Antares coven when he killed them all—save Nat. Black witches were among the wealthiest in the world, and I was now sitting on a significant fortune that was continuing to profit in high-profile investments, now that Sienna was managing them on our behalf.

"And the Illuminati?" Dahlia asked. "Taking care of the humans will buy loyalty among some. Complacency with even more. But you know better than any of us the way some injustices are too hard to swallow or turn your back on. What about the ones that don't choose to go forward, and instead take revenge?"

I flexed my fingers slowly, letting the joints crack one by one.

Would I punish them? Would I end them for taking supernatural lives? Would I truly be fair in all regards?

For once, the answer was easy.

Yes. Yes, I would.

"Any person—supernatural, human, or demon—that breaks my laws will be punished according to the crime. While I will leave you to choose how to punish your own, any humans you employ, their infractions will need to be reported to me. I will decide the consequences for their actions. For those that won't end up working with any of you and somehow manage to get by under the radar . . . I'll deal with them myself."

Dahlia nodded, the slightest of smirks tweaking her lips.

She didn't ask that question for herself; she asked it for the other factions. So they would know where I stood in the gray areas we were wading through. My reputation as a hunter made me a name, but it was a name supernaturals learned to fear. I needed more than that now. I needed their respect.

"Anything else?" I asked them, looking around the table.

From left to right, I scanned, noting the pride in Ronan's eyes. Rafael, and his succubi mate, Rajvi, seemed appeased by the answers I'd given. There was a reluctant acceptance on Eidelyon and Etheria's faces. Whereas respect radiated off the banshees, both Siobhan and Aoife. I suspected that had more to do with me being a female than anything, but if it meant this transition went smoothly, then I didn't care what the reason was. Comparatively, Thaddeus and Ephraim, his second, had tentative hope written all over them. They came here needing something from me, which made them one of the easier and less risky people I was taking on today. The unquestionable ease from Dahlia was strange, and even her second, Diego, seemed to think so. She didn't know me, but it seemed she knew enough that her mind was made up before we even sat down. The air of importance that Isadora still managed to hold was amusing, but it grated at old wounds. She acted as if being chosen to be here meant she was superior to others, and it riled my long-held prejudices like no other. Her second, Antonella, at least appeared to have some humility as she dipped her head, eyes cast down when I came to her.

Leonard and Kai, our werewolf representatives, were last.

Kai somehow managed to hide whatever he felt behind a cocky, overconfident smile. He winked flirtatiously. It was a poor move, regardless of who was here—but especially in front of Ronan.

The room shook. Dust drifted in the air as sediment and sand dropped onto the table.

I lifted a hand to stop my atman.

The room stilled.

"We'll start with you."

A flicker of unease ran through him. Beside me, Sasha smiled, a touch wicked. I pushed my chair back, the wooden legs dragging on the smooth stone floor. I walked around Sasha's chair and stood beside Kai's.

His eyes looked from my face to my wrist as I lifted it with purpose and pulled a blade from my blazer's inner pocket.

"I ask for unyielding loyalty. That you will be loyal to me above all else. That you will never lie or deceive me. That you will never plot against me or any that share my blood. That you will uphold my laws and decisions, even if you don't agree with them. That you will never undermine my power or make any attempts, direct or otherwise—to weaken my stance as your queen." I lifted the blade to my wrist and cut a line across the back of it, blood welling around the blade. "In return, I give you my blood for power and purpose, so that you may rule the shifters with fairness and might. I will not forsake you or your kind, should you need me. Nor will I knowingly abuse the trust you've placed in me."

Magic seeped from my skin, wrapping around us like a cloak. It formed a binding between Kai and I, one that if he accepted would never be broken.

"Kai Winters, alpha of the West Elsdon Pack, do you accept this bargain?"

Perspiration formed on his dark skin. His tongue swept across his bottom lip, nervous despite the cocky stare he was giving me.

"I do," he declared, voice booming through the secret meeting room. It echoed off the walls. I lifted my wrist over his head. He leaned back in his chair, lips parted.

I tipped it to the side, letting a single fat drop roll off my skin.

It fell in slow motion. The room seemed to pause and hold their breath when it hit his tongue. A second passed as we all waited to see what would happen.

His pupils dilated.

His hands slammed down on the wooden table, claws growing at his fingertips and fur sprouting in patches. He choked, the sound reverberating, a foreboding beginning to the first blood oath and transformation.

Kai pressed his palms into the table, trying to lift himself and push back against the chair at once. He faltered, falling face-first and smacking his head on the edge as he went down. Leonard moved to help him, and I lifted my hand.

He paused, confused as to why I'd silently told him not to move.

Fire erupted along Kai's skin. White and rageful from his dishonesty.

I knew the moment my blood touched his skin his words were deceitful.

Now he was paying the price.

"Watch and learn what happens when you attempt to lie under a blood oath," I said, having to speak louder to be heard over his screams. "While the transformation of my power entering you will be painful, and some of you may die from your bodies rejecting it—this is what happens when you take my blood but intend to overthrow me. Promises are binding with demons and blood—mine will burn you alive."

His screaming died out. His body turned to ash.

Still, his death filled the room—a stark reminder for each of them what awaited them if they lied.

With a look at the flames, they winked out instead of spreading further.

I turned to Leonard Daunte, who had been his second.

There was no small measure of terror behind his eyes.

I hoped it made him loyal. I hoped it kept him alive.

"Are you ready?"

He pressed his lips together and took a deep breath, then nodded.

"Very well. I ask for unyielding loyalty . . ." I began, reciting the same oath I'd just made. It was going to be a long night.

19

PIPER

"Ten out of fourteen," Bree commented, kicking her feet up over the armrest of the couch. "That's really not bad, considering Kai only died because he was a liar."

I fell back on the sofa across from her with an audible 'oomph.' My head craned back against the cushion to look at the ceiling. "Is it bad I was hoping Isadora would follow behind him?"

Nat choked on her tea. The twins snickered.

"Isadora is haughty. You'll butt heads, but she'll yield every time when push comes to shove," Bree said, running her hand along her jaw. "But I don't disagree. Antonella would have been better. She's more docile. Moldable. She can be shaped into a good leader. There won't be any shaping Isadora."

"She's a cunt," Nat added bluntly. "But a useful one, unfortunately. Be thankful witches have short lifespans compared to the other species. You'll only have to deal with her for a few decades at most."

She had a point. While it was difficult to grasp right now, Isadora was hardly the worst choice given how temporary she would be in the grand scheme of things. Antonella too, by that logic. If Antonella had children, though, they'd be born of my blood and easily guided to what I wanted them to be. Much as I didn't care for most witches, I'd be spending a good deal of time with that one going forward.

"It's unfortunate the banshee second wasn't strong enough," Sasha said, standing at the kitchen counter. "They'll be our greatest allies in hard times."

"I feel bad for Thaddeus," Sienna sighed. "Ephraim was like a son to him. He's going to struggle all the more grieving his loss while transitioning."

They were both right. Neither second in those factions made it, which sucked. It was the risk you ran with demon's blood. There was no guarantee it would take. If it didn't, death was inevitable. At least I'd made theirs quick when I realized which way it would go. I had no desire to make them suffer. Not when they meant no harm and simply weren't strong enough.

"We should consider ourselves lucky that at least one representative from every group survived," Bree pointed out.

Nat nodded in her direction. "She's right. It would have been a nightmare if neither did for some of these groups. I suspect the fae would have rebelled outright."

She wasn't wrong. Eidelyon didn't make it. His death wasn't quick because Etheria wasn't willing to let go. She cried, demanding that we wait to see if he could push through. After all, the vampire second, Diego, managed to. I was certain he was a goner when he pulled through to the other side. Eidelyon wasn't even close.

He died because his blood turned to poison.

He felt pain every second of it because of her selfishness.

I stood by and shook my head, wondering if it made me worse for honoring her wish instead of putting him out of his misery. She screamed so violently that the ceiling cracked. It was the first display of my power running through her veins, and yet another reason I questioned myself. If what I was doing was truly right.

I didn't know, and I suspected I never would—I didn't choose for right and wrong—I picked the choice I could live with.

"Etheria will be in a delicate state," Sasha said. "I will help her through it and see that she picks a second that's stable."

"Your help won't be welcome," Nat murmured into her cup. Her long sweater sleeves went over her fingers as she gripped it between both hands. "Fae don't care for shifters, and you might only be half, but that won't matter to her."

"She's also my second," I pointed out. "She may allow it just because it could suit her needs if she thinks she's getting more of an 'in' with us."

"Exactly," Sasha said with a flick of her cat tail. "Thanks for telling me that before we went in there," she added with a sour pucker of her full lips.

"Wasn't my original plan," I said. "I was going to talk to you afterwards, but when they started fighting over it, saying it then was the best way to shut them down."

She nodded. "I know it was, but next time, just a little bit of heads-up would be nice. Just saying."

"I'll see what I can do." I leaned forward to tug off the black blazer. It stuck in spots where sweat pooled, making the fabric cling to me.

"So," Sienna said in a lilting voice. Her golden eyes

reflected keen intelligence and curiosity. "Are we allowed to talk about the baby yet?"

I sighed. Should have ended social hour as soon as we came back to my place. I doubted I could feign exhaustion now and get out of it.

"Babies," I corrected. Sienna let out a delighted squeal and Sasha's eyebrows lifted.

"Twins?" she asked.

I nodded. "How long have you two known I was pregnant?"

"Since the vampire den," Sienna said. "I could feel it when I was next to you in the void, just before we went in." She came and plopped down on the opposite side of the couch from Bree, crossing her legs. "How far along?"

"Second trimester," I said. Her eyebrows drew together, then dropped to my stomach, trying to do the math. "Demon babies don't progress the same as other species. They mature based on how strong their magic is."

Sasha appeared skeptical at that explanation. "When exactly will you be due, then?"

I grimaced and Nat patted my knee. "About a month is the estimation Señora Rosara has given us. Because there's no true timeline for demon pregnancies, it's impossible to pin down an exact date."

"Right around my challenge," Bree said lightly—her voice hiding what her expression betrayed. "Lorcan knows," she added. "That's why I'm here."

"For the smartass comments?" Sasha asked, still not the biggest fan of my sister after the whole bombing incident that almost killed Sienna. I didn't blame her. I would be the same, or worse, if the roles were reversed.

"To guard Piper." She appraised Sasha like she would an ant beneath her boot. Isadora might be haughty, but she had nothing on Bree when my sister was in a fighting mood. "Lorcan can't get to her if I'm with her always—at least until our challenge."

Like the tried-and-true asshole Sasha was, she looked at me and said, "My condolences."

Nat twisted her hand and a slight wind slapped Sasha in the back of the head.

"Don't be a Piper. I've already got one to deal with," she said.

"Hey—" we both protested. She lifted her hands in mock surrender.

Bree let out a rasped chuckle. Her legs dropped to the floor, one after the other. She rolled her neck, letting out a series of pops. "Fun as this is, I need my beauty sleep—especially if we're paying a visit to the ghouls tomorrow. They're so droll." She groaned, getting to her feet, then disappeared without another word.

"Does she always have to be dramatic?" Sasha asked. "I mean the room is right down the damn hall. It's all of twenty feet." She motioned to the hallway that led to our room and the soon-to-be nursery. For now it was Bree's, recently furnished by Anders and Ronan.

"You get used to it," I said.

"Nope," Sasha said, putting her hands up then crossing her arms. "Can't say I will."

"I wouldn't be so sure," Nat said, blowing across the top of her tea. "Not so long ago you couldn't stand Piper either. People are complex. You've only seen one side of Bree. Something tells me there's more beneath the mask she shows us."

She wasn't wrong.

"One, Piper saved Sienna," Sasha said, holding up a manicured fingernail that was filed to a point. "Two, she wouldn't have needed to save her if not for Bree." She lifted a second one. "And three, Piper proved herself."

"After she killed the man you loved," Nat pointed out.

Sasha's expression went flat. "There's a difference between love for a partner and my twin—my family." She faded to shadow, then disappeared.

"And into the void she goes," I said quietly, shaking my head. "Did you really have to press her?"

"Growth is good for everyone," Nat replied. "Not just you."

I snorted. "Has it occurred to you that if you'd let it be, they'd figure it out on their own?"

"Of course," Nat said, looking between me and Sienna to address us. "Both of your sisters are too stubborn, though, and that would take more than my lifetime." I started to laugh, until her words really sunk in.

Nat was a witch. Unlike demons, vampires, shifters, or succubi—she wouldn't live forever. In the same way we only had a few decades of Isadora to deal with, I only had a few decades with Nat.

She must have noticed the shift in my mood and where my brain went, because she squeezed my knee again. "It's okay." She smiled, wise beyond her years in a way that few others were. "Bree is right. You have a busy day tomorrow. We all do, and I still need to check on our siren before bed." She got to her feet, and the long sweater dropped halfway to her knees over her sweats. The ears on her fuzzy bunny slippers flopped up and down as she made her way to the elevator.

"I should be going too," Sienna said with a sigh. "Sasha's going to be a nightmare tonight. We'll have to talk baby stuff soon, though. I have a bunch of parenting books you can borrow—"

"Okaaay, Sienna. Time to go," Nat said, holding the elevator door for her.

I met my best friend's gaze across the room. Sadness reflected back at me. She tried to smother it, but I saw it there in the depths of her light brown eyes.

It was the realization that while I might be immortal, she very much was not.

Sasha was right about one thing; romantic love was strong—but the kind you felt for someone ingrained in your very soul and sense of being—that was something else entirely. If we all survived the next three weeks, I'd spend the following decades searching for a way to buy her the one thing I couldn't change.

Time.

20

PIPER

"My," the Señora murmured as she bent over my belly. Her magical goop was slathered across it, making my skin turn translucent and allowing her to see the babies beneath it. Their bodies glowed like iridescent opals brought to life. Tiny hands and feet, grasping at each other in a mishmash of limbs. "They've grown so much in only a week."

I didn't comment, instead staring up at the ceiling. I focused on the cool table beneath me as a way of grounding myself. While needed, these appointments were a little too invasive for my comfort. I hadn't been to a doctor since I was a child. I wasn't touchy-feely in general, not even with my family growing up. My parents always thought I was emotionally damaged from watching my world change. I saw the president murdered on TV and then proceeded to live through the Magic Wars. They were probably right, of course. Logically I knew it was impossible to live through what I had without suffering trauma, but I'd lived it so long that it didn't register that way. Instead, it simply *was*. Any lovers I'd taken before Ronan were closer to fuck buddies. I never slept over. I never stayed.

To have someone touching me, using magic on me, looking *inside* me—it was a step that I didn't think I'd ever be truly all right with.

"How is Mist's training coming along?" I asked, pretending that she wasn't hovering over me and that my stomach wasn't lit up like a disco ball.

"It's coming."

I frowned, waiting for her to continue. She didn't. "Can you elaborate?"

"She's a gifted seer, able to connect with both short- and long-sight, but she's afraid of what she'll see. Her fear makes her power difficult to control. She's working on it." That was both more and less than what I'd hoped for.

"And you still think you can help her?" I asked, hedging carefully.

"I'm still working with her, aren't I?" It wasn't exactly an answer, though she seemed to think so. "I do not waste my time. If I didn't think I could do it, I would have said so. I can—but it will take time. Months. Years. Who knows? But it won't be instant."

I nodded slowly, counting the cracks in her ceiling. "And the death magic?" I asked. "You think you can help that too?"

"No," she said. "She needs to heal to be able to get a hold on that, and only time will do it."

I paused in my counting. Her answer was candid. Not what I wanted to hear necessarily, but it was the truth. In the same way I'd had to work through the worst of my issues to be able to harness my magic, so would Mist. I didn't want that for her, but I also did. I wanted her to heal, but I needed her to have control over her magic. Until she did, she was a danger to herself and others. But after everything she'd lived through . . . time would be the only thing that could help. Still, I worried there would never be enough.

It's not as if time erases the past. It just lessens the pain. Scars may fade, but it's not the scars themselves that are painful. It's the way wounds heal, if they ever do.

"How's Mist's baby?" Nat asked, leaning against the edge of the table. She shifted side to side before hopping up and pushing my feet behind her.

"Almost to term," Señora answered, squinting her eyes as she examined something. Her thin lips pressed together as she mulled over it. "She only has one, so it's simpler. Hers also isn't growing anywhere near this fast. If anything, the growth seems slower than the norm—although, who is to say what the 'norm' is anymore. If there's anything I've learned about supernaturals, it's that we're all different, and every pregnancy has its own issues."

"Do sirens often grow slower?" Bree asked, leaning against the opposite wall of shelves. Her white hair was bound in a simple crown braid around her head. She wore a ripped T-shirt and dark jeans. A pendant sat in the hollow of her throat, a clear vial with silver liquid that I strongly suspected to be mercury.

"I don't know," Señora answered. "I've never treated one before. They've been hunted for their gifts since I was a girl. Mist is the first one I've seen in decades."

Her answer put Mist's situation in a sort of difficult spot. I had no idea what we were going to do if the kid came out a siren. She didn't want it and it's not like I was up for raising three at once. Two was already going to be difficult, but we couldn't just abandon it.

"Can you tell what her baby is?"

"No more than I can tell your two," Señora said. "The girl is fine. Her baby is fine. At the moment, it's yours I'm concerned about. How's your appetite?" she asked, measuring my stomach. The stark outline of my upper ribs seemed to draw her attention.

"Never-ending," Bree answered on my behalf. I turned my cheek to purse my lips in her direction.

"She's eating like eight meals a day," Nat added from down by my feet.

"Good," the Señora remarked. "You're most of the way through the second trimester and haven't gained much." She frowned at me, like it was somehow my fault. "What little you have gained is all here."

"Not going to argue there," I muttered. In the last week alone, I'd gone up two sizes in jeans and five inches around the waist. I knew because I started measuring myself around the middle.

"Her stomach has definitely grown, even if the rest of her hasn't," Nat said. "I just assumed she wasn't showing as fast because she's tall. More room for them to stretch out."

"I'm concerned she's not getting enough nutrition," the Señora said as she wiped the goop from my stomach. "The babies are developing right, but her blood pressure is low, her skin looks pale. Gaunt. I'd guess she's lost weight if not for the twins' size and added water weight."

"She's likely in a caloric deficit," Bree said, "Demons have a difficult time during pregnancy. The stronger the child, the more they draw from the mother. She has two, and they're progressing faster than any other demon chil-dren in history. I'm surprised she isn't skin and bones yet."

"I've been offsetting the draw of power," Ronan said. He stood by the door, leaning against it. "Helping replenish her each night."

"You can do that?" Nathalie asked.

"Blood and sex," Bree replied. "Mated demons can share power by exchanging blood. Most don't very often outside circumstances like this, where the female is having too much taken by the fetus and needs more before they both starve. It speaks to his power that he's actually been able to offset this much. To my understanding, multiples often don't make it because the mother's body gives out before they're born."

My face heated. I thought it was normal for atmans to regularly share blood with their partners given that's how the bonding process worked. Apparently not. I'd have to ask her more about that when it was just the two of us, without an audience.

"You know a lot about demon children and pregnancy," Ronan said, not sounding completely thrilled with her. I had a feeling it had to do with her voicing the final piece of information. While he didn't lie to me about the dangers of pregnancy, he didn't bring them up unless asked either.

"I helped deliver the few that were born when I was at court," Bree replied.

"Is that the norm for women in the Otherworld?" Nat asked, genuinely curious.

"Not necessarily. I made a point to learn as much as I could about politics, magic, science, and health—the more I knew, the more useful I was."

The more likely Lorcan would be to take her as his atma.

She didn't say it, but she didn't need to. I read the truth between the lines.

"All in all, you look fine, and the babies are all right," the Señora said as she used a damp washcloth to wipe her hands. "But I'm concerned about your health the further along you are. I want you to weigh yourself morning and night. Limit exercise. We'll need to do check-ins every other day going forward."

"But—"

She stopped my protests with a look that could kill, or in my case, judge. If not for the fact it was the cold, hard truth, I wouldn't have given two shits what she thought I needed. But she wasn't wrong. While I might've felt huge, part of the reason I was taking measurements already was because my muscles ached. I felt like I'd run a marathon when I'd only walked a few miles. I was tired all the time but still struggled to sleep.

Muscle atrophy. Insomnia. Fatigue.

I knew it was the pregnancy but didn't realize how bad it was—or would be as I continued.

"I understand this is not your favorite place to be," she said neutrally. "But you're doing the growth of a week in a single day." She held up one finger with two rings on it. "One day. That's all. Your body isn't handling it well. If it gets much worse, you will have a hard time giving birth."

I sighed, then searched inside myself for the strength to power through.

"All right. I'll take it easy and come back in two days."

She nodded once, knowing she'd sufficiently gotten her point across.

"What exactly do you perceive as being the problem as this continues? Since there's no way it won't. If the issue is her being pregnant, then the solution is to not be pregnant, but that's not an option." Nat slid off the table, crossing her arms over her chest. Her brow pinched in concern.

"She'll be too exhausted to give birth," Bree said. "Too weak. The babies will continue to drain her energy until there's nothing left."

Bree's eyes cut across the room to Ronan. I sat up on the

table, my legs dangling over the edge as I pulled my shirt down.

"Demons die when their magic is drained. Their magic is their soul. It's why the Harvester is the only one that can kill other demons . . . usually." Ronan's voice was low and gruff, his expression closed off. "There are exceptions, like when the witches killed Lucifer by taking too much of his magic to try to create a direct channel to the Otherworld—or pregnancy. Human children need food to grow and thrive, but demons need more than that. They need magic."

"If they're born too early, they'll die. But if they're born too late . . . I will."

The thought was sobering to say the least. But it wasn't debilitating. As it was, I felt like I was living on borrowed time. With only two weeks left till Bree's challenge, the future was uncertain as ever. Even before this, I'd lived every day not knowing if I'd see the next. This was no different.

I'd either make it or I wouldn't, but I'd fight tooth and nail to the very end either way.

21

PIPER

"You look unwell," Isadora said diplomatically. Her keen eyes dropped to my stomach before she feigned a smile.

"Tired," I answered somewhat gruffly. My throat was still dry and my voice groggy from sleep. It was the truth, albeit a simplified version. I'd grown another five inches around the middle in three days. In no time at all, my body went from strong and lean to heavily pregnant. Exaggerated more so because it was two and not one.

"I suspected you were expecting, but it looks like congratulations are in order." She smiled, clasping her pale hands together. The thin gossamer dress twisted around her legs as she walked, shifting in the sunlight. "May I?" she asked, descending the steps from her front door with ease as she reached for my belly.

I moved my hand to block hers. "No."

She blinked, lips parted. "I-I'm sorry," she stumbled over the hurried apology. "I meant no harm—"

"I know." She'd be dead if she did. "I don't like to be touched, pregnant or not. Rubbing my stomach won't bring you luck. I'm not the Buddha. Wrong kind of demon." He had spirit magic. Only after the Magic Wars did that become known—on top of the cult he started in the Himalayan mountains. They'd grown in numbers over the last ten years, or so the rumors were. It was hard to tell what was true or not with news the further it was from the city. "And frankly—it's weird."

Nat turned her cheek to hide her laugh, but the subtle shaking of her shoulders completely gave her away. On my other side, Bree smirked.

"I see . . ." Isadora stammered, trying to find a polite response.

From the doorway, her daughter Antonella said, "If we can be of any assistance to you during your pregnancy, please let us know. I understand that witches don't have the best reputation right now . . ." Antonella was in a modest periwinkle dress, her auburn hair flowing behind her as a gentle breeze swept through the quiet street of McMansions. The white porch with dark wood double doors painted an antiquated picture. "But I'd be honored to help with your labor, if you need it. I'm a good healer that ascribes to the old days of *do no harm*. I could help make the process easier."

Isadora turned to reprimand her. Over the last week, word had spread through the grapevine that I was pregnant, and the white witch had surely planned this introduction to get on my good side. It seemed Antonella had gone off script after seeing my reaction to her mother.

Yet another reason for why I was here. To interact with the daughter.

"Ella, our lady just said—"

"Thank you," I replied, answering for myself. "I'll consider it. Because of the nature of my pregnancy, it may not be safe to have you there, blood oath or not. I'll speak with my atman about it and get back with you."

I wasn't necessarily the most comfortable with her, but I wasn't with Señora Rosara either. At least this witch had taken the blood oath and couldn't harm me or my children. She'd die if she ever tried to.

Antonella smiled and dipped her head. "Of course."

Isadora stilled, debating how to deal with me. I opted to take the lead and walked past her, up the steps to the porch. Twenty-foot-tall pillars held up the extended roof that covered it, wrapping all the way around the house. It was hard to call it that. I'd grown up in a two-bedroom apartment in the city. I still lived in one. But up here, in witch country, the houses were bigger, grander. Their size bordered on that of a mansion. Each one had a decent plot of land and a long driveway with large sweeping trees on either side that gave it the appearance of a tunnel from the main road up to the house. Instead of driving, I brought us through the light realm. Upon arrival, I'd taken a walk around the property before approaching the door. I wanted a feel for what I was getting into with the white witches. Unlike their counterparts, they often tried to hide behind a facade of goodness that wasn't realistic. It was the reason why I'd asked Nat to come, especially when Sasha was busy with Etheria. They may not be able to lie to me, but that wouldn't stop Isadora from bullshitting her way around my inspection if I wasn't careful.

Bree let out a low whistle when we stepped through the front door.

Admiral-blue stone spanned like a great expanse of sea. Streaks of lighter blue and cracks of silver ran through it. I couldn't tell one slab from the next. There were no edges to mark where the inlays had been placed. Somehow they'd made it look natural, beautiful, if immoderate.

A staircase wrapped around from the right side of the room to the left, creating an archway with baroque crown molding where they met in the middle. Large pillars that mirrored the exterior columns acted as structural components on either side of the stairs. A glass and opal chandelier finished it off, refracting light into rainbows across every shadowed corner of the entryway.

"Pietersite," Nat remarked, with a sweeping glance across the floor. "This wasn't here last time."

"We've remodeled."

"Clearly." She glanced skyward at the chandelier. A rainbow prism of color danced across her face. "Where to?"

"We'll be in the tearoom," Antonella answered, waving a hand toward the archway. The tearoom was right on the other side and aptly fit its name. Ostentatious furniture lined in gold with patterned cushions sat in a stiff arrangement on a sheepskin rug.

I took a seat on the small loveseat, letting out a small 'oof'. Nat sat beside me, and Bree remained standing.

"Feel free to sit," Isadora said as she entered the room behind us.

"I'm good where I am," Bree replied with a tense smile. She paced behind me, vigilant as she took in every nook and cranny in sight. I didn't bother telling her to play nice with the witches. She wouldn't have listened to me, anyway.

"All right." Isadora looked down at the tea set she'd arranged. She made a motion with her hand and murmured a command in Hebrew.

The kettle began whistling as it heated in no time. She lifted the top off of a dainty porcelain box. Inside tiny paper bags filled with tea perfumed the air.

"What kind of tea do you take?" she asked lightly. "Cardamom? Green? Oolong? Chai?"

"Jasmine, if you have it," Nat said, crossing one leg over the other. Isadora's lips thinned, and I had a feeling she wasn't asking Nat. She didn't say anything as she silently reached for a pouch that was near black and placed it in the cup, filling it with hot water.

"For you?" She lifted her head toward me while silently handing the cup over to Nat.

"I'm not familiar with them beyond Jasmine. That's what Nathalie always makes."

"You should try peppermint," Antonella said. "It helps with energy but doesn't have caffeine."

Nat tipped her head after inhaling the scent of hers and letting out a happy groan. "Peppermint is a good choice. It's often given to witches when they're pregnant."

"I'll try it."

"And for you?" Isadora asked Bree while making mine. My sister lifted her eyes to the ceiling, examining it while she said, "I'm good. You won't have what I like."

"Are you sure? We have many—"

"The plant it comes from doesn't grow on Earth."

That silenced the witch coven leader. Internally, I sighed. While she had significantly warmed up with me and even Nat, she was still very guarded with everyone else. Witches and vampires in particular. I suspected it had to do with our parents. Mom had essentially been a blood slave, and then they were murdered by witches. She often pretended things that happened on Earth before didn't affect her, but I knew they did. Her defense against everyone was a haughty air of superiority and indifference. She cut them down with a cruel word or look, just as she'd done to me when she first came through the portal.

"We need to discuss your budget," Nat said after taking a long sip of her tea and humming in happiness. "I've reviewed your books and found a number of problematic things."

Isadora stiffened in her seat. "Such as?"

"Write-offs, for one. Half of your tax credits aren't categorized properly. You purchased a ski resort last fall and deemed it a business expense because your coven goes on 'retreats' there."

Antonella grimaced, avoiding our gaze by looking at her hands. A faint blush crept across her cheeks in embarrassment. Her mother, on the other hand, lifted her eyebrows and pinched her lips.

Here we go.

"It allows them to decompress. We deal in many difficult matters, from birth to healing life-ending wounds—and it doesn't always work. The coven needs that as a mental health expense."

I couldn't stop myself from rolling my eyes. "I'm not counting it. You need to go through and reclassify things more reasonably. You want mental health expenses? Find appropriate outlets. Get a hobby. Go buy some bath bombs. Hell, I'd even let a reasonably priced bathtub slide—"

"What do you consider reasonable?" she interjected. "I understand you grew up less fortunate, but it is *unreasonable* to expect everyone to live that way."

I blinked. My lips parted.

Red tinged my vision.

I bit the inside of my cheek, taking deep breaths. Nat saw my expression and a worried frown crossed her face.

"That was an ignorant statement. You don't know the poverty that over seventy percent of the population lives in," Nat began.

"And you do?" she shot back. "You're the wealthiest person in this city. On this side of the country. You bring in more money than our entire coven combined by several multipliers—"

"And I employ several hundreds of thousands of people," she snapped and cut her off. "I live in a two-bedroom apartment and grow my own food. I don't have a staff of hundreds just to maintain my property, unlike your coven. I don't have an entire floor of pietersite, for fuck's sake." Gold flashed around her, like glitter. Her voice echoed, carrying her anger with it. "I know the going rate for that stone. You would have spent, at minimum, five million to have that installed. Do you know how many families that would take care of? How many children could go to school? How many meals that would buy?"

Isadora turned white as a sheet, whereas Antonella's rouge cheeks only darkened.

"I do. I donate millions of dollars a year to food banks and shelters and resource centers. I hire human staff and provide them with in-home healthcare—through doctors *I* pay for. I get blood donors for my vampires and fresh flesh for the ghouls. Witches get free schooling for their children if they can't afford it and are not part of a coven. I have done more in the last decade to help this city than your coven has done in the several hundred years of its existence. *Do not* talk to me like I don't understand the plights of the poor. I'm *very* well acquainted, and the only reason the percentage of those suffering isn't higher is because of the work that I do."

It was a rare thing to anger Nathalie Le Fay. Not only did she have one of the mildest temperaments of anyone I'd known, but there also wasn't much that truly riled her. She took most things and rolled with them, whether it be sadistic vampire dens, kidnapping, riots . . . but everyone had a line, and Isadora had just crossed it.

"I understand that this blood oath is new to you," I said quietly, violence breathing into every word. "But you will never, *ever* speak to me that way again."

At my command, the bond between us flared, tightening around her neck like a noose. If she continued on this path, she'd hang herself before her several decades were up.

"I lived in poverty for a very long time because that is all the humans of this city are afforded. That I could even keep an apartment with running water and working power was not only incredibly difficult, but fortunate—if you don't count the fact I was a bounty hunter to make those ends meet. Many people weren't able to do it then, and they certainly aren't able to do that now. That you are so removed that you can't see that . . ." I shook my head, trying to calm the raging storm in my mind. "You'll fix your books and reassign the business expenses. You'll also be creating a women's shelter and healthcare provider that is *heavily* discounted for anyone that falls below the poverty line. To get an understanding of what is needed and how to do it, you will personally be volunteering for the next month at *All Vaginas Are Equal* and report to Sienna Loren every day."

I'd planned on telling them they needed to find a cause to help with, but after her previous statements, I changed course. Isadora needed to be taught a lesson in humility.

"Every day?" she repeated, hands fisting in her iridescent dress, her thin lips pressed together in a hard line.

"Consider it a warning. Should you not learn to have empathy for the struggle of others, you'll be staying in one for six months—and volunteering there while you do."

Bree snickered to herself, loud enough we all heard it.

I might have cut her a look if it wouldn't have taken away from the point I was trying to make.

"Very well," Isadora answered, dipping her head in subservience.

"Antonella will be assisting Sienna during that time so that someone in this coven understands what *reasonable* expenses means. We'll reconvene in a month about your revised taxes and volunteer experience. Provided everything is in order, I'll approve the request to start construction on a private hospital."

Isadora had assumed we were here to discuss their plan to build a for-profit healthcare network. While it was something that the population as a whole desperately needed, it wasn't something many of them would be able to afford without going into indentured servitude. While it hadn't been called that in their proposal outline, that's essentially what it was—and it wouldn't fly with me. We would revisit that once the hospital was actually built, and we'd determine a pay scale that would profit them and those they employed. I wouldn't support a backhanded way to retain slaves.

I supposed I should've been happy Etheria was too busy grieving to submit bullshit projects like Isadora. She'd submitted three times more than any other faction, most of them I'd outright rejected.

"Thank you," Antonella said, slowly lifting her head. "I won't disappoint you." Her eyes were dark brown, like the bark of a cedar tree. Amber freckles splashed across the bridge of her nose. While a mere eighteen years old, she seemed even younger compared to the other women in the room. For all the white witch leader's faults, she'd sheltered her daughter from the harsher aspects of life a great deal. I didn't envy her ignorance, but I understood her mother's reasoning. The world was a difficult place, and innocent souls were few and far between.

"I believe that." I sighed, struggling to be upset with a girl that was eight years my junior and carried a certain purity I hadn't encountered in a long time. The last of the anger that was riding me drained away as I looked at her.

Nat, however, narrowed her gaze at the younger witch.

"I know what you are." Her eyes glowed gold for a moment, letting her chaos shine. "What I can't tell is if you're doing it on purpose or struggling to control your power."

Antonella's lips parted, face draining of all color.

Before she could respond, or react, or do anything at all —a knock came at the door.

Isadora sighed. "Ella, get that."

She rose to feet unsteadily. Her steps were quiet as she went to the door.

A knock sounded again.

She grasped the brass handle just as the double doors blew open. She stumbled and Nat's jaw slackened.

Her doppelgänger stepped forward, wicked black heels clicking on the stone floor. Her light brown hair swayed at her waist as she moved. I recognized the determined expression on the intruder's face. I'd seen it a hundred times on my best friend.

"I don't know who that is, but it's not Lorcan," Bree said with absolute certainty, even though she'd stepped closer to me and took on a protective stance.

That meant it was really . . .

"Katherine."

Nat's twin.

22

NATHALIE

SHE IGNORED ME.

A passing glance as she entered the hall was it. No welcome. No acknowledgement. She entered with a single-minded purpose, and I wasn't it.

It stung. While I didn't often wish for apathy like Piper and Sasha could manage, I did now. After the ritual, when Lucifer died . . . it was chaos. I didn't know where she went, whether she'd lived or died. It was only in finding her magic at the vampire den that I even knew she was alive.

I could live with her never searching me out.

But for her to come to Piper . . .

I swallowed, squaring my shoulders as I got to my feet. Across the room, an amber gaze watched me, tracking my every movement, the slightest inhale of breath and every shaky exhale I managed.

My devil. My demon. His ghost followed me always as my ever-observant shadow. Somehow bound to me, and yet not alive or existing on this plane of existence.

"Why are you here?" To my own shock and approval, my voice came out flat and unwavering. I was a good liar when I wanted to be, but it was harder with Katherine. We had a bond that could never be shaken.

"To speak with the demoness in charge."

Katherine stopped under the archway, her arms crossed over her chest, and she lifted an eyebrow. "They call you the Queen of New Chicago."

"I'm not hearing a question," Piper replied. I hid the smirk that threatened to show. Katherine and I may have a bond like no other, but so did Piper and I. She always had my back, even against my shitty family.

Especially against my shitty family.

"You formed a council, but no black witches were invited."

"Again. Not hearing the question."

Beside her, Bree snickered. While she butted heads with almost everyone, Piper included, she did delight in her sister's smartass comments when they were aimed at someone else.

They had that in common.

"I've come to offer myself as the black witch representative," Katherine replied through gritted teeth. She wasn't familiar with people that didn't bend to her whims. Growing up privileged as she was . . . the new world order must have been something of a shock. I had to give it to her, though. She had a pair of brass ones for coming in here and all but demanding a blood oath.

"I'm not looking for any more representatives," Piper said. "As you can see, both witches survived the oath, and therefore, there isn't a spot open. Check back in a couple of decades."

Bree choked on a laugh, and despite my own warring feelings, I cast a sideways smile at my best friend. Katherine's features darkened. The veins around her eyes turned a shade bluer. Her full lips tightened as she sucked in a taut breath, smudging her tan lipstick on her front tooth.

"Black witches are cut from a different cloth. The white coven leader will tell you that." She nodded in Isadora's direction, and Piper turned to her.

"Is that so?"

Isadora gaped for a moment before recovering, then nodded. "Yes, we are. Even more so now that black witches have lost their power." It was an underhanded jab; one that Katherine wouldn't take well.

My sister wasn't known for controlling her temper. That was my job.

She was the fire. The glory of our house.

I was the air that fed her. The foundation that kept her standing.

Dark blue magic rose at my twin's fingertips. Shadows swirled in her eyes. Dark magic and ire. "Break," she hissed.

To my own shock, those sapphire threads struck at the windows behind her. They shattered, and the wind swept them up, letting them drift around her in a wicked wall of glittering shards and edges.

"How did you . . ." Antonella whispered from behind her. Fear lit her up, sending her empathetic gift spiraling. The very gift she'd used on Piper only moments ago.

Fear leaked from her in black, billowing clouds. It reached for Katherine.

"Crack," my sister commanded.

The floor beneath her groaned before snapping with a clap of thunder that shook the house. From where Katherine stood, spiderweb splits branched out from the spot like a star crack.

"Do I look powerless to you, Isa?" she demanded.

The white witch stared with abject horror, and all the

while Antonella's empath ability slowly settled over Katherine, making her shake as fear that didn't belong to her crept in her veins. Fear wouldn't diffuse the bomb that was my twin. When Katherine got scared, she got angry.

This situation was going from bad to worse. One poor move, and someone would pay the price.

I reached out, gold sparks lighting at my fingers. They touched Katherine's magic and the gold spread, taking over. It turned from blue to shimmering aurous metal midair.

I seized her magic and then Antonella's.

Both women stopped in their tracks and turned to me.

"You've found new magic," I said to my sister. "I've never heard a witch cast in English."

"I've *made* new magic," Katherine replied with a bite. She didn't appreciate me taking over. "There's power in words. In tradition. But that power came from somewhere before it was tradition." She motioned to the glass that dropped to the ground at my command. "Lucifer may have died and cast my kind into the darkness with him—but we're not all dead. We've formed a new coven, and we seek to serve this city's new mistress."

Piper regarded her coldly. "I don't care for black witches."

"But you like power," Katherine said, not deterred by Piper's prejudice. "We'll either stand with you or find someone else to serve that will give us what we want. I'm giving you the choice."

The breath hissed between Bree's lips as she drew them back, fangs elongating. "You dare threaten a demon?"

"I could kill you all and be done with it," Piper pointed out. She placed a hand on Bree's shoulder, silently telling her to calm down. "I'm inclined to go that route when you make demands of me."

"You won't," Katherine said, completely assured. She flicked her eyes toward me and smiled coldly. "Because say what you will, but you'd never kill Nathalie's psychic bondmate."

I shuddered.

Check mate.

We were twins, and if that weren't enough to bind us together, the universe made us each other's psychic bonded partners. Just like werewolves had a mate, vampires had a bride, demons had an atma or atman . . . we witches had psychic partners. It wasn't a romantic bond, though some of them ended up that way. It was a soul bond. An anchor in the vast universe of power that stood between us and madness.

Katherine and I never completed our bond. It would have stopped her magic from growing. Stunted her, our parents said. We were forbidden to do it. Now, something told me she wouldn't want to. Not with whatever new magic she'd discovered to power her spells.

Piper looked at me, expression torn. I hadn't told her that bit about us.

"Well, well, little witch," Lucifer crooned from his shadowed corner. "So many secrets." I bit my bottom lip in an effort to not look at him. Now was not the time for his commentary.

"I'll consider it," Piper said eventually. "You'll have my answer in a week."

"Tomorrow."

"A week," Piper repeated. Her eyes shifted from violet to maroon. "I may not kill you, but that doesn't mean your coven is safe. Remember that, since you're so keen to serve me."

Katherine narrowed her eyes but didn't argue it.

"Very well."

My sister, my twin, my psychic mate . . . she turned on her heel without a second glance in my direction and walked right through the same double doors. They slammed closed behind her. Antonella collapsed, her body sagging to the floor. Isadora was raging, curses flying out of her mouth the moment Katherine walked away.

Piper turned to deal with her while Bree continued to survey the cracks in the floor, as if concerned there was residual magic still in them that might strike.

Not an ounce of Katherine's sapphire-colored power remained. I walked to the door and rested my hand on the knob. Was she still here? Did she drive?

Questions ran through my mind, one after another.

I gripped the brass tightly, knuckles white, and gave in to the urge.

My face fell, and I immediately regretted that decision.

She was gone. Not a trace of her as far as the eye could see.

But that wasn't what struck me. Instead of the lush green lawn and vibrant trees that had been there, dead grass and shriveled branches took their place. Every leaf had fallen. Every tree trunk split. Not a single bud of fresh growth remained in the half mile that spanned between the mansion and its property line. It was as if all life had been stripped from the earth.

I had no doubt in my mind Katherine was the cause, but the question was, why?

Why kill the grass and trees? It seemed too petty for her.

Too mild a way to unleash her anger. The cracked floor and broken windows? That rang true. But this?

I gnawed on my bottom lip, mulling over the reasons.

A phantom touch ghosted my lower back. I stiffened.

"Tell me, little witch, what would you give to know your sister's secrets?"

23

PIPER

WHERE ARE YOU?

Ronan's mind brushed against mine.

Dahlia's bar, I answered. The air crackled with power a moment later. A familiar ripple of darkness swept over me. I leaned into it as Ronan appeared out of the void. A burning hand slid across my lower back, scorching me with delicious heat.

"I'd tell you to get a room, but I'll be subjected to hearing it either way," Bree muttered. The red and blue lights reflected off her white hair, staining it to match.

"How long do you have left?" Ronan asked me, ignoring my sister's comment.

"We're still working our way through this proposal." I nodded to the documents spread out across the low table. Dahlia sat reclined back in one chair, Diego in the other, Sasha and Sienna took the couch, and both Bree and I had opted to stand.

While standing for long periods wasn't great, getting in and out of a chair so low to the ground sucked even more at the moment.

"We can wrap this up," Sasha said, highlighting a section in red, meaning it wouldn't work and needed to be cut or adjusted. "I'll give you the abbreviated version tomorrow. Go. Enjoy yourself for once." She flicked her pen toward the door in a shooing motion.

"Are you sure—"

"You work too much," Sienna said. "And the stress isn't good for the babies."

I pressed my lips together in a firm line and pointedly looked at the two vampires and back at her. They weren't supposed to know. While it was obvious I was pregnant, that I was carrying twins was not.

"Don't mind us," Dahlia said, smirking. "We can hear their heartbeats. I already knew."

Of course they did.

Because vampires.

I sighed. "If you say so—"

Ronan tugged me tighter, and the void closed in around us before I could finish speaking.

"I was still talking."

"The conversation was over," Ronan replied. We were only in the darkness for a second before a chilled breeze blew my braid away from my face. I blinked, taking in the wide-open field and night sky. After being surrounded in true blackness, the stars were dazzlingly bright—as was the aurora borealis.

"What's this?"

A large blanket was spread out at our feet with a picnic basket sitting on the corner. My brows drew together.

"Dinner," he answered. "And a date."

He stepped around me and settled down on the blanket to dig through the picnic basket for a thermos. The lid cracked as he unscrewed it and poured hot chocolate into two mugs. He took in my T-shirt and jeans, then nodded. "Right, forgot about those." Without a word or movement, a puffy jacket enclosed my upper half. A knit hat covered my head, and gloves warmed my fingers.

"What?" Ronan asked when I didn't immediately sit down.

"You. This." I motioned to it, swallowing past a lump in my throat. "Why?" This gesture was very . . . un-Ronan. He didn't do love. He wasn't the hearts and flowers type. I didn't mind. Those things didn't matter to me. Labels. Gifts. He gave me what I truly needed, and we didn't question it.

But this, it bordered on too much.

I could only think of one reason why he'd go out of his way to set it up.

"It occurred to me that we've never been on a date," he said, silver eyes swirling with some unnamable emotion I couldn't place.

"Navy Pier. We had dinner on—"

"Doesn't count. You wanted to kill me, and the boat blew up."

"There was the weekend we did this," I said, pointing to my distended belly. I shifted from side to side, eyeing the spread. "Or the time we fucked in a church and then you cooked me dinner?"

Ronan lowered his head and let out a rumbling chuckle. From not far off, the sound of my sister choking on something alerted me that we were not alone. I scanned the field, but there was no one else there. Just us and the endless sky.

"Bree's giving us this moment," he said. "I'm confused why you're not wanting to take it." He set the mugs aside.

"Did I do something wrong here? Both she and Nat insisted you'd like this . . ." I groaned.

Taking care not to step on the blanket, I dropped down onto one knee and twisted around to flop on my butt. I was beyond the ability to be graceful in my current state. "It's not that. I love it. Really." I leaned over him to grab one of the mugs. It smelled of peppermint and sugar. I drained it in one go. The heat filled my chest and defrosted the cold creeping in.

"Then why the need to justify the time I fucked you for three days straight as a date?" His directness had a different sort of heat running through me. We'd held off from sex anywhere except in the void since Bree had moved in. It was a new kind of hell when my body craved him anytime we were alone. But we never were for more than a few minutes anymore, not really. And I wouldn't subject Bree to that when she was here to protect me from her own atman.

Stolen moments in the darkness were all we had.

"Are you doing this because you think it will be the last time?" I asked him quietly, setting the empty mug aside. "Are you that convinced she'll lose? That this is the end?"

I understood it. It was the very reason I refused to hide. With the possibility of only weeks left, I wanted to *live* as much as possible.

But for some reason, this felt different. It felt . . . like a goodbye.

Ronan's silence didn't help.

"I don't know," he answered honestly, leaning back on his elbows. Shadows lined his eyes, but they had nothing to do with the void or his power. His raven hair was longer than he usually wore it. Unruly and wild. "I'm not sure if this is the last time or not. I can't predict the future, and even if I could—it's ever changing. I just know that if this is the end, if the next week is all I have left with you . . . I wanted to give you this."

I didn't describe things as 'touching.' I didn't cry from happiness. I didn't believe in that fluttery heart bullshit.

But my eyes watered.

I sniffed, wiping it away.

"Stupid pregnancy feelings and horm—"

Ronan ran his finger down my cheek. "It's okay."

"No," I breathed, exhaling that heavy feeling that made my throat constrict. "It's not. It's crap that this may be the last week we get. That you waited thousands of years for what? Six months?" I shook my head. "It's not right. None of this is. Bree shouldn't have been bonded to that sack of shit or trapped for a decade. I shouldn't have been a bounty hunter. I should have embraced my magic sooner. Nat shouldn't be stuck as mortal. Mist shouldn't have been raped and forced into having a kid. New Chicago shouldn't be this fucked." I put my head in my hands.

"You can't change the past," Ronan reminded me.

"I know that," I said. "I do. I just can't help but feeling cheated out of everything we should have had. Out of what could be . . ."

"She may win," he said lightly, but there was a strain behind it. He didn't believe it any more than I did. We might have hope, but that's because it was the only thing we could have.

"He's a chaos demon. The Source chose him."

My sister may be powerful and crafty, but she wasn't the Harvester.

She may have thought he wouldn't kill her, but I knew from experience that what he planned was so much worse.

"If she wasn't your sister, I would have drained her myself already," Ronan confessed. I turned slowly, lips parted. "I won't. Even if everything in me says that's the better way. I could make it painless, and then their challenge would never come to fruition. Lorcan would never be powerful enough to win."

"He would still come for me."

"I know," Ronan sighed. "I know."

The lights above us shifted from blue to green, shimmering across the sky. If magic had a form, that's how I imagined it would be. Perhaps it was magic itself; a different kind we'd never seen before. A kind we couldn't touch. Contaminate. Ruin.

"All we can do is trust that she knows what she's doing," I breathed. "For better or worse, if this is all we have . . ." I shuddered, not wanting to finish the sentence. "I'm happy I got to have it with you. That we got these few months."

"You were worth it," he said. He put a finger under my chin, lifting my face away from my palm. "All the pain. The death. The destruction. The endless years of existing. You are worth every second."

He might not have said the word love, but he showed me so much more. His actions were louder than any words, and I was drowning. In him. In the moment. In this slice of time that I would have liked to stay in forever.

But time didn't stop for anyone, not even a chaos demon.

I leaned over and kissed him hard. Our lips met in a clash of passion. I grabbed his hair, pulling him to me, just as he pulled me to him. I swung one leg over his, straddling his waist. Ronan let out a pained sound, his hands gripping my thighs with crushing strength as he attempted to control himself.

"You have no idea how hard it's been for me to keep my

hands to myself," he grunted. His length pressed between my legs, and I shifted, dragging myself across him.

"I want you," I whispered.

"I need you," he answered. Our foreheads touched. "But unless you've changed your mind about doing this in front of your sister . . ." He left it there, not needing to explain more.

I grumbled under my breath. "We'll need to stop in the void tonight."

Ronan let out a deep laugh. I loved the sound of it. Genuine. Not fake or forced. How many more times would I hear it before Bree's challenge? Was this the last?

"Don't focus on that right now," he said quietly.

I must have been thinking loudly. Literally.

"It's hard not to."

"Then I'll give you something else to think about." My mind automatically went to the position we were in. Ronan shook his head in amusement. "Turn around."

With his help, I twisted and resettled between his legs, my back to his chest.

"I brought you here because this is what the Other-world looks like every night. Lights dance in the sky, changing to colors that you can't even imagine. They come from the Source."

"Do these?"

"No," Ronan said, his lips speaking softly into my ear. "They're something else. Some magic I've never seen before."

"They feel . . . pure." I imagined what it would be like to wade through them. Part of me shuddered because it was the opposite description of myself.

"They are," he said. "Bree told me of them. This place."

"She's been here?"

He nodded. "She was right that I've never seen anything like it. On the surface, it's so similar to my world, but utterly different. These lights are something impossible. They shouldn't exist. That gives me hope." I turned, lowering my eyes from the sky to my atman. "If there are still things in this universe that I've never seen before, perhaps it's not so impossible for Bree to find a way. This world has secrets. Maybe whatever you both are, is one of them."

I wanted him to be right. I would have given anything.

But as much as I might have hoped, I still feared.

Lorcan had nothing left to lose.

I had everything.

24

PIPER

I rested my elbows against the cool stone. A fraction of New Chicago lay before me. Graffiti buildings and blood-stained concrete. Wicked winds that screamed down the alleys, twisting and twining in clothes that hung on lines, making metal fans clink as they spun around at its behest. People quietly shuffled, darting in and out of the streets, going about their business. The city was quiet. Peaceful.

"Penny for your thoughts?" Bree said, sauntering over to my side. She leaned against the waist-height ledge that wrapped around the top of our building.

"I'm enjoying the sunset."

She hummed in response. "You wear the same expression when you're contemplating doing something you shouldn't."

"Says the woman that thrives on doing things she shouldn't."

Bree shrugged. "I lived in cages long enough that I enjoy true freedom."

My brows drew together. "True freedom?"

"When we were kids, supes ruled. We existed inside cages of their making."

I nodded along. "The Otherworld?"

"Was one of my own making," she said quietly. "I had power, but I was always under Lorcan's thumb. His bitch at his beck and call."

"You shouldn't call yourself that."

"It's true," she said, not bitter but . . . sad. "I didn't love him. I've never loved him. But I felt something for him—attachment, perhaps? He's my atman. No matter what I did, I knew he'd never truly harm me. He killed several demons for overstepping their boundaries. If a male touched me, even if it was the most innocent graze—he cut off their hands."

I lifted my eyebrows. "That's intense. And unhealthy."

Great. Now I sounded like Nathalie. The thing was, she wasn't wrong.

Bree smiled faintly, not looking at me. "I liked it. Makes me a shitty person, I know. But I liked that I was that important to him. That I could do literally anything, and he'd strike anyone down that tried to hurt me. If I stepped out of line at court, he would punish me, though if anyone else dared to say I should be sent away, or hurt, or even killed—well, it didn't end well for them. He claimed he didn't recognize the bond, but he still acted like a male that did. I could live with that. I was unloved and mostly unacknowledged, but I was still important to someone. I mattered."

"You still matter." I reached out, grabbing her hand in a firm grip. "You will always matter to me."

She nodded. "At the time, it was different. I didn't know there was a way back. I assumed that's where I'd be forever. It was a lonely existence, but it was still existence. I had to find some meaning in it, something that made it worth living—and Lorcan was that for me."

Part of me hated hearing her truth. It made the guilt I harbored stretch its claws, as if awakening from slumber. It was my fault she was sent there in the first place. It was my fault she was brought back and forced into this situation.

You didn't challenge her, a small voice said in my mind. *You didn't tell her to reject him. You didn't cast the spell that sent her to Hell.*

Then there was the other part of me. The part that was learning. Growing. Getting louder and louder with every hard choice I made.

Ultimately, I wasn't the only reason for her situation. I was one of many.

"He was your cage because you made him one."

Bree nodded. "But then you opened a portal and brought me back. Everything I knew was turned upside down. Ten years had passed, and this city wasn't the place I remembered it to be. Neither were you." She smiled at the setting sun as it sunk below the buildings on the horizon. "I'm jealous of your relationships. You have an atman who loves you and respects you. You have friends who would give their lives for you. You have children on the way . . . I'm so incredibly envious, but also happy for you because you *deserve* it."

"I disagree," I said. "I don't deserve it—and no, I'm not throwing myself a pity party." The flash of annoyance in her expression vanished. "I don't think anyone deserves those things. The universe doesn't owe them to us. It doesn't care. It doesn't look at someone and say, 'you're a good person so I'm going to give you X'. Fate. Destiny. It's all bullshit." I shook my head, my blonde ponytail swinging around me. "You got the short stick with Lorcan. I'm not going to pretend otherwise. It's not fair that you were paired with someone so horrible. Just as it's not fair I got Ronan and that we actually work. The rest of it, though . . . those are things you can choose. You want friends? Make them. You want territory? Take it. You can't control what the universe doles out, but everything else, that's up to you."

She snorted. "That was a good pep talk. You'll need it one day for those kids of yours."

I chuckled. "It was, wasn't it? I'm getting better with words."

"You're getting better with everything," Bree said. "I'm really proud of you. Of who you are. I may not say it or show it, but you are who I'd look up to if I were a better person."

She turned her cheek, her light blue eyes settling on me. They were my eyes, before Aeshma. Before I became a demon. But they were wise beyond their years.

"You're not a bad person," I said. "You've made mistakes, but haven't we all?"

"Tell me this, why did you decide to rule New Chicago?"

I sensed a trap in her question but answered anyway. "Because someone was going to do it no matter what I did. At least if I stepped up I could decide how things would be run and actually try to fix this mess."

She nodded. "I wouldn't rule a territory because it was the right thing to do. I would rule one because I *like* power. I *like* control. I *like* fear." I didn't know what to say, so I didn't. "If not for you, I would still take Lorcan as an atman. As horrible as he is—he's also mine. I feel territorial over him. Not from love, but because he's a possession to me as much as I am to him."

I grimaced at her words.

"I can see you're starting to get it now," she said.

"You're right that you might not be as good as I thought, *but* you forget that no one is wholly good or bad. I've killed out of anger. I'm sure I will again. I've lost control of my temper and tortured—"

"It bothers you, though. When you do it."

"Actually, it doesn't," I admitted. "If I were a better person, it would. I don't lose sleep at night over most of the people I've killed. Torture? The vampire was the first of what will likely be many, and I don't regret it."

"You tortured him for what he did. It was a punishment befitting the crime," Bree said. "I threw a girl in the pit for lusting after Lorcan."

I lifted an eyebrow. "The pit?"

Bree smiled wickedly. "It's a giant hole in the ground. Hole understates its size. It's closer to the Grand Canyon, but deeper and fewer pathways out. Some of the worst monsters in the Otherworld live there."

Okay, then. Perhaps I was more like Nathalie than I thought.

"I take it you don't feel bad about this?"

"Guilt is a useless emotion," she replied. "Sometimes I feel it, but that's rare. I've seen so much torture and death that it doesn't faze me anymore. Every single action has a consequence. I couldn't challenge her, so I got rid of her."

"Why couldn't you challenge her? If that's an infraction worthy of being thrown into a pit?"

Bree smirked, a Cheshire smile. "It wasn't. Technically, she was supposed to have acted on it before I would have been allowed to challenge her—which is the 'correct' route in the Otherworld. I pissed off some council members with that one. They wanted me thrown in the pit as well. Lorcan silenced them and whipped my ass for it." Something like fondness filled her face. Sadness too.

"Unless you're the Harvester, every action is supposed to be handled with a challenge. Rejection. Stealing. Cheating. If I wanted your territory, I could challenge you for it. Or if I was making moves to acquire it and you wanted to put a stop to it, you could challenge me. Everything in Hell is decided by who has the most power. Right and wrong aren't even subjective, they're meaningless. Worthless."

"It sounds like a terrible place to live." I'd said it before and I'd say it again, the Otherworld was not for me. Everything I'd heard about it screamed that it was the personification of the worst parts of humanity—Hell itself.

"For the weak," she agreed. "I'm not weak."

The way she said it almost sounded like longing. "Do you miss it?"

"Sometimes," she admitted. "I wouldn't change the decisions that led me here because I'm truly free, not bound by another's laws or my attachment to Lorcan. But as horrible as it was, it was also familiar and comforting in some ways. I understood the dynamics. I fit in with their world. Here, I'm floating. Aimless once more."

The sun slipped below the horizon and Bree's face turned wistful as the sky darkened. City lights clicked on, one by one.

"You have me."

"I love you more than anything. You're all that remains of what humanity I have left . . . but you aren't a purpose."

"Neither is Lorcan." I shifted side to side, adjusting my weight when it became uncomfortable.

"True," she agreed. "When Lorcan and I duel . . . no matter the outcome, it's going to be difficult. I may go away for a while."

"To the Otherworld?" I kept my tone neutral, but inside,

claws scraped against my chest thinking of her leaving again.

"No." My chest released, making it easier to breathe again. She eyed me warily, like she could tell how I'd reacted. "But it may be for a long time. I'm going to be in a bad place. When one loses their other half . . . it's not good. I don't want you to see me like that—but I also won't want to see you."

Hurt flashed through me, but I smothered it. She was being honest. It wasn't my fault any more than it was hers.

"I understand."

She nodded. "I'll come back but give me time. Don't push it. Don't look for me. Okay? Promise me?"

Promise her. Bree knew what she was asking. Promises were binding. Unbreakable for demons. She was serious.

"On one condition."

The door to the roof banged. We both looked over. Nat peeked her head through. "Are you growing the cucumbers from a seedling? We've been waiting for twenty minutes. Mist wants to play charades and got the twins to agree. I asked you to get some cucumbers for the hummus, but I'd have done it myself if I knew you two were going—"

"For fuck's sake," Bree muttered. "We're coming."

Nat eyed us both. She lifted two fingers and pointed them at her eyes, then ours. "Two minutes. Then I'm sending Sasha." I nodded, and the door closed. She made a show of tromping down the stairs. Bree rolled her eyes.

I put my hands on her shoulders.

"Live," I said hoarsely, naming my condition. "I promise I won't go look for you if you live. Find whatever purpose you're looking for."

Bree put a hand over mine, squeezing it tight.

"I will—and just so you know, don't be scared. I won't lose."

My mouth opened, then closed, words failing me. Eventually I settled on, "You can't promise that."

"I can," she disagreed. "I promise you that I won't lose. So just focus on you and staying alive until then."

Our magic flared around us. Two promises made. Both binding.

Our connected hands burned where they met, new brands forming to signify them.

"What happens if you lose, when you've made a promise?"

Bree smiled sadly. "I won't."

"But *if* you do," I insisted. A creeping feeling told me that I knew the truth already. That she'd just changed the future with those words.

"I'll die," she said softly. "And my magic will die with me."

25

PIPER

Three days.

I wanted to scream sometimes. Cry others. The desire to burn and break was nearly overwhelming. Having this time *was* good. I'd always asked myself what I would have done different if I'd known it would be my last day with my family.

At least this time, I wouldn't have to wonder.

I wouldn't have regret.

Bree had given me the greatest of gifts. I would never be able to repay her for her selflessness. Or be able to tell her the relief I felt. If she lost, she wouldn't be tortured. He wouldn't be able to abuse her for eternity. I'd said death was kinder, and I meant it.

These thoughts circled round and round in my brain for days, keeping me up at night despite my exhaustion.

"You're distracted," Nathalie said. She stood across from the bar, arms crossed. "And you look like shit. Have you been sleeping?"

"Some."

Her lips pressed into a thin line. "The pregnancy is

taking its toll," Bree grunted from the other end of the counter. She'd turned to the side to lean her head against the wall, eyes closed. Black coffee in one hand, newspaper in the other.

"Are you sure you should be doing this right now?" she questioned aloud. "Katherine and her coven can wait—"

"If we delay, how long will it be until they find someone else?" I said, setting my spoon down in the bowl of oatmeal. "How do we know they haven't already? She wasn't exactly keen on waiting this long to begin with."

"She's mortal. She can wait."

I rolled my eyes, ignoring Bree. "You know her better than anyone. If I tell her we need to wait till after I deliver, what do you think she'll say? Would she wait?"

Nat sighed and looked away.

Yeah, I didn't think so.

"Patience isn't a virtue she possesses."

"No shit," Bree said. "Apparently she has no sense of self-preservation either."

"I won't kill her," I said, twisting in my seat to look at Bree. She cracked her eyes open, narrowed and apathetic. Somewhat like a sleeping dragon that was perturbed to be awoken by nonsense. "She was right. Not only is she Nat's twin, but her psychic bondmate . . . I won't risk that."

My best friend smiled in apology and gratitude. It wasn't her fault her sister was pulling this card. We don't get to choose our blood, or even who our souls are part of. Bree should understand that better than anyone.

"Didn't you already think she was dead?" Bree asked. "Why does it matter if she actually is now?"

I sighed. "Because it's her *sister*," I said, pinning her with a glare. "Her anchor, should they ever choose to bond. Nat thought she was dead, and it wasn't an option then. It was beyond our control. Now I know she's alive. That *is* within my control, at least to some extent."

"She's a bitch," Bree muttered.

"You won't hear an argument from me," Nat said, holding her hands up. "But that doesn't seem like a good reason to kill someone."

"Says you."

"This is why you're not in charge," I grumbled, rolling my eyes at my sister. Bree huffed in return. "I've weighed out the options here. If I don't do the blood oath with her, nothing stops them from going to Lorcan or another demon."

"If you *do* do it, it may be what pushes you over the edge." Nat's gaze traveled from my face down my shoulders. In a T-shirt, you couldn't see how much my bones were jutting out, but they were. My appointments with Señora had moved to daily because I was dropping two to three pounds a day.

She may not be able to see beneath my clothes, but they were baggy everywhere other than my stomach—and my cheekbones were now sharp enough to cut someone.

"Usually she's too conservative for my tastes, but in this case, I agree," Bree said, leaning forward. "I've seen pregnancies get this close to the end." She held her forefinger and thumb an inch apart. "But their body gave out too soon. I don't think you'll make it another two weeks, but we're at the point that every *hour* matters. You need every bit of your strength at this point because even giving up a drop might make a difference in how this plays out."

"I see your point," I acquiesced. "But that still doesn't leave us with a better solution—"

"I'll do it."

My eyebrows should have hit my hairline. "You'll take the blood oath with them?"

Bree nodded. "They're not willing to wait? They get me. I can handle a coven of ingrate witches."

Our conversation from a couple of days ago played through my mind.

I like power. I like control. I like fear.

"Your challenge is right around the corner," I argued. "If a few drops makes a difference for me, it could for you."

"It won't," Bree said, the picture of utter certainty.

"If you die, you'll take my sister with you," Nat said. "That's part of the reason they want Piper. And even if you weren't coming up to a challenge, I'm not sure you're the best influence over them, if I'm being completely honest."

Bree lifted a white eyebrow. Dark amusement dancing in her eyes.

"Me?" she said innocently. Mocking.

Nat wasn't amused.

"I won't lose. I already promised Piper that."

It was my friend's turn to have her eyebrows hit her hairline. "You can't promise that."

"I can." She lifted her hand, the one now adorned with a brand from her promise. "I did."

Nat's lips parted. She shook her head, muttering to herself.

"The future isn't set in stone. You have no way of knowing if you will or won't."

"Do I look like a liar?" Bree said sharply. At the expression on Nat's face, she lifted her coffee mug and said, "Let me rephrase. I'm confident. Not cocky. I have no desire to die, but I wouldn't be reassuring you if I knew I was going to."

"That's the problem. You don't know either. You can't. It's impossible to predict—"

"I know Lorcan. I know his strengths. I know his weaknesses. I know him better than he knows himself—but he doesn't know me. Not like he thinks he does."

"Care to elaborate?" Nat said dryly.

"Not really."

Nat took a deep breath, letting it go. The look she gave me matched what I was feeling. "She wants us to just trust her."

"Actually, I don't care if you do or not," Bree corrected. "Your opinion of me doesn't change the outcome. It also doesn't change that we need a solution if they won't wait for Piper. I've presented one. It makes little difference to me whether you accept it."

"Ronan would do it," Nat said. She tilted her head toward me. "We both know he would."

"He's giving everything he can to keep her alive right now," Bree said. She drained her coffee, then sat the mug down on the counter with a thump. "I don't recommend it."

"Beyond that, I don't want Ronan doing a blood oath with them," I said, mulling over my options. "He's the most powerful demon out there. That's not the sort of magic I want to hand over to a black magic coven with few scruples and even fewer morals."

"Fair," Nat agreed reluctantly. She chewed the corner of her thumbnail, then paused, realizing what she was doing. Her hand curled into a fist that she dropped to her side. "I don't like it . . . but I don't think we have another viable option if Katherine refuses to see reason."

I nodded. "It's settled then. After I eat this, we pay them a visit at"—I paused to glance down at the parchment paper that showed up on my counter last night—"A Wicked Haunt." I frowned. "That's the cathedral with the giant cemetery on the edge of town. It was converted years ago for forbidden rituals. I thought Lucifer put a stop to it . . ."

"Lucifer isn't here anymore," Nat said, eyes cast downward as if avoiding *someone's* gaze. "I'm not surprised they resumed using it since his word is no longer binding. My family put a lot of work into making that hallowed ground prime for necromancy. The souls of my ancestors were laid to rest there and used to increase the channeling ability of any magic used."

Great. It was a supercharged battery to give them extra 'juice'. Just what they needed.

"On second thought, I want Sasha here for this one. I don't trust Katherine not to pull a fast one."

"Good," Nat said. "And if she tries anything—don't hesitate to stop her, okay?"

"Nat," I sighed.

"I'm serious." Her eyes glowed with that strange chaos that moved through her. "Twin or not, psychic bondmate or not—there are lines that people can't cross and expect it to be okay. I've not completed the bond with her. It won't shatter my mind."

Yet.

The unspoken word hung between us.

HEADSTONES LINED THE GRASSY WALKWAY, a macabre marker for where it was okay to step. They led up to the stairs of a small cathedral. It had two spires, the middle one larger, more imposing. In the center was a glass window with black filigree running through it—creating the image of a pentagram. It was a witch's symbol.

We were in the right place.

"Your ancestors were creepy," Sasha said, surveying the rows and rows of dead beneath an open, cloudy sky. What few trees remained, were dead or dying, the same as everything else in this place.

"The Morrigan made us. I assumed that was a given." My best friend donned her outfit like armor. Between the shoulder pads on black velvet material and short boots with a chunky heel and steel tip, I couldn't place whether she fit in with the gothic display or not. I'd long since realized that she, like my sister, chose clothes with a purpose. Today she commanded authority, the French twist that bound her chestnut hair accentuating it. "You don't have to be here," I said. "If it's too much to face her right now. We've got this."

Nat took a deep breath. "I'm good." She ran her hands down the tight black shirt that clung to her stomach like a second skin, skimming the edge of her pants. Sweaty palms, I assumed. One of her many tells that showed how nervous she was.

If she said she was okay, then I took her word for it. I'd learned my lesson in deciding what was best for others.

"All right," I nodded, starting down the aisle. Black and brown blades of grass crunched under my feet like fallen leaves in the winter. It was just like what Katherine had done at Isadora's mansion. We'd all assumed it was a slight . . . but maybe not.

"Let's get this over with," Bree sighed. She trailed at my side, only a foot behind. Dark sunglasses covering her eyes. A cup of cheap coffee in one hand, a thin strand of metal weaving between her fingers on the other. She wore a number of rings and metal spikes in her braid that looked like delicate thorns. Instead of heels, she donned boots with metal soles.

"Expecting a fight?" I said lightly as we approached the double doors.

"Always. Being unprepared would be asking for it," she replied. "But in this particular case—yes. They're black witches. I'm hoping a show of power will keep them from pulling a stunt."

"I rarely wear sleeves anymore for that reason," I said as we slowly climbed the steps. "My brands speak for me. As do my guns." I patted the thigh holster. Usually I wore one around my waist, but that wasn't exactly doable with the giant beach ball that was my stomach.

"They'd speak louder if you had a different dress code. Something that didn't scream 'homeless and struggling,' or 'blind grandma' perhaps," Bree said smoothly. She knocked on the door with a closed fist, thumping it twice.

I glared.

"What?" She tilted her head and motioned behind us. "It's true. Ask the witch."

I turned to Nat who was very purposely looking at the sky.

"Anyone else think it's going to rain?" she said lightly, omitting a reply.

"Oh fuck you too," I muttered. "I'm practical." I glanced down at the T-shirt, jeans, and combat boots. I didn't see the problem. Just because I preferred to dress for safety instead of show. After enough years pretending to be a human bounty hunter, some things were ingrained in me.

Always wear pants because being dragged on concrete was a bitch.

Boots or sneakers only. Boots were preferable for the ankle support.

Leather jackets were actually convenient in a knife fight. My turtleneck sweaters I wore exclusively for years? Not so much. Those had been a necessity for a different reason.

These things were practical. That Nat could run in heels and Bree could fight in them was the closest thing to devil magic on this side of a portal.

That they could do it wearing corsets, shoulder pads, halter tops, and every other kind of moronic piece of clothing . . . I shook my head, accepting that I'd never understand.

"Piper is a work in progress," Nat said. "When she tears holes in things or burns them, I replace them with more . . . professional pieces."

I snorted. "That's what you call the lacy scraps you gave me for underwear?"

"No, that's what I call bribing Ronan."

"For what?" I asked, more curious than anything. It was true he did like the expensive lingerie she got me. I knew because even though he burned or ripped it every time, my supply magically never ran out.

Nat opened her mouth to answer when the cathedral door shifted, screeching as it dragged across the floor.

Katherine crossed her arms over her chest.

"Why the entourage, demoness?" She tilted her head, assessing Bree in particular, like she somehow knew that despite my sister's bored expression that she was the biggest predator here. I might have rage, but Bree had something far worse. Cruelty. "One might think you either came here to kill us or were expecting to be killed."

"Given your family's coven murdered Lucifer, I'm not going to insult us both by justifying an explanation."

Katherine bowed her head slightly, a small smirk on her lips as she stepped to the side, motioning us through. As I passed, she said, "Murdered what was left of him. We wouldn't have been able to if you didn't do ninety percent of the work for us."

I ignored her, remembering Nat's warning about how her twin worked. *Disregarding her comments is the fastest way to cut her down. If she can't rile you, it throws her off. She doesn't understand a power dynamic where she isn't the aggressor.* Katherine just couldn't help herself from kicking the hornet's nest. She'd been raised to be mean. Merciless. Their mother taught her how to get under people's skin.

At my lack of response, a pout crossed her full lips. She closed the door quietly and went around us without another word.

I met Nat's gaze and she smirked, nodding once as if to say, *see? I told you so.*

It seemed she was right. Not that I'd doubted her.

Twelve others milled about in A Wicked Haunt. Five warlocks. Seven witches.

They lay on the tabernacle and reclined back on the steps of the dais. A younger man with gnarled fingers and scarring across the left side of his face played a violin. The strings sang a deathlike song. Eerie, and yet interesting. It made you want to stop and listen.

"This is your coven?" I asked, surveying the faces. They were young. None of them could have been past thirty.

"We call ourselves The Ouroboros," another voice said. A robed figure that had a distinctly high feminine voice stood from one of the pews. "From death comes life, and life gives way to death. On the backs of our ancestors we have been reborn—and with our union today, we will never end." Her hood fell back, revealing an aged and withered Carissa Le Fay. Nathalie's oldest sister.

Her once brown hair was gray and stringy. Skin that was soft and supple only months ago now stretched around her mouth and the corners of her eyes. Her cheeks looked hollowed out. But her eyes, those had changed most of all.

Whatever stared back at us from inside her was dead. There was no spark of life or passion. Only cold, unwavering nothingness.

A chill skittered down my spine.

"Carissa," Nathalie said with distaste. "You've seen better days."

Sasha couldn't stop the laugh that escaped her, though she tried to smother it with a cough. The black witch narrowed her eyes on the succubus shifter. "You've found yourself new friends. A whore hybrid and two demons. If only you could have done that sooner. Things would have gone very differently."

Sasha let out a hiss, her cat ears flattening back against her hair.

"Perhaps." Nathalie's voice dropped an octave. "But I'm not here for your approval any more than I was four months ago when you took it upon yourselves to bind me and use my magic. To use another creature that way . . ." She looked down and shook her head. "You crossed a line. One you can't uncross."

"Necessary sacrifice," Carissa replied, those same dead, unfeeling eyes staring out. "We wouldn't have had to if you'd cooperated, but many mistakes were made that day. We're willing to look past that and let you retake your place in the family . . . we've lost too many. That Katherine found you now is a sign that it's time for you to re-enter the fold."

"We are not family." Nathalie's nostrils flared in anger. She sneered in disgust. "You may be my blood, but you are not my sister."

Carissa smiled. It was slight, without teeth. "Blood is the only thing that matters in this world. One day you'll remember that."

"Enough with the vague threats," I said, suppressing my annoyance. "You asked to have a place on my council. I came here to tell you that I accept, but there are some complications that need to be considered."

"Such as?" Carissa asked, her high voice as cutting as it was cold.

"I can't do the blood oath today."

"That's not what we agreed—" Katherine started.

"We didn't *agree* on anything," I snapped. "You asked to represent the black witches, and I'm accepting that request. I won't be able to do a blood oath for a couple of weeks, if that is not acceptable, I have a solution."

Katherine crossed her arms over her chest. "We're listening."

"You'll take the oath with me," Bree said, stepping forward. She tilted her head to the side and slid off her sunglasses. Katherine looked back and forth between the two of us.

"You're not in charge of this city," she said.

"Being under her oath will still grant you protections," I said. "It just won't be my power flowing in your veins."

"Why can't you do it?"

She narrowed her eyes, dropping them to my stomach. My hand clenched into a fist. This part was a gray area. If I wasn't strong enough to give, I wasn't strong enough to protect. In that sense, the Otherworld and ours weren't so different.

"Pregnant witches don't partake in serious rituals. Pregnant shifters don't join hunts. Pregnant succubi don't even leave their homes because their pheromones become irresistible to all that come near them. Demons have their own set of rules," Bree said, answering the question without giving much away. "Your choice is me or wait. If you're dead set on Piper, you won't mind waiting. If it's just power you're searching for . . ." She lifted a hand, and the metal winding between her fingers turned to a thin dagger. "Count yourselves lucky I'm deferring to Piper because I would have wiped out your coven for how you spoke to her last week."

Katherine's lips pinched together. It was the same look Nat had when she wasn't thrilled with something.

She turned to look at Carissa. The action intrigued me.

Contrary to how she'd acted before, Katherine wasn't running this show.

The eldest Le Fay was.

Carissa nodded once, her face stern. Unreadable.

Katherine turned back around and said, "Very well. We'll accept this solution."

"Who's your second?" I glanced over the options, but her choices were sparse. Half of the people present were horribly scarred—the side effects of losing so much of their power. Their souls. It was no surprise Carissa appeared soulless when she was probably the worst off for it.

"Marcel," Katherine said after a moment of pause. Hesitation. I half expected her to say Carissa, but there's no way she would have survived. She was barely hanging on to life as it was.

"A male?" Bree crooned as a tall, black-haired man with skin the color of desert sand stood up. "What a surprise."

It was to some degree. The witches were matriarchal in

their covens. However, I had the distinct impression that Katherine didn't *want* him as a second.

Beside me, Nat stiffened. I glanced over. "Is there an issue with him?"

All she had to say was yes. I would have dismissed the choice and told Katherine to pick another. But Nat stared straight ahead, not looking at the dark-eyed warlock who stared at her with raw hunger.

"Nope."

My eyebrows lifted as I glanced between them. Something happened there. Judging by Nat's white-knuckled hand at her side . . . it wasn't insignificant.

"What is your last name, Marcel?" Bree asked, walking around the male in question.

"Abernathy."

Her brows rose. She and I instantly made the same connection. The woman who'd kicked off the Magic Wars, who'd killed the president on live TV . . . she was an Abernathy. "Dryanda, a relative of yours?"

"She was my grandmother," he said, speaking easily as if Carissa wasn't on the precipice of death beside them. "I was born in the witch camps. The Sirius Coven had me removed at birth and raised me."

The witch camps.

They were barbaric. Horrifying.

Concentration camps specifically for their kind, lobbied by humans and supported by supernatural factions with a prejudice against witches. They'd cut out the tongues, preventing the most dangerous of spells, giving humans the upper hand. Most had been abolished or turned on those that had built and supported them.

Dryanda's daughter had been sentenced to one, and it was the very reason she chose to act out.

Bree circled him like a shark waiting for blood. She leaned only inches from his face and sniffed. "You're stronger than this coven. Than her." She jutted her chin towards Katherine. "Your magic is substantial. Yet you stay here? You accept your rank being below hers?"

How she could measure his strength, I wasn't sure. It wasn't a talent I possessed. Occasionally I had a sixth sense-like knowledge, but nothing so concrete.

"This coven is all that's left of my kind."

"Here," Bree added. "New Chicago is but one city among many. There are other black witch covens that would accept you."

"They are *my* people," he said, a possessiveness coming through in each word. "I don't walk away from what's mine because there's an easier path." Dark eyes, like embers in coal, focused on Nat. A shiver ran down her spine. It wouldn't have been visible to the witches, but I was close enough with heightened senses to see the slight quake.

"Loyal," Bree mused. "Stupid, but loyal. I can accept that."

She backed away from him. "Are you ready, witch?"

Nat's twin nodded. "I am."

"Katherine Le Fay," Bree started, walking forward. Her boots clicked against the smooth stone floor. "I give you my blood in return for your *subservience*. You will be *obedient* to me and those of my lineage. You will be loyal to my line above all costs. Honest and unwavering in your *devotion*. Should you show any form of *disrespect*, you will feel the burn of cold fire through your veins, and only once you have truly repented and realized the error of your ways will it abate." Bree smiled coldly. The slender metal blade in her hand biting into her palm. Blood welled. "Do you accept this bargain?"

Every oath was different. Where I'd demanded loyalty, Bree was all but bringing her into servitude. Nathalie murmured something that sounded like a prayer under her breath. Even Sasha cursed, seeing the difference between us starkly in her demands.

Katherine swallowed hard. "That's not the bargain she made with the other factions."

"You're not making one with her. If you wanted kindness, you should have had patience."

She took a deep breath and glanced back at Carissa, who nodded again. Her face stone-cold and empty. No empathy for what she was signing her away to whatsoever.

"If Piper Fallon, the Witch Hunter, the Demon Queen, promises her protection and to bring us back into the fold."

Katherine dropped to one knee but stared up at me instead of the demon poised above her. Part of me could recognize the strength it took to make this vow. Her commitment to this coven and its demands was almost admirable.

"I promise protection to the Ouroboros Coven and to bring your community into the new age, under the same rights and laws I've imposed upon all the others."

She nodded once, the action stiff.

"I accept the blood oath."

Silently, Bree extended her hand. Red ran down the knife, still gripped in her fist.

Katherine tilted her head back, lips parted. Two drops fell. The first on her cheek, the second on her tongue.

A strangled cry echoed off the cathedral walls.

She curled into a ball, not caring for how her clothes gathered dirt and grime against the floor, or how her cheek smudged with dust. Tears ran down her face, black mascara smearing with them.

Meanwhile, Bree turned to Marcel, dismissing the writhing witch at her feet. Bree's tongue clicked. "Marcel Abernathy. I give you my blood in return . . ." She began the vow anew while Katherine arched her back so far I thought she'd snap her spine. Sweat dotted her brow and ran down her face. It didn't escape my notice that she left out the clause about disrespect in Marcel's. She'd put it in there as an inherent punishment for the way she'd already acted.

How much of her suffering was being caused by it now?

I grabbed Nat's hand, squeezing it tightly. She squeezed right back, not letting how much it affected her show.

"She's not going to make it," Sasha said when Marcel bowed his head but didn't collapse as Katherine had. "You should kill her—"

"She'll make it," Bree replied, walking around her. Seconds turned to minutes. She screamed and screamed and—

Then she went quiet.

Panting. Breathing.

Bree nudged her body with the toe of her boot. "Get to your feet."

Muscles still twitching, Katherine had no choice but to pull herself up. Every inch was a strain. She nearly fell again twice just getting to her knees. "Bree . . ." I started.

"She wanted power. She got it. I want to have a look at her."

It was a long couple of minutes as Katherine dragged herself to her feet to stand. Her cheeks were white. Her eyes dazed. She survived all right . . . but it pushed her body to the very edge in doing so.

"You're the first I've ever given blood to," Bree said, appraising her. I hadn't realized that. "Do you know why that is?"

Nat's twin didn't have any fight left in her. She shook her head, fingers clawing at the wooden pew to stay upright.

"Because I hate your kind," she said softly. "I don't mean witches. I mean supernaturals like you that believe power is owed because of your privilege. I've never taken a blood oath because I don't want to share even a drop of my power. In most cases, I like the challenge of making someone bend by their own will." She tilted her head, lifting a finger to caress Katherine's dirty cheek. "But for you, and people like you, I'll make an exception."

Katherine shuddered but didn't dare let her knees give out.

By comparison, Marcel stood with ease. His face neutral, if not for the way his dark eyes kept straying to Nat. "We're done here," I said, calling my sister off. If I'd realized exactly how much she despised Katherine, I might not have agreed to this in the first place. She was equally icy to most people, but this went a step beyond that. I hadn't seen this side of her since the night Ronan opened a portal for her. It was all too easy for me to forget that she wasn't simply my sister, but a demon whose teen years were spent in Hell.

Katherine made demands of you. Disrespected you, a small voice in my head said. *Bree's territorial. She said it herself. If Lorcan is a possession, she doesn't even love. For you, she'd do anything* . . . even make a promise that would end in her death so Lorcan couldn't use her power against us.

I swallowed hard.

To the coven, I said, "Get your financials together. In the next week, Sasha will start onboarding you with how things are done." I released Nat's hand and turned toward the door, motioning for her and Sasha to go first. Bree lingered, and I cut a glare in her direction.

As if sensing my eyes on her, she dragged them away from Katherine.

"Ugh. Fine." She sauntered around the pews and toward me. At the doorway, she twisted to say, "Be careful what you ask for, mortal. You might just get it."

With a wicked smirk on her lips, she walked out of the cathedral. Katherine collapsed the minute she wasn't in sight. No one turned to help her.

I sighed, wondering if any kindness would only be used against me. To my knowledge, Katherine hadn't truly done anything wrong other than being a pain in my ass. I walked over and glanced down at the trembling witch.

Silently, I extended my hand. She stared at me, confused, yet defiant. Her reserve wavered, and she slowly extended a shaking hand. I grasped it with ease and pulled her up, then helped her to a pew. The other witches watched in silence.

"You almost didn't survive that. It's going to take a few days for your body to bounce back. I'll send Antonella over with something to help it go faster."

"I'm fine—"

"I didn't ask," I replied. Stupid stubborn witch. "No necromantic summonings or human sacrifice," I added, starting for the exit. "For any of you."

Silence followed in my wake.

I made it halfway across the room when the cathedral doors slammed shut.

I blinked, mentally reaching for Ronan on instinct—

"He won't hear you."

I wheeled around. My heart pounded. Skin flushed. That voice was unmistakable, as was the power filling the church—enough to smother my own.

Still, I called on the elements as I screamed bloody

murder down the bridge between Ronan and me. His name filled my mind so loud that the bridge itself trembled.

But true to Lorcan's word, he didn't respond.

He couldn't hear me.

"I told you not to involve Bree," he said, blood-red eyes assessing me. "You've been so smart up to this point, always having one or the other nearby. Usually both. But now you've slipped up—and I've got you all alone."

He smiled, and whatever cruelty I thought Bree had was nothing compared to the viciousness that lurked in his gaze. I glanced at the door, commanding the wind to open it. It blasted apart—wood splinters flying everywhere.

I opened my mouth, ready to call out. To get their attention.

But Lorcan came up behind me. A cold hand wrapped around my throat.

"Bree," I croaked.

"I'm afraid my atma is indisposed at the moment," Lorcan whispered in my ear. One of the pews flipped off the ground, coming right at us. I registered Marcel's command just a moment before it hit. With a wave of Lorcan's hand, it stopped midair—then launched back across the room, knocking the warlock unconscious.

Before another witch could intervene, before I could get another word out, before anyone could do anything, Lorcan whispered again, "I look forward to playing with you, but first—*sleep*."

At his command, the darkness closed in.

And for the first time in a long time, I didn't welcome it.

26

NATHALIE

"You shouldn't feel bad for her."

I ignored him. Grass crunched beneath my boots despite the warm spring air that stirred the looser strands of hair from my French twist. "You only know a fraction of the things she's done," Lucifer continued. "While you, *my* little witch, are a good person—Katherine Le Fay is the furthest thing from it."

"I'm not *your* anything," I said quietly.

"Lies sound all the sweeter when they come from your mouth," Lucifer murmured. Phantom lips brushed my earlobe. My breath hissed between my teeth. "I find it intriguing that *that* is the part you focus on."

Sasha paused and looked back at me, her eyebrows knit together in confusion. "What?"

"Nothing," I shook my head. "That was just . . . a lot."

Sasha nodded empathetically. "Piper has a temper. One I wouldn't want to be on the other end of, but Bree . . ." Sasha pressed her lips together. She already wasn't a fan of the demoness, but this afternoon likely sealed that opinion. "I don't like her. I never will—but today is the first time I felt *fear* toward her. I hope Piper knows what she's doing letting that monster loose in this city."

I wanted to disagree. Piper's methods were more brash than my own. Where I liked to slowly move pieces on the board, Piper moved them quickly. She was queen, able to move in any direction, doing as she pleased. But she was also king. If she was taken out, it was game over for everyone.

What complicated it was that Bree was a queen in her own right as well—and that made this a whole new game.

"She did it so Piper wouldn't have to," I reminded Sasha.

"Did she?" Her green gaze slipped sideways as she asked her question in response. "Because from where I'm sitting, that oath was a far cry from the one Piper would have given her. Your twin's a bitch, but Bree's oath was fucked up."

I swallowed. "Katherine had a choice. She could have waited. She could have said no. I don't disagree that what Bree asked in return was not right—but she made her bed."

Sasha's dark eyebrows lifted. "I'm surprised."

"By?"

"You. I would have thought you'd take issue with it more."

I shrugged, focusing on her instead of the shadow at my side. The golden eyes that burned my skin. "I don't *like* it but feeling bad for her is pointless when she chose this. Katherine is a lot of things, but she isn't stupid. If she didn't want to bargain, she didn't have to. Piper wouldn't have made her. Neither would Bree. She knew the terms and agreed anyway. I can't help someone that won't help themself."

Sasha let out a low whistle. "I don't think I'd be able to be that way if Sienna had agreed. Even if it was her choice."

I couldn't tell if it was shame or judgment that colored her tone.

"You and Sienna have a special bond." It was a vague comment, but I didn't have more to give.

"So do you and Katherine. Piper told me she's your psychic bond mate."

I sighed. "You and Sienna are different. You're more than blood or magic. You'd die for her, and she for you. Kat and I . . . we aren't like that."

Sasha opened her mouth to say something.

"We're not alone," Bree said. No more than a foot behind us, she stood surveying the graveyard. I squinted, following her line of sight. There was nothing, though. Not a wisp of magic or scent on the wind.

"How do you know?" I asked.

"Run, little witch," his voice whispered over me. Bree didn't answer. I waited.

"I said *run*," Lucifer said louder, his beautiful voice turning dangerous. When I didn't move, that phantom touch grabbed my shoulders. "Damnit, Nathalie—"

Bree's lips parted. Her eyes narrowed.

"Get back to the cathedral."

A shot rang out.

It cut through the air like a clap of thunder, hitting Sasha in the chest before either of us could turn. She dropped to her knees, ears pinned back and tail stiff as a board. Her canines were extended. The pupil of her cat eyes were slitted as thin as a piece of paper.

Pain.

She was in a voiceless, endless pain.

All at once, people appeared around us, as if they'd

come out of thin air. Clothed in black with masks on their faces—I couldn't tell one from the next.

"Leave her," Lucifer demanded as I crouched beside Sasha.

I glared at him. "No."

"*Yes*," he growled.

I tore my gaze away from the demon that burned in my periphery and focused on the living one at my side. "He's right," Bree said. The ground rumbled beneath our feet. "Leave her. Run."

My mouth gaped. *She could see him?*

Not the problem at hand.

"I can't leave her," I insisted.

"They're here for Piper," Bree replied. She said, quite possibly, the only words that would have gotten me to move from that spot. "I'll protect Sasha. You need to go to her. Tell her to go into the light realm until Ronan says it's okay."

My indecision drained away. I got to my feet.

"Promise me," I said. "Promise me you won't leave her—"

"I promise," Bree ground out. "Now *go*."

I didn't let myself think about it. About Sasha wavering on the edge of consciousness from a wound I couldn't see. About the masked people closing in. About the ground rumbling, shaking, shuddering.

I sprinted for the cathedral to the double doors. I was only halfway back when they slammed shut. Magic wove between my fingers. The wind gathered beneath my feet, propelling me forward, faster.

I slammed into the doors, but they didn't shudder. Not an inch.

Palm open, I slapped it against the hardwood, cursing

when the handle refused to turn. "Piper!" I yelled. The wind howled, carrying my voice across the graveyard. Turning it from a single cry into the voice of a hundred.

"You can't save her," Lucifer said.

"Piper!" I screamed again. I raced to the side where the windows were, trying not to trip on the uneven ground. I fell on a rock the size of my fist.

"You're not strong enough, Nat—"

"Shut up," I said. My fingers latched onto the rock, gripping its rough surface. I got to my feet and cocked my arm back. Golden strands seemed to illuminate all around me as I funneled all my strength, all my magic, all my measly power into that throw.

The rock hit glass.

The window shattered. With the added wind I could manipulate, the fracture spread until the entire thing blew out. I ripped my shirt over my head and threw it down on the sill, over the rough edges.

"It's too late," Lucifer said as I tossed one leg over.

"Shut up," I repeated. Harder. Meaner. I couldn't believe that. I refused—

My other leg went over. I turned, facing the cathedral.

My best friend stood, facing the door. At her back with one hand around her throat and the other fisted in her hair was none other than Lorcan.

He smiled at me. Only feet away.

"Tell Bree I look forward to our challenge."

"Tell her yourself," I spat, wishing for one moment that I'd accepted her offer to teach me to shoot. To fight. To defend myself. Maybe then I wouldn't have been so useless. Maybe then I could have stopped him, not from ending the world, but from taking her.

Buying her time.

Anything but the sad reality of watching them disappear and not being able to do a damn thing about it.

27

BREE

Nulls.

They'd brought fucking nulls.

Where supernaturals had magic and humans had nothing, nulls were the opposite. They were the absence of nothing. Not magic itself, but anti-magic. The antithesis of it. Magic couldn't hurt them. It couldn't touch them at all.

Fire? It wouldn't burn.

Air? It wouldn't choke.

I couldn't stir the anger in them into a frenzy where they'd kill each other.

But there were other ways to kill.

I'd long said that my talent with metal was my greatest ability—because it was my most flexible. And here, now, that ability was going to mean the difference between life and death for them.

My lungs filled with the sweet spring air, its crispness melting as it sat right on the cusp of summer. The clouds overhead were pregnant with rain, casting us in their shadows.

It was a beautiful day for a massacre.

I released my breath and pulled every last scrap of iron out of the ground around me. I stole the silver and the bronze that decorated the tombstones. I ripped the gold from the dead, rings and necklaces and other forms of jewelry that adorned their bodies.

Then I molded it into throwing knives.

"There's one for each of you," I called. "If you want to live, turn around and report to your betters that you failed."

In a predictable, and if I were being honest—not a sad turn of events—they advanced on us.

Bullets rained left and right. They stopped midair before reaching me, breaking apart into liquid metal before merging with others and forming more knives. More weapons.

It was laughable.

If I were Piper, I might have given them another chance. Maybe made an example of one to show the others reason.

I wasn't Piper.

The knives went flying. Their wicked blades a flash of light followed by a spray of crimson. They aimed for the eyes, striking true as they went through, then into the brain, and ended up sticking out the back of each of their skulls.

The bullets stopped.

The gunfire ended.

Nine people collapsed on the ground, their bodies food for the maggots.

At my feet, Sasha Loren had lost consciousness from the gun that stole her magic. It was temporary. She'd feel weak for a day or two, and likely nursing a migraine through it— but nothing she couldn't come back from.

From the tree line, Robin started across the field. Her

verdant green hair turning a shade darker beneath the clouds.

I met her halfway.

"You make it look easy," she said, pointedly staring anywhere but at the Illuminati members I'd just murdered.

"That's because it is." She shook her head, letting out a heavy sigh.

"I'd say, I hope that one isn't a friend of yours, but all things considered she got the better deal here." Robin nudged Sasha with her boot. The succubus didn't stir.

"You're here for Piper," I said, putting myself between the cathedral and her.

"No, I'm here so the Illuminati don't get suspicious," she corrected. "*They* were here for Piper, but you took care of that." She holstered the gun on her thigh and crossed her arms.

"How'd they know we were here?"

Robin thrust her chin in the direction of the cathedral. "Tip-off this morning. My guess? You got a mole."

I swore under my breath in the demonic language. Robin lifted her eyebrows, eyes squinted. "It can only be someone in the coven. Outside of them, no one knew we'd be here. The succubus twins are blood sworn to her. The witch might drive me crazy, but she'd never betray her. This was a setup." I rubbed a hand down my jaw, working over the tense muscles. "They had to know I'd be here, though. Last time they tried to bind me, and I killed their agents. Did they really think a hit squad of nulls would do this?" I shook my head. "I think they're testing you. Something's not right."

Robin bent down and picked up one of my knives. She held it out to me.

"Stab me."

"What?"

"I agree with you," she said. "It's going to look suspicious if I'm not hurt at all. You need to stab me and then get Piper out of here so I can call my CO." I blew out a harsh breath, not liking my options, but not seeing a better one that she'd actually take.

"They may still not believe you."

"That's a risk I have to take, but you still haven't dealt with your asshole mate, and now they're stepping up the hunt for Piper. You need me on the in right now. So stab me and get it over with."

I grabbed the knife, twisting it between my fingers. "You'll need more than one wound. I killed the rest of them in a single shot. They need to believe you had to fight for your life."

Robin swallowed and then nodded. "Do it."

"Who is that?" a quiet voice said not far off. I'd been so focused on Robin, I hadn't realized the witch came back.

"Where is Piper?" I asked, surveying the graveyard. My sister's blonde hair and telltale scent was nowhere to be found. "I told you to go into the light realm with her—"

"Who is she, Bree? Why does she have Sasha's magic?" Nathalie repeated, the wind stirred, lifting the loose strands of hair that had fallen out of her French twist. Her shirt was missing, and blood dotted her skin. Tiny surface cuts, nothing more.

"It's not what you're thinking, so calm the fuck down and tell me where my sister is."

That was the wrong answer, apparently.

Nathalie's eyes glowed gold like headlights. Robin reached for her gun and Nat barked a spell in Hebrew. Magic wrapped around Robin, binding her in place. "What are you really doing here? Were you working with him—"

"Him?" Everything in me froze. Time slowed. She couldn't be talking about—

"Lorcan," she spat. Fire raged in her eyes. "He was here. Waiting. While you were doing god knows what—*he took her.*"

My jaw tightened, teeth pressing together so hard they should have cracked.

He was here. Feet from me—and I didn't even know it.

"Tell me everything."

"Not until you tell me who the hell she is and why she has a gun that can steal magic—a gun I've been hunting for, for over a month."

My hands curled into fists. The urge to stick metal pins and needles through her hands and feet until she told me what I wanted to know ran strong. It was only who she was to Piper that kept me in check.

"Her name is Robin, and she's my contact in the Illuminati."

Nathalie shuddered. "You're still working with them?"

"I'm helping her get out," I said. "They're pissed with me for leaving, and they want Piper. Robin's been feeding me information so I can better protect her." It wasn't the complete truth, but close enough. Still, the witch looked between the two of us, suspicion still clouding her.

"Well either she sucks at her job, or she double-crossed you because Lorcan was in the church. He barred the entrances. By the time I got there, it was too late. He told me to tell you that he looks forward to your challenge. Then he disappeared with her."

Rage surged through me, making my brands light up. I knew my eye color had shifted from blue to green as I shoved my power down, holding it in tight. Being explosive and losing control wouldn't help us find her.

"Release her binding and Robin can tell us herself what she knows."

Nathalie's lips pinched together. "Fine, but if you double-cross me, there will be hell to pay."

I couldn't help the caustic laugh I let out, because she was wasting our time with idle threats. "Will there?" I said condescendingly. "Because last I checked, you're a witch with only moderate power that's threatening a *demon*."

She didn't crack a smile. "If you think I don't have contingency plans in place for things like that, you are sorely mistaken and not half as smart as I gave you credit to be."

Something about her unwavering confidence made me wonder, but now wasn't the time for this. "Robin's with us. I promise I am not double-crossing you and had no knowledge Lorcan would be here. Now unbind her so we can get some answers before Ronan shows up and starts his interrogation by instantly killing the entire coven."

She let out a tight breath and shifted her gaze. Her fingers twisted, undoing the spell. Robin sagged, taking in a deep breath.

"We were contacted this morning and told Piper would be here today, likely with Bree. That's all we knew—or at least what I was told. They sent me with a team to apprehend her. I shot your friend here so she wouldn't be implicated while Bree dealt with others in my squad." True to who she was, Robin didn't waste a breath. She knew how I worked. How much I loathed this back and forth. We trusted each other enough to have each other's backs and not question motive.

"If that's true, then Lorcan is working with the Illuminati," Nathalie said. "We're so screwed. If he drains her—" She shuddered again.

"He won't," I said, not entirely sure myself, but not willing to go with that train of thought. "He knows what Ronan will do to him if he touches her before the challenge. He'd have no reason not to end him if Lorcan hurt her."

Nathalie wasn't convinced. "We need to track him down and get her back."

"We won't be able to. He can shield magic."

"But he can't hide his blood."

I narrowed my eyes. "Lorcan wouldn't have given anyone his blood. He hasn't even given it to me—"

"I cut him. The night we were going to send you back. My athame nicked his cheek. I kept the blood from it, just in case."

I opened my mouth, closing it quickly to hide my shock. "You're only mentioning this now?"

"I told you, I have contingency plans for *everything*." She crossed her arms over her chest. "If she's on our side, then I vote we send her back. Let her watch and listen. You and I go back and get Ronan. We do the locator spell and go after Lorcan."

It wasn't a bad plan. All things considered, it was actually pretty good.

Piper was in danger no matter what, but if we could get to her within a few hours . . . how much damage could he do?

I grimaced because I already knew the answer to that.

"You ready for this?" I asked Robin, holding up the throwing knife.

She nodded, trepidation making the corners of her mouth tighten despite her fighting spirit. "I can't blow my cover for nothing, but if I have a chance to get her out, I will. Watch for the ravens." She looked to the skies and then back to me, her expression grim. "I'll send word if I hear anything."

"This is going to hurt," I warned.

"Make it believable. It'll be nothing compared to what they'll do to me if they find out I double-crossed them."

Her cries of pain chipped away at my armor, but there was more on the line than Robin's safety now. There was Piper's. The twins. The entire world's—because I knew exactly what would happen if we lost her.

I'd seen demons lose their other half and what it did to them.

Killing sprees. Suicide. Complete and total self-destruction.

It was the Harvester's job to end them if they didn't do it themselves when that happened.

And Ronan? He wasn't just bonded to Piper. He was completely and utterly in love with her. Devoted to her. He would end the world for her and there wouldn't be a damn thing anyone would do about it.

28

PIPER

Bleach.

It stung my nostrils, the scent raking over my throat. I swallowed, trying to clear it away, but it only made the feeling worse. My eyes cracked open, and I winced at the harsh fluorescent light.

Why was it so bright?

I coughed, rubbing my eyes with the back of my hand.

"I wondered how long it would take you."

I stilled. Memories surfaced. The graveyard. The Ouroboros Coven. The doors slamming shut, and then—

"Where am I?"

My head fell back against something soft. I turned, searching for where that voice came from. Lorcan sat in a high-backed chair with red velvet cushions. He wore a suit. Something fancy that Ronan might have. Likely some designer Nat would know of with one look. His hair was combed to perfection, not one white strand out of place. Crimson eyes watched me.

"Bree's apartment," he answered, much to my surprise.

I sat up, swallowing down the grunt. "It's a nice place,"

I said, looking around. Cold. Clean. Nice all the same. "Thought she moved around. Didn't know she had an apartment of her own."

"You don't know her," he said, still watching me. Dissecting me. "You might have before, but not now. This game you're playing . . . you will lose. You know that, don't you?"

I sighed, shaking my head. "Spare me the speech and let's get to why you kidnapped me and what you plan to do."

His features hardened. Lips pressed into a thin line. Eyes narrowed.

"You're weak from the pregnancy, but still stronger than many demons. Your magic will make a nice hors d'oeuvre before I bond to Bree. I can siphon it slowly, keeping you alive until I've dealt with Ronan."

I didn't shake. I didn't shudder.

I refused to show fear of any form.

"That's all?" I asked, irreverent at best. "You kidnapped me to siphon my magic when there's an entire city of supernaturals, not to mention my sister—who you think you beat so easily?"

He didn't react to my taunting, and instead just smiled like the sadistic fuck he was. "It's a shame you're his. I would have liked to keep you both. Pitting you against each other for my affection." His gaze turned fond, as though he were looking at a lover and not a woman he planned to torture then kill. "Rip that last shred of humanity away from her, bit by bit. Bree would be my queen, of course, but you would be a concubine truly worthy of me." His eyes snagged on my belly as he perused me. "And if you have a daughter, I could have her too when she's old enough." Disgust made my stomach acid churn.

"Has anyone ever told you you're a sick fuck?"

He kept smiling. "If you somehow survive the birth, and Ronan's death, I may keep you anyway. Not here—you have too much power here. Too much sway. I plan to make this world mine as well, but in the Otherworld—I could put you there. My prize in all of this."

I lifted my eyebrows. "I'd rather die than fuck you."

"I know, that's what will make it so much better."

Bile climbed up my throat, threatening to make an appearance. I swallowed it down, putting the back of my hand to my mouth in an effort to keep it there.

"There's just one problem with this little plan of yours," I breathed, queasiness throwing me off-kilter.

Lorcan leaned forward, batting my hand away and grabbing my chin. He forcefully turned my face to him. "Enlighten me."

Oh, I planned to. Overconfident ass. Little did he know that I'd been learning these past three weeks. About him. About Hell. About our magic, our culture, our rules.

"I, Piper Fallon, Queen of New Chicago, Hunter of Witches, challenge you, Lorcan, son of Eris and Anhur. You've declared intent to take what is mine—either submit now or accept my challenge for power."

Lorcan froze. The slight smirk on his lips fell.

Magic wrapped around us, mine and his, waiting for his answer.

"You fucking bitch—"

"Your answer, asshat," I snapped back. He inhaled deeply, nostrils flaring as he closed his eyes. Then he leaned forward, putting his face only inches from mine. I resisted the urge to try to bite his nose and rip it off his face. I wasn't sure how the magic would react to that, and I didn't have much energy to fight it off.

Lorcan opened his eyes. At such a close range, I could see the way they shifted like blood. Brighter around the edges and darker toward the pupil. Where some demons shined when pissed off, he emanated darkness—and not the good kind.

"You just decided your future," he said quietly. His icy breath ghosted over me. "I was going to be nice. Keep you in comfort given your current state. Let Bree tend to you. Deliver your children." He shook his head. "You're just as stupid as her, it seems. Not knowing when to bow for your own good."

"You're still monologuing."

Lorcan dropped my chin and whispered, "I accept."

Our magic bound tight, stifling me for a moment as it threatened to crush my windpipe. It eased just as fast as it came, settling back as a brand appeared, snaking its way up my neck, just over my jaw.

"You should let me go. Run while you still have the chance," I said, leaning back against the cushions. "You may be able to block my mind, but Ronan is not only my atman, but the *true* Harvester. He will find me, and when he learns you can't touch me—he'll end you."

Lorcan sneered a laugh. "You think I didn't have a backup plan in case you decided to try this?" He lunged, grabbing my wrist painfully. "You're about to learn a very hard lesson in trying to play me."

Our bodies disappeared even though I could still feel him. He yanked me to my feet and our surroundings changed. It wasn't the light realm or the void that he carried us through. "You can astral project," I said. "You steal that from Bree?"

We reappeared in a lab of some sort.

White walls.

White tiled floors.

A single metal chair with wicked-looking cuffs around the arms, legs, and middle.

In it, five people were waiting, wearing white lab coats to match.

"She's yours. You have three days to do what you want before I'm taking her back."

He shoved me toward them, throwing me off. I twisted, grabbing the end of the chair to stop myself from falling. Latex gloves grabbed at my arms, forcing me onto the seat. I struggled, pulling my arms, kicking, thrashing—doing anything to stop them. It was like my demon strength meant nothing as they strapped me down. First my arms, then legs. Chains wrapped around my middle, my neck. When I couldn't do much more than wiggle my fingers, they shoved a gag in my mouth, then pulled out a big-ass needle.

I tried to shake my head, to stop them.

I called on fire and air and water and wind.

The elements didn't answer as the needle plunged into my right arm.

"This might hurt a little."

Understatement of the century.

29

RONAN

"How much longer?" Bree asked for the fourteenth time. I knew because counting was the only thing keeping me together.

"A few minutes," Nathalie said without looking up. "The time hasn't changed."

Bree paced for another thirty seconds. Her boots clicking against my hardwood floor were like nails being driven into my skull. My hands wrapped around the ends of the armrests, trying and failing to ignore her.

"You're certain there isn't a faster way?" Bree said, pausing in her pacing.

"I'm certain," Nathalie said. Her patience was a far longer leash than my own at this moment.

She resumed walking, her steps counting the seconds. It wasn't even a full minute before she stopped again. "It's been hours. Every second she's with Lorcan—"

I exploded out of my chair.

Red had tinged my vision since the moment they appeared without Piper. They told me their excuse for why she was missing—no, not missing. Taken. Kidnapped.

"She wouldn't be with Lorcan if you'd done what you were supposed to and stayed by her side," I hissed. Dark energy, like thunderstorms on the horizon, made my power push and pull. It stretched its claws and retracted them. Searching. Seeking. But no matter how loud I called down the bridge between our minds, no one answered.

I followed it to the other end, but mist shrouded her thoughts. I'd wander into it and find myself walking back out, no matter how many times I tried.

She was alive. I knew that much, but nothing else.

"I did," Bree replied, her voice dropping an octave. Not from remorse or guilt, but anger. Rage. "She was only feet behind me—"

"Yet he still managed to snatch her—only feet behind you."

I crowded her. Towering more than a foot above Piper's petite sister. Despite the sheer size difference, Bree didn't cower. Chin up and eyes blazing, she stared me down like a bull ready to charge.

"It isn't my fault that she has no mental defenses."

"Excuses."

"That she can't protect herself from psychic attacks—"

"Do you ever take responsibility for anything?"

"Or that she's too weak because you decided to not use protection, thinking you could just knock her up to tie her to you—"

A growl let loose. I didn't realize it was me until I was lunging for her.

Bree disappeared, then reappeared across the room. Throwing knives circled her as she tilted her head. "Is that the best you've got?" Her voice dripped with scathing condescension. "The rumors of how you handled yourself when you ruled the Otherworld must simply be that. Rumors. No wonder the Source chose another."

Her knives turned midair, then fired.

A flash of light, they came at me head-on. I threw up a wall, and the blades dematerialized as they passed through it. Nothing more than metal bits the size of a grain of sand, they formed a pile at my feet that scattered as the pieces hit the floor.

I dropped the shield and conjured an orb of black fire.

If she wanted someone to fight, I'd give her—

"If you throw that, I'll have the unfortunate job of telling Piper her atman couldn't control his temper and killed her sister." Nathalie's voice broke through the air, just strong enough to pierce the blazing inferno that roared inside me. "She won't forgive you, Ronan. It's not worth it."

Pain registered in the back of my brain. I looked down. A throwing knife embedded itself in the hard muscle of my thigh. Blood oozed profusely from the wound. I lifted my head, all thoughts of stopping myself became smoke in the wind when Bree smiled viciously.

"Got him."

In our periphery, Nat pointed to a spot on the atlas. Bree vanished again, reappearing next to the witch. I swallowed down the flames that were begging to be unleashed as I ripped the throwing knife from my leg. The wound healed faster than the time it took for the blade to fall and hit the floor with a thunk. The sharp end burrowed in the wood, handle sticking up. I left it there and walked over to the kitchen bar. Peering over Nathalie's shoulder, I saw where the drops of blood had gathered.

"That's my apartment," Bree said quietly.

"We should come up with some sort of game plan—"

I ignored the witch and walked into the void.

Lorcan was waiting when I stepped out.

"Ronan," he smiled. The scent of smoke and roses was all over this place. It tasted of Piper's magic, a particular kind of burn that I was addicted to. "What a pleasure—"

I traveled the space between us in a single step, grabbing him by the throat.

"Where is she?"

"Safe, for now."

My nails turned to claws, pressing into the flesh of his throat. Demons couldn't suffocate to death, but I'd like to test that theory in great detail on this son of a bitch.

"I need a location, or I'll pull you apart limb by limb until your mouth tells me what I want to know."

Lorcan smirked, fangs bared in warning. "Then you'll never see her again. She's with friends—and if something happens to me, they'll be keeping her. Insurance policy."

My fist tightened. I wondered if I drained him, would he feel the same? Would he break? Would I learn where it was inside his twisted mind that he was keeping her?

Could I risk it? Could I not?

My options were few and the outcome of her survival was growing slimmer every minute.

"Stop," Nathalie said quietly. "She's not here. Wherever he's keeping her, we need to put our energy into finding that." Lorcan laughed, an emotionless sound.

"If we lose our chance by killing him, what's the difference between today or in three?" I asked, more to myself than anything. "If you won't tell me now, you won't tell me then." My fingers tightened, the flesh around them turning a splotchy purple. Red veins burst just below the surface. "Might as well finish the job."

Beneath my hand his skin turned hard. A red sheen

spread over it, carrying a distinctive prismatic aura that disoriented the person looking at it.

Rubranium.

He was an organic metamorph.

It was an extremely rare ability to change one's composition into another compound or material altogether. I'd encountered metamorphs that could change to pure fire, or rock, or even light—but never Rubranium. He hadn't possessed that ability when we were in the Otherworld.

I unfurled my fingers as he reached up, grasping my wrist. His grip tightened as I attempted to pull away. The result was a stalemate. "Still want to play this game?" His voice echoed, a side effect of his entire body changing on an atomic level. Instead of flesh and blood and bones, he was made of the strongest metal the Otherworld had to offer. Capable of absorbing strength and redirecting—it was impenetrable. Infallible. Without breaking it down to the quantum level, not a single hit would make a dent on him. "I didn't think so."

"Release him." I wasn't sure if the cold-hearted woman at my back was speaking to me or her atman.

Lorcan took it as aimed at him. His pupilless eyes moved, likely looking past me at the white-haired woman approaching. "You don't command me."

"I'm here to make a deal," Bree replied, stepping in between us. Her head was tilted back far enough I could see her eyebrows as she faced him. "That's what you wanted. I'm giving it to you."

Lorcan's grip eased, then his fingers opened. I stepped back, watching the demoness warily. I didn't know what her move was here, but if there was anything I'd learned about Bree—it's that she always had a reason for the things she did.

Lorcan stared down at his atma. The reddish metallic tint fading into alabaster skin.

He reached up, touching a lock of her hair. The breath hissed between his teeth as the skin of his finger singed everywhere it touched.

"You shouldn't have rejected me," Lorcan said quietly. "We've always played our games, but you went too far this time. I've been denied from what's mine for long enough. You will pay for that."

"I'm only yours if you win," Bree responded.

Lorcan's face tightened. "Yield to me, or you'll spend the next few centuries watching the many ways I can break her."

My fists tightened. His death was a need I couldn't stop. A thirst I couldn't quench.

Banging on your chest like an alphahole won't save me.

It wasn't Piper. Not really, but her voice was like a conscience that whispered through my mind. If she were here, that's what she'd tell me.

I know Bree. She only hurt me to save me. We have to trust her.

My breathing was loud in my ears, the sound of my blood roaring made everything except that quiet voice and the two demons' conversation disappear.

"I'll yield on one condition."

My head snapped up. She couldn't be serious. After all of this, she would yield? Knowing what it meant? Knowing how much was riding on this challenge—

"You bring Piper and her children to our duel, unharmed and in good health."

Lorcan stared at her for minutes. His crimson eyes searching for something only he could see beyond the impenetrable expression of Bree Fallon. "You can't make the bargain binding. The magic of our challenge forbids it," he said, settling on a condescending tone.

"I know what the rules are," she said coolly. "If I make a deal, I follow through. I don't need magic to keep my promises."

He considered her for a moment. "No guarantee not to harm her after? To spare her or her unborn children in the future?"

"These are my terms," she said, giving nothing away.

Meanwhile, something in my chest tightened. If she made this bargain, she was all but signing away her life, but I couldn't stop her. I wouldn't. Piper might hate me when she learned what happened, but she'd be alive and here to do so.

"I'll deliver Piper and her children to our duel, unharmed and in as good of health as her pregnancy will permit, in return for your submission." He leaned forward, only a hairsbreadth from the woman who was playing him like a fiddle.

I regretted my earlier rage toward her because this—this sacrifice was something I could never repay.

"Take care of my sister," Bree said, stepping away. "I'll see you in three days at the Underworld." The lock of hair wound around his finger, dropped as she did so, revealing the horrible scarring that touching even just her hair during the wait for their challenge had caused.

"I'll be waiting."

30

PIPER

The one where I was with Ronan. Happy. Attending Sunday family dinners at Nat's place. Stargazing and exploring every mystery this planet had. Raising two tiny dictators, and the hardest thing I had to figure out was how to be a parent. I knew how to fight and kill and enforce peace over New Chicago. But how to be a *good* parent? Not so much.

It was a beautiful world.

It was the one I should have lived in.

Instead, my body was grounded by reality.

The faint drip nagging at my attention, forcing me to stay here—where my body was secured to a chair. Not that I could stand anyway. The fatigue was so strong. The desire to sleep overwhelming.

But I couldn't sleep.

There was something to do. To fight for. The heavier the exhaustion weighed, the more I struggled to remember it.

A door closed. The telltale whir of the room pressurizing made me dizzy. My head swam as I tried and failed to open my eyes.

Voices drifted in and out, carrying small pieces of conversation.

"... had to sedate ... couldn't contain ... induced coma ..."

I tried and failed to hold on to those words. To process them. What they meant. The happier world called to me. Reaching out like tiny hands, begging to be held. Embraced.

I fell into it for a time. Settled into a better place. Where Nathalie was giving me grief over something ... what was it? I tried and tried to focus. To think. Why couldn't I remember? It was all a blur. A fuzzy outline of a real conversation.

I pushed harder, trying to recall what I was forgetting.

"... blood pressure dropping ... severe blood loss ... decreased fetal movement..."

Those voices were new. I'd never heard them before. Why hadn't I heard them?

Why was it dark? Where was Ronan and Nathalie and the twins? Where was Bree and Sasha and—panic kicked in. I tried to open my eyes. It didn't work. I pushed harder. The faint shine of the light from behind my lids was just out of reach. I had to grasp it. To see. To understand. I had to—

"... remarkable healing ... replenishing despite increased severity of symptoms ... patient nearing consciousness ... increasing propofol ..."

Propofol? I'd never heard of it before. I'm sure Nathalie would have been able to tell me what that meant. I searched for her, falling back into the better world. We were in her apartment. She was cooking, and I was cleaning my guns. I asked her about Propofol.

She stared blankly.

I asked again.

Again.

Again.

Why didn't she know? Nathalie knew *everything*. Something wasn't right. I searched for Ronan, and he appeared. One of the kids in each arm. They reached for me, and I took them, staring at the faces I loved so much—

Faces. They had no faces. No clear features. The closer I looked the more they shifted. My skin. Ronan's nose. Blue eyes. Black hair. Darker skin. My lips. Blonde hair. Silver eyes. I dropped them. They screamed.

Their hair turned white.

Eyes red.

Like two tiny versions of Lorcan . . . *Lorcan.*

I repeated his name over and over. With every syllable the world around me broke apart and slipped away into total darkness. It wasn't real. It wasn't right. I had to get back. To find them. To fight—I had to wake up.

I grunted, trying to push to the surface again.

Monitors started beeping like crazy. The door opened and closed. Opened and closed.

The pressure flip-flopped back and forth, making my head swim and my stomach turn. I tried to fight through it. To hold onto my tenuous grasp of will. To resist.

" . . . she's pushing back . . . power fluctuation . . . not safe . . ."

That's it, a familiar voice whispered through my mind. *Try just a little harder.*

I reached for that voice. Flinging everything in me, every scrap of strength, every bit of magic. Glass shattered. That incessant beeping went silent. Grunts and shouts followed.

Then nothing.

Blissful silence.

My eyes cracked open—

"PIPER!" the voice screamed. It rumbled. It howled. A sound of anguish and rage. Loss and desperation. I reached for it and the bridge appeared.

Mist surrounded me, but it was clearing with every second.

"Who's there?" I mumbled. The words came out scratchy. A rasped question that couldn't have been louder than a whisper.

The mist cleared instantly.

Ronan appeared. His eyes blazed with fury and fire. Dark, terrible fire. His brands pulsed, the lines shifting and turning and forming, only to reform moments later. I'd never seen brands do that before.

Despair hit me.

"This isn't real," I croaked.

Hands touched me. Rough, magnificent hands. They grabbed my shoulders and shook me so hard my teeth rattled. *"Where are you?"*

I frowned. "Right here."

Alarm went through him, I felt it in me. The bond stretching thin. Mist pouring down. I had to find him. The real him. I had to find the real world—

"You need to think, Piper. Where are you? What do you see? Give me something. Anything—"

My eyes snapped open. I gasped, a choked inhale of breath.

31

NATHALIE

His fist went through brick.

Early morning light spilled into the apartment. Bits of clay and drywall and dust falling to the floor. He didn't care. I wasn't even sure he noticed. It was the third hole he'd put in their living room today.

"She was there," he said hoarsely. "I saw her. She spoke to me."

"Where?" Bree demanded, striding down the hall from the temporary room where she'd been holed up the last two days. I lifted my head from the world map I'd been scrying over. I'd tried blood and hair to find her. I used Ronan's magic. Bree's as well, though she didn't know it. Nothing had worked. The pendulum kept swinging. The blood never moved. Wherever the Illuminati was keeping her for Lorcan, their methods of hiding her were alarmingly good.

That Ronan somehow made contact spoke to their bond.

No other method had worked.

"I . . . don't know." His head fell forward, hidden in

shadow. I closed my eyes, trying to hold on to hope that we'd find her. That Lorcan would hold true to his bargain.

Bree seemed to think he would, but I had doubts.

That's why I continued searching. Hour after hour. For nearly three days.

Maybe he'd come through and she'd be unharmed. But I wasn't betting on it.

"She didn't tell you?" Bree asked, her voice rising. Green magic swirled through the apartment, a tempest waiting to be unleashed.

"She didn't know," he replied. I recognized that tone. That voice.

This wasn't Ronan, my sort-of friend, or even the demon who'd made a bargain with me those many months ago in return for keeping an eye on Piper. This was the Harvester. The threat of losing his mate had brought him right to the edge.

I couldn't let myself think about what would happen if he went over it.

The devastation that would occur. The billions of people who would die.

It was the reason I stepped in when Bree went to make a comment that would push him further. I'd noticed that when her own worries were riled, she went on the attack. Flinging hurtful words and venomous accusations left and right. I didn't believe he'd kill her now. Not after the deal she'd made with Lorcan. That didn't mean I was going to test it.

"Have you heard from your contact?"

The look she gave me threatened violence. "She knows the Illuminati have her, but not where. As best she can tell, Piper isn't in New Chicago."

I'd suspected as much. A demon of her power? They'd

want her as far from here as possible to be able to stand a chance of covering her signature. That they'd somehow succeeded in it . . . I clenched one hand in a fist, my nails biting into my palm.

I thought I felt hopeless when I couldn't take on Lorcan.

After three days of doing the one thing I should be able to . . .emotion clogged my throat, threatening to make me cry. I swallowed it down, refusing to show that here. Not when Bree was looking for anywhere to put her own feelings—in the form of a blade to the head.

"I should have killed him." Ronan's voice was lethally quiet, but also distant. "In the Otherworld when I saw his greed. His ambition and cruelty."

Under different circumstances I would have reminded him that focusing on what he should have done wasn't helpful. It wouldn't do him any favors.

"Yeah," Bree said. "You should have."

My mouth fell open as she walked back down the hall. Her door slammed shut, rattling the frame. I couldn't believe she'd actually said that.

Ronan didn't seem to share my shock, then again, I wasn't sure he was fully paying attention. His mind was quite literally elsewhere as he tried to search the planet for Piper.

"You made contact," I said, thinking on how to phrase my question. "She didn't know where she was, but was she okay? Did she seem like Piper?"

"You shouldn't ask that," another voice said from the couch. Lucifer sat there with his arm across the back of it. White hair falling into his eyes. His pure predatory gaze was set on me. I'd ignored him for three days and he wasn't thrilled about it. But this wasn't about him.

I shot him a look for saying it, despite the fact I was thinking it in the back of my mind.

It was the sort of question you were scared to ask. You wanted to know the answer if it was good, but if it wasn't . . .

I had to know. Either way it would eat at me until I asked.

Ronan didn't respond for so long I wondered if he heard me, or if he was too far steeped in his magic while searching for Piper that what I said didn't reach him.

"She said, *this isn't real.*"

I jerked, my attention swinging back to the chaos demon. "Where she is, or you?"

"I don't know," he said. Shadows clung to his form, shielding parts of his body. "But if I had to guess, I'd say she meant me. That she didn't think I was real."

"What does that mean?" I asked before I could stop myself.

Ronan hesitated before repeating, "I don't know."

Broken. Defeated. I'd never heard such a thing come from this man.

I swallowed hard, because despite his words, we both knew. If she couldn't tell what was real and what wasn't . . .

My eyes watered again, and this time I couldn't push it down.

"I told you, you shouldn't have asked," Lucifer said quietly. I blocked him out as I picked up the vial of Piper's blood and started scrying again.

It may have been useless, but I wouldn't give up on her.

Piper always found a way.

I just hoped it wasn't too late when she did.

32

PIPER

"Let's take a walk."

The man at the door motioned beyond it, to a hallway where I couldn't see the end. I opened my mouth, then closed it, repeating the action a few times before I was able to speak. "What?"

His mouth quirked up. Not exactly a kind smile, but not cruel either. He was dressed in a nice sweater and slacks. A pendant hung from a metal chain around his neck, a stained-glass bottle with dark liquid that was likely blood. His pale skin was even starker than the sterile lights, almost sickly so. He had dark hair and wore his beard long. I couldn't see any brands peeking out from his clothes, nothing on his neck or wrists, but I'd long since learned that didn't mean anything. Not where magic was concerned.

I regained my senses quickly and reached for the light dimension, drawing it to me. It oscillated back and forth, flashing between where I was and where I wanted to be. In seconds, it stopped, and I was still here. In this metal chair surrounded by bodies and fractured glass.

Either he'd somehow blocked my magic, or I truly was that weak.

Swallowing down the lump in my throat, I reached for the IV on my wrist. The tape ripping off barely registered next to the dribbles of blood that followed the needle exiting me. I clapped a hand over it and the flow staunched, then stopped. When I lifted my thumb, blood-smeared skin was all that remained. Which meant my magic still worked.

I lifted my head, reassessing the man in front of me. "Who are you?"

He inclined his head. "Take a walk with me and I'll tell you."

I blew out a tight breath and lifted one foot. The bindings on my body were ripped open. From what? I didn't know. I could only assume it came from me, but what exactly happened here was knowledge I didn't have.

I stepped down off the chair. My head swam, but I kept a firm grip on the arm of the chair until it stopped. When the world was no longer wobbling, I took my other foot down and turned to the stranger.

He motioned again for me to go first, and I didn't question it this time. I needed to find a way out of here as quickly as possible, and he was the best way to do it.

When I reached the hallway, I didn't waste any time, reaching for the light realm once more. Again, it warbled in and out. Never fully transitioning from one place to another. I let out a strangled grunt of frustration.

I hadn't experienced issues with my magic ever since Bree and Ronan started training me. I'd forgotten how much of a pain in the ass it could be.

"I'd heard rumors about your ability to access another realm. A world within a world. I didn't believe them until now."

He watched me with curious eyes, but they weren't harmless. A child looked at the moon and saw dreams and stars. A scientist looked at their experiment and asked themselves what other variables they could test. This man looked at me like the latter, and it was every bit as unsettling as the fact I couldn't leave.

"You said you'd tell me who you are."

"So I did." He nodded and started walking. I followed, ignoring the twinge in my stomach as one of the twins kicked in protest. "My name is Grigori. You might know me as Rasputin."

I lifted both eyebrows, assessing him more closely. My knowledge of history was pretty good. My dad was a high school teacher before the Magic Wars, but we didn't exactly focus on Russia. Let alone men that were thought to be charlatans. "Where are we?" I doubted he would answer, but it was worth a shot if he felt like talking. The more I knew, the better.

"Nowhere," he replied. "But also everywhere. It's a fascinating thing."

I squinted my eyes at him. "I don't understand."

"You will," he answered. "All in good time, my dear."

My hairs stood on edge at the term of endearment. It wasn't spoken with condescension, which made it more concerning. I was beginning to think Rasputin might be mad.

"What are you?" I asked. Every species had their issues. He was white enough to be a ghoul, but there was a heartbeat. Which also eliminated vampire. While Grigori had wrinkles, it wasn't the kind you would see on someone over a hundred years old. He was mid-forties at most, in appearance at least. Which implied someone changed. Shifter perhaps? He didn't give off that aura, but little else made sense.

"A warlock."

My pace slowed. That was impossible.

They didn't live that long. They were the one and only species that didn't gain immortality with the change. With the exception of Morgan Le Fay, no witch had ever found a way. Though they'd certainly tried.

Then there was the other snag. The Illuminati were a human rebel organization. Why would they allow a warlock into their ranks? One they trusted enough to move a prisoner without any bindings or guards. Let alone a demon? It made no sense.

I wasn't sure which was more troubling at the moment.

"You look awfully young for a man that supposedly died a hundred years ago." Give or take a few.

He didn't slow his pace, lips still curled. "And you're very alive for a woman that should have died five times over the last three days for how much blood we took."

I'd ask why, but I already knew. I'm a demon. Power was in my blood. They were trying to siphon it. For what? That was the real question.

"Why did you let me out if you were trying to kill me?"

"Not kill," he corrected. "Test. I had to be certain." Grigori didn't turn as he added, "You let yourself out. I simply decided to welcome you."

I blinked. This hallway seemed never ending, and I was becoming more tired by the minute. "How long was I asleep?"

"Drug-induced coma," he said as we came to a stop outside an unmarked door. "You were fighting too much. We put you under so that we could better test what you are.

If you're indeed the very thing I've been looking for." He smiled wider.

"A demon?" I asked. Why did my voice falter? Hesitate?

He chuckled. "Among other things. If you were simply a demon, I would have let them continue draining your blood until you eventually ran dry."

"Isn't that what you did?" I replied.

"Did I? Last I checked, you're alive."

An unspoken *for now* hung in the air.

Grigori reached for the doorknob. I wasn't sure what to expect. He wasn't exactly leading me around in chains. Would there be more torture on the other side? A different kind of test? Another experiment? My mind spun out of control, trying to ready itself for the unexpected.

In reality, there was no way to prepare myself for what came next.

Not for what was on the other side.

The door swung open.

I stared and stared. "What is that?" I said softly.

Grigori stepped forward and turned to face me. For the first time since we'd started talking, I saw something maniacal behind his eyes. An evil that was shrouded by a pleasant facade.

"This," he motioned to the gaping void beside him, "is the reason you're here."

I looked around, but there was nothing else in the room besides a small nightstand, an athame, and the portal.

They were rare, but having seen them before, I had no doubts about what stood before me. Large and looming, it seemed to emit a cold, terrible energy that had me backing away.

"I thought the Illuminati wanted to end magic. Yet

you're working with Lorcan to open a portal." My head shook, and I reached for my guns on instinct.

"Your perception of them is what they want you to see," Rasputin said with a wave of his hand. "If the world truly knew who they were and what they did, well, it would be so much harder to strategize. So much harder to put the pieces in the right place. The human rebels provide excellent intel, and with such limited life spans, they don't possess the ability to learn any better. So long as they believe that they're fighting for the end of magic, they'll do what they're told. It gives them somewhere to put their hate and aggression, all the while providing a common enemy for supernaturals. With that as their focus, no one was looking for the *real* rulers of this realm, or thinking about who filled the gaps in power, or whispered in presidents' and monarchs' and emperors' ears. It's rather clever, don't you think?"

My stomach turned, but Grigori Rasputin continued. "As for Lorcan, he was a means to an end. Chaos demons are problematic at best. Too tricky to keep control of for long. I used him to gain access to you and your sister, but in the end, he delivered you right to me. For beings so ancient, you'd think they wouldn't let arrogance cloud their judgment."

Yellow. His teeth were yellow like rotten squash. For some reason, out of all the absurd things I could focus on, that was it. The thing that grounded me enough to say, "You keep saying them. Are you not the Illuminati?"

Annoyance surfaced for the first time. "No . . ." he said. "Only the strongest of witches and warlocks make it to the council. Figuring out the key to immortality wasn't enough for them. They need a show of power. Of strength." He looked away, the skin around his eyes tight with tension. "New Chicago was my test."

My eyebrows rose. "This," I waved my hand, motioning to the room around me. "Is all part of your fucking application to get into a secret society of assholes?" I probably should have bit back that response given the flash of anger that crossed his face.

"They wouldn't have me," he snapped. "Despite the work I've done there, they deemed me 'unsuitable' for the council."

"So you're pissed at them and want revenge. All right, what does that have to do with me? You've already got a portal. I don't see what I could possibly give you that my blood hasn't already."

Rasputin twisted his hand and an invisible push shoved me forward into the room. The door slammed shut behind me. Before I could stumble or fall, bony fingers grasped my shoulders, keeping me up.

"Your blood is only one component, a rather small one in the grand scheme. Still useful for this first part, but not critical. The real thing that makes you special is something no one can take away." He turned away, toward the small end table, and went to pick up the athame. "It's the reason I had to test you. To make sure. Your kind are incredibly rare. To find two that were strong enough to become demons from the same family . . ." He let out a low whistle. "I wanted Bree, but Lorcan made obtaining her more difficult. Your pregnancy was an added bonus that was worth the agents I lost. Should you survive this and give birth, there are great odds your children will also inherit your genes. They will be valuable assets and well treated."

My skin prickled. Something other than bile rose in my throat.

Anger.

What was it with men thinking they had any sort of claim over me? Over my kids? Disgusting, vile men.

Power. It's what they wanted.

People say that power corrupts, but I didn't believe that anymore.

There was already something evil in them. A seed of contempt that burrowed in their hearts and grew with every terrible act in their pursuit of power.

And for this power that I held at my fingertips . . . they'd do anything.

No matter how despicable. How inhumane. Not for the pursuit of something better, but for the strength to rule over others and impose their own dominion.

My fingertips sparked as my thoughts turned. I didn't completely understand what I was reaching for. Only that I did.

Rasputin tsked, not seeming to understand the danger he'd put himself in. I may not be able to call on the light realm—but I was far from weak.

"We can do this the easy way or the hard way, my dear. I'd rather be allies. Friends, even. We're going to do incredible things, after all. I don't mind sharing the glory—I'm not as high and mighty as those assholes, as you called them."

I reached for him. Not sure if I was going to crush or rip or tear. All I knew was that he needed to break. To crumble.

My feet moved faster than my mind, crossing the distance between us with ease.

Grigori sighed. "Always so resistant."

My hands stopped midair. My breath lodged in my chest.

He tapped the tiny pendant bottle on his chest. "Lorcan's blood to bind. My blood to control. Your blood to seal the deal." Rasputin handed me the athame, and to my own horror, I took it. He smiled, though it was filled with false pity. "If it's any consolation, you won't be able to stop yourself."

"From?" I ground out.

He motioned to the portal. "Finishing the infinite corridor." Everything in me hardened. My muscles locked up. My chest clenched tight. What he was talking about, it couldn't be done. To create a portal was hard enough, but a corridor?

Witches had tried and failed. Lucifer's death was the price.

"I can see that you're dubious. Morgan tried this only months ago, but her desire to see Lucifer suffer clouded her judgment. She hurried the process. You see, to build a corridor, you have to build it piece by piece. Thousands of supernaturals have gone into this one, their magic fueling it just a little bit further each time. With yours, we'll finally reach the end."

I shook my head, something he must have allowed me to do since I was still holding the athame despite everything in me wanting to stab him with it instead.

"There are easier ways to get to Hell. If you're so all-knowing—you know that much."

He seemed delighted that I pointed that out. "Except I don't simply want to go to Hell. I want to steal the Source, and then conquer every world between ours and theirs. I'm going to show the Illuminati where they can shove their opinions about who is 'unsuitable' to rule."

I thought it was bad when Lucifer took over New Chicago. Then when Morgan Le Fay and the black witches wanted to go to Hell, I'd felt a new kind of terror. The more we knew, the more dangerous a place the world was becoming. When Lorcan came here with intentions to enslave all humanity, I'd thought surely it couldn't get any worse than that.

It seems the universe had to prove me wrong.

Whoever the Illuminati were, they'd been the real threat, building over time.

The true danger, hidden behind a veil we didn't see through.

The worst part was that Rasputin wasn't even one of them.

He was just a madman. A warlock corrupted by his own magic until he'd well and truly lost his mind. What other reason could someone have for thinking this was the response to being rejected?

I bit the inside of my cheek, trying to find a way out of my predicament, but without the light realm to transport myself, and him controlling my body, there were few options. My smartass comments wouldn't do anything but rile him further. This was one of those times I could really have used Nat. She had a way with people. Specifically, she had a way of manipulating them.

All I had were my words and my mind.

My dad used to say that knowledge was power.

But this was unknown territory, and I had neither.

"You say that I can get you the rest of the way, but what happens then? You're a witch and I'm a demon. We can't steal the Source—and the creatures that will be there to greet us are far more powerful than either of us. This is a suicide mission."

Grigori shook his head. "If you were only a demon, yes.

It would be. But you, Piper, my dear . . . you're so much more. You're a conduit—and this is your destiny."

Against my own will, I cut my palm with the athame and offered my blood, my magic, *myself*, to the portal.

It devoured me.

33

BREE

LIQUID METAL PAINTED MY BODY.

It adorned the braids in my hair. It covered my hands in thin gloves that ended in pointed claws. It coated my eyelashes like mercury mascara. It molded around my legs, waist, and chest, ending at my neck. Goosebumps dotted my bare arms.

The late afternoon sun was low in the sky.

Dusk was approaching as my internal timer counted down to our final minutes.

The chaos witch approached from the sidelines where she, Ronan, and the shifter-succubus with an attitude stood; my temporary allies as long as I was protecting Piper.

Her footsteps were quiet, but every step squeaked against the glass ground of the Underworld.

Once it had been an arena. A battleground where super-naturals fought for the entertainment of others.

Now only ruins remained.

Which made it the ideal place, should Lorcan try something.

She breathed heavily compared to the other immortals

around us. Her chest heaving with emotions she couldn't shove down so easily. Cheeks pink and eyes sad, she stopped next to me.

"I just wanted to say thank you."

"No need." I pivoted to walk away, and she grabbed my arm.

"Yes, there is. Piper isn't here to say it, and she probably won't when she realizes what you've done—but *thank you* for saving her." She spoke in earnest, her eyes revealing too much. I knew a steel core lay within this girl, but her heart was still soft. Kind. She wasn't broken like the rest of us or jaded by time like Ronan. I was happy Piper had someone like her, however fleeting their friendship would be when her mortal body failed her.

"It wasn't a choice for me."

She quirked her brows, and a pucker formed between them. "Of course it was."

I shook my head. "No, it really wasn't. She may not be my bondmate or twin . . . she's something deeper than even that. I couldn't let her die. I won't risk it."

Nathalie tilted her head. "It's not because she's your sister?" The witch was dubious. I smiled wryly without looking at her.

"No."

"You won't tell me?" she pressed. "When Piper asks me why you did it, and feels guilty for centuries—because let's be real, she will—you won't give me a better answer to why? For her?"

I looked up at the sky. There were decent odds that I'd overplayed my hand, and this would be the last sunset I'd see. It wasn't as brilliant as it was in the Otherworld. The colors more limited. The hues almost pastel by comparison.

But it was home.

"She's my humanity."

For as much as she'd like to believe herself someone who existed in the gray—she didn't know what that meant. Not truly. She fought for what was right and protected people even when she didn't have to. She was going to fix this world, whether she knew it or not.

My home hinged on my sister's very existence.

Her death and her happiness both hinged on mine.

It was an easier choice than they made it out to be.

Lorcan would never be mine the same way Ronan was hers. We'd forever be possessions to each other and nothing more. An immortal life as someone's possession, with him obsessed with the total destruction of the last inkling of light I had in me . . . that wasn't living.

Unlike Piper, I wouldn't fight for better days.

I'd succumb.

Which left me with one option.

Win or die.

The scent on the wind shifted. A hint of something familiar. Something piercing. I turned toward Lorcan and lifted my head, a knowing smile gracing my lips.

He'd astral projected and was waiting to make a reveal.

And they thought I was dramatic.

"Where is she?" I demanded upon seeing him empty-handed.

He smiled, and I read its meaning. I knew him like I knew the back of my hand. He was in a *mood*.

"Hidden. Safe. I decided there was no reason for Ronan to behave if I brought her. I prefer the challenge anyhow. You're so much more fun when motivated." His tongue flicked out to lick his top lip in a salacious way.

Lorcan wanted to play with me until I broke, then force the pieces back together so he could do it again.

Little did he know, this game ended one way or another tonight.

Right now.

I hummed. "Why haven't you challenged Ronan if you're so concerned about him 'behaving'?" I openly questioned him in a way I rarely did before. His crimson eyes flashed with malicious intent. "I can see every reason for him to not challenge you, not when he can just strip your power at any point. But to leave yourself so vulnerable?" I tsked, using irreverent indifference as my mask. "You're either arrogant or stupid." Lorcan could handle my rage. He could twist my jealousy. But he'd never had to deal with this side of me, the side he so loved to use against those that spoke out against him.

"Every word," he said quietly, his face bathed in terrible shadows as the sun slipped below the horizon, "every fucking insult—will be another whipping for you."

My skin pebbled, but not out of fear. The messed-up part of me liked it. The pain and punishment. It meant somewhere deep down in that twisted heart of his—he cared. Lorcan killed what he didn't care about. He only tortured when it was personal.

In Hell, I'd been his favorite subject. His muse.

He was my painter. My master and disciple in one.

Lorcan lived to dominate me as much as he craved my attention. Jealous didn't even begin to describe our toxic relationship.

"Don't threaten me with a good time." I winked at the second our six hundred and sixty-six hours ran out.

He was on me the moment that our magic released its binds.

Pupils dilated. Fangs extended. He grabbed me by the

throat and pulled me to him. "You always did like to mouth off when you wanted it harder."

He towered over me, face only inches from my own.

I leaned up. Our lips met in a clash of teeth. From the sidelines, a growled, *"what the fuck,"* from Sasha made me smirk. Lorcan's grip closed painfully around my throat. His body pressed into my own.

I pulled back a fraction, only to bite his bottom lip.

Before he could pull away, I sucked on it, my chest caving in as raw hunger ran through me—mouth to chest to cunt.

This was the shakiest part of my plan. The most difficult to accomplish.

I had to withstand the pull the blood oath demanded when my body very much wanted to give in.

The grip on my neck loosened as his other hand came around to grab my ass. I released his lip and whispered in his ear, "Maybe you just hit like a bitch."

He didn't, but nothing riled him more than being told he was weak.

Lorcan snarled as I shoved against his chest, leaving metallic handprints against his shirt that dissolved beneath it.

He roared in outrage, like a dragon that was pissed off about stolen treasure. It was an apt description for what was happening here. I stepped into the astral realm, knowing he could see me but not touch.

Time. All I had to do was buy it.

Lorcan's eyes blazed with fury as he recovered his footing. His lids turned thin as slits. "Why are you dragging this out, *ashefleri?*" I kept the grimace off my face at his condescending term of endearment. Little monster. No different from calling me a kitten with claws. Ultimately harmless, even when hissing mad. He used it to get under my skin, knowing I hated it. "You know you can't win, and now that you've taken my blood, the mating process begins. When I catch you, I plan to drink my fill and fuck you while that faery-boy watches."

I lifted my eyebrows. Faery-boy. *He couldn't mean . . .*

I'd been careful. Never expressed interest. Never interacted too long or let my gaze stray. Not during the month that he and I played cat and mouse. Not when I ran into him on 'accident', pretending to feign disinterest and not notice the way he looked at me. How could he possibly know about him?

Lorcan grinned wickedly. "Did you really think I wouldn't be able to tell?"

I scoffed, rolling my eyes. "What are you going on about?"

His smile sharpened, seeing through my mask. "He's here now, you know?" I didn't let my gaze waver. Not once. "Your seven o'clock. The poor bastard couldn't stay away from the demoness he found so *fascinating*." Lorcan laughed. "I will admit, my ego was hurt that you showed any interest in a weaker male like him. I'll have to remind you that you're *my* atma. Come up with something innovative for this transgression."

My metal claws sharpened. I smiled cruelly back at him, at ease that the man he spoke of couldn't hear me. Not in the astral realm. From their perspective, this was a one-way conversation.

"A real atman would have claimed me years ago," I replied. "It's a transgression for me to seek pleasure from another when you were too weak a male to hold my attention."

My words landed true. Lorcan cracked.

He stepped into the astral realm but disappeared instantly.

I turned, dread filling me when I knew what I'd see.

Anders leaned against a blackened pillar.

His dark brown hair pulled back in a low ponytail. Sharp blue eyes focused on the spot I'd disappeared. I could have sworn he saw, stared straight into the unseen dimension at my soul.

I'd never fucked him. Not like I led Lorcan to believe, but we had touched . . . kissed. The day I was supposed to return to Hell, I'd gone to his apartment, drunk and spiteful. I'd goaded him by telling him that I always knew he was there. He was only able to follow my trail because I let him. When he would pretend to be a stranger at the same coffee shop or getting groceries from the mini-mart on the corner—I always knew.

I told him he was a sad, pathetic man who stalked me because he had nothing better to do. That he was Ronan's bitch because he was too chicken shit to rise above. That he'd lost his wife and son because he was weak.

I was mean. I was vile. I was cruel.

Angry that I was leaving. That I was bound to another. Shackled to a man that didn't give a fuck about *me*. Not in the ways that mattered.

I wouldn't call it love. I didn't know him. I'd barely spoken to him before that night. But we'd been playing a game back and forth, studying each other silently. Reading between the lines.

I said quite possibly the worse things I ever could to him, and he pinned me to a fucking wall, then *devoured* me.

Until that moment, every fuck, every kiss, every ounce of sexual pleasure had been with Lorcan. I'd never realized how much of it the bond created. How much our magic forced it. Not until that kiss.

It changed everything for me because he never said a word.

He just kissed me like I meant something—like I was more than an object, more than a possession—and then walked away.

Anders looked at me that night the same way he looked at me now.

As if his eyes were telling me to make a different choice.

To not bow to fate.

"Here's how this will go, Bree. You're going to step out of the astral realm and get on your knees. You will *beg* me to accept you despite this." The S hissed between his lips as he hovered beside Anders, who had no idea the devil that was waiting to end him stood by his side. "*Beg*. Do you hear me? Because if you don't," he paused, squinting his eyes to look around. He pressed a hand to his head before turning his glare on me. "What are you doing?"

Hope unfurled in my chest.

So close. He was so close.

"I don't know what you mean," I said mockingly innocent.

He frowned, doing a double take of my body. "Where did your gloves go?" Lorcan asked, as the truth started to dawn on him. "And your pants? They were longer—" At that exact moment, he turned corporeal.

I crossed the hundred yards to the ruin just as Lorcan turned on Anders. He was already siphoning magic off of him when I slammed my body into his—sending us both flying off a thirty-foot drop.

Lorcan landed first with a grunt, his back cracking the

glass beneath him. I didn't even have time to brace myself for the impact as my knees slammed into the already fissured surface, sending glass shards flying all around us. I locked my hands around his neck, silver crawling down my skin onto his.

It was now or never. This would either be enough, or it wouldn't.

Lorcan's eyes flared for a brief second.

"You actually"—he struggled with words—"p-plan to kill me. You th-think you c-can."

"I know I can." The silver liquid seeped into his bloodstream, poisoning him with every breath. "You always thought that my abilities mirrored yours because we're mates. You were so arrogant in assuming that because the Source branded you that I would always be under your thumb." I squeezed tighter, my rage growing with every second. Every memory. "You never stopped to question how a human gained the power of a demon. How I stole magic from all of the Otherworld, including *you*."

Lorcan's face was contorted from pain and violence. He managed to grab hold of my wrists. The reality that he was going to lose finally settling in.

"I only gained the ability to astral project when I came into contact with you."

He wouldn't have killed me. Not if he had any other way.

But that's where we were different. Some might say I was crueler.

I wouldn't just choose myself at the end. I chose myself *always*.

"You're an incredible telepath, and you gave me incredible shields. Ones that will stand up to anything—even you. That's why you never saw this coming."

He reached for his magic then and tried to pull from me. To steal my power. To harvest me.

"You can turn to Rubranium, and I gained the power to control metal—like the kind poisoning you now." I let the last of it on me fall from my hair and form spikes that nailed him to the ground. Four to the chest, surrounding his heart. "Magic is in the blood, and right now, yours is filled with mercury. Little known fact—too much won't kill you, but it'll cut you off from your magic."

If not for my ability to control it, he would have turned to Rubranium right there and obliterated me. But I was his complement. Made from his own magic. Created to be part of him in every way.

Lorcan started to tremble. To shake.

He was one of the strongest demons in existence, and I'd reduced him to this. The sense of power it gave me over him was incredibly seductive. Tantalizing. I wanted more. I wanted all of it.

Straddling him in nothing but shorts and an old T-shirt now that every bit of metal was stripped from me, I leaned in close, inhaling the scent of his blood like it was a fine wine for tasting.

"What"—his teeth chattered—"are"—his body convulsed—"you?"

My soul cried out as I breathed it in and began to pull.

"Human," I groaned. "Completely and utterly human. A sponge for magic. A *conduit.*"

It was true. Every word.

Just as nulls had come out of our world, conduits came too. While their DNA rejected magic in all forms, we were the opposite. People whose body took from anyone it came into contact with once the circumstances were right.

My trigger was rage.

The more I riled the violence in him, the more I could take. The angrier I became, the easier it was to pull. Piper survived Aeshma because she was pissed off that she'd been deceived and was going to die for it. I survived Hell because every awful, horrible thing that happened to me made me that much stronger.

Strong enough to become a demon.

Deadly enough to kill one.

Wicked enough to destroy my own soul.

34

PIPER

Falling.

Flying.

I wasn't sure which it was as stars and galaxies wrapped around me.

Arms flung wide, I reached for something that wasn't there. Grasping at anything that might anchor me. Droplets of blood drifted, somehow suspended in time. Pain ripped through me like a knife tearing through my chest. It was as if hands had reached inside and pulled back my skin. Slowly, torturously, they peeled my muscles, tendons, and ligaments. They snapped the bone cage that protected my immortal heart.

Thunder.

That's what it sounded like when they ripped it from my chest.

Booming claps of raw power that seemed to ache with every beat. Cavernous roaring that never ended as it echoed above and below.

Yet the pain didn't stop.

Lightning arced through me as every last drop of magic

I held was wrenched from my body. Like a plug pulled from a drain, it ran freely until there was nothing left.

Only silence.

Never-ending. All consuming.

Or maybe it was the antithesis of silence. When the thunder was so deafening and raucous that it blended together endlessly in a suspended note.

I wasn't sure which.

Only that I was barren. Empty. *Human.*

It took me hitting the ground to realize that the reticence was inside me.

My head smacked into something hard. I rolled to the side and groaned. Eyes closed tight, I strained to inhale enough air. My breaths came short and quick as my lungs attempted to expand but didn't have room. Bright light made my lids glow orange where before there had been only darkness. I flinched away from it as nausea roiled through me. Every muscle and bone in my body felt weak. Limp.

I couldn't explain it, but I knew without a doubt my magic was gone.

Not gone. Stolen.

"You did it." The awe in his voice was unmistakable. The glee of mania as he realized all his illusions of grandeur were possible. "You finished the corridor, just as I knew you could."

I swallowed hard, then found the will to open my eyes.

Hell was blinding.

Bree had told me it was like nothing on Earth. That there were colors that didn't exist. The sky wasn't blue, but purple. Periwinkle. Three suns poised in it. One on the horizon where there seemed to be mountains with snow-capped peaks, one directly above, and the third—

I froze with my cheek pressed into the dirt where I was laying. Across reddish brown dirt and a sea of pebbles was what I could only guess to be the Source.

I'd thought it was a sun from how bright it shone. Lights of every color imaginable twisted and twined, dancing in the open air around a literal wall of power.

I rolled onto my back, following iridescent light to the sky. It stopped, but I couldn't tell where. Distance was relative from the viewpoint of the ground.

A part of me wanted to lay there and never get up. To stop fighting. To let the exhaustion take me.

I'd fought for a long time. Tooth and nail; bullet and claw. I'd never been given a damn thing. I'd earned or stole every scrap. Now here I was, in the very place I never wanted to step foot in—magicless, heavily pregnant, drained of energy and blood.

Giving up would be easy. So fucking easy.

I couldn't reach Ronan. The odds of making it out of this were slim to none, and even if I could—I'd never find my way back. There was no reason for me to keep going . . . and yet, I couldn't stop. I couldn't give up. Everything in me screamed in pain and *fury*.

For my magic. For my home. For my family.

This son of a bitch pulled me out of my world because he wanted to throw a goddamn temper tantrum. He didn't get into some secret club and lost his mind over it.

And now, he wanted me to steal the source of all magic.

I pushed up on my elbows, biting back the groan as I reached for the fallen athame.

Grigori Rasputin stood on the edge of the chasm where we'd landed, facing the wall of pure magic. I didn't need to see his face to know that greed was written all over it. My hands bit into the rough terrain as I forced myself into a sitting position.

Every inch I moved was like fire in my veins, and not the kind I wanted.

It burned to lift a finger. To twitch. To shift. Let alone force myself to stand.

But I did. Bit by bit, I pulled myself up and got to my feet.

Swaying in the gentle breeze, I lifted my chin, taking in the sheer size of the Source. The ground dropped off right at the edge, but it was impossible to tell how far down it went. The edge of it alone had to be miles long.

I looked back.

The portal suspended midair. Ready. Waiting.

Beyond the corridor, a single sprawling estate sat on the edge of a forest, like something out of a fairytale. It wasn't a cottage by any means, but neither was it a castle. Some sort of pink-veined white stone made a large house with pillars and filigree. Smaller buildings in the same matching stone sat roughly around it. The windows were large and covered in a thin film that changed color the longer I looked at it, while the doors seemed to give off a metallic shimmer that I could only guess to be a deep, rustic red metal. It wasn't like anything I'd ever seen before. I really hoped there weren't demons inside. My grip tightened on the handle, not that a small blade would do much good. It was laughable, but it was all I had.

"Come," the mad scientist commanded.

My feet moved on their own accord. Gravel crunched beneath my soles as I approached the edge of the ravine. The Source simultaneously seemed to be pulling me closer and pushing me away. The intensity of the contradiction increased with every step.

I grit my teeth against the heat bearing down on me the closer I got.

"Look at it—"

"Oh, I'm looking, all right."

He turned his cheek, and it was hard to read his expression, but I sensed displeasure. "You need to embrace your destiny."

I let out a single, sharp laugh. "This isn't destiny. It's madness." I pointed toward the chasm with the athame. "You're messing with forces you don't understand, and it's not only going to kill us, but everyone else too."

"Every great mind in history was called mad at least once," he replied, eyes only on the abstract force he wished to control. "It's simply another word for visionary."

I shook my head, not even arguing. He was too far gone. I needed to find a way to break that pendant and get the hell out of here, pun intended.

Nathalie would be so proud. I bit the inside of my cheek, tasting blood.

Think, damnit. You spent two decades learning about magic. There has to be something that can get you out of this.

But the harder I tried to reach for it, the more any sort of solution evaded me. The exhaustion weighed too heavy on my mind, making it foggy. Disoriented. Whatever the answer might have been, it was just out of grasp.

Footsteps behind us made me freeze. I turned my head toward the estate.

"We've got company."

"Ignore them."

The glare I gave him would have lit him on fire if I had my magic. For once, I missed the smell of burning flesh. It would be a welcome stench knowing I took out one more power-hungry asshole on the way to my own death.

"They're demons—"

"Ignore them," he repeated, voice hard. "Reach for the Source. Embrace your power—"

"I have *no power*," I snapped. "You *stole* it to create a corridor that never should have been created."

"You're a conduit," he said, in a patronizingly patient tone. "All you need to do is seek out the magic and take it. *Now reach for the Source.*"

My heart hammered as I waited for my body to move against my will.

The footsteps drew closer. Voices were shouting.

The skies turned volatile.

But my hand didn't move.

Our eyes locked the moment he realized that his spell was no longer working. I didn't spend time questioning why or how as I stepped around his foot, hooking it with my own then grabbed the collar of his sweater. I pulled on the thick material as I swept my foot outward.

My strength wasn't what it had been, but he went down all the same.

Rasputin's knees hit the dirt. He let out an oomph as I twisted, pressing the athame to his jugular.

As much as I wanted to just kill him and be done with it, the two demons between me and the portal home were now a problem.

"Who are you?" a female called out. Her brands glowed white against her dark pink skin. That didn't bode well.

"Just passing through," I called. She said something to the man beside her that I didn't understand. Then again, how she knew to speak English was beguiling. I tried not to focus on that as I attempted to piece together what they were saying. It was definitely *not* in English. I probably looked worse for wear with blood all over me, a bulging stomach, and dirt smeared into my skin. If my understanding of Hell was to be believed, demons were all about dominating each other through force. I wasn't going to stick around and let that happen to me. "If you let me go back through that portal, I'll give you this asshole." I flicked my chin toward Rasputin, who looked about ready to curse me if not for the blade at his throat. "He's not a demon, but I bet it would be fun to watch him in the pit."

The couple paused in their conversation and turned to me.

"You know of the pit?" the male asked. He had to be over eight feet tall with blue skin and pink eyes that narrowed in distrust. I swallowed hard.

"Yeah, my sister used to live here." I debated whether or not to mention Bree's name. It wasn't likely she was on good terms with them if what she'd told me about her time here was true.

"Bree?" the female asked. Based on the tenseness on her face—I'd been correct in my assumption that mentioning Bree was unwise. I imagined they didn't get a lot of new people here.

I nodded. "She came to my world looking for the Harvester." This part was harder. To think of Ronan was worse than Nat or Bree or anything else. While it hurt to think of them, it was suffocating to feel like I'd never see him again. "Ronan—he is—was—my atman."

"Was?" the pink demon asked quietly. Her bright blue eyes softened.

How did I explain that I lost my magic? No magic meant no soul. No soul meant no mate. Right as I opened my mouth to respond, Rasputin barked a single command I couldn't make out.

The female demon yelled, "No!"

Air left my lungs. I choked, but couldn't seem to breathe no matter how hard I tried. All that came out was a rough, gagging sound. He grasped the wrist holding the blade to his throat. I tensed as he yanked on the hand that held the collar of his shirt, pulling me down as he thrust the athame up.

The blade pierced my throat, ramming straight through to the hilt.

Blood drenched me. My mouth opened and closed, like a fish seeking water.

Gurgling sounds rattled from my throat with grave inflection.

I reached up, wrapping my hand around the end. My vision was beginning to fade as my slick fingers pulled it free.

The athame hit the dirt.

I stumbled.

The ground swayed, then tilted. I lost my footing on the edge of the ravine and couldn't regain it.

Falling.

Flying.

I wasn't sure which.

All I knew was that my heart was pounding its final beats. A funeral march. A death knell.

This was the end. The real one.

Thump . . .

As I descended into the chasm, I beheld the Source in its infinite glory.

This *thing*, this entity, had chosen Ronan and then Lorcan. Had been the cause of so much pain and destruction. It destroyed my home and would now be the end of the universe if Rasputin had his way.

Thump . . .

My hands clenched into fists. My heartbeat slowed.

With every breath, it weakened further. With every second, I bled more. By all accounts, I was at death's door—but I wasn't ready to open it. I refused.

I'd have to reach the bottom of wherever this abyss ended to be forced through it.

Even in pain, dying, I reached for the tiniest ember inside me. The glowing speck amid the ashes that were all that remained of my power.

And I kept falling.

Down.

Down.

Down.

Thump . . .

My heartbeat sounded like thunder, one long suspended note signaling it was my last. I let out a convoluted scream that whistled through the air from having my vocal cords cut. Then . . . that ember caught fire.

35

RONAN

I knew Bree had to have a secret hidden up her sleeve. There was no way she'd guarantee her own death. She had to have *something* she believed was strong enough to kill a chaos demon chosen by the Source.

But I never would have guessed this.

Her trick with the mercury was clever. I'd realized about halfway through the fight that her suit was slowly peeling away. Burrowing past his skin. I didn't put together why until his power began to falter.

By then it was too late.

"She's draining him," Nathalie whispered. "How?"

"I've never heard of a conduit," Sasha murmured.

"*Me neither*," Anders said across our mental link. He stood on the ruin where he'd been for the entire challenge, staring down at Bree as she pulled every last bit of magic from Lorcan. His flesh began to decay, turning ashen, then brittle.

She didn't let up.

In all my years as Harvester, I'd only seen a challenge actually end in death a dozen or so times. Demons that were incredibly old. Demons that saw yielding as a weakness they couldn't bear. Demons that longed for death and therefore refused to bond, knowing they would be killing their other half.

Never in my time had I seen a toxic relationship where the opposing party didn't eventually give in. They always decided life, even in shackles, was better than nothingness.

Only one other atma who'd refused the bond for similar reasons won out in the end—but she couldn't do it. Even without the ties of the blood oath, she couldn't find it within herself to kill her atman.

Bree didn't hesitate.

I wondered if she stopped to think at all before she finished the job, but it wasn't something I would ask. Not for the price she paid so I could find Piper.

In a matter of seconds, Lorcan's life force winked out. A strong wind whipped through the Underworld, sending his desiccated ashes across the city.

I expected her to break down. To snap. To collapse in on herself upon realizing what she'd done.

I should have known better.

"He lost her," she said quietly. "Piper challenged him so he couldn't tap into her magic." Fear gripped me, and I was not accustomed to being scared. Part of me was proud. So fucking proud that she found a way to stop him.

The rest of me knew the story didn't end there.

"Where is she?" I demanded.

Bree sagged, falling back. Her thighs smearing in the remains of her atman. "He gave her to the Illuminati thinking he would just retrieve her when needed."

"They double-crossed him, didn't they?" It was the witch that asked it, the sinking tone of her voice echoing the one in my chest.

Bree nodded. "He went back, and the place was deserted. She wasn't anywhere to be found. None of them were. But . . ." She hesitated, brow furrowed. "Where he took her wasn't associated with any of the Illuminati locations I know of."

"What are you saying?" Sasha asked.

"I don't think the Illuminati—"

The earth shuddered.

It creaked. It groaned, like it was a giant beast awakening. The skies turned wicked as winds blew hard enough to cut through stone. The ruins Anders was standing on cleaved in half. He jumped down, tucking into a roll at the bottom so that he didn't break the glass any further and end up with viscous edges implanted in him. The fae grunted as the hulking mass of concrete collapsed behind him, covering the destroyed arena in a plume of broken rock particles. He coughed hoarsely while waving his hand in front of his face in an attempt to clear it away.

He didn't have to wait long. The wrathful wind did it for him.

Clouds filled the previously clear sky, making the city lights reflect off of them, casting us in an ominous shadow. From one second to the next, rain poured, flooding the city. I glanced at Bree to find her already staring at me.

"Piper."

There was no other possible cause for such violent displays of elements.

But when I cast my power far and wide, I couldn't find her. Traces existed all over the country. Beyond the oceans and across the continents, wisps of her magic seemed to be everywhere—but she was nowhere to be found.

A chunk of ice fell from the sky, slamming into the ground with a wicked crack.

In the beginning of June, hail the size of baseballs started raining down.

Bree's eyes turned verdant, and she waved a hand, throwing up a metal disk easily fifty feet in diameter above us. The ice clanged against it, but she fixed the dents as soon as they were created.

"Earth. Wind. Water. Ice," she yelled in an effort to be heard over the din. "But where's the—"

Fire.

It started as a spark. Then turned to a coal. The glass between us began to melt around a ring of fire that was steadily growing. It slid over the edge in liquid form, falling into a black abyss. Both Bree and I stepped back, not sure what to make of it.

"Run!" she yelled at Sasha and Nathalie. They didn't need to be told twice. She turned as Anders came to a halt beside her, grabbed his arm, then disappeared. I was prepared to follow suit when I felt a distant presence. Then a whisper came from the gaping void.

"*H . . . help . . .*"

I'd never felt panic and relief so strong and at the same time in my incredibly long life. "*Piper?*" I called, turning inward to the bridge between our minds.

Whatever mists that plagued her side before were suddenly gone, replaced by a raging inferno of white fire that made it look like every interpretation of Hell that the humans had created. The emptiness around the bridge was pure flame. Every inch from her side to mine was singed black. It stopped at the edge of my side but was slowly breaking down my barriers.

There was no crossing this, whatever it was. I had to find her in person, and I had to do it *now*.

"*Ronan.*" Her mind seemed to call from the growing

circle of fire. I peered over the edge, finding stars and galaxies in its depths. Magic. Her magic. The Otherworld's magic. Immense and awful. Great yet harrowing.

It was a portal unlike any other *and it was growing*.

Somehow Piper was causing it. I was certain. The weather and earthquakes around the globe; it was the only explanation. What I didn't know, was how.

My atma was a powerful demon, but this . . . I swallowed thickly.

No one in the known universe was strong enough to do this. No one.

And yet . . .

I stepped over the burning circle into oblivion. The fall was short, but longer than I remembered. This wasn't a portal. It was a corridor.

My concern grew as it spat me out on the other side. I landed in the dirt. My knees were skinned from the tiny rocks and pebbles that lined the Rift.

I peered past two demons. One pink. One blue. Both had spirit magic. I recognized them as Ailaine and Morfayus, the guardians of the Rift. They had their hands locked together, and Ailaine whispered, "Source help us."

Beyond them, on the very edge, a warlock was on his knees, facing the Source.

I looked around, but despite feeling her in every breath of air and pore of my skin—I couldn't find her. "Where is she?"

The guardians jumped. Morfayus looked me over once, eyes wide. "Where in Tartarus's name have you been?" I hated that curse. My father was regarded as a god among these people, and he'd been dead for over nine thousand years. "Things have gone to utter shite ever since you left. The council let every chaos demon they could find approach the Source, and now the son of Eris and Anhur bears the—"

"Lorcan is dead," I said. "Where's Piper?"

"Piper?" Ailaine repeated. Her eyes widened. "The woman with child. She said she was your atma, but she wasn't of the Source."

I didn't blink. *Wasn't of the Source . . .*

"Where is she?" I repeated. My magic coiled around me, waiting to strike. I held it in, trying to force it into submission.

Ailaine looked at the warlock on his knees. Morfayus pointed to the man. "He came through the portal with her. She wanted to go back. She tried to bargain with us." Of course she did. Even out of her element, Piper wasn't stupid. She would have used anything she had to her advantage.

"I'm so sorry, Ronan," Ailaine whispered.

The wind roared.

"Where is she?" I repeated again. She looked down, eyes watering. I turned to Morfayus, waiting for an answer.

It was the warlock that spoke.

"She is becoming," he said, voice raspy from age and tinted with madness. "Only through pain could she be reborn."

I stepped around the guardians, turning to the warlock. Violence simmered in my blood with murderous intent. "What have you done?" I whispered, knowing there would be no reply. Instead, I cut through his shields and sifted through his thoughts and memories.

There was so much blood.

"Get me more. I've never seen anything like this."

Drip.

Drip.

Drip.

"Initiate the Theta protocol . . . you'll need to significantly overdose the patient to combat healing . . ."

Cracking.

Breaking.

Shattering.

"Subject seems to feed on anger. . . vitals weak . . . need to use her while she's still strong enough to complete it . . ."

Blood. Blood. Blood.

Three to bind.

"You're a conduit . . . it's your destiny . . ."

Spurt.

Splatter.

Splash.

Red dripped down his fingers where the knife pierced her neck. She pulled it out and painted her body. The athame fell.

Piper followed.

Horror ran through me. Revulsion at what he'd done to her. Unbridled savagery made me react. I ripped the warlock up by his throat.

"You wanted immortality? You'll have it."

I tossed him to the ground, ignoring his cries as his skin began to blister and bleed, flaying itself, revealing muscle, sinew, cartilage, and bone. He screamed while his cheeks peeled over his head, his moans becoming nothing more than a muted mumble as he swallowed his tongue and his vocal cords pushed to the exterior of his body. Organs exposed themselves, while nerve-endings worked at breakneck speed, rapidly firing pain all over the body. The transformation was complete when he turned into a living lump of fleshy meat, existing in this excruciating state for eternity. Never able to scream. Never able to escape. Always feeling. Always writhing. Every layer of his existence peeled back like an onion, turned inside out, with his beating heart on display, forever racing as non-stop adrenaline coursed through his visible veins in agony.

Inside out. Outside in.

It was the worst punishment that could be given. Reserved for crimes that hadn't been committed in so long, I'd lost memory of them. But for what he'd done to Piper, there would be no less.

I heard retching that I assumed to be Ailaine. She didn't have the stomach for cruelty. What I'd done to him? It was beyond punishing. It was barbaric. I didn't care.

"Ronan," Morfayus began. "The woman fell into the Rift. No one could survive that—"

"Piper will."

He didn't answer, not wanting to contradict me after what I'd done to the warlock, but I knew she wasn't dead. Not when her voice had called out to me. She opened a corridor through the Underworld to get to me. Some part of her was still there, and it was reaching out—trying to get home.

She is becoming.

His words replayed in my mind. I looked at the white-stained sky, as if leached of color.

A sponge for magic. A conduit.

The hairs on the back of my neck lifted. A chill skittered across my skin. Deep within, the Source was rolling, boiling, writhing—becoming.

And it tasted like rage.

36

PIPER AND RONAN

I'M NOT SURE WHEN THE PAIN STOPPED, OR IF IT EVER REALLY DID. Maybe it changed, or maybe the soul-eating rage eclipsed it. After all, what's a stubbed toe when you have a bullet wound?

Sure, my throat was slashed open. But I was human again, and whatever was happening now very much wasn't.

The process of becoming immortal was brutal.

I could never forget it the first time, and that was nothing compared to the incomprehensible energy that was flowing through me. Into me.

My head pounded as it stretched to fit power inside every bone, cartilage, and tissue, filling my atoms, even coating my hair. No part of me was left unchanged. Not a single cell unaltered.

But it didn't stop.

Not when I was filled to the brim and bursting with power. Not when it was leaking from me like sweat. The fullness turned painful. Pressure built in my chest and my back strained from how hard I was arching. I let out a bloodcurdling scream that echoed the sound of storms. Thunder and wind and rain.

Or maybe those things sounded like me.

All I knew was that the pressure was too much. It was going to tear me in half.

The Source obliterated my heart, creating a fracture in my sternum. A crack snapped as my back bent too far. Searing agony lashed through me. I shattered.

For a moment, it was only white.

Pure, yet glaring. Untainted, but harsh.

I blinked slowly, half wondering if I'd somehow found my way back to the light realm. But the white faded. The brightness dimmed.

Darkness spread from the chasm below me. It spanned miles and miles. Since the dawn of time, it was the home of the Source. Where the inception of the universe began, creating planets and dimensions that overlapped.

Now only nothingness remained. A deep, endless pit that never stopped.

I stared at that darkness with burning eyes, knowing that should have been my fate.

"Piper," a voice brushed against my mind, coaxing me gently.

I slowly lifted my gaze from the schism. The edge of the ravine teetered within view. The large and still growing corridor behind it. I moved closer without thinking or realizing what I was doing.

"That's it," he murmured. His presence wrapped around mine as if trying to comfort me. I wasn't sure why, given not an ounce of fear remained in me after the fall.

Nor worry or panic or pain.

It was as if almost all emotion left me. Good and bad. Leaving only anger and wrath behind for me to feed on.

I was the apotheosis of rage and quintessence of power itself.

Yet a lone figure stood on the edge of the universe, speaking to me like he knew me. A demon with skin black as night. Silver horns curled over his head into jagged points. His brands were painted in that same silver, their color illuminating beneath my light as I approached.

Behind him a male and female crouched in the dirt, heads bowed. The blue one lifted his eyes briefly to look at me, then flinched.

"Piper," the obsidian demon said. He spoke quietly, but that name drifted, echoing off the never-ending walls of the chasm.

"Do you know who I am?"

I tilted my head. Lips curving down.

Alarm made his eyes widen.

I'd heard that voice before, but I couldn't place it. I'd felt that presence . . . but I didn't remember. The parts of me that were once human or demon didn't exist anymore. I was something else now. Something *other*. So far removed from emotion and feeling, yet consumed by the entity existing inside me—there wasn't room for anything else.

Still, this male seemed familiar somehow.

The harder I tried to place him, the more it evaded me.

Irritation banked my curiosity. The ground began to tremble at my annoyance, pebbles bouncing against the rocky cliff. Some of them fell right over the edge. Their tiny pings against the rock face trailing off the further they fell.

"It's okay," the obsidian demon said. He was still speaking in quiet, gentle tones. There was an undercurrent of concern that made him sound hurried. "It's not your fault. I'm Ronan. Your atman." When I didn't respond, he let out a curse. His fists tightened. I didn't like the sight, but

I couldn't understand why. "You called me to Earth through a summoning and then ran from me at every turn. But you're a hunter. A fighter. I took your sister, Bree. You remember her, right?"

A wisp of a vision showed me a brown-haired girl feeding tiny white creatures with webbed feet. She was pale with eyes the color of the blue veins on her chest.

Before I could build a timeline around that memory, it was whisked away—lost in the infiniteness of time. I reached for it, my failure to grasp on made the skies darken, then bleed in fire and fury. Raging balls of flame and light hurled toward the ground. It shuddered on impact.

I regarded the male with a cool expression. Unhappy that his presence was stirring emotions in me I didn't understand. Instead of sadness or confusion or longing, all I felt was anger.

And it fed me.

~.~.~Ronan~.~.~

SHE FLOATED ABOVE US, an avenging angel with wings of fire and a crown of light. Her body glowed so brightly that any lesser being wouldn't have been able to even look upon her. The hair I'd always thought was so reminiscent of sunshine, now poured down her back like molten gold.

It was her eyes that concerned me the most.

Wholly white, no color or pupil to see.

She was rage incarnate.

I thought I knew terror before, but nothing came close to seeing her merge with the Source. *Become it.*

If she were simply an all-powerful being, akin to the gods of legend on Earth—that would be one thing. I was not fragile enough to be threatened by my atma's power.

But absorbing the Source didn't just come with magic.

I was merely bonded to it—chained to it. Subjected to the apathy that taking on so much magic does. Forced to lose parts of humanity that I didn't know I had until they were gone. As the Harvester, I was the in-between that stood in the middle of it and demon kind. Chosen by the Source to bend to its will. It infused me with terrible power, once thought to be the greatest in the universe.

But my magic was not even a tenth of what now resided inside Piper.

The immense weight of taking in such a force of raw creation, it was stripping her of everything that made her, *her*.

And that ignored the very reason only chaos bonded to it.

Piper was all rage, and just as she was becoming the Source—it was also becoming her. Chaos had balance. It was a combination of every magic. But rage magic was simply destruction.

Every thought, every feeling, every action—would be wrath.

I'd once thought that her realm wouldn't survive her anger if she ever truly lost it. But no world would survive this.

I had to bring her back from the brink somehow. She had to remember. It was the only way.

"You were raised by your parents. They were teachers. They lost their jobs when the Magic Wars hit, and your world collapsed. Your mom became a blood donor and your dad helped form human patrol. You hated seeing them suffer trying to make a better life for you and Bree, so you did something about it." She tilted her head, regarding me. "You tried to become a vampire, but they wouldn't take you. You tried to get bitten by a wolf, but they didn't want you. So you went to the witches. You made a deal. You'd be their offering in a summoning, and a demon would give you the magic you needed to protect your family."

Her glowing hands curled into fists and meteors rained down on the Otherworld, threatening its extinction. But I kept going.

"They lied to you. The summoning would have used your life force to allow them to call the demon into your world. You learned too late, but your rage called the demon named Aeshma. She answered—and in a battle of wills, you *won*." I stalked toward the very edge of the abyss, my toes just over the line. She was only feet away, but it still felt like miles.

"But I didn't win."

My chest expanded, forcing air into my lungs because some part of her was still here. I couldn't stop now.

"No. When the summoning failed, they came after you. Both of your parents were killed, and Bree's conscience was sent to Hell. You blamed yourself for years, that in trying to help you made things worse. You still blame yourself, even though you try to say you're past it. I know the truth. I always know with you." The faintest shadow of her lips turned down. Cracks started to form in the Rift. I held in my curse. Minutes was all we had. There was no clock, but I sensed that she would reach her end before too long.

"You became a hunter. First with human patrol, and then working for Lucifer. You took every job with a witch so you could interrogate them and find out how to get Bree back. For ten years you searched, and then you ended up in another demon summoning." She drifted closer, her flaming wings beat softly, and the heat singed me from a distance. "Except this one you did on purpose. You were trying to save that girl, thinking that if you were there to help, she wouldn't die. She still perished in creating the portal that brought me to you, and that bothers you."

"She shouldn't have," Piper said. Her voice was a whisper, but it still managed to reach every corner of the Otherworld. "I should have been enough."

"You can't save everyone, but you still try. Just like you can't win every fight, but you still put up one. Do you remember the bargain we made? You asked to live and for me not to kill Claude Lewis. I agreed, and in return I asked for—"

"Me." The brightness dimmed. She came forward another few inches. Slowly, piece by piece, she was taking her mind back. "I shot you."

I smiled. It was one of my fondest memories. "That's the moment I knew you were it for me."

She frowned again, but the shaking calmed. The meteors stopped. While the sky hadn't cleared, and she was still burning with the heat of a million suns, it was progress.

"That's not right." Her voice almost sounded like herself that time. It still echoed with power, but it wasn't so emotionless. So empty.

"That's us. I'm a heartless bastard who chased you, then manipulated you into chasing me. You're a bounty hunter that tried to kill me as often as you kissed me. I had to learn to be what you needed. To understand that my smart, cold, stunning atma could take care of herself—and that even though I wanted to fix all your problems, that wasn't the solution. I needed to *help* you fix them yourself."

Closer, closer. She couldn't have been more than a foot from the edge. The raw power radiating from her blistered my skin, but I refused to move even a single inch.

"Do you know who I am now?"

The light in her eyes finally died down enough to see the pupil, surrounded by a ring of white flame that was edged with violet.

"Ronan."

~.~.~Piper~.~.~

I REMEMBERED.

Him. Bree. My parents. Nathalie. The twins. The knife. The blood. The darkness.

Just as I started to slip once more, he reached out and grabbed me. His skin charred, smelling of burnt flesh as he pulled me to him.

"I won't be able to hold on," I said into his shoulder. "I'm here, but the Source—it's too much. I'm going to lose this battle eventually."

He threaded his fingers through my hair, pulling me back just far enough to see my face. My light radiated, but his darkness absorbed it. Just as the Rift stood against the Source for billions of years, so he stood against me.

My equal. My atman.

"You won't," he insisted.

"I can't stop it."

"You will," he disagreed. "You will because you have to. Everything happening here is already happening on Earth. The corridor is complete. The door to every single world between here and Earth is wide open—and if you don't win, we all lose."

I shuddered, and the world shuddered with me as if reiterating his point.

"I don't know how to win," I said. His silver brands flared to life beneath my palms.

"We'll do what we've always done. You have the tools." He tapped my temple. "I'll help you use them." I swallowed hard, trying to hold on to my memories and sense of self.

"Tell me what to do."

He pressed his forehead against mine, our lips brushed when he spoke.

"Bree said you're a sponge for magic. I'm going to bite you and try to siphon it until it's bearable."

"We won't be able to carry the weight between the two of us—"

"We will," he insisted. "Because we have to. We don't have another choice."

Tears leaked from the corners of my eyes, burning droplets of starfire. "What happens when you lose yourself and can't walk me back?" I demanded.

"I won't."

"How do you know that?"

"Because I've been close to the edge before, and you brought me back. We're soul bound. Two halves of one whole. Light to dark. The perfect balance. We can do this."

I stared, seeing him for the first time. On Earth his body became like ours, but in Hell—he wore his truth in every way. From the black skin to the horns to the silver brands that matched his eyes.

No matter what he looked like, in any form, he was still Ronan.

"I trust you."

. . .

~.~.~Ronan~.~.~

HER BLOOD TASTED LIKE FIRE.

A raging inferno that wreaked havoc on my insides from the first sip. I embraced it instead of fighting. Letting her magic run rampant in my veins, scorching every corner of my body and soul.

Her head tilted, and a moan of relief escaped her lips.

It was all I needed to hear to keep going. To keep drinking.

At first, it was painful. Addicting still because it was her, but too much. Too sharp.

Slowly, the magic unfurled and mingled with mine. Rage met chaos, but instead of exploding in misalignment —they merged.

They settled.

I turned inward to our minds where the flames had been worse. They were still there. Still burning. Instead of consuming everything in their path, they remade it.

The bridge between our minds glowed like it was made of burning coals. Sconces of light dotted the sides. Miniature stars, confined in globes the size of my fist. They lit the way, guiding me through the fire to the other side.

I broached the double gates of her mind.

They were wreathed in flame, but open. In the center of a blackened isle where no life could grow, sat Piper. Her knees were pulled up to her chest, arms wrapped around them. Wings of fire stretched around her in a protective manner. Her crown of light sat canted on her head, hair streaming down her back.

I approached slowly, letting her know I was here.

She lifted her head.

Our gazes locked.

I dropped down onto my knees and her wings unfurled. I reached under her naked legs and around her back. Every part of me burned that touched her, but I didn't let go.

Piper shuddered when I picked her up. Head against my chest, arms wound around my neck, she closed her eyes and *finally* gave in.

I carried her out of the burned remains of her mind, never looking back.

~.~.~Piper~.~.~

I SAGGED AGAINST HIM.

The fragile pieces of memories soldered back together. My body shook from the exertion, but together, as one, we balanced the Source between us.

It was an impossible weight, yet we carried it.

It was a soul-crushing responsibility, but neither of us let go.

They say a house divided cannot stand. But to hold the literal Source of creation, it took every single piece of both of us fused together. Anything less and only chaos or rage would prevail.

Ronan released my neck and licked the wound clean as it healed.

"I need to get you home. I can feel the contractions.

You're in labor." He wrapped an arm around my back, pressing a cool hand to my skin.

I wasn't sure what he was talking about. I couldn't feel a thing beyond the pounding in my head.

"What about Rasputin?" I murmured.

"He's been dealt with." Ronan's tone of voice turned dark, edged with lethal intent. Whatever had happened between us when he took my blood and stabilized the Source, I saw in his mind what happened. What he did to the warlock.

"Gruesome, but fitting. I like it."

My entire body tightened. I didn't feel pain, but I felt *something*. Ronan let out a growl before hauling me into his arms, just like he'd done on the psychic plane of our minds. My flaming wings were limp on my back, the tips of them dragging the ground—leaving trails of white fire behind.

He turned around to carry me to the corridor. My chest tightened. I hated that I felt fear when looking at the gaping void. But the way Rasputin had stripped me of my will . . . forced me to complete it . . .There were some sins that left a scar on the soul where no one could see it. A stain that would forever cast a shadow. My forced excursion to Hell was one of them.

"I won't let you go," he said, speaking low enough that only I could hear. "It's not going to be like last time."

I pressed my lips together and dipped my chin. The only thing I hated more than that corridor was the Otherworld.

"Can you close it?" I asked. "Make it so no one can ever use it again?"

Ronan nodded. "I can. When we're in it, I'll close off every entryway then seal it shut on Earth."

"Do it."

He approached the infinite corridor and the two

demons stepped in front of it. From his memory I heard their names. Ailaine and Morfayus. Guardians of the Rift. They were meant to protect the Source for all eternity.

"I don't wish to kill you, but I will if you don't let us pass." He spoke with the voice of the Harvester, but I wasn't afraid. It was just another face of his, just like the burning entity inside me was now one of mine. One that I would always struggle to control, but with Ronan's help, I'd manage. I had to.

"We don't want to stop you," Ailaine said. Her blue eyes turned sad. "We want to come with."

I sensed Ronan's reaction. The lift of his brows. I couldn't see it, but I felt it as if the movement was my own.

"Why?"

It wasn't Ronan that asked it, but me. Both demons looked down, from his face to mine. Simultaneously, they each dropped to one knee.

"We were created to be guardians of the Rift, but without the Source, we don't have a purpose," Morfayus said, bowing his head in respect. "We want to follow so we can protect it."

"You," Ailaine added. "Your children. Each of you carry it. We failed here because we never expected an attack from another world."

"We will not make that mistake again," Morfayus swore.

Ronan looked at me and I stared at him. We didn't need to speak with our minds. There was an understanding that formed without words or thought between us.

"You will swear an oath," Ronan said.

"Of course—"

"And take no territory," I added. "Nor create supernaturals without good reason."

"We understand," Ailaine said. "Until our end of days, we swore our lives to protect the Source. You are it now, so now we will protect you and your children until death. We'll make no gambles for power or claim territory. Nor create supernaturals, as you call them, without due cause."

Morfayus repeated the same oath with slightly different phrasing.

My body tensed again. Hot liquid erupted between my thighs. I looked down and then back up. "Unless they know how to deliver a baby, I need to get to the Señora *now*."

37

NAT

When the earthquake stopped and the skies cleared, I let go of a breath I didn't know I'd been holding.

"They're not back yet," Bree said. "This isn't over."

From the side room next to us, Mist's screams threatened to tear the walls down as she went into labor. If not for Piper's command that she couldn't hurt us, we'd all be dead ten times over from how often she'd cursed us to Hell and back. Despite it all, Sienna stood by her side as her support while Señora waited to catch the baby.

The timing wasn't good, but when it rains, it pours.

"That the elements have stopped raging is a good sign," I insisted. My arms were crossed as I leaned against the wall, staring out the window.

Bree wasn't exactly known for her positivity, and Sasha shut down completely when confronted with feelings she didn't like. She and her sister's existence was reliant on Piper's survival. It was a hard pill to swallow.

On my couch, Anders sat with his legs splayed and fingers threaded together behind his head. "Pip is a fighter. She's faced worse odds in the past."

That was easy to say when we didn't know *what* exactly she was facing. Still, I appreciated the better outlook. It made it easier for me to hold on to my own.

"Not while pregnant," Bree responded.

I focused on the window, trying to tune them all out. Mist's screams hit a pitch that made the glass warble. I winced.

"She'll be fine," Lucifer said. He stood too close for comfort. His ghostly chest pressing into my back. While it wasn't solid, I felt something when he touched me. "And if she's not, you won't know until right before. None of this will matter."

He wasn't wrong. That didn't mean I liked to hear it.

I'd been ignoring him for three days, and his impatience was growing. It didn't matter that Piper was kidnapped, or that the world could end at any second; Lucifer wanted my attention. It was selfish . . . but part of me also understood it. If it was going to go that way, and everything ended, I was the only one he could communicate with.

"Wherever you are," I began quietly, humoring him while distracting myself, "is that where we go when we die?"

I felt his gaze on me but didn't look. "I don't know."

"I hope it's not."

"Why is that?"

"Because wandering aimlessly, not able to have any impact on the world or interact with the people we care about sounds like a horrible way to exist."

A phantom touch wrapped around my forearm as he leaned in. I could have sworn the scent of blood and sex washed over me.

"You grossly overestimate how many people I actually

gave a shit about in life," he breathed. "As for being unable to have an impact, I'm talking to you, aren't I?"

"That's not the same. You can't feel the sun on your face or the wind in your hair. There's no job—"

"Why on earth would I want to work?"

"Because doing nothing is boring," I argued. "Your mind will become a pile of slush. Lack of engagement is terrible for the brain, and it does nothing for preventing dementia."

"Forgive me for not being worried about dementia when I'm several thousand years old."

"But you're not anymore. You're dead. Before you ruled the world. Now . . . you can't even enjoy tacos, or read a book while drinking Jasmine tea—"

"While I enjoy reading on occasion, there's only one thing I wish to taste that I cannot." Heat made my cheeks flush. "And I intend to change that."

"It's also depressing to think I'm the only person you can talk to given I don't even particularly like you," I continued, clearing my throat.

A soft laugh brushed against my skin, leaving goosebumps in its wake. "You don't know me enough to like or dislike me, little witch, but that will change."

"Pass."

He chuckled, unperturbed. "As you pointed out, I have nothing to do and no one to talk to except you—and you'll find I can be quite persuasive when I want to be. So pretend to be unaffected all you want, but I know the truth, and I'm not going anywhere, Nathalie. Not if you beg. Not if you scream. And trust me, love, for how long you've been ignoring me—I'll want my pound of flesh."

The wail of a baby crying broke through the air. I

glanced over to the double doors of my study where Señora Rosara was holding up a red-faced child with wings.

"It's a girl," she said, cradling the child while clamping the cord so Sienna could cut it. She took her in a towel to clean her while the Señora finished delivering the placenta.

The baby made little squeaking noises while Sienna smiled down at it, swaying softly. "Do you want to hold her?" she asked, looking up at Mist. The girl seemed confused. I could only imagine the complicated feelings she must have been having. The child was conceived against her will, but she still carried it to term and delivered it from her own body. Whatever she did, there would be no judgment from any of us.

"I . . . I don't know."

Sienna twisted to take a seat beside her, holding the baby so Mist could see it. They both stared; Mist at her child, and Sienna at Mist—trying to gage what she needed. It was a serene moment.

Shattered between one second and the next as Piper and Ronan appeared in the middle of the living room. If not for her magic signature, I wouldn't have recognized the being in his arms.

Her skin was radiant. Brands starting from the bottoms of her feet and stopping around her hairline. They glowed like pure light. Massive wings of fire draped over Ronan's arm, burning his skin. He didn't show any signs of pain, despite how hot they would have to be to injure him at all.

"What happened?" I demanded, springing forward and narrowly dodging her wings as he turned with her in hand. Two other figures appeared beside them. The one closest to me was female. She had dark hair and prominent, wide set blue eyes. Pale pink brands ran down her arms and chest as she stood naked. The other one was male, nearly as tall as

Ronan, but stockier in build. He had blue brands that popped against his mahogany skin. "Who are you?" I continued. The man turned toward me, showing magenta eyes.

"Explain later," Piper hissed, eyes scrunched shut. "Babies are coming."

"Put her in our room," Sasha said, jumping to her feet. Anders disappeared around the corner, likely pulling out the flame-proof blanket Ronan helped me make in preparation. When your best friend had a tendency for exploding into flame on a moment's notice, I expected no less while she was giving birth. We just didn't expect wings as part of the equation.

The living room became a flurry as Piper was moved into her old room and laid on the bed. Bree grabbed the tools she'd need from Señora Rosara, while she finished stitching Mist. I rounded the corner, heading into the bedroom when Ronan blocked my way.

"She can't control herself right now," he said. "Her powers are not under control. If she hurt you because—"

"I'll redirect her magic if it happens."

His eyes darted between me and a writhing Piper. "She consumed the Source. It may not be enough."

She consumed the . . . "It's either that or make me fireproof somehow."

He was too busy debating when Piper screamed. We both turned to the bed fully when a tiny blonde head popped out between her legs.

"Oh shit—"

Ronan was kneeling in front of her before I could finish, just in time to catch as the baby came sliding out the rest of the way.

There were no cries. No screams. No squeals.

"It's a boy," I told her softly. His squishy face was prune-like and blue despite his flailing arms and legs.

Worry tugged at me.

"Why isn't he making a sound?" Piper asked through gritted teeth.

Ronan didn't answer.

Bree appeared next to him, blocking my view as they dealt with the first one. I stepped around them to go to Piper's side. Sweat dotted her brow. White fire surrounded her pupils, the outer edge lined in purple. She panted heavily. Her wings snapped outward as a contraction hit, and I grabbed her hand.

"I'm right here," I said. "Keep your breathing slow. In. There you go. Now hold it." Her brands turned hot, threatening to scald me as she squeezed her eyes shut again. I had to redirect her magic back into her so that she didn't hurt me like Ronan thought she would.

"What is wrong with him?" she demanded on a heavy exhale.

From the bottom of the bed, Ronan stepped to the side, holding the first baby while Bree bent between Piper's legs. "Push and count to ten," her sister said, ignoring Piper's distress.

"Why isn't he crying?" she asked, getting more panicked by the second when neither of them answered her. I brushed the hair away from her eyes and cupped her cheek.

"Ronan's got this," I said. "His job right now is to take care of your son. Your job is to get your second baby out."

"Tell me what—"

Right as she started to waver, a tiny cry came from beside the bed. Ronan knelt next to her, holding out their boy for her to see. Instantly, I noticed that the flush, round-faced baby looked very little like the child that came out of her only minutes ago.

I looked from the kid to Ronan, but he was focused on his mate and child.

Instead of saying anything, I just kept holding her hand. She squeezed me back, letting me know I was doing what she wanted.

"I need you to work with me here," Bree said. "I really don't want to have to cut you open to get the other one out. You need to push."

Piper swallowed hard and nodded. "On three. One. Two. Three . . ." Piper did as she was told, repeating the process over and over again while never taking her eyes off her son.

"You're doing so good," Bree said after another fifteen or so minutes had passed. "Just one more. Baby's right there—"

A wet smack sounded, followed by Bree lifting up her second child and plopping it on Piper's stomach. "You did it, sis. You've got a daughter."

38

BREE

I wasn't sure whether I should feel relief or despair as I cleaned my hands of blood and all other sorts of bodily fluids. My index finger sharpened to a point that I used to get into the crevices of my cuticles and under my nails.

I tried to focus on the action itself. On my niece and nephew one room over, sleeping on their mother's chest after surviving impossible odds. There was something different about them. They carried magic I'd never seen before.

The boy . . . he'd nearly died in the first few minutes. Then somehow sprang back to life. Growing and changing rapidly into a child that was arguably months older than the one that came out of her.

The girl's heart stopped partway through birth. She shouldn't have lived. But when she popped out, she looked like a healthy nine-month-old baby. Wrinkly and pink, exactly what you'd expect of a newborn. Not the premature twenty-sixish weeks they were maturity wise if how the growth Señora Rosara had been seeing was accurate.

I'd never seen anything like it.

Twins born a mere month and a half after conception . . . I shook my head.

They had the brands of demons, but their magic was something else entirely. I just couldn't place what. Either way, Piper would have her hands full with them the next few months. It would help. She'd hopefully be too tired to miss me much while I was gone.

I shut off the sink.

In the background I could hear people talking. Sleeping. Crying. But inside, it was so unbearably lonely.

Lorcan was gone.

He may have been a horrible abusive monster, but he was all I had. Now, not even the magic I stole resembled him anymore as it rested dormant in my veins.

People often said that they weren't given a choice when in my shoes. I wondered if it was easier for them to believe that. A nice lie for why they had to endure being alone. The truth was I had a choice. It was me or him.

I chose me.

I would always choose me.

But there were still consequences for not choosing him.

My magic had grown to impossible heights, but in doing so, I was infinitely closer to the tipping point.

All magic corrupted. When I stole it from the demons of Hell, I'd already taken stuff that wasn't pure for the most part. Very few found their mates early on. Had I finished the bond with Lorcan, it would have stabilized, never corrupting further. Now that the option was gone . . . it was only a matter of time until I lost myself to it.

My sanity. My mind.

So I'd chosen myself, but I was really only buying time. It might be a thousand years. It could be more. Less. But eventually, time would run out.

I dried my hands on the teal hand towel.

A knock came at the door.

"I was just leaving," I said, as it swung open.

"I know," the witch replied. "Piper told me you'd do this if you won. Run away. Take the time to be sad and mopey, make bad choices she can't drag you out of." I raised my eyebrows, and she shrugged.

"I doubt she said it like that."

"She didn't," Nat agreed. "I read between the lines. You two are a lot alike. That's what she would have done, before working through her shit."

"You have no idea what it means to lose your soulmate."

"More than you might think," she said vaguely. "Complicated feelings aren't the issue. It's how you deal with them, and isolating yourself is a rather poor way—which you already know. That's why you made her promise not to come looking for you. That's neither here nor there."

"What do you want?" I sighed, debating just leaving in the middle of the conversation. I wasn't in the mood for one of her lectures, and I no longer had to listen now that I wasn't on guard duty.

"Two things." The witch lifted a finger. "The first is that I have a position I want you for, when you get back."

"You want me to work for you?"

"I have a job you'd be good at, and I think you'd enjoy it. It's a long-standing offer."

"What is it?" I leaned back, crossing my arms over my chest.

The witch smiled. "Let's just say acquiring magical weapons has become an interest of mine. The places these weapons come from aren't somewhere I would send Sienna."

I arched an eyebrow. "You can find cheaper paid muscle than me."

"I could," she agreed. "But you have mental shields. You can't be turned as easily, and if you swore a promise to not betray me, you'd have to actually follow it."

I laughed, a bitter sound. "Why would I promise that?"

"Because I think I can find the *real* Illuminati."

That was a high claim. One that had my interest piqued, just like she'd planned. The Illuminati were hunting both Robin and me. While it was doubtful they'd ever be able to actually apprehend me, Robin was a different story.

I could move her a dozen times and they'd find her again if they really wanted.

"What do you want with them?" I asked, keeping my tone neutral.

She only smiled. "Take the job and we'll talk."

I twisted my lips, mulling over that. "I'm not just leaving to be an angsty shit." She lifted both her eyebrows, seeming surprised I'd offer up any explanation. "I grew up in another world. Like it or not, Lorcan was all I had. Until two months ago, I thought I was going to be ruling Hell by his side. It's an adjustment. I have some stuff I need to figure out."

Which was true. Yes, some of it might be self-inflicted punishment. I was choosing to leave, isolating myself. I hated being alone. After years as nothing more than a ghost . . .I shook my head. There was more than one way to be alone.

Nathalie lifted her hands. "I'm only judging a little bit. Come find me when you're ready."

"What's the other thing you wanted?"

She wasn't as forthcoming this time. Her hesitation answered for her. "Ahh."

"You see him."

I nodded. I'd wondered how long she'd hold out before asking me ever since I'd revealed that I could see the aura of a demon attached to her.

"How?" she asked, then held up a hand. "I've never seen another ghost, but I see him. Is it the same for you?"

I shook my head. "I can see anyone that occupies the astral realm. That's what we call the place where he exists. It's something like an in-between. A layered dimension that sits on top of this one. Where some with a magical signature inhabit."

"There's others?"

"Many," I said. "Others like him, that not enough of themselves remained on this plane, so what was left went there."

"Then why can I see him, but not them?"

"Because they're not tied to you."

Her lips parted. "He's dead—"

"Not quite," I corrected. "Some part of his magic lived on. Not enough to let him inhabit this realm, but enough to cling to that one. Like a wisp of life. It's there, but not corporeal. That piece is attached to you. Anchored here because you hold it. How did that happen?"

She ran a hand through her hair and tugged at the end of her sleeves. "I may have . . . attempted to make him my familiar."

My jaw slipped, but I caught myself. "You made a demon your familiar?"

"Well, I didn't think I'd succeeded. Clearly I did a half-assed job if only part of him is here," she grumbled. "How do I release him?"

I tilted my head, assessing her. "Why did you do it if you didn't want him?"

She sighed. "It's not that. Well, somewhat. I don't want to trap him here," Nathalie confessed. "I did it because I was trying to save him from dying, but he died anyway. Now he's stuck here because of me."

Beside her, the said demon chose to appear and leaned against the wall, giving her a cool stare. "I already told you, I'm not going anywhere."

Nathalie pressed her lips together and waited for me to reply.

"You know the rules," I said. "You gave a piece of yourself to save a part of him. There's no undoing that. Till death do you part, or however the line goes."

She looked a bit queasy as she tilted her head back to look at the ceiling, then closed her eyes. "I was worried you'd say that."

I almost smiled. "All magic has a price. Next time, consider that before you try to save some asshole." The demon's glare turned on me and I glared right back, unintimidated. "She may ignore you, but I'll say it. You're a selfish ass."

"Says the pot to the kettle." The arrogant bastard cocked his head. "You're willing to die for Piper when it suits you, but not stay when she needs you."

My lips thinned. I pushed past Nat and started down the hall.

"That was uncalled for," she said to him quietly.

"She was being a condescending bitch," he replied.

In the living room, Morfayus and Ailaine were drinking tea and cooing over Mist's baby. It was strange to see them in this form instead of their shapes in the Otherworld. Neither had been big fans of me in Hell, so I didn't feel compelled to speak to them.

Sasha and Anders stood in the corner conversing in hushed tones.

I paused, part of me wanting to say something to him. The rest of me didn't know what to say.

Why did you come to my challenge?

Why do you care at all?

I wish the Source gave me someone like you, but it didn't.

I'm still grieving the man who abused me.

I shook my head. It was stupid. I was being stupid.

One kiss didn't constitute anything. Sure, I didn't want Lorcan to hurt him, but just because I grew a conscience for a few seconds didn't mean anything.

I was still me. Powerful. Capable. Alone—because I chose it.

I didn't need anyone.

Anders paused mid-conversation. His eyes settled on me. Waiting for something I didn't know how to say. I could see it there. An expectation. A disappointment. A goodbye.

Instead of waiting for the words to come out of his mouth, I turned for the door.

He didn't owe me anything. Nothing.

At least that's what I told myself as I closed the door behind me and started down the hallway. I made it halfway when the door opened behind me.

"You're running. Again."

I bit the inside of my cheek. *Why didn't I just use the astral realm to leave?* I only had myself to blame for this.

You wanted to see what he would do, a small voice whispered.

I pushed her aside, not liking the feelings behind it.

"I have things to do."

He laughed. A deep chuckle that came out cold and detached as I wanted to be.

"Sure you do. Find a purpose and all that."

That had me gritting my teeth. *Did she tell everyone what we talked about?* For fuck's sake.

"It's more than that," I ground out. "And it's none of your business."

"Lorcan thought it was," he whispered against my neck. I didn't know how he crossed the hallway so silently that he was now behind me, all the burning heat and passion he carried radiating from him.

"Lorcan's dead."

"And I'm not, even though I should be."

There it was. The truth.

Lorcan should have killed him, but I intervened.

"Lucky you," I said passively.

"You could stay."

"Are you asking me to?" I shouldn't have asked that, but I couldn't stop myself.

His breath made something in me shiver when his lips grazed my ear. "Would it change your mind?"

Yes. No.

Fuck. That teetered incredibly close to uncharted territory that I wasn't ready to enter. Not yet. Maybe not ever.

"I have things to do," I repeated. "I don't know why you followed me. Are you just so desperate for attention because your wife is dead that you'll take anything? That succubus whore? A woman that doesn't want you?" I turned on my heel, facing him. "If Lorcan, a demon chosen by the Source itself, wasn't strong enough to keep me, what makes you think you have a chance?"

I lashed into him, unable to let go of the cold, bitchy demeanor. The demon attached to Nathalie was right about that. I was a condescending bitch, but that's because it was all I had left. My power and my mask. I didn't know who I was behind it. I'd been wearing it so long.

It had the desired effect. Anders backed away, his features neutral and his emotions closed off like the doors to a house that I was no longer welcome in. He shook his head and went back into the apartment.

It was what I'd wanted . . .so why did it make me feel so shitty?

I swallowed thickly, looking around the hallway like it would tell me what was wrong with me. Why I pushed everyone away.

But there were no answers here. There never were.

Not wanting to make the same mistake twice, I stepped into the astral realm before someone else could stop me.

I needed to find Robin and get out of this city, away from all the people and memories it held.

39

PIPER
ONE MONTH LATER...

I PLOPPED DOWN ON THE BARSTOOL, WIPING MY HANDS ON MY shorts before reaching for the pita. Ronan dropped his arm over my shoulders, pressing a kiss into my temple.

"You're late," Nathalie said.

"Take it up with Isadora," I sighed. "She cursed one of the women in the shelter today and then wouldn't back down when Sasha tried to talk to her."

Sasha groaned. "That woman is a nightmare—"

"Ah-ah-ah," Sienna chided as she scooped hummus onto a cucumber. "You know the deal. No shop talk at Sunday dinners." Something we'd instituted after everything calmed down was a weekly dinner where we all got together. Nathalie, Sasha and Sienna, Anders, Ronan and I, as well as the babies.

Sasha's ears flattened against her head, tail flicking in annoyance. "Easy for you when all you're doing is mentoring Antonella in taxes."

"I've also got a baby, and when Morfayus is out with Piper, I've usually got the twins too," Sienna reminded her with a cool look.

She'd adopted Mist's baby, but they were keeping the agreement open so Mist could still see her daughter if and when she wanted to. While she wasn't ready to be a mom, she didn't want to cut off all contact. It worked for them. Sienna got to be a mother without needing a man to do it, and Mist didn't have to worry about where the child she'd carried went in the end.

"Speaking of," she continued, twisting on her stool toward me and Ronan. "Have you noticed anything odd about the way Orson is with Hallie?"

I glanced over to the floor where we had a large foam mat laid out. All three babies were down there playing. Honor, my daughter, smiled up at me with one tiny tooth sticking out. My heart squeezed knowing that one short month ago she was so tiny and could barely hold her head up. Now she was sitting up and playing with toys. True to form, our demon children grew at different rates than humans. My kids were continuing to grow over a full week in a day's time, meaning they were more like eight-month-olds in size and milestones.

Across the mat, our son, Orson, was sitting with Hallie's head on his lap. He was petting her wings softly while she slept. His eyes turned from ocean-blue to soft petal-pink as he looked at the little girl in his lap.

"He loves her." I shrugged. "Why wouldn't he? They were born on the same day and haven't been separated since."

Sienna frowned, but it was Anders looking very intently at something else that made her suspicion grow. "Unless there's something you know that I don't?"

Ah shit.

Nat took a sip of her water to clear her throat. "Do you want to tell her or should I?"

Sienna looked between us, lifting her eyebrows. "Tell me what?"

"If Anders can't control his face, you might as well."

"Hallie is Orson's atma," Nathalie said in a rush of words then gave an awkward grin.

"I . . . what?" Sienna pointed at the babies on the floor. "They're a month old. They can't have soulmates yet."

"Called it," Sasha said in a singsong voice. Sienna turned to her twin.

"You suspected? Why didn't you say something?"

Sasha lifted a dark brow, loading her pita up with chicken shawarma and tzatziki. "You're not exactly the most easygoing parent."

Sienna flushed. "I don't know what you mean by that—"

"You won't let tap water be used for baths because you're worried it will 'contaminate her' even though she's probably got more magic than you and I combined. I wasn't going to say shit."

Sienna stewed. Her lips pressed into a firm line.

I put my head in my hand. Ronan rubbed the muscles in my shoulders comfortingly. It's not that we'd wanted to lie to her exactly . . . but Sasha was right.

"Soulmates aren't the same at this age," Ronan explained. "They feel close to each other and are very affectionate, more like a best friend than anything. It's nothing to be worried about. We were concerned if we said something you'd want to separate them—"

"Because they're a month old," Sienna said, green eyes hard. Hallie might not have come out of her, but that didn't mean anything. She was her mother. As far as Sienna was concerned, that little girl was as much hers as Honor was mine.

"It would backfire," Ronan said calmly, not letting himself be riled. "Their bond would feel strained, and it would cause attachment issues for both of them. Even if you wanted to ignore those consequences, Orson is protective over her. She is aging at the same rate as the twins because he's making it so."

Sienna frowned. "He's a baby. How much could he really—"

"Need I remind you he can control time?" Nathalie said. It was fun learning that when he was a week old and liked the sound of his play mat barking like a dog to the tune of Frere Jacques. He started rewinding time for the same song to play over and over again. It was reminiscent of rewinding tapes in a VCR. "The twins each have part of the Source. He's not exactly a normal baby. None of them are. Hallie's a siren, but like a demi-god version. Honor can literally change reality. I mean we've basically got the next rulers of the world drooling on the floor over there."

She took a deep breath then let it out. Clearly pissed, but starting to see reason. "So they're soulmates. Great. Well that explains that." She motioned to the way my son was petting Hallie's wings like she was a cat and making soft cooing sounds at her. His color-shifting eyes turned gold a moment later. His stuffed raccoon appeared on my lap, followed by his mind brushing against my own, wanting to understand what was wrong.

They say kids don't see it, but they're more intuitive than people give them credit for. My son was a remarkable empath, sometimes to his own detriment, like now.

I turned on the stool and got up, carrying over the stuffed animal. "No one is mad at you, baby." I set it down beside him and bent to kiss his blonde head.

"Ma!" Honor yelled. She hadn't gotten the hang of

mama yet, but she knew that yelling 'ma' would get my attention. I turned, taking in her outstretched arms and big blue eyes. When I didn't bend down fast enough, she disappeared then reappeared in my arms.

Having a kid that could alter reality was about as chaotic as it sounded. Time sucked bad enough, but when Honor wanted something, all she had to do was think about it and she'd make it so.

The two of them were doing me in. It was a good thing I only wanted two kids, because I might've changed my mind after having them. It wasn't like I didn't love them, raising two children with incredible powers was just *a lot* on anyone, and I had Ronan to do it with me.

I couldn't imagine being in Sienna's place, but I admired her for it.

Putting Honor on my lap, I took a seat back at the table and finished loading up my pita for dinner.

"As much as I *love* being right, they're also right," Sasha pointed out as she licked shawarma sauce off her fingers. "There's not exactly much you can do when the wonder twins will find a way around it. Ronan said it's not the same as when they're adults, anyway."

Sienna glared sideways at her sister.

"How long have you all known?" She asked us.

"Ummmm . . ." I trailed off, taking another bite so someone else would answer.

Nat frowned at me, totally seeing through what I was doing. "Ronan and I saw it the first time Orson and Hallie met. We told Piper. Anders was eavesdropping."

"It's not my fault you were speaking in a public place at normal conversational volume," Anders said.

"Really?" Nat asked. "You weren't standing on the other side of a closed door?"

Anders had the decency to look away. "Insignificant details."

"Nope, you're full of shit on this one," I said, throwing in my two cents before stuffing another bite of food in my mouth while trying not to accidentally drop any on Honor's head. She was laying against my chest, both hands up over her curly raven-haired head. Tiny brands marked her body all over, from her fingertips to toes, the same as mine had done after taking in the Source. Where my brands still glowed like I was holding a sun inside my chest, hers changed color the way Orson's eyes did.

"Next time, just say it. Please," Sienna said after an extended moment of silence. "I've felt I was seeing something that wasn't there, and that I was the creep for even thinking like that."

Nat's face softened. "That wasn't our intention."

"At all," I confirmed. "We just know you have strong thoughts about how Hallie is raised. We respect that, but we also don't want Orson separated from her. To find their soulmate this young makes them incredibly lucky."

Ronan nodded. "I've only seen it happen one other time. Morfayus and Ailaine. They found each other so young that their magic wasn't corrupted. It's why they were tasked to guard the Source."

Sienna sighed. "I understand that. I can even see it. Sort of. It's just weird to think of my daughter as basically betrothed and she can't even walk yet."

I gave her a sympathetic smile. "If it helps, the bond doesn't force anything. It just means that they have a best friend, right from the start. That's what I remind myself of when I think about it."

"Now that the cat's out of the bag, we should plan a celebration," Nat said. "Nothing huge," she added when I narrowed my eyes. Neither Ronan nor I were a fan of crowds. "Except there'll be cake, obviously. I figured we could invite Mist, Señora Rosara, Morfayus, and Ailaine."

I nodded, and she went into planning mode, tentatively pulling Sienna into the details. Meanwhile, sadness colored the moment because there was a name missing on that list, and also nothing I could do about it.

"She'll come back when she's ready," Ronan reminded me.

"I just wish I knew when that would be. I know she's a conduit too, but I worry about her with the Illuminati running around."

"Bree's strong. She can take care of herself."

He was right. I knew he was right. But it didn't make it any better in the moment.

I had everything I wanted in life. A family. A home. A semblance of stability. I just wished she could be with us to share it.

"Speaking of plans," Anders said, leaning back in his chair after he threw his napkin down. "How's the house building going?"

"Well. The foundation is down. They start framing next week," I said. After the twins, we decided that we needed a bit more room than our building was able to accommodate. As a belated baby shower present, Nathalie was building us a house. Right next to hers. Mind you, an acre separated the two, but never let it be said she was basic when it came to gifts.

"Morfayus and Ailaine still moving in?"

Ronan and I shared a look. "We're back and forth about it."

"So Ronan likes the idea of bodyguards, and you like your privacy," Nathalie said, summing it up.

"Pretty much."

"I can relate. I'm looking forward to telling people to get off my lawn with a megaphone." The way she deadpanned that statement had the whole table rolling.

"You aren't actually planning to use a megaphone, are you?" Sienna asked.

"Oh she is," I said. "I'll be shocked if she doesn't lay wards that stop solicitors from knocking on her door. Maybe wards imbued with a spell to shock them."

An entire world had changed with magic, but death, taxes—and apparently solicitors—would somehow remain.

Nathalie appraised me. "Now that is a damn good idea. I could sell it too." The wheels were turning in her mind before she got up to clear the plates. I shook my head, a smile curling my lips. I leaned into Ronan, enjoying Honor being sound asleep on my chest. Her mouth making little blowfish faces as she dreamed about the bottle.

I glanced over at the mat. Orson was passed out. One arm over his face, the other starfished to the side. "My kiddos are looking about ready for bed. We need to get them down. Thanks for coming over and making dinner."

"Of course," Nathalie said as she rounded up the dishes. "Sasha, you mind helping me clear the bar so we can head out?"

"Sure."

They got to work putting up leftovers and clearing the plates. I loved that she took the time to do that. With twins, I felt like I blinked, and a mess suddenly appeared.

"I'm going to take Hallie back to our place," Sienna said. She got to her feet and picked up the baby siren. Her light brown skin illuminated warmth beneath the lowlights of our kitchen and living room combo. Her dark brown hair was pulled into twin pigtails, so it didn't get twisted up in her wings. Sienna held her to her chest, humming softly under her breath as the baby frowned. Even in her sleep, she didn't like to be away from Orson any more than he did her.

"I'll be quiet coming in," Sasha said as she grabbed the last of the plates. Since Sienna now had a kid, they'd put a bassinet in the room they were in. In a few months, when our new house was done, Ronan was giving them our apartment so they had more room, and Nat could finally get some of hers back.

"Any chance you can take me back to my place when you're done?" Anders asked Sasha.

"Yeah, just give me a few."

Over the following fifteen minutes, our apartment steadily emptied. When it was just us, I got to my feet and started carrying Honor down the hall. Ronan followed behind, pausing to pick up Orson off the ground.

We laid them down in the joint bassinet that sat next to our bed. They immediately rolled, gravitating toward one another.

Ronan wrapped his arms around me from behind. "You did a good job."

"Damn good job," I agreed. His hand cupped my stomach.

"Still thinking you only want two?"

I turned my cheek to look over my shoulder. "If you're telling me you've already knocked me up again—"

His chest heaved as he laughed, burying his face in my neck. "No. I haven't. Nathalie had me add my blood to the contraceptive she made, so until you stop taking it, that won't happen."

"Good. As for only two, yeah, I think I'm good. At least for a long, long, *very long* time. Pregnancy was brutal." That was putting it mildly. I still wasn't back to feeling like myself because of all the muscle loss. "I almost died a few times, and I want to raise these two without the world trying to end every other month."

"I think we can manage that. When you get to a place where you're comfortable having Nat watch them for the weekend, I want to take you somewhere." His voice turned deep and gravelly. The kind of sound that did wicked things to me.

"Oh yeah?" I asked, pushing my backside against him. "Where did you have in mind?"

His breath hissed between his lips. "Norway. I'm going to get us a place with a glass ceiling so I can fuck you beneath the stars and see what shines brighter. You, or the northern lights."

I stifled a groan. "I need to shower. I'm gross from . . . today. Why don't you come with me and tell me all about this vacation you have planned?"

His fangs brushed the column of my throat in answer.

"Are you sure you can be quiet?" he asked, fingers teasing the rim of my shorts. "You don't want to wake the twins."

"If I can't, you will just have to find a way to keep me quiet."

"Is that a challenge, Atma?" His fingers slipped down the front. *Warm, rough, seeking.*

"Depends on how good you are at *talking*, Atman."

He took me twice before he came down my throat, making good on finding a way to keep me quiet. The twins were still asleep when we crawled into bed, and the moon was large and round in the sky. Ronan pulled me onto his chest, our legs weaving together while he rubbed circles in my lower back.

"Thank you," I whispered into the night. My confession. "For?"

"Becoming what I needed. Fighting for me, even when the person you were fighting was me. Thank you for saving me." We never talked about the Otherworld. Not outside of the brief discussions with Nat and the others. We didn't speak about the Rift or what happened there. That I forgot who I was.

"I didn't save you," Ronan said. "I just reminded you who you were. You saved yourself." A heartbeat passed. "You saved me too. I don't want to live in a world where you don't exist. If you'd lost the battle with the Source, I would have taken you into the Rift."

My lips parted, staying open before I could speak. "The Rift is never-ending. We'd be falling forever until one of us killed the other . . ." Understanding washed over me. "You'd sentence yourself to that sort of eternity even though I might have never been me again?"

"Where you go, I go. If there was even the smallest chance you were in there, I wasn't going to leave you in the darkness forever. Not without me too."

My eyes watered. I blinked the tears away. "I love you. I know love doesn't mean the same thing to you as it does me—"

"I love you too, Piper," he said, shocking the hell out of me. "It doesn't matter what it means to me. I know what it conveys to you, and I love you so fucking much. I told you once, I followed you from one world to the next and that I'd do it again if I had to. It doesn't matter if it's a world or the light realm or the Rift. Where you go, I go—and that's never going to change."

The end.

. . .

THANK you for reading FORGED BY FURY! I hope you loved Piper and Ronan Fallon's love story as much as I do. If you want to read about Nat's story with Lucifer, you can check out here series Her Immortal Monsters with Kissed by Chaos now!

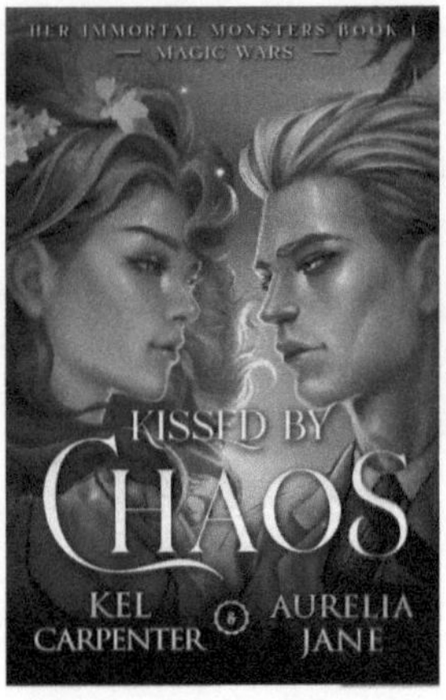

COMING from a powerful line of black witches doesn't mean anything if they've abused you your entire life.

I'm a broken witch.

Born with weak chaos magic, I exist on the fringes of society as a fixer of people and their problems.

Until I tried to save the Devil.

Instead, I accidentally created a blood bond between his soul and mine.

Whoops.

Lucifer whispers filthy promises of all the things he'd do to me if I brought him back, but I won't sacrifice another life to restore his playboy throne.

What's worse, my ex-fiance won't stay away.

He broke off our engagement. It was his choice. So why won't he leave me alone?

You'd think I'd have learned not to trust my taste in men by now, but when a one-night stand with a sinfully arrogant stranger turns into something more, the only thing I know for certain is that I'm screwed.

Love almost killed me once, and I'm determined to keep my distance from them.

But as they say... the road to hell was always paved with the best intentions.

Chapter One of Kissed by Chaos:

Latex was overrated.

Sure, it clung to all the *right* places, but it clung to all the *wrong* ones too. The dress felt like a glove suffocating my body for the sake of sex appeal, and the boob sweat was real.

I wasn't sure if it was a blessing or a curse that it had large cutouts along my hips, waist, and thighs. While it gave those parts of me a tiny bit of relief from the sweltering, nonbreathable fabric, I couldn't help feeling like a busted can of biscuits.

I hid my snort behind the martini glass pressed to my lips.

My legs were crossed, appearing long and sleek despite my actual petite stature, thanks to a magically enhanced body oil infused with succubus pheromones. It would make me irresistible to my date for the evening.

Hopefully enough so his lips would come loose and let slip the location of an incredibly powerful magical artifact I was searching for.

Throughout the dungeon of Bliss, no clock ticked, but I sensed the passing of time. Keeping up with the seconds in the back of my mind as I waited.

An incubus approached, no doubt caught in the lure I'd cast out.

On another night, I might have sidestepped his attention. But with this particular target, having his interest would suit my needs.

I smiled demurely but with unmistakable interest, teetering on that line between being a flirt and too forward. His own smile widened. "Hello, beautiful," he purred. The incubus bent at the waist, extending his hand toward me. "May I?"

He was blonde—ashy, not golden. Once upon a time I might have taken him to my bed. Now I avoided blondes. Even if his blue eyes were pretty. High cheekbones. Full lips. He had a face I could sit on.

The subtle scent of my arousal hit him, and those eyes darkened a shade. "You may." I dropped my hand in his, letting him pull me from my barstool. The moment our skin touched, I got the feeling of yearning. A raw, unbridled ache longing to be soothed or forgotten entirely. He was so lonely, lost in a darkness that left him *empty*.

My heart sighed, deflating a fraction, even though he'd never see. I related to the poor man and the way he sought to fill the void that grief and resentment left in his soul.

The *tink* of my martini glass touching the counter was the last I knew of it as he pulled me through a crowd and away from the main room. Deeper in the dungeon, play chairs, crosses, and sex swings waited.

"Does anything pique your interest?" he asked me, a glint of sexual excitement in his gaze.

My lips parted and I leaned forward a fraction to point when a presence appeared behind me. I knew he was there despite being unable to see or touch him. He had no body, but his entire presence filled the space.

"What are you doing, little witch?" Lucifer rumbled; his voice dark. Gruff. The hairs along my nape stood on end in answer, but I refused to acknowledge his presence. Not anymore.

In an effort to keep him at bay, I severely limited my magic use. It seemed to work. But the small touch of skin led to my premonition about the incubus and gave Lucifer just enough of a crack to open the door and make his presence known.

Should have worn gloves, I thought, making a mental note to not make that mistake again.

I swallowed, then pointed at the cuffs hanging from the ceiling.

The incubus in front of me shifted his attention to them, completely unaware of the ghost in our midst or my unease due to it.

A sly smile spread across his face. He licked his lips, looking back at me with hunger. "You or me?" he asked.

The target whose attention I wanted liked pretty things. Submissive things. Seeing me bound and on display for another? He wouldn't be able to resist.

"Me," I answered with a wink.

The incubus smirked. "Hands up, beautiful," he murmured as he guided me closer. At my back, that presence grew. Silent, but not indifferent. If anything, his lack of speech said a great deal. I ignored it. Ignored him.

The ghost was dead. Gone.

Sure, I could hear him, but he wasn't *here*.

I offered my wrists, raising them high above my head. The incubus's fingers were cold to the touch, but soft. They weren't working hands, that was for sure.

The leather cuffs wrapped around my wrists, restricting my movement. If not for the heels of my boots, I would have struggled to stand.

"What's your name?" my partner for the evening asked,

checking the grip. Months ago, I would have appreciated the care he took to respect my boundaries. Seeking permission. We would have had lots of fun together, a creature that fed on sex and a witch that liked to have it. It really was a shame so much had changed.

"Ophelia," I lied smoothly. I may not be the strongest witch by a mile, but I was a fantastic liar. "And yours?"

"August," he answered as he rolled up the cuffs of his button-down shirt. "Tell me what you like, Ophelia."

I opened my mouth to answer, right as my gaze slid past him. Nothing came out as golden eyes, bright as the sun itself, focused on me. Lucifer's white hair seemed to reflect the lights of the dungeon, but that was impossible. My mouth went dry at the look on his face. The sheer intensity with which he stared was startling.

"Two weeks," Lucifer said, not revealing a hint of emotion. "You've refused to use magic for two weeks just to shut me out, and when you finally slip, it's to fuck one of my children."

Stomach acid climbed up my throat, but I kept it down.

"Ophelia?" the incubus asked, drawing my attention back to him. I blinked, remembering myself. Lucifer was being dramatic. The incubus wasn't his child. He couldn't be. At least by blood. Magic was another story.

"Sorry," I murmured. "I thought I recognized someone."

The incubus glanced behind him, then turned back, brows pinched together. "Would you prefer—"

"Choking," I said, interrupting him. His mouth snapped shut, that dark hunger coming back. "Spanking. Biting. I like some pain, but not so much it leaves more than a mild bruise. My hair being pulled turns me on." I focused on him, refusing to look elsewhere, even if it meant I wouldn't see when my actual target approached.

"How do you feel about toys?" August wondered, studying a rack of options.

"Impact toys are okay. No canes. No clamps. I can't do pinching at all, but I'm all right with restraints. Hard no on any kind of hook."

The incubus glanced over his shoulder and lifted an eyebrow as his fingers hovered over a velvety eye mask. I shook my head. "Not here."

While a sliver of disappointment went through him, he acknowledged it. It wasn't uncommon for people to be uncomfortable with masks when taking a partner for the first time to play. My reasoning had more to do with needing to see the door, but there was no need to elaborate.

When he selected a single black feather, I tried to cock my head but couldn't, and settled for a lift of my eyebrows.

"Interesting choice."

"I'd rather start slow and find your limits than accidentally overstep," he said thoughtfully.

A ghostly tingle ran from one shoulder blade to the other as Lucifer stepped around him, circling me. "I wouldn't need to ask," Lucifer whispered in my ear. "I already know all your likes. Your dislikes. Your limits. Your boundaries."

My heartbeat intensified, filling my ears with the sound.

"May I feed from you?" August asked. The question grounded me.

He wasn't talking about blood. He wanted my pleasure. Normally I said no. While I wasn't inherently opposed, that was something I preferred only with partners.

Just as I was about to answer, Lucifer snapped, "No." The word was a growl. Possessive, though he had no right or reason to be.

Just to spite him, I said, "Yes."

Lucifer's golden eyes burned like solar flares. August dipped his head in thanks. "I'll be gentle," he murmured.

"I'm sure he will," Lucifer scoffed. "You guard your blood and magic carefully. You won't even give him your name, but you'll let him feed from you?" Lucifer asked me. I didn't answer. I refused. "What happened to not wanting to taunt the devil?"

So much. Yet so little.

Was it cruel? If I owed him anything, yes. But I didn't.

He was simply a ghost, and I was just the very unfortunate witch who'd been tied to him. While annoying, he couldn't do a thing to stop me.

August leaned forward, letting the tip of the feather touch me. A sheen of silvery blue magic covered him, letting me know he was disguising his actual appearance with a glamour. It didn't bother me. Half the people in the club opted for one. I didn't like the feel of glamours, the way they rubbed against my skin, stifling me. I preferred to use a fake alias when possible.

Under other circumstances, he would have asked me for a safe word before getting started, but that wasn't needed in this establishment. Not when they used the universal colors of red for stop and yellow for slow down. It was simplistic and easy to remember.

It also meant that magic enforced the rules.

"You have beautiful eyes," August said, letting the feather trail over my collarbone. "I've never seen eyes such a light shade of brown." The feather drifted over my abdomen, skimming the edges of where the dress cutouts let it touch my skin. Another kind of itch erupted in me.

My breathing slowed.

He leaned in and licked a trail up the column of my neck.

I gasped at the contact, and he groaned.

"You taste delicious. You shouldn't use the succubus pheromones. You don't need it."

My lips parted. How did he know that?

August lifted his eyes to me once more. "I have a *very* good sense of smell. I can scent magic and other things . . ." I heard the truth in his voice and let it lie. While uncommon outside of demons, I'd heard of some creatures inheriting a demon's ability to scent magic—since all magic came from them. I was an oddity myself for being able to see it.

He leaned in again, inhaling around my neck. He kissed a spot and despite it being nothing more than his lips, it felt tender, with a bite of lust entwined that I wasn't used to. It had been a while since I'd been with an incubus. The feather trailed across my abdomen and my stomach twitched.

Lips falling open, I lowered my guard a little, letting my eyelids flutter closed as I let the pleasure wrap around me.

"Nathalie."

I bit the inside of my cheek.

My eyes flew open to see a person on the other side of August, just over his shoulder. I couldn't say the newcomer was the very last person I wanted to see, but he was certainly near the top of that list.

The incubus touching me froze, stepping back a fraction. He glanced over his shoulder, expression neutral to the point of distaste. "We're in the middle of a scene." A polite dismissal if I ever heard one.

"Consider this production canceled." The not-welcomed guest unbound my wrists with a flick of his hand. "Scene over. Move along."

The incubus worked his jaw instead of dropping the topic and deciding it wasn't worth his trouble. He looked at me. "What would you prefer, beautiful?"

I gazed at him. He had to have known I lied about my name, but he was still interested, and unwilling to walk away unless I wanted it.

Regret tasted like ash on my tongue.

"Unfortunately, I can't ignore this."

He dipped his head. "Perhaps we'll meet again, then." He stepped away, walking backward to keep eye contact with me.

"Maybe," I repeated, knowing the odds of that were incredibly unlikely now that my cover was blown and that meant I couldn't return to this club without a glamour—which pissed me off even more. They were worse than the latex dress by a mile.

Turning to the man who'd interrupted me, I shook off all desire, letting a familiar mask drop into place. He grabbed my wrist without permission, making me instantly wish for my incubus companion. We disappeared, rematerializing in a graveyard outside none other than the Wicked Haunt, a church turned summoning center owned by the only existing coven of black witches in New Chicago.

"Marcel," I said curtly, yanking my wrist back. "I was in the middle of something important. I hope you have a good reason for interrupting."

I doubted he did. Severely doubted.

The heated look he practically branded me with solidified that thought.

But his words made everything evaporate.

"Your twin is missing."

START KISSED BY CHAOS NOW

Kel Carpenter is a master of werdz. When she's not reading or writing, she's traveling the world, lovingly pestering her co-author, and spending time with her family. She is always on the search for good tacos and the best pizza. She resides in Maryland and desperately tries to avoid the traffic.

instagram.com/authorkelcarpenter
patreon.com/kelcarpenterandaureliajane
tiktok.com/@kelcarpenterauthor

Acknowledgments

This book took everything from me. It took nearly eight months from start to finish, with over fifty straight days of writing in the end. I worked on it when I was so pregnant I couldn't even sit in my office chair, and I got back to it when my son was three weeks old. I absolutely love and adore these characters. What started as a passion project has turned into a universe I don't want to leave.

I hope you enjoyed where Piper and Ronan's journey went as much as I have. While there are still many stories to tell, I know this one will always hold a very special place in my heart because of the journey Piper goes on to becoming a better person.

First and foremost, I should thank three people. My best friend/co-author, my husband, and my son. Without their support and love, this book never would have been half as good (or finished, in all likelihood). They've been my anchors that got me through this 100%, and I love them for it. My boy has been such an amazing baby, napping while I work. While still so young, his personality inspired what little we've seen of the twins, and no doubt will continue to inspire others in future series.

Thank you to my publishing team: Analisa, Maegan, and Dom. Your hard work and dedication has made this series all the better (and me so much saner).

I can't go without mentioning Emigh, Amanda, Court-ney, Heather, and Lexi, who let me vent at odd hours of the day and never once got upset with me for it. They cheered me on and gave me advice when needed and gave me their ears when I just needed someone to listen. We all need friends like them.

My mom also played a huge role in helping me keep my mental health together through the transition I made from pregnancy into motherhood. Certain growth points that Piper underwent were also inspired from my own journey with her, and it showed me that strength can come in many forms. Not all of them are pretty or easy to understand, but that doesn't make them any less.

And finally, thank you, dear reader. Your love and support of this series has breathed new life into my writing. We authors often joke that the things we love never sell, and the things we don't go gangbuster—but this series defied that. It's because of you that we'll be seeing so much more from this universe, so thank you for giving me the excuse I needed to continue. I hope to see you next time in New Chicago.